THE SUMMONED ONES

DARRYL A WOODS

Brelsford Ridge Publishing
3481 Dixie Highway #218
Franklin, OH 45005

All characters and events in this publication are fictitious and any resemblance to real persons, living or dead, is entirely coincidental.

Printed in the United States of America
ISBN 978-0-9979059-0-8

THE SUMMONED ONES

DEDICATION

I'd like to thank Jim Effler for bringing my vision to life in the cover art. Thanks to my wife and daughter who put up with me reading the same paragraph to them over and over again during multiple rewrites. I want to thank all of my early readers, especially the ones who stuck with me during the very early and raw material. Of those readers, one stands out: my good friend, Mike. He faithfully read first-draft chapters the same evening I gave them to him and offered comments the next morning, always ending with much-needed encouragement.

The person who deserves the most thanks is my editor, Kelly. She endured some pretty bad copy without complaint, was always encouraging, and offered suggestions beyond those of a typical editor. The changes she made, from the ever-so-subtle to the not-so-subtle (more times than I care to admit) were nothing short of magic.

PROLOGUE

"Rally to the general! Rally to the general!" shouted the tall, lanky soldier as he fought his way toward Darnon.

Kail thought to himself that if they survived this battle, General Darnon would likely discipline him for issuing commands. What he did not know is that Darnon greatly admired his skill with a sword, and regarded Kail as the best he had seen in his long military career.

Over the last nine years of war, the two had engaged in an odd sort of dance. Darnon was keenly aware of the respect his troops had for Kail. A respect not only for his individual prowess in battle, but for his uncanny understanding of the battlefield. As he was now demonstrating, Kail instinctively knew where he and the others were most needed at critical junctures in a battle.

In the beginning, when Kail first joined his army's ranks and began to positively affect the outcomes of battles, General Darnon decided to reward his new soldier with a promotion. But each time he prepared to issue Kail a field commission, the rogue would do something that forced the general's hand and demanded reprimand. Darnon came to realize that these altercations were no accident. Over time, he learned what Kail already knew: that he could serve best as a rank-and-file soldier in the thick of battle. So, the two played out their game. Darnon would dole out light punishment and Kail would act indignant, then reluctantly accept his penalty.

"Fight your way to the general!" Kail bellowed again and again over the din of battle.

His general was indeed in trouble, as was the army's position in the overall battle. Only minutes earlier, Darnon's command post had been overrun. The enemy was countering in near-perfect fashion the battle-plan drawn up that very morning. The general now found himself surrounded on three sides. His skillful use of his massive two-handed sword was the only thing keeping him from being overwhelmed. Three of his officers fought frantically to protect his back, but two were so slowed by wounds, they could barely defend themselves, let alone their commanding officer.

"The general, the general," Kail continued to scream, as enemy after enemy fell to the savagery of his blades.

Kail fought as he often did, with a medium-length sword in one hand and a long dagger in the other. His blades were literally a blur, the speed and uncanny accuracy of their wielding unmatched. A wedge of soldiers followed in the wake of Kail's lethal blades. Many of the men owed their lives to the fighter as he mercilessly dispatched the enemies that came toward them. Those not killed outright by Kail were quickly dealt with by the throng of soldiers growing behind him.

"To the general, to the general!" Kail heard his entreaty taken up by soldiers across the battlefield.

The shouts took on a cadence that seemed to cause Kail to intensify his frantic fight to reach the general he respected and admired. Darnon had been so intent on his own fight for survival, it was only now that Kail's shouts began to register. Allowing himself a quick glance, Darnon made eye contact with his tall soldier. That brief exchange gave both the exhausted warriors the boost they needed to close the gap.

Kail finally reached the ring of enemy soldiers surrounding Darnon. As the skillful swordsman attacked them from behind, each foe quickly fell in turn. The last two made the mistake of wheeling to face their new threat, only to be cleaved nearly in two by the wide arc of the general's long sword.

The shouts imploring the men to rally to their general continued unabated even though Darnon was temporarily out of harm's way, surrounded now by dozens of his men. The shouts persisted in no small part because of Kail. Darnon couldn't comprehend why his usually astute tactician continued to encourage the troops to rally to their general. The only affect apparent to Darnon was that his troops were collapsing into the center of the battlefield, now completely surrounded by the enemy with little hope of escape.

"To the general, to the general!" continued the shouts from Kail and the mass of troops surrounding Darnon. Such conduct exasperated their leader, and he began to second-guess the man he had once trusted implicitly. In this moment of despair, when Darnon thought the lives of the troops he commanded and his own forfeit, he heard the sudden thunder of hooves and the clash of steel. The Jerimassian cavalry exploded into the enemy with such force, the sounds of new battle drowned out the localized fighting. Darnon's army began cheering as they realized help had arrived, seemingly from nowhere.

The enemy, so sure of complete victory only moments before, now found themselves caught in a vice. Darnon's surging troops pressed them from the inside out, and they were completely surrounded by the formidable Jerimassian cavalry. The skillful horsemen darted in and out of the enemy's ranks, inflicting heavy casualties then disappearing before any defense could be marshaled.

As they had done in several prior battles, the enemy troops now turned their aggression on their leaders. Darnon's troops aided these common soldiers as they attacked their superiors. Darnon and his men knew that the bulk of the enemy fighting force was made up of men coerced into fighting to keep their families alive.

For the last nine years, their foes had served under an evil entity named Zybaro. He overran villages and captured their inhabitants, forcing anyone capable of serving into his army and enslaving the rest. The new soldiers were forced to fight or witness the murders of their loved ones. Enforcing his brutal siege with the aid of powerful, mutated magicians called nollax, Zybaro swept across Malabrim, amassing an immense army. Malabrim was the country General Darnon and Commander Namir now fought, hoping to free as many souls as they could and disrupt Zybaro's methodical march to total domination.

When the conflict was at last over, the remaining enemy troops dropped their weapons and placed their hands, fingers interlocked, on their heads. Over the years, Darnon and his men had seen this scene play out many times. Without waiting for orders, the soldiers began corralling their now-placid enemy towards an empty area of the field. They would next begin the long process of removing their enemy's armor and searching for hidden weapons.

Kail set out to help the troops with their task, but made it a point to pass close by the general en route. He spoke softly so that only Darnon could hear.

"I'm sorry for the confusion back there. I saw Commander Namir's scouts on the ridge. I thought it best to get everyone away from the perimeter."

Darnon couldn't help but return the soldier's unrepentant grin.

The general heard a commotion and turned to see Namir reining in his horse a short distance away. The commander dismounted in the fluid motion of one who has spent a lifetime in the saddle. Leading his well-disciplined steed forward, the reins slack between them, Namir approached

Without offering a formal greeting, the commander got right to the point. "My scouts reported they saw you having a hard time." Not waiting for a reply, Namir pressed on, genuinely concerned.

"Darnon, you know I was ordered north. We stumbled across a mine being worked by the most wretched souls. We couldn't allow their agony to continue. If we hadn't taken the time to liberate them, we would have been well over a league from here."

Darnon face reflected his regret but not shame. He inclined his head, indicating acceptance of just how dire the situation would have been without his friend's aid.

"The state of those miners was the worst I've seen yet. Children as young as four or five years, piled like cordwood, dead of malnutrition and exhaustion. The condition of the ones left alive was so deplorable it made the dead seem like the lucky ones." Namir paused as he struggled to deliver his dark narrative.

When he continued, contempt edged his voice. "When the guards saw the overwhelming odds and realized they had no hope, they turned on their captives. If not for some of the stronger miners defending themselves, the slaughter would have been far worse."

Darnon's pained look and glistening eyes were reflected in Namir's countenance.

"Between the captured soldiers and those you rescued, at least we saved a few," Darnon all but whispered.

Namir gestured to the surrounding battlefield. "I agree my friend, but at an ever-increasing price. How long can we keep this up?"

"What alternative do we have? We can't just leave these people to their own fate. Besides, how long will it be before those miners are replaced by our own families?" Darnon demanded.

"I know how you feel about the prophecies, Darnon, but if the clerics of Hinloose really have found the means to bring the Summoned Ones to our aid, don't you think we should at least try?" Namir asked, expecting the same skeptical response he had heard so many times before.

Darnon replied in a matter-of-fact tone, "The air has grown cold. This will be the last of this year's campaigns. Let's get these people healthy enough for travel and back to Bericea. Once there, we can make plans for the summoning as we await the spring."

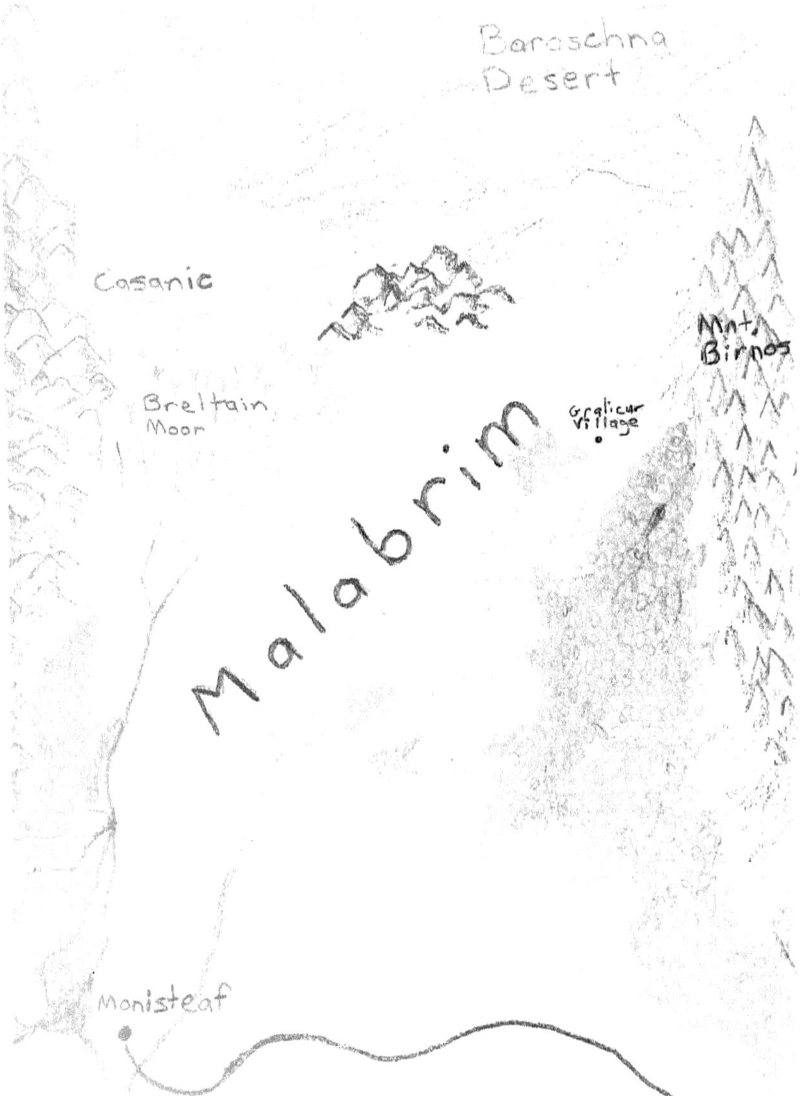

Baraschna
Desert

Casanic

Mnt.
Birnos

Breltain
Moor

Gralicur
Village

Malabrim

Monisteaf

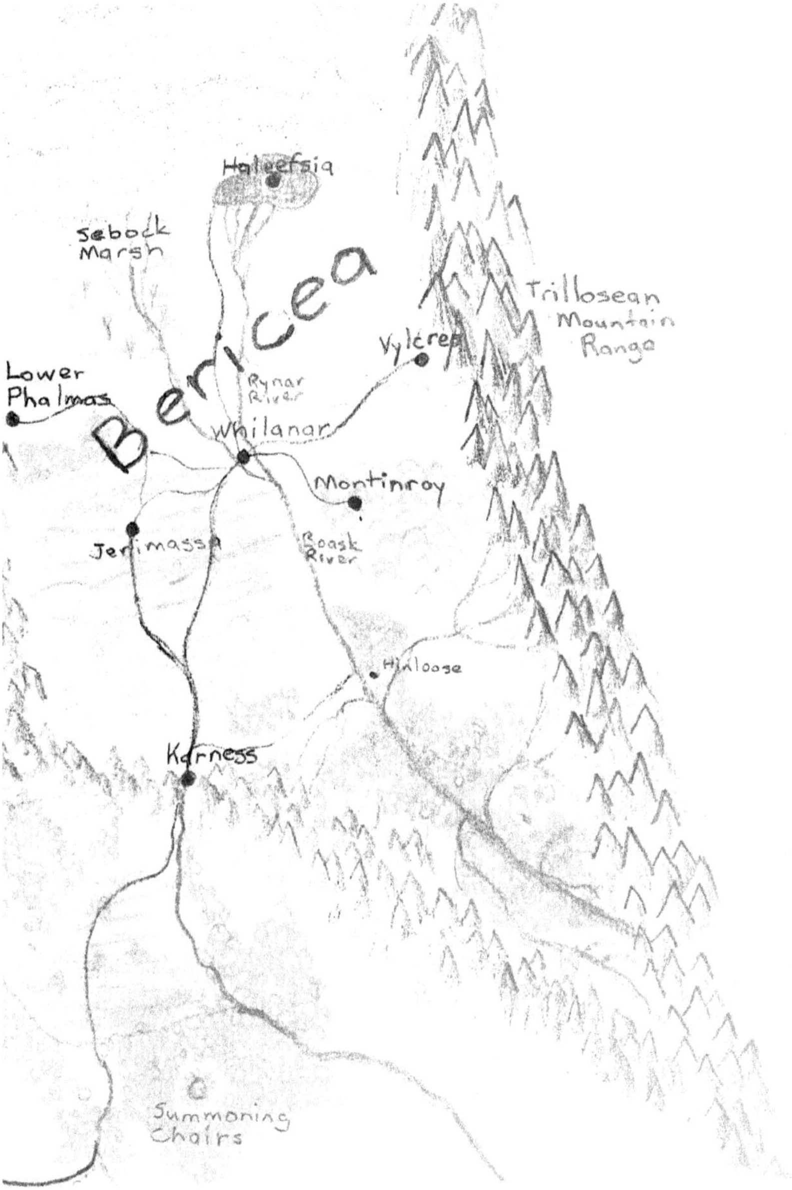

Haleefsia
Sebock Marsh
Bericea
Trillosean Mountain Range
Vylcrep
Lower Phalmas
Rynar River
Whilanar
Montinroy
Jerimassa
Boask River
Hinloose
Karness
Summoning Chairs

CHAPTER 1

INVITATION

The night air was brisk as Pattie and Mike stood by the sidelines of their old high school's football field. The weather had turned cold a few weeks ago. The days had been clear, filled with blue skies, sunshine, and trees showing off their brightest autumn hues.

Tonight, the stars and crescent moon in the clear sky hung unseen above the glare of the bright lights. Pattie, a pretty young woman of 20, was dressed in her typical garb—old blue jeans, a loosely tucked and rumpled button-down shirt, and a denim jacket. Her straight, black hair fell below her shoulders, her large brown eyes taking in the action on the field. She had a natural attractiveness that required no makeup.

Pattie O'Keenan and Mike Wilson had been friends since they were kids. They'd grown up a few miles from one another, in the countryside surrounding the small town of Irvine. From the age of 12, they'd biked to one another's houses for visits over the long summer breaks. Pattie's family owned a small horse farm, and she spent a lot of her spare time alone, working with the horses or doing chores. Pattie had grown up a bit of a tomboy. She insisted on doing the same chores around the farm as her two older brothers and didn't take advantage of being the youngest or the "little sister." Because of this, her brothers respected her and they all got along well together. Unfortunately, they rarely included Pattie in their inner circle, leaving her too often to her own devices. Luckily, whatever loneliness she felt was eased by her friendship with the boy down the road.

In stark contrast to Pattie's casual attire, Mike Wilson was well-dressed in a sports jacket and khakis. Although of average build and height, he carried himself with the air of someone who knew what he wanted and how to get it. His dad, a former Marine Corps boxer, had taught him to fight at an early age, and Mike knew how to take care of himself. His air of confidence could also be attributed to his days spent leading teams on the paintball field. He had been playing since the age of 13, when his uncle took him to a local paintball venue. Already an avid reader of military history (tactics, logistics, maneuvering, and overall strategy, in particular), the boy had a keen desire to see whether the techniques he studied in books could be applied first-hand on the playing field.

Since the age of seven, Mike had been interested in all things military. One late night, awakened by a loud noise coming from the living room, he crawled out of bed to investigate. Mike found his dad asleep in front of the TV. George C. Scott was leading the troops through battle in Patton, and the little boy became riveted. He was still in front of the set the next morning where his parents found him sound asleep.

A shrill whistle broke through the crisp night air, immediately followed by the deafening roar of the Mighty Engineers fans. The football team was good this season and had already won five of its first six games. Tonight, however, the game itself was being overshadowed by the return of a former football hero.

"Brandon doesn't have to enjoy all this so much," Pattie told Mike wryly.

"He knows he's the biggest thing that ever happened to this wide spot in the road. No doubt, the biggest that ever will happen," Mike replied. "As much as he hates the attention, he'd never deprive the folks of this moment."

Just the week before, Brandon Rollins had made the cover of Sports Illustrated, even though he'd shared it with three other Heisman Trophy hopefuls. Most of the article was devoted to Rollins, however, and his decision to announce early he would play out his senior year at The Ohio State University instead of entering the NFL draft.

"Do you think he had us meet him here for sympathy, moral support, or some far-flung hope we might be able to get him out of this," Pattie asked.

Mike grinned. "All of the above."

Now in his junior year, Brandon was already on track to break Ohio State's all-time rushing record before the season came to an end. The 6-foot, 1-inch 230-pound running back had already surpassed OSU's total yard record with his catches out of the back field. In his high school days, he had shattered every Mighty Engineers record on the books, not to mention most of the high school records in the state.

Ruggedly handsome, with a defined physique, Brandon often caught the attention of admiring females, though his shyness around women was obvious. His graceful way of moving despite his size was also attractive to the girls that always seemed to surround him. Brandon had more going for him than sheer athleticism, however. He was maintaining a 3.8 GPA in business at Ohio State, his devotion to his studies almost as rigorous as his workouts. He knew if he made it to the professional leagues, with his background in business, he'd be able to manage his own career and finances.

Brandon had learned about responsibility and the importance of making good decisions at a young age. His parents divorced when he was only eight, and Brandon helped raise his younger sister after his dad moved out of their house in the northern section of Irvine. He still called her two or three times a week from college. Despite their divorce, Brandon remained close to both his parents and often sought out his dad's advice. Brandon's mom remarried when he was 14. His dad remained unmarried and lived close by his children. Brandon and his sister stayed with him every other weekend, and Brandon spent his summers with him.

"Does he still practice his martial arts?" Pattie asked.

"What? Oh, yeah, some," Mike replied, distracted by the game and the large crowd surrounding Brandon. "Well, he did cut out the sparring, but you know him, disciplined as ever. No matter how much school work or how long practices run, he gets up at 5:00 a.m. every morning and does that ritual workout of his, walking through all those forms. Not during the season, but off-season, he still works with all those weird martial arts weapons."

Brandon had been working aggressively in the martial arts since the age of 12, having advanced to a black belt by the age of 14. He had a room full of trophies from martial arts tournaments but had decided to stop competing at 16. Major colleges had started noticing him when he was only a sophomore. Taking his dad's advice, Brandon decided that risking injury and a full athletic scholarship was not worth it. Even so, despite dropping out of competition, he had not abandoned his martial arts training.

"I drag myself up at 5:00 or 5:30 a.m. every once in a while and high-tail it across campus to watch his "famous" workouts. Besides, letting all the girls that hang around the gym know I'm his friend doesn't hurt," Mike laughed.

"I still can't believe you ran off to that huge campus with Brandon and left me here to go to community college."

Pattie was kidding, of course, knowing full well that Brandon's chance to play on scholarship at a major university and Mike's academic scholarship were once-in-a-lifetime opportunities. "Who'd have thought all that reading about war and fighting would have landed you such a sweet deal?"

As Pattie chatted with Mike, she looked around expectantly, waiting for the arrival of another old friend. Earlier in the day, Pattie and Mike had met Steve Oliver at Rise and Shine, the local coffee shop. Steve brought his new girlfriend, Gloria, whom he'd been seeing for the last two months. He'd met her at a party he'd organized for his fraternity at Brown University and their sister sorority. Pattie had taken an instant dislike to the girl and was not pleased to see her hanging on Steve's arm as he pushed through the coffee-shop door that morning. No doubt, he'd have her in tow again this evening, she thought with disgust.

Of all the members of the group meeting tonight, Stephen William

Oliver III was the most out of place. While the others had gone to public schools, Steve attended Lexington Prep. His parents sent their only child off to the top-tier boarding school when he was eight years old. Before that, he'd spent much of his childhood alone in the family's Colonial Revival mansion on a 300-acre estate. His father's political career was beginning to take off, and his parents traveled extensively, leaving their young son at home in the care of their head housekeeper, Carmela. The Mexican woman practically raised the slender blond-haired, blue-eyed boy as her own and soon had her charge speaking Spanish like a native. Because of Carmela, Steve developed an early appreciation for language and a love of linguistics.

When Steve came home from boarding school during holidays and summers, he began to take advantage of the estate's riding facilities to fill his time. The estate had been in the Oliver family for over 120 years. Backing up to the Daniel Boone National Forest, it was now a working farm producing grain and thoroughbreds. Steve learned he had an aptitude for horsemanship and soon became an accomplished rider. He began competing in stadium jumping and other English equestrian events, honing his skills on the family's private course.

When he was old enough, he began to travel. Other than Mike, who had taken two fishing trips to Canada with his uncle, Steve was the only one of the group who had been outside the United States. He'd made several trips to Europe and visited nearly every country, even spending some time in Russia. He'd also been to Japan, Australia, New Zealand, South America, and most recently spent a month touring China and Tibet. For last few years now during his travels, Steve had shied away from the more touristy locales, preferring to hang out with the locals and hone his language skills. He even went so far as to take odd jobs, hanging out in the pubs in the evenings and sleeping on the floors of farmhouses or barns where he had worked that day. Such exposure to the local color, the languages, the sounds, phrases, cultural influences, and mental processes associated with the spoken word and its regional variations, all fueled Steve's obsession with language. Because of Carmela's early influence and his subsequent travels, he chose linguistics as his major at Brown.

Although Pattie had figured that Steve would arrive on time, the Reinard brothers would be another story. With Jeremy just in from the University of Kentucky, his brother Will would be monopolizing him, describing all the new projects and inventions he had dreamt up during Jeremy's absence. Will had decided long ago that college was not for him. Though of above-average intelligence, Will was content to work in their father's metal fabrication shop, and his after-hours use of the shop equipment allowed him to pursue his real passion: inventing. Jeremy had the same inventive drive, but he loved mechanical engineering and (though he would never admit it) the routine and discipline of acquiring a formal education. If Pattie didn't miss her guess, the brothers wouldn't make the game. However, she knew they wouldn't ignore Mrs. Stayton's request to stop by her house this evening.

Mrs. Stayton was Joshua's mom. Josh was one of the old gang, the one who made sure everyone kept in touch after graduation. He had died this past Tuesday after a six-month battle with cancer, and his passing was the reason they were back in town after 2½ years. The last time they'd all been together was the summer after graduation, when they gathered for their annual week at camp. It seemed like only yesterday that Josh had called each of them, begging them not to visit but rather to remember him in better times.

Mrs. Stayton's request came as a bit of a surprise to the group. Only Will had remained particularly close to her. He had spent a lot of time with Josh after high school. The two had discovered caving, a common hobby in the local area, where caves were abundant. Will also helped the Staytons by taking on household and automotive repairs. Josh's father had passed away several years earlier, and to say that Josh was not mechanically inclined was an understatement.

Pattie scowled, "There's Steve now, with that woman trailing him like a hound."

"Hey Pattie, keep it civil for Steve's sake," Mike said in a placating voice.

Pattie could hide her jealousy well enough around Steve, but with Mike, her lifelong friend, she knew better than to try. She (and everyone else) was convinced, and with good cause, that Gloria Stenner was out for two things: money and power. Pattie had never treated Steve as the son of a wealthy state senator, but she always knew he would follow in his father's footsteps despite his disdain for politics. Forced to attend more and more of the senator's functions over the years, Steve began to resent his father and the perfect image he cultivated for the press and his contributors. Senator Oliver still harbored hopes that his son would enter politics, but despite his natural talent for leadership and organization, Steve had so far resisted his father's attempts to steer him toward a political career. Pattie wondered briefly if Steve's aversion to the limelight would dampen Gloria's affections.

Before Steve spotted her and Mike by the sidelines, Pattie allowed herself a few moments to look over her old friend. She saw he was parting his fair hair on the side now, and his 6-foot, 2-inch frame, though still on the thin side, was more athletic now that he was on the college fencing team. Catching sight of her, Steve raised a hand in greeting, flashing a quick smile. He wasn't handsome in the conventional sense, but Pattie thought that smile could light the entire football field.

Over the years, she had taken great care to hide her true feelings for the senator's son, believing that a tomboy from a very average family could only hold him back. One thing was certain, though—a person like Gloria was definitely not what Steve needed.

Mike spoke up just as Pattie was about to address the couple, aware that any remark she might make to Gloria could get the evening off on the wrong foot.

"Hey, glad to see you two. I know you just arrived, but we need to get Brandon out of here before the end of the game, or he'll never get away."

Mike continued as everyone glanced toward Brandon, "Halftime was an absolute madhouse. Kids wanted autographs, long-lost friends wanted their pictures taken with him, you know how it goes."

The foursome was finally able to get Brandon's attention by waving and shouting his name, giving him the excuse he needed to break away from the large group surrounding him. The four turned and started toward the exit gate where Brandon was finally able to catch up. They were a somber group as they headed for their cars to make their way to Mrs. Stayton's house. Pattie was already on her cell phone to remind the Reinard brothers of the unusual invitation.

The brothers were just pulling up in the driveway as the others rounded the corner and eased in to park behind them. The house was a bi-level, part of a 30-year-old subdivision just off the main drag. Mrs. Stayton was proud of how she had kept the place up after her husband died. Even among all the other well-maintained properties, the Stayton home stood out. Mrs. Stayton had always worked extra jobs and, with Josh's help, had kept the yard manicured and the flowerbeds perfect; the exterior of the house always looked freshly painted. Will was a great help on the overall maintenance of the place, but it was Mrs. Stayton's perfectionism that made the property a showplace. Josh had lived his entire life in this home.

Silently the group gathered on the porch, the chill of the night more penetrating now. Pattie knocked on the door.

Mrs. Stayton answered almost immediately, smiling at their familiar faces.

"I'm so glad to see you all. Please come in."

She was trying to project a strong, upbeat mood but they could tell she had been crying. The loss of her husband, then her only child, had devastated her. She directed them to the always-spotless living room and invited them to sit. After meeting Gloria and exchanging pleasantries with Josh's old friends, an awkward silence settled on the group.

Then Mrs. Stayton began to speak.

"I don't know how to ask this without being blunt. And I don't want to offend any of you. I hope you understand that is not my intent."

She paused, choosing her words carefully.

"It's just that I feel I need to know what drew all of you together. Why my son felt so close to you right up until the end."

The group, with the exception of Gloria, looked at one another with a mixture of surprise, concern, and relief. Gloria's interest was piqued, as she had been wondering the same thing. This particular group of friends seemed to have nothing in common.

"Go ahead, Mike. I think you should be the one to tell her," said Brandon. The others nodded in agreement.

"Well," began Mike, "as you know, we all met for the first time when we were 12, at the South Fork Summer Camp."

Mike fidgeted in his chair as he glanced at the others, then continued.

"That first year at camp was awful. The counselors were young and more than eager to abuse their authority." Mike paused and looked at the others for encouragement before continuing.

"We were spread out across several cabins and met one day quite by accident, when we went to investigate a big ruckus."

Mike focused his attention back on Mrs. Stayton and started anew.

"That ruckus was Brandon saving Pattie from the camp bully."

Mike turned to Jeremy.

"You remember, you and I came down the same path just as Steve and Josh were coming down another, and we saw Brandon facing a bully twice his size. Pattie was on the ground nearby with a bloody nose."

Brandon and Pattie nodded in agreement and Mike proceeded.

"All of us newcomers to camp, even though we were barely acquainted, looked at each other without a word and decided to a person that we were going to help. Just as we started forward, Brandon flipped the bully onto the ground and had his arm twisted in what would best be described as a pretzel. With a few not-so-idle threats from Brandon, the bully left in short order."

"I didn't miss the fact that you all were coming to help me," Brandon chimed in.

Mike was becoming more comfortable telling the story now, as the others hadn't interrupted with any criticism. He continued his narrative, relating that only two days of camp were left at this point. After helping Pattie up and making sure she was OK, the newly-formed group decided to meet after lights-out.

That night, they began sharing their negative experiences at the camp and quickly fell into an easy camaraderie. They began relating their life stories and soon realized their backgrounds were very dissimilar—in another setting unlike the close confines of the camp, they would never have started hanging around each other. And before the night was over, the eclectic group had formed an almost-instant bond.

They met the following night as well. Because this was their last night together, the group was under pressure to form an alliance against next year's enforced campout. They knew two things: one, their parents would almost certainly send them to this terrible place again, and two, they wanted to hold on to their newly formed friendships.

Josh and Steve came up with a plan.

"We all love the outdoors, we all love camping. So, why don't we just make up our own camp?"

After the others stopped laughing, they realized the two boys were completely serious. Josh came up with the idea of form letters written on fictional camp stationery. Steve added that he was sure he could get a post-office box set up using his dad's campaign as a cover. With the P.O. box, they could get their parents to send checks to the imaginary camp, and Steve was sure he could get them cashed.

"And that's when Camp Wyanet was born," Mike finished proudly.

The group was concerned over Mrs. Stayton's reaction, but she smiled in genuine amusement. For those who had been around her for the last few months, it was the first time they'd seen her happy.

"So, you never went to camp all those years," she said, almost chuckling.

"Well, not exactly," replied Mike. "We did go to camp, just not where you thought."

Mrs. Stayon's smile was contagious. Mike couldn't help grinning as he offered more details of their deception.

"We picked Camp Wyanet because it was near the state park. There was a side trail near the entrance that cut straight over to the campgrounds in the state park."

"I remember several times calling and getting a camp recording. I left a message, and later that day, Josh returned my call from the same number. How did you manage that?"

"That was easy, Mrs. Stayton," answered Steve. "We bought one of those cell phones with prepaid minutes and used the number on the flyers we sent out. I had my older cousin record the message so it sounded like an adult."

"So, you kids used up all that money we parents sent along with you to go to camp. You must have had a grand old time," Mrs. Stayton commented, as amused as ever.

"I sure wish I could have thought of something like that when I was that age. I see now why Josh was so close to all of you, even though later he didn't see all of you that often."

Mrs. Stayton seemed to grow more reflective. "You must have grown very close spending entire weeks together over six summers."

She stood up. "Please wait here a moment. I have something for you," and she walked slowly out of the room.

Mrs. Stayton returned a short time later with an envelope in her right hand. Her eyes were glistening as the sadness fell over her again. The all-too brief-respite Mike's camp story had offered her was over.

"I have a letter that Josh wrote a few months ago," Mrs. Stayton offered as she fought to control her emotions.

"He made me promise to bring you all together and give this to you the night before his funeral," she added so softly, the friends had to strain to hear her words.

With a little more strength in her voice, she continued, "I don't think I can stay to hear its contents, even if Josh would have wanted me to. I'll just go on to bed now. Please make yourselves at home."

Without replying to their good nights and thank yous, she handed the letter to Will and hurried off up the stairs.

Without any ado, Will opened the envelope and began reading the letter, printed in Josh's distinctive handwriting.

If the Camp Wyanet Gang is reading this, I've already been cremated. I have a final request of you. I've been thinking of all the places people scatter ashes, or how they set urns on a hearth. Nothing like this seems quite right for me. As you all know, Will and I have done some serious caving. We've explored most of the caves in the park and several on private land. Other than my music, this has been my greatest passion. So, the spot I've chosen for my final resting place is in the far reaches of a cave in the very park we all used to meet in.

I've put a lot of thought into how and where I would like this to come about. I would like all of us to have one last adventure together as a group. I want you to take my ashes to a cave that Will and I found just before I got sick. You have to remember, Will, it was that place we called Spur Cave.

Will nodded to the others as he lifted his eyes from the page. He remembered the cave well; they had both commented at the time how much the entrance looked like a western cowboy spur. He also recalled that the entrance to the cave was deep in the park, and it had taken them a long day's hike just to reach it. Josh had become unusually tired that day, and they hadn't taken much time to explore the cave itself. It wasn't until later that they learned how ill he was. Afterwards, Will never had the desire to return to the cave to explore it without his friend.

Will suddenly realized that his thoughts had drifted and the others were waiting for him to continue. He returned his attention to the letter and continued reading.

I've been planning this for a while, really not too long after my diagnosis. While I still had my strength, I took camping supplies to the Three Forks campsite. You remember, Will, we've used it several times. I carried all the equipment each of you will need to the entrance of the cave.

I asked my mom to have my funeral early in the morning. She must have thought that was odd. Ever since high school, with playing in the bands and all, I seldom got up until the afternoon. But by having the funeral so early, all of you should be able to make the first camp well before dark. Then you can leave early and make it to the cave before noon. I'd like you to place my urn in the cave on a secluded ledge, as far in as you can get in three hours. That way, you can get back out and to the camp before nightfall.

I know this is a lot to ask, but I feel this strange pull that we all need one last adventure together.

Love, Josh

CHAPTER 2

LAST WISHES

The funeral the next day was well-attended. Irvine was a small, close-knit town and nearly every resident had attended a wedding or party where Josh's band had played. The highlight of the service was Pattie's a cappella arrangement, her voice so beautiful and clear that the only dry eyes in the church were Gloria's. She sat close by Steve's side, seething with jealousy.

After reading Josh's last wishes, Will worked late into the night preparing daypacks for everyone. Each pack would hold enough food and back-up supplies to get its owner to the cave and back. Josh had always been thorough when planning their caving expeditions, so Will didn't need to assemble much. One thing Josh hadn't planned for, however, was a last-minute addition to the group. Gloria informed the others after the funeral that she would be accompanying them, and Steve did nothing to dissuade her. Although they hid it well, Will and the others weren't pleased with her intrusion into their solemn and personal trek.

The group had shown Mrs. Stayton the letter before the funeral, and she seemed to reach a sort of internal acceptance of her son's last wishes. At the end of the service, Will placed Josh's urn into a container that he stored in the light daypack he'd prepared for the hike. The group planned to take three vehicles, including Will's pickup with the daypacks, to a small parking lot near the trail leading to Will and Josh's old camp. After saying their farewells to Josh's mother, they left the service, going home to change before heading to the park.

Steve, driving Gloria and Brandon, caught up to Pattie and Mike en route, so they all arrived at the lot at the same time. As they pulled into the parking spots near the trailhead, they found Will and Jeremy unloading the daypacks from the back of Will's truck. As she got out of the car, Gloria, feigning fear, demanded Steve's protection in a voice all could hear.

"Stay near me, I just know there are snakes and animals out here."

Gloria was quite pretty when she wasn't sneering or complaining. Her sandy-blonde hair fell just past her shoulders, and she took great pains to maintain her bouncy, wavy curls. She kept fit, and her slender 5'7" frame showed off her curves to great advantage. Undoubtedly, her physical beauty had attracted many men, and Steve was her latest conquest. As a child, she had watched her mother use others to get what she wanted, and Gloria was a quick study. She could turn her contrived flirtatiousness on and off like a switch, and Steve fell victim to it that night at the fraternity party. She had done her homework, and it was no coincidence that Gloria snagged an introduction to the senator's son that night. She craved power and money, and Steve offered plenty of both.

Gloria had a plan: meet and marry a wealthy East Coast businessman who would give her a financial safety net for life. Brown had accepted her application only because of her current stepfather Bill Willington, an alumnus who had been more than generous to his alma mater over the years. When Sylvia Stenner first met her fifth husband four years ago, she wasted no time in moving her family to New York City and snaring the rich bachelor executive. Gloria soon had her stepfather wrapped around her finger and saw him as a means to get into Brown or another Ivy League school where she could mix with young men from the right types of families: old money, powerful, influential. His ties and contributions to the university eventually ensured her admission to Brown despite her mediocre grades and sparse participation in school and community activities.

After her first husband left her, Gloria's mother decided to use any future marriage as a tool to improve her station in life. Sylvia wasn't above using Gloria in her battles, teaching the little girl to manipulate her dad and bring in a little extra cash to supplement her child support payments. Gloria's father came to resent her as she matured for her part in Sylvia's ploys, and Gloria no longer had a relationship with him.

Her mother's marriages never seemed to last. Gloria was the product of a second union; she had an older half-sister four years her senior, the result of an early teenage pregnancy and brief marriage. Her older sister and Sylvia did not get along; the girl was addicted to drugs and lived with her dealer boyfriend. Gloria didn't miss her one bit. They had never spent much time together to develop much of a kinship. She also had several other step-siblings from other relationships her mother never settled into. Gloria wasn't close to any of them and didn't care. They weren't the type of family she could exactly be proud of if she fulfilled her ambitions of marrying into wealth.

Despite Gloria's frequent complaints, the first hour of the five-hour hike to the camp went well. The views in the Daniel Boone National Forest were dazzling any time of year, but now at the peak of autumn, their surroundings were simply breathtaking. This time of year was perfect for the hike they had in front of them, with the temperature in the mid-fifties and the sky a perfect azure blue. The terrain in this part of the park could be rugged, adding to its beauty, but the trail that led to the camp and on to the cave was relatively level. Their path went around the mountain, not over it as the adjoining trails did.

It was soon apparent to the group that the cool hiking weather and relative ease of the trail would do nothing to lessen Gloria's constant grumbling. For Steve's sake, the others tolerated her frequent demands for rest.

Near the halfway point of the hike, Gloria made a sudden announcement to no one in particular.

"I will not walk one more step. My feet are killing me, my legs are like rubber, and I'm all sweaty."

"We're only about a 100 yards from a small mountain stream. It has grassy banks, we can cool our feet and have some lunch," Will said with as much civility as he could muster. The thought of getting her hiking boots off, even if just for a moment, enticed Gloria enough that she grudgingly continued down the path. She was not the outdoors type, and her brand-new boots were rubbing painfully.

The stream was exactly as Will had described it. The morning sun had burned off the dew from the knee-high grass, helped along by a slight autumn breeze. The water was cutting the far bank in an ever-changing path, leaving a nice shelf of grass a foot higher than the water and right near the edge. The group jumped to the other bank at a point where the stream narrowed and spread out on the grassy shelf. Within minutes, they had their boots off and were resting with their bare feet in the cold, moving water as they ate lunch.

Gloria was nursing the big toe on her right foot, moving it gingerly as she soaked her feet in the stream. Noting Gloria's discomfort, Pattie hesitated only a moment before approaching her with a first-aid kit from her backpack.

"Gloria, I've got a bandage here that should help with your toe."

"I don't need any help from….well, thanks," Gloria started to rebuff Pattie's offer, then thought better of it.

"Use this gauze. Make sure it's good and dry, then put the open center in the middle of the sorest point. It'll help until those new boots have a chance to break in," Pattie instructed.

Steve relaxed back onto an elbow, pleased with the brief exchange. Pattie seemed more like her old self, and Gloria was at least being civil.

When Pattie moved back over beside Mike, he said quietly, "That was downright decent of you. Always the nurse, no matter who the victim is."

"Well, no one should have to suffer with that, even her," grumbled Pattie.

She was in her second year of nursing school at Berea College and also worked as a nurse's aide at the Irvine Convalescent Hospital. She couldn't stand to see anyone or anything suffer if she could ease their pain.

After a brief lunch break, the group's trek to the campsite continued without incident. Gloria's whining even seemed more intermittent, as Pattie's bandage eased the pain in her toe.

The trail thus far had been well-worn and easy to follow. Park volunteers did a good job maintaining the path and clearing away fallen debris. About a mile from the camp, Will called a halt.

"We're going to be leaving the main trail now," Will explained. "We all need to make certain no one falls behind. If you do, don't panic, just call out and we'll wait or come back for you." Will added the last bit for Gloria's sake.

"If something should happen and we do get separated, just make your way straight down the mountain and you'll find a creek. Follow it downstream, and you'll run into a ranger's cabin," he said to the group.

Following the ever-prepared Will, the group set out down a small, all-but-hidden side trail. The self-appointed protector of the group, Brandon, brought up the rear. It was immediately apparent they were no longer on a trail policed by the volunteers. The path was narrower and strewn with rocks and fallen limbs; this slowed their pace somewhat, but they still made steady progress. The group arrived at the camp with over an hour remaining before nightfall.

"The waterproof containers we used to stage supplies should be over here under this brush pile," said Will as he headed toward the spot. "Why don't you give me a hand, Brandon? Be careful of snakes. They'll be sluggish if they're out this late in the fall, but let's not take any chances."

"Here they are," Will called out a moment later. "Good old Josh, just where he said they'd be. Now, let's see what he has for us."

Josh was true to his word: he had bedding and blankets in one tub, cooking supplies in another, and tents in the last one, although tents wouldn't be needed on such a mild fall night.

The old friends were all experienced campers and had already started preparing the campsite for the evening. Mike was gathering firewood while Pattie repaired the fire pit and cleared the area where they would bed down. Jeremy had gone over to help Brandon and Will with the supplies. Steve was helping Gloria ease her hiking boot over her sore toe.

In no time, the friends had the campsite in order. Mike made a small fire, and Pattie arranged their bedrolls nearby. Dinner was soon cooking over the small fire, its warmth permeating the chilly night air. Mike had made sure he gathered enough firewood to last all night and through breakfast in the morning.

Will knew as well as the rest of the group that camping with a fire outside of designated park areas was not permitted. However, because they were all locals and had grown up in the area, the friends knew every ranger in the park. More importantly, the rangers knew them, and of their dedication to leave the park in better condition than they found it. Even though Will was fairly certain the rangers wouldn't give them any trouble, the group kept their fire as small and smokeless as possible.

After dinner, the friends cleaned their dishes and pans with a minimum of conversation and without Gloria's help. They stowed everything away for the night and sat on the edge of their bedding nearest the fire to glean what warmth they could before turning in.

"What's Mrs. Stayton going to do with Josh's collection of instruments? It was huge" said Jeremy, as he poked at the campfire with a small stick.

"I think they should all be donated to a museum. They're way too cool to be left collecting dust," Steve mused.

Josh had inherited his musical talent from his father. Mr. Stayton never played professionally, but he had been the leader of the local, award-winning church choir. He often played a variety of musical instruments at the services. Josh's father also enjoyed discovering instruments from different cultures, and over the years had accumulated a small but impressive collection.

Even before his father's death, it was obvious Josh was born to be a musician. On his seventh birthday, his dad had given him a Hohner #842 Blues Chromatic harmonica. His mother had argued at the time that Josh was too young and couldn't possibly appreciate the expensive instrument. Later, she was glad her husband had insisted. The harmonica was Josh's constant companion, and he rarely left the house without it in his shirt pocket. The Hohner was on the stand beside his hospital bed when he died.

After his father's death, Josh threw himself into music and, in particular, the mastery of each of the instruments in the collection. Over the years, with the aid of the Internet, Josh almost tripled the number of items.

Much to Mrs. Stayton's aggravation, who was growing tired of the expanding collection taking over the house, even Will helped out. He often put his formidable woodworking skills to use building replicas of instruments Josh couldn't afford to buy.

"Wherever the instruments end up, I hope they're played and loved, that's what would make Josh happy," offered Pattie.

Will's thoughts turned back to their journey. "If we've any hope of getting to the cave and back to the cars before nightfall, we'll need to leave early. It'll take us about two hours to get to the cave, then three or four hours to explore. If we leave around 8:00, that should get us back here around 3:00 p.m. That should give us just enough time to get back to the cars before nightfall."

Hearing the 8:00 a.m. start time, Gloria snorted and crossed her arms as the group turned as one to stare at her. She glared back at them defiantly, muttering "country hicks" under her breath before falling silent. Only Will, the closest to her, overheard.

Turning back to the group, Will ignored her and continued, "So, we'll get up at 7:00 a.m., that'll give us time to have breakfast, and break camp by 8:00." It really wouldn't take that long, but after Gloria's insult, he couldn't resist moving up their start time.

Soon after this exchange, they turned in. They were all tired from the events of the last few days, and still saddened by thoughts of the funeral service. They couldn't force themselves to stay awake talking into the night like they used to.

When the group woke early the next morning, Brandon was not in his sleeping bag. The others weren't too concerned, knowing he had likely slipped off to perform his morning ritual of martial arts exercises. Sure enough, he came strolling into camp moments later with his hair wet from a dip in a nearby stream. "How was working out in the dark, in the middle of the woods?" asked Mike with a grin.

"Not bad. Bet you missed the girls, though," Brandon parried.

Will and Jeremy had already brought the small fire back to life from the banked coals. This added a little illumination to the scant early dawn light. The mountains were gorgeous yet eerie at this hour, the spooky effect compounded by a light morning fog and the flickering firelight.

Gloria remained unaware of the beautiful landscape, merely complaining as she rolled back into her blankets, "This is crazy, it's still dark."

The morning ritual of preparing the camp breakfast went smoothly: the friends had gone through the motions together many times before. Gloria fell back to sleep, unaware of their orchestrated movements as they cooked the simple but hearty fare, ate quietly, and quickly cleaned and stowed the cooking and camping equipment. She missed eating breakfast as well, finally rising only upon Steve's insistence.

The sun was just coming up as they made their final preparations to leave, and Will briefly explained the next part of their trek.

"The trail is about the same as the last mile into the camp, but it'll only take us a little over an hour to get to the cave." Although they had nearly reached their destination last night, he knew why Josh had arranged for them to set up camp here instead of forging on to the cave. Will and Josh were both very protective of the park, and with inexperienced spelunkers, damage to the caves was a real possibility. Also, Will suspected that Josh wanted to keep the cave a secret, and keeping the campsite away from the cave entrance would make it less likely to be found by others.

The group hoisted their packs and headed for the cave in the same single-file order as the day before, with Will in the lead and Brandon bringing up the rear. It wasn't long before the others could hear Gloria hissing at Steve. After 20 minutes of this, she flounced away in a huff, leaving him behind. She had been chastising Steve for forcing her to come on this dreadful trip. However, that wasn't the real reason she was so upset with him. He really earned her ire when he pointed out that he had tried repeatedly, but in vain, to convince her to stay behind. Unable to dispute his account, she stormed off to the front of the column. Steve watched her go. He was quite content to walk alone, relieved that he no longer had to deal with her incessant whining.

Lost in thought, Steve was going back over the events of the past few days when Mike came up behind him, catching him off guard.

"Why in the world are you with someone like that?"

Steve wasn't sure how to respond at first, but decided to be honest with his old friend. Gloria was well out of earshot, up the trail somewhere out of sight.

"She wasn't at all like this when we first met. We were introduced at a fraternity/sorority mixer. She was a sweet girl for the first two months we dated but, little by little, she changed. The first time I really saw it was the night she demanded we go to a very expensive restaurant. I told her I couldn't afford it. She couldn't believe it. My parents insist on paying for my tuition and my trips abroad, but I work on-campus jobs for spending money. I hate asking my parents to pay for anything I can handle myself."

"Gloria couldn't understand how anyone could be that stupid and pig-headed. That night, she insisted I put an end to my 'silly behavior' and ask my parents for what amounted to an allowance, and a very generous one at that. She wouldn't stop talking about it, finally becoming downright insistent. She refused to see my side, and finally I had my fill of it. I was ready to break up. I had actually set up a time to meet with her and end it the day I got Pattie's call about Josh. I just couldn't deal with her that night."

Mike interrupted. "If you felt that way about her, why in the world did you bring her along?"

"It wasn't my idea. My parents invited her; more specifically, my father. It seems that her stepfather is a big donor to the national committee. When I got out to my car to come down here, she was standing beside it with all her luggage. She and my father arranged the whole thing. I argued and argued with her, because I knew this wasn't her type of thing. I felt so bad about Josh, I ended up just giving in to her."

Mike started to say something, then stopped. He finally blurted out, "None of this would have been an issue if you weren't such an idiot about Pattie."

"Pattie?" Steve asked, genuinely surprised.

"I've seen how you look at her when you think no one is looking, and she's always had feelings for you. The day she first saw you at camp when we stopped that bully years ago, she went on and on about you. Ever since then, she's been interested, we all knew it. So, here comes the big question. Why haven't you ever let her know how you feel about her?"

Steve was stunned by Mike's directness. He didn't answer right away, concentrating instead on the trail as if his life depended on it. Finally, he ventured a response.

"I always thought you and Pattie were…"

"Pattie and me? Are you kidding? We grew up together. We're more like brother and sister than we are with our own siblings!" Mike said disbelievingly, unable to fathom how Steve could get it so wrong.

"Then why haven't you said anything before?" Steve asked

Mike said earnestly, "She made me swear to never tell you. Now don't laugh, but she felt you were destined for 'greatness.' She really believed she'd hold you back because of her rural upbringing and lifestyle. I've tried countless times to tell her she needed to let you make that decision for yourself. But our conversations always ended with her reminding me of my promise. But I can't do this anymore. I can't let two of my closest friends go their separate ways without getting this out in the open."

The two friends walked on, an uneasy silence between them.

After a few minutes, Mike said, "I'm not sure what else I can tell you. I don't expect you to act on this while Gloria is with us, but you need to think seriously about what I've told you."

Mike clapped Steve on the shoulder. Quickening his pace, he moved on up the trail to join the others, leaving Steve with his thoughts. Thirty minutes later, Will called a halt.

"This is where we leave the trail. Josh and I stopped in this same spot. He went over in that direction to relieve himself." Will pointed off to the side toward what looked like a game trail. "He shouted for me to hurry over—he'd seen an albino deer, a small doe. She ran off in that direction, up and over the steep terrain, and Josh wanted to follow her. I thought it strange that the doe chose a route with such difficult footing."

"Shortly after we started tracking her, about 100 feet from here, the trail opened out into what's called an eyebrow plateau. It's actually a shelf in a very steep part of the mountain," Will explained.

Till now, the group had been picking their way slowly along a mere pig trail. This next portion of the hike, although brief, would force them up the same sharp incline the doe had followed. Though he thought it unlikely, Will instructed the others, "Try to avoid leaving any sign that we've left the trail. I don't want anyone following us." It was only through a series of coincidences that he and Josh had even stumbled upon the place, and Will wanted to keep their destination private.

"You should be used to this cloak-and-dagger stuff, Mike. Are you still into paintball like you used to be?" Steve asked, using his body to hold back a wind-blown branch so that Gloria and Mike could pass.

"Nah, I only got to go out three times this summer, and two of those were just to help Millie. I purposely never sought out any fields in Columbus, I knew it would take too much time away from school," Mike answered, following Gloria through the opening Steve had created.

When he was 14, after a year of pestering the owner of Lockland Fields, Mike had convinced Millie to hire him part-time. Millie never regretted her decision. She was pleased with his work and often called Mike to fill in when teams needed more players. He had an uncanny ability to develop winning strategies for his teams and before long, players were asking for him almost every weekend. As he gained experience on the paintball fields, Mike began incorporating the battle techniques he read about. His successes on the paintball course were not limited to strategy and tactics. Mike also had an instinct for choosing the right person for the role needed, and, despite his young age, could inspire his players to achieve more than they thought possible.

The hikers pushed on, grabbing onto trees and undergrowth to stay on the hillside as they progressed upward. The going was very slow, but they eventually found the plateau just as Will had described it. It started just as a flat spot only a few feet wide and curved out of sight. After following the welcome flat path for just a few yards, the group discovered a grassy plateau fanning out 30 feet at its widest point. Jeremy found himself picturing the albino deer grazing peacefully and second-guessed once again his decision to go away to college. If he hadn't gone, no doubt he would have been with Will and Josh when they found this beautiful, secluded spot.

Will, Jeremy, and Josh had grown up together and become close friends, but Will and Josh had really bonded once Jeremy went away to college. He had initially tried commuting the 40 minutes to school and keeping his job at his dad's fabrication shop, but it was too much. Jeremy found working at the shop far too distracting and moved into an off-campus apartment halfway through the semester.

Jeremy was the opposite of Will in physical appearance and personal grooming habits. Jeremy was 5 feet, 8 inches and a compact 165 pounds, and stayed fit doing regular workouts. He kept his dark-brown hair clean and cut to a medium length. He was always well-dressed and aware of his appearance, making sure even his shop clothes were clean and ironed. He couldn't wait to shower and change if he got dirty while he was working. Will, on the other hand, couldn't be less concerned about his appearance. Slightly overweight, he stood an even six feet, weighing in at 230 pounds. His light brown hair was always just a bit too long and shaggy, and it was obvious he didn't often trim his beard or moustache. If he would devote some time to his appearance, he wouldn't be bad-looking; however, the best way to describe Will most of the time was frumpy.

Despite their differences, Will and Jeremy were close. Both brothers learned the techniques and mechanics of fabrication while working in their father's shop and loved inventing and experimenting with different fabrication methods. Mr. Reinard always encouraged his two boys, but often let them figure things out on their own, especially how to work together. He was very proud of their abilities and the time they devoted to the family business.

Where Jeremy picked up enough to be handy, Will would go further and master a technique. Will was also the better of the two at practical mechanical skills. Always a prepared individual, as evidenced by his preparations for the camping trip, when it came to inventing and tackling fabrication projects, he tended instead to wing it. He liked going through the materials in his head and the tools needed, then gathering all of them around him before he started a project. He seldom made lists or drawings; instead, he could plan a construction project out in his mind and make adjustments as he went along.

Will's ability to "wing it" drove Jeremy nuts. Jeremy approached projects with a detailed plan, including sketches and lists of materials. He took a more cerebral approach to high-end engineering concepts, and loved math and drafting. Jeremy would rad engineering textbooks by the hour. Will, on the other hand, read tech manuals and Popular Mechanics. Rather than driving the brothers apart, these different approaches actually worked well for them, and they found a way to play off each other's strengths.

On a big project, Jeremy would lay out the overall being as specific as time permitted. He knew that Will with his creativity and technical slills could fill in any details that were omitted. Once, when they were boys, they entered a competition and built a go-cart. Jeremy sketched the desired design and made a list of the major components, including drive train, steering, seating, safety equipment, etc. Will took on the design of the steering and constructed a rack-and-pinion system they were able to use in future projects. Jeremy had introduced the rack-and-pinion concept to his brother, but it was Will who turned the concept into reality.

Jeremy shook off his recollections and resumed his assessment of the grassy plateau before him. The mature trees both above and below the plateau hid the shelf from either vantage point. The rock face at the back of the plateau, its widest point, was about 40 feet high. A large portion of the face had fallen, the slabs of granite forming a massive, jumbled pile. The granite chunks must have tumbled down a very long time ago, as the substantial roots of an old-growth oak wove their way through the side of the rock pile nearest the group.

The cave could not be seen from the south end of plateau where the group now stood. "We'd have never found the cave if we hadn't stopped for lunch," Will recalled.

He began leading them to the other side of the plateau as he continued his story. "After lunch, Josh (always exploring) was searching for deer tracks on the north side of the landing when he came upon the entrance."

When they were nearly to the far side of the plateau, Will motioned for them to turn around and look back the way they had come.

"Wow, that's cool," Jeremy said with astonishment.

They were all looking at the entrance to the cave. "It does look just like a western spur," said Pattie.

The entrance started on the right-hand side with an opening only a foot high that led to the left, toward the fallen granite slabs. It gradually increased in height as it ran for eight or nine feet, where it abruptly opened into a circular entrance seven feet in diameter. This larger entrance was almost perfectly round, with cracks radiating out all the way around the perimeter, giving it the look of a spur.

"I brought you all over here so you could see what Josh and I saw that day," clarified Will.

"Let's go see what Josh has for us in the cave" urged Jeremy. They began following him to the opening until Will stopped them.

"Hold on a minute, I've got a few things to talk to you about. Josh and I lived by the first rule of spelunking: always, always leave the cave as you found it. So, before we go into the cave as a group, let's bring the equipment out into the sunlight and I'll go over its use."

The sunlight was intense now, shining out of the cloudless, blue sky. It was close to 10:00 a.m., and the sun was warming this eastern side of the mountain.

Jeremy and Brandon ducked inside and soon re-emerged with two large, sealed tubs. Josh had stored them far enough into the cave that they didn't need to be waterproof, but the sealed lids kept any curious varmints out.

"Let's see what he has for us this time," Jeremy said as he set the tub on the ground and started to open it. This tub contained several lengths of heavy-duty climbing rope, harnesses, rappelling gear, caving helmets with built-in headlamps, and several unopened packages of batteries. In his tub, Brandon found coveralls, knee and elbow pads, caving backpacks, and six L.E.D. flashlights.

"Josh spent a lot of money—this is high-end equipment. He must have made several trips to get it all here," observed Jeremy.

"I agree, and it had to be long after he started feeling the effects of his chemotherapy," added Will. He began sorting through the supplies and issuing instructions before his emotions got the better of him.

"Let's get the coveralls, pads, and helmets on, then I'll go through the other gear. I've got some extra equipment for Gloria here in my pack."

Will started handing the items out to her. Once everyone had their gear on, Will helped them adjust their harnesses and ran through some brief instructions on the rappelling gear.

Each member transferred their food and any other gear they thought essential into the caving backpacks and stowed the rest into the tubs. When everyone was finished equipping themselves for the next leg of the journey, they stored the tubs back inside the mouth of the cave. With that done and headlamps lit, the group was ready, standing in the mouth of the cave and anxious to get started. That is, with the exception of Gloria. The thought of going any further into the slimy cave was truly dreadful to her.

Will led the way, recounting the earlier trip, "We didn't have much time before dark to explore and had no equipment. Besides, Josh was getting tired, so we planned to return in a couple of weeks and examine the place thoroughly." He added quietly, "That was the week he was diagnosed, and we never came back."

The first chamber was bigger than the group expected, 12 feet high and over 20 feet deep. Will led them toward a fissure in the back and disappeared between its sides. The opening was wide enough that even Brandon fit through comfortably. Once they were all through, the group resumed its now-familiar, single-file order and began the trek into the cave.

The passageway was narrow but manageable, and led consistently downward. Will was impressed by his environs already. Many caves in the area that he and Josh explored had only a small first chamber and nothing more.

About 100 feet into the cave, they came across their first obstacle. The pathway had widened to over ten feet but then suddenly ended. Will gauged it to be roughly a 12-foot drop to where the path resumed. He and Jeremy rigged some rope and lowered the others slowly. Steve quietly but insistently managed to convince Gloria there was no turning back. Reluctantly and ungraciously she relented, allowing the men to lower her slim form but cursing under her breath most of the way down. Will then lowered Jeremy before climbing carefully down unassisted.

Once on the lower level, the passageway narrowed again and continued as before, downward and straight into the mountain. After only a short distance, the group encountered another drop, this one only four feet. Brandon nimbly jumped down, then helped the others. They continued on like this for over 40 minutes. Will's favorable first impression of the cave only grew as they went on.

The passage didn't contain stalactites or stalagmites; although the surface was limestone, there was very little water, meaning the key element required for the creation of the structures was not present. Small traces of water were apparent at times, but it seemed only to be working its way through small cracks to a lower portion of the mountain.

"This passage appears to have been cut by water, even though it's dry now," observed Jeremy. He clarified, "It has a relatively smooth, flat bottom and little debris." The passage walls slowly tapered upward to form tall, arrow-shaped ceilings.

At last they reached a drop of over 40 feet into a large chamber whose ceiling was only ten feet above the passageway floor. They couldn't see the far walls of the chamber with the amount of light cast by their headlamps, so Will broke out one of the L.E.D flashlights.

"That has to be over a 100 feet across, and 50 feet from floor to ceiling," Will calculated, clearly impressed. "I see no opening other than this one up high, but some of those fissures near the floor have promise." He continued with a note of caution in his voice, "Jeremy, help me with the rigging, we need to be careful and get this right. We don't want to get anyone hurt this far back in."

The brothers had worked together all their lives and soon had rigged the ropes to Will's satisfaction. Still, he insisted on being the first to be lowered. When Gloria's turn came, she allowed herself to be lowered down without a fuss, too frightened even to curse this time. Jeremy was the last to rappel down; they left the rigging in place for their return trip.

"Let's explore those fissures. If you find any with promise, don't go far. Meet back here, and we'll decide which one we want to try first," instructed Will.

The group split up and started exploring the dozen fissures around the chamber. After several minutes, they all returned to the center, reporting dead ends.

"It looks like the end of the line" said Will disappointedly.

"Thank God," Gloria chimed in.

Ignoring the remark, Will said, "We may as well break for lunch. It's after 11:30, and the walk back will be harder than the hike in."

They took off their packs, made themselves as comfortable as possible, and began eating their cold lunches.

"Well, I guess an impressive chamber, this far into the mountain, is a fitting resting place for Josh," said Mike thoughtfully.

"I agree," nodded Will. "And up there on that small shelf would be a great place for the urn." He pointed to a narrow shelf ten feet above the floor of the chamber.

"How about you boost me up there, Brandon, and I'll make sure that it'll work." Brandon had just finished his lunch, so he jumped up and met Will at the bottom of the shelf. With little effort, he lifted Will up until his head and helmet light was above the lip of the shelf.

"Wait a minute, there's a horizontal crack large enough for me to fit through," Will said with newfound excitement "Can you lift me up further?"

The shelf was just to the side of where they had descended into the chamber. They could hardly see the shelf, let alone the fissure, and the fissure was not visible from the floor of the chamber.

With Brandon's help, Will was able to pull himself up onto the shelf. He disappeared until a few minutes later, sticking his head over the lip of the shelf. Full of excitement, Will exclaimed, "You gotta see this! Throw me some rope and I'll set a rigging for you."

Within no time, the energized Will had the rigging in place and the group lined up to begin squeezing through the fissure.

Will called to Jeremy, the first to disappear into the fissure, "Just go into the chamber ahead and wait for the others." He turned back to help the others onto the narrow shelf. Brandon was last to approach the fissure. Will observed, "It looks like you'll have to take off that pack and squeeze a bit, old buddy."

Brandon, feeling no small amount of apprehension, slid the pack off his back as Will instructed. It was a very tight squeeze for his large frame, but with some guidance and encouragement from Will, he was able to squirm through.

The others were waiting in a chamber just big enough to hold them all, below the passageway that led to the opening. A large vertical fissure ran down the right-hand side.

Will pushed forward through the group to resume the lead, still animated by his find. "I only went a short way from here, but the path leads away from the chamber and the passageway above."

The passageway was so narrow at this point, Brandon was forced to hold his pack in front of him. Will's excitement was contagious, and the entire group, even Gloria, was eager to press on. They moved forward as one, and the narrowness of the passage eased only slightly. They advanced roughly 100 feet before Will halted abruptly.

"My God," he breathed.

Jeremy, right on his heels, said anxiously, "Come on, let us have a look."

Hardly able to believe his eyes, Will moved forward into a massive chamber and stepped aside, allowing the others to enter. They regrouped, adjusting to the extra space that suddenly surrounded them, and began shining their headlamps in all directions, trying to find a surface that would reflect the light on either side of the entry or the floor. Neither the far wall nor the ceiling was visible. The ones with the more powerful flashlights were already digging in their packs as Will pushed forward into the large space, using his headlamp to light his path.

Fifty feet into the chamber, the ground began gradually rising, the smooth floor giving way to small debris that appeared to have fallen from the ceiling. The mound of rubble continued to rise in the beam of the more powerful flashlight Will had retrieved from his pack as he walked further into the chamber.

He pressed on alone, curious as to the height of the ceiling and the overall size of the underground hall. The debris that Will stepped over was made of various-sized chips of limestone. It was packed down, but still gave way slightly as he walked. Because of this, he proceeded with caution after his initial charge toward the center of the chamber.

Up to this point in the trek, Will had been the protector and leader of the group. Now, his curiosity and excitement had gotten the better of him—reaching the top of the debris mound was his only thought. The rest of the group broke into two groups and started exploring along the walls of the chamber. Pattie, Mike, and Jeremy fanned out to the right of the entry, while Steve, Gloria, and Brandon took the left route. Each group made sure to keep the wall within sight of their flashlights at all times. Judging from the radius of the walls as they proceeded around the perimeter, it was soon apparent to them all that the chamber was massive. They had discovered a geologic wonder.

For some time, the two groups continued exploring the perimeter, weaving around slabs of limestone that had fallen from the ceiling, expecting at some point to meet at the back of the chamber.

Will continued to climb the mound. He was now more than 200 feet into the chamber and 50 feet higher than the entry below. He still couldn't see the ceiling using the flashlight's powerful beam. The others had proceeded far enough around the chamber to guess that it might be as large as 800 to 1,000 feet across.

Will's cry broke the silence of the cavernous space, "You have to see this!" His voice floated far above them.

"Where are you?" Jeremy shouted back.

"I'm in the center of the chamber on a massive mound of debris." Will was so excited he could hardly contain himself. Casting aside his typical cautious nature, he shouted to the others, "Hurry, you'll never believe what I've found!"

CHAPTER 3

CHAIRS

Jeremy was already scrambling up the massive debris pile, ignoring the unsure footing. He had thrown aside all caution, as he often did to his older brother's consternation, and Will was concerned for his safety.

"Are you all right?" shouted Jeremy breathlessly as he continued his dash.

"I'm fine, just slow down," Will instructed his brother. "Everyone, be careful, but you have to get up here, you won't believe it!"

The others began following quickly, but not with Jeremy's reckless abandon.

"Just come to the center of the mound, it spreads out in all directions," yelled Will, his voice displaying the same level of excitement as before.

Jeremy crested the top of the mound and stood in disbelief. The only sounds he made were harsh intakes of breath caused by his hurried ascent.

Pattie and Mike were the next to make the summit. They had been slowed by the constant shower of loose limestone chips Jeremy generated as he raced up the mound in front of them. They, too, stood breathing hard and speechless.

Brandon came next, having taken the time to help Steve with Gloria, who was struggling to cover the debris field in her new boots. Finally, just past the halfway point, Brandon could contain himself no longer. He took off up the mound, shouting over his shoulder, "See you at the top!"

Just as Brandon was saying, "My God, what is that," Gloria and Steve reached the summit and gaped, open-mouthed. Even Gloria was speechless.

At the top of the mound was a flattened level radius, 60 feet in diameter. After just five feet of leveled debris, three stone steps rose around the entire circumference of the mound. At the top of these steps was a flagstone platform nearly 45 feet in diameter. Will was standing near the center of this stone platform facing the new arrivals, his arms spread wide in a gesture of disbelief.

Eight large empty stone chairs sat atop the flagstone platform, like mute spectators to some drama played out long ago in this dark, cavernous space. The chairs were arranged in a circle, facing inward. Mike began running his hands over the closest one, using the light from his headlamp to examine it as the others approached.

"How could this have gotten here?" said Mike in astonishment. The history major had received scholarships to a number of colleges, but had chosen OSU for its outstanding military history program, aside from the fact that Brandon would be playing football there. Mike knew full well that no one had ever made a finding like this.

"The workmanship of the stone is astounding," Jeremy said in awe. He would notice that aspect before anything else, thanks to his father. Mr. Reinard had taught both his sons at an early age to appreciate fine craftsmanship.

The stones were perfectly set, not in the way the Mayan temples were set, with perfectly cut stones. Instead, these had been painstakingly chosen to fit perfectly, one stone into the next, and looked as natural as if they had always been there.

Jeremy noted the lack of mortar, or maybe the fit was so tight there was no gap for mortar. Even the perfectly smooth flagstone surface the chairs sat upon, composed of much larger stones, was perfectly matched.

Henry Reinard, Will and Jeremy's uncle, was a master stone mason; they often helped him on big jobs during summer breaks. Jeremy understood the enormity of the task of setting these stones this way. He thought it truly impossible.

The chairs were perfectly spaced in a circle, 15 feet apart. Mike noted that each chair was much like a throne in size, though lacking ornate carvings. He resumed his examination of the chair nearest him. The back stood over six feet and ran all the way to the floor. The seat was a solid slab and standard height from the floor; straight armrests continued up the sides another ten inches. The chairs had been crafted with precision and were covered in what appeared to be runes.

"These runes appear to be Celtic or Nordic," offered Mike.

"They're similar, but they're not like any runes I've studied," Steve said, curious as to their true origin. "I studied Celtic extensively last year in school," he added matter-of-factly, without bragging. "We also covered Nordic, Elder Futhark, and Gothic for comparison, and I've seen rune-like writing from several other cultures. I've never seen any like these."

"These are carved from a single piece of stone," said Will, speaking almost to himself.

"The circular base is also part of the same stone," he added as an afterthought. "That base is more than five feet in diameter and has to be pretty thick to support the weight of the chair," he concluded. Will was on his hands and knees now, closely examining where the base met the chair. Jeremy made his way over to the chair near Will.

"Have you ever seen stone like this around here?" Will motioned for Jeremy to join in his inspection of the chair. Jeremy bent down beside his brother and lent the additional aid of his flashlight. The stone appeared to be a pale-cream color, with a hint of red veining throughout.

"It's definitely like nothing I've seen around here, or anywhere else for that matter," concluded Jeremy. "It has the coloration of marble, but the texture of granite. I'm no geologist, but I've never seen anything like it working with Uncle Henry, or on any buildings I can recall."

"That's exactly what I was thinking," Will said, perplexed. "So how did these massive carved seats, or the stone to carve them, get all the way down here?"

Gloria collapsed into one of the chairs and let out a big sigh. Even she couldn't be bored with a find like this, thought Pattie, who had been quiet since reaching the summit of the mound. Wanting to put some distance between herself and Gloria, she followed Brandon's lead, depositing her pack beside one of the chairs and making her way towards the center of the circle.

As she approached Brandon, Pattie remarked, "The stone in the floor here is the same as the chairs."

Brandon nodded. "And runes much like the ones on the chairs are carved into those stones."

"See how the same stone connects the base of each chair in a circle, and then a line radiates to the center from each chair," said Pattie, using her flashlight beam to point out what she was describing.

"Looks like a wheel and spokes," concluded Brandon. The band of stone was eight inches wide and cut very precisely into the naturally fitting flagstone floor.

The group spent the next few minutes milling around, examining the chairs and floor. Finally, Mike asked the others, "What do we do now?"

"We can't exactly keep this a secret," said Steve as he made his way over to Gloria. He felt a twinge of guilt as he realized he had forgotten all about her for the last several minutes.

Jeremy observed, "This will definitely change the entire region."

"I see what you mean," agreed Brandon, realizing the impact of such a discovery.

"Archaeologists will be crawling all over this place," mused Pattie.

"Don't forget linguists. Those runes may be unique or a transitional breakthrough," added Steve.

"You'll be famous for your great find," Gloria said to Steve in a calculating voice. Embarrassed, Steve shook his head slowly as the others stared at her in disbelief.

"My concern's for the park and all the other caves," said Will, redirecting their attention to the matter at hand.

"I mean, they'll likely shut down at least this part of the park, if not all of it, but that'll do little or nothing to keep treasure hunters from trashing every cave around here."

Pattie and Brandon turned and made their way back to the chairs where they had left their packs. Both of them sank slowly onto the stone seats as they thought about the impact of the find.

"Even if we're discreet about this, word will leak out eventually, and the results will be the same," Jeremy mused as he sat on the front edge of his chair without removing his pack.

"The historical impact of this is nothing short of spectacular," Mike stated, making his way to the empty chair between Jeremy and Brandon.

"I'm not an archaeologist, but I think these definitely pre-date Columbus, and the runes are similar to a form of runes used over 1,000 years ago, but not the same as any Steve knows about. That means...Hell, I don't know what that means," concluded Mike. He fell silent, sitting in the vacant chair lost in thought.

Will had stowed all of his gear on one of the seats after he reached the summit and called to the others. After he completed his examination of the chair, rather than move his pack, the bag that held spare batteries, and the pack that contained Josh's ashes, he moved over to a vacant one and sat down heavily. He was overwhelmed by the findings of this morning and had abandoned his plans to make it back to the cars before nightfall. It was now past noon, and if they had any hope of making it back before then, they needed to leave immediately. Leaving, however, was the last thing Will wanted to think about right now.

Steve was kneeling by Gloria's chair, talking to her in a low voice as the others considered the ramifications of disclosing their find. He straightened and addressed the group.

"It's now a little after 12:00 p.m. I say we rest a bit and then explore the rest of the cave."

Steve walked over to the last vacant chair. Gloria huffed, making no attempt to hide her disappointment at his proposal.

"We can look around for another three or four hours and still make it back to camp before nightfall."

The others nodded agreement but maintained a contemplative silence.

"Don't look so glum. This is a great find," Steve said encouragingly as he looked around at his friends.

"It looks like Josh tied us all together in a way he never could have imagined," he said, turning to sit.

At the precise moment Steve relaxed into his chair, the entire cave and the very ground itself began to rumble. The sound was deafening.

CHAPTER 4

SUMMONED

His ears were ringing, as if he had just been subjected to an explosion. His eyes ached as if he had just witnessed a bright flash. But Josh couldn't recall either of these things happening to him. He vividly remembered his mother crying at his hospital bedside and trying to console her. He wanted to smile at her and tell her everything would be fine, but his voice would not obey. From that point on, he seemed to be moving through a disjointed, confusing dream.

He recalled floating above his bed as a nurse shouted "Code Blue!" He watched from above as several hospital personnel raced into the room. Just as in a dream, events shifted and he suddenly saw his mom standing over a casket, putting his harmonica into the shirt pocket of a man wearing a suit. He couldn't see the man's face. "Am I dead? Was that me?" he thought.

Images shifted again, and he saw all his friends gathered in the living room of his house. Next, he was entering the cave he and Will had found a few months ago.

Now he was surrounded by semi-darkness, looking at an odd chair spotlighted by flashlights. Again he saw his childhood friends, all sitting on similar chairs in a circle surrounding him.

Josh's thoughts jolted to the present. "Where am I now? This doesn't feel like a dream. It seems real, except I can't see or hear."

He became aware of a slight, cool breeze and the sun warming the side of his face.

Josh's hurried thoughts continued. "I must be outdoors in an open field; no, I smell forest, a wooded area is nearby." He also detected a fresh scent, like just after a storm, but he couldn't smell rain and was not wet.

He then realized he was sitting on something hard, cold, and uncomfortable. "I can feel."

His arms and hands were resting on something hard and cold. Josh moved his fingertips lightly over the surface and thought it felt like smooth stone. His feet were also upon on a hard surface and something crunched under his shoes. "Shoes, I have shoes on?" thought Josh as he moved his feet ever so slightly. He became aware of a shirt collar against his neck and ran his hands over his chest.

"I'm wearing a suit; I haven't worn a suit since dad's funeral when I was 12."

The ringing in Josh's ears had changed to a buzz; his hearing was returning sooner than his sight. His mind raced, "This must be what death is like. Damn, I hope this buzzing doesn't continue."

The first thing he heard clearly was the uncontrolled screaming of a woman. She seemed to be 15 feet away and completely terrified. "

What the hell is that?" he thought, then caught himself.

"Oh Lord, please don't let this be Hell"

He could hear chanting a little further way. It sounded like a foreign language, and much like the chanting of monks.

"Maybe this is Heaven," he thought, more hopeful now.

Josh could see dark silhouettes taking form in the bright whiteness. A shadowed movement caught his attention, and he turned his head to follow it. More defined shapes started taking form.

The chanting stopped, and now he heard a lot of frantic shouting in a foreign tongue. Josh thought the foreigners were trying to shout over the screaming of the terrified women.

"Wait, that was Brandon shouting to stay back," Josh thought, more confused than ever.

His mind was whirling with confusion, doubt, and concern. "Why would Brandon be in heaven? My God, he can't be dead, I just saw him play in the big Michigan game only a few days ago."

Josh's sight was improving rapidly now. The dark shapes in the field of light were taking definite form. He could make out large, square shapes, maybe those chairs, and some shapes that might well be people.

His eyesight almost completely restored now, he leaned forward, stunned. He was opposite a screaming woman he had never seen, but what confused him more were the other sights before him. His childhood friend Steve Oliver knelt beside the frightened woman, trying to console her. Brandon was in a fighting stance behind the woman's seat.

Josh realized he was sitting on a massive stone chair, as were the others. "The others," he thought. His closest friends sat surrounding him in the chairs he had seen in the darkness of his dreams. They hadn't noticed him yet; their focus was on the screaming stranger.

"I wish she would shut up," thought Josh.

The ring of chairs they occupied sat upon a flat, flagstone platform at least 60 feet in diameter, stepping down to a narrow shelf of knee-high grass. This shelf gave way to a rather steep incline trailing off in all directions. By Josh's calculations, they were sitting atop a high grassy mound, about 70 feet tall, in the middle of a vast forest.

Josh saw the source of the chanting he heard earlier. It was a ring of what seemed to be clerics, judging from the coarse cloth robes they wore tied at the waist with braided cord. Josh counted eight men, one for each of the eight chairs in the circle.

All but one was standing just a few feet behind their respective chairs. That individual was near the screaming woman and the reason Brandon had assumed his fighting stance and threatening demeanor. From what Josh could observe, the man meant no harm, as he was backing off quickly from Brandon. It seemed to Josh that his intent had been merely to quiet the hysterical woman.

Josh sensed movement to his right. As he turned calmly in that direction, he saw the cleric behind his chair approaching him. Josh was calm for two reasons: he did not feel threatened by the cleric, and he was still quite disoriented.

The cleric was speaking a foreign language. Josh was not the expert Steve was on languages, but he was certain he had never heard its like. The man cautiously and gently held out to Josh what looked to be a large, intricate coin, slightly larger than an old silver dollar. Josh flexed his fingers experimentally and took the coin in his right hand.

"Please, Summoned One, you must get this woman to stop screaming," said the cleric intently. To his surprise, Josh understood each word. The sensation was a bit overwhelming. It was not that Josh heard the words first in a foreign tongue, then their translation into English. Instead, he felt he understood the meaning of the words at the level of conscious thought.

"What do you want from me?" Josh asked, disoriented.

"Please, she must be quiet, the enemy is near," the cleric pleaded. "And get the others to accept these language tokens."

Josh understood one word above all the others—enemy. Because of this, he acted with no further prompting from the cleric. He stood and shouted to his friends, "Take the coins from these men. Steve, I know you're trying, but you've got to shut her up."

Josh's friends were still dealing with their own out-of-body experience. Suddenly they found themselves in another place and time, surrounded by what seemed to be chanting monks. Behind the monks were apparent soldiers. Gloria could not stop screaming. Brandon moved to intercept one of the robed figures as he began to approach her. Then, something even more unbelievable happened.

Between Gloria's screams, they all heard Josh's voice, as close as if he were right there with them. But they knew that couldn't be. His ashes were in Will's pack on one of the chairs. They turned in unison toward that chair and froze at the sight of Josh standing before it in an ill-fitting suit, very much alive and repeating his commands for quiet and ordering them to accept the coins offered by the monks. Even Brandon let down his guard. Gloria's screams dwindled to sobs as she took in the group's stunned reaction to the young man.

The friends wanted to approach him and touch him, hug him, prove to themselves he was alive, but their surreal surroundings and the urgency in Josh's voice stopped them. They nodded and gestured their acceptance of his instructions, holding out their hands to the monks. Gloria, who had finally stopped screaming, managed to follow suit.

The clerics assigned to each member of the group hurried forward and handed out their tokens. Josh realized they must have understood what he said to his friends. As a matter of fact, his cleric had responded when Josh asked what he wanted of him. It suddenly dawned on him that the strange tokens must be two-way translators.

"Hear me, Summoned Ones." A heavyset cleric in his early sixties addressed the entire group, speaking quickly and forcefully. "I know you're disoriented and afraid, but you must listen. We haven't much time."

The friends, though skeptical, perceived no immediate threat from the man and remained still, listening.

The cleric rushed on. "The noise of your summoning will have alerted the enemy to our position. We are deep in their territory and must depart now."

"What enemy? Where are we? How do we know you're not the enemy?" interrupted Brandon as he stepped forward in an obvious attempt to protect his friends.

"Enough of this, Varis, there is no time!"

The speaker stepped forward. Brandon thought distractedly that the man was dressed as if he had just come from a renaissance festival.

"I am General Darnon. You four with me, the rest with Commander Namir," the man continued, clearly upset that no one was moving. He was pointing toward Brandon, Steve, Gloria, and Pattie, the only ones forming a tight group. Brandon had come over to Steve and Gloria earlier to protect them, and Pattie had followed. She was hoping to calm the still-sobbing Gloria, who seemed to be in a state of shock.

Mike assessed the self-proclaimed leader using knowledge acquired through years of studying history. The man's garb was clearly that of a ranking officer, a fact that was borne out by the way in which the soldiers behind him (also officers, based on their attire) followed his lead.

Mike had a difficult time dating the general's outfit. It seemed to be a collection of items from several different periods in history. Mike noticed that the man wore them with the same ease that he himself might wear a pair of old blue jeans and a T-shirt. The man's knee-length, chain-mail hauberk ran all the way to a hood. This style was pre-1400s—an officer of this status would be in plate-mail after that. However, his weapons seemed to be of a later date. He wore a six-foot great-sword of exquisite workmanship sheathed diagonally across his broad back, the hilt protruding a foot above his head at his left shoulder. Mike noted that the workmanship of this sword and the long-bladed Basilard dagger the man also carried had to have been from far later in the Middle Ages, as late as the 1600s.

After a quick assessment of the general, Mike glanced at the man General Darnon had identified as Commander Namir. This man's attire was quite different from Darnon's, as were those of the soldiers standing near him. They wore finely crafted leather, from their specialized knee-high boots to their gloves. It was clear to Mike these soldiers were cavalry. The only chain mail each soldier possessed consisted of small patches in critical places, including a four-inch strip from under the arm to the waist, elbows, knees, forearms, crotch, and a narrow strip along the outer thigh. Mike knew the chain mail was used sparingly to lighten the burden of their steeds. Each soldier also wore a leather shirt with a hood sewn into the leather. The soldiers wore the hoods pushed back and draped across their shoulders.

Mike's eyes came to rest on the most unusual member of the group before him. The lone female member of the company was strikingly beautiful, with long, curly red hair that fell across her chain-mail vest. Her armor was similar to that worn by Darnon, who was apparently the ranking officer. Her most prominent feature aside from her beauty was her height. Mike calculated that she had to be at least 6 feet, 2 inches. It was obvious from the assortment of weapons she carried that she was an accomplished warrior.

Her weapons consisted of three maces, one massive as a good-sized cannon ball, attached by a short length of chain to a metal billy club. The other two were made in a similar fashion, but were half the size. Because she did not carry a bow as the others did, Mike assumed she used the smaller maces as throwing weapons. His assessment of the female warrior was interrupted by Darnon's impatient shout.

"You have your orders, now move!"

"If they don't start moving, persuade them, gentlemen," the general said menacingly to the officers behind him.

But before the officers or the friends could act, a cry sounded from a wooded area at the bottom of the grassy knoll on which the platform and chairs stood. The cry was followed by a scream of agony and the clash of metal. Suddenly, chaos erupted all around them.

"Please, you must come, there's no more time!" Darnon changed tactics, his menacing threats giving way to desperate pleading.

Darnon, four of the clerics, and the 12 remaining foot soldiers moved to encircle the group he had indicated earlier. As they moved to surround Brandon, Steve, Gloria, and Pattie, the strangers began pulling their weapons. Half the soldiers brandished swords and shields, while the others took medium-length bows from their back and notched arrows. Darnon pulled the massive two-handed great-sword with impressive ease and speed.

Much to the relief of the small group of friends, the clerics and, more importantly, the armed soldiers were facing outward as they ringed the group.

Darnon took control and began shouting, "Here they come! There's no time now to make a break. We stand here. Protect the Summoned Ones at all costs. Sound the alarm!"

A soldier sounded a piercing blast from a polished animal horn that hung from his neck. Then, from 400 feet down the slope, at least 20 armored men on horseback broke from the woods and started charging up the hill at full speed.

The cavalry soldiers had acted more quickly and with more force than their foot soldier brethren. At the first sound of conflict, Namir, 12 of his cavalry soldiers, and four of the clerics closed in on Josh, Will, Jeremy, and Mike. A soldier grabbed each Summoned One by the arm and began pulling them quickly down the slope. The four were too stunned to put up any fight, allowing themselves to be spirited away. As fate would have it, Namir had chosen a path that led them away from the charging horses they could not see, only hear.

Left behind on the platform, Steve felt helpless to prevent his friends' abduction or the impending annihilation of those with him. He knelt beside Gloria, offering what comfort he could to his terrified girlfriend. Pattie and Brandon anxiously looked past the surrounding protective force to see their friends being force-marched rapidly down the hill. Both were still struggling to assimilate what was happening around them, including the fact that Josh was seemingly alive and well enough to run away from them.

Roughly halfway down the hill, Mike, last in the line of racing friends, suddenly tripped and fell hard. The fall knocked the wind out of him, nearly rendering him unconscious. The cavalry officer who had been beside him continued on his flight, running several steps down the hill before he realized the Summoned One he was assigned to protect had fallen.

"Commander!" the soldier shouted as he turned to head back to Mike.

Namir looked back and saw the Summoned One push himself to his knees and struggle to rise. He ordered seven additional soldiers and one of the clerics to head back up the hill, then continued on, leading the others toward the protection of the woods.

The commander knew that the cleric he sent back was the best healer among the clerics who had come to the summoning chairs. He fervently hoped that Balose's skills would not be needed, but "always prepared" was his canon. He also knew without looking that the mace-wielding warrior Elisibrin would accompany Balose back up the slope. The healing cleric never went anywhere without his shadow—Elisibrin had been assigned by the cleric's order to protect Balose with her life.

Back on the platform, Brandon had recovered his senses and was quickly corralling his friends toward the center of the ring of chairs, accurately assessing that the interior would be a more defensible position than the perimeter. Steve had enough wits about him to grab what he could from the nearest seat, which just happened to be Will's gear, left on the chair where Josh had first appeared.

Darnon was relieved to see the Summoned Ones moving to the center of the chairs without prompting. He immediately deployed eight of his men to cover the gaps between the chairs. He and the remaining four soldiers then stepped into the grass to face the first wave of the assault.

Three of the soldiers who stepped forward with General Darnon to protect the group in the center of the platform were his immediate officers. The fourth man, Kail, was not an officer. In fact, he was far from it, more a constant thorn in the general's side. Darnon was routinely forced to discipline the soldier, but he considered Kail to be the best fighter by far of all those he had met or served with in battle. He felt reassured by the man's presence, suddenly glad he had overruled his officers to allow Kail the honor of meeting the Summoned Ones.

All the clerics, with the exception of Varis, their spokesman, stepped into the grass on the right flank of the general. They began singing in a rhythmic chant while staring at the hillside between the platform and the charging horses. The cleric's voices rose and fell over the thundering hoof beats. Their chant emphasized a strong beat, sounding much like a military march to the four friends who remained on the platform.

The horses chewed up the long distance as they bounded up the hill in a fury. The friends stared at the sight, transfixed; none of them could foresee the men on foot withstanding such an attack. Steve couldn't understand why they didn't pull back into the relative safety of the chairs, but Brandon knew the reason: they needed room to use their long swords and the general's massive two-handed great-sword.

The horses were now only 50 feet away. Amazingly, the general and the others seemed prepared but unconcerned, even calm. Just then, the ground immediately in front of the horses exploded in a shower of earth, rocks, and sod. The three in the lead tumbled head first, their front hooves disappearing into the hole left by the explosion and their riders literally launched toward the waiting defenders. One of the officers closed the gap in an instant and dispatched the horsemen before they ever had a chance to rise.

Directly behind their fallen brethren, six horses threw their riders, rearing onto their hind legs as they pulled up short in response to the explosion. Of the six riders that fell, five were able to regain their footing. Before they could draw weapons or get their bearings, four died with arrows sticking from their chests. The lead defenders around the chairs had armed themselves with medium-length bows they had secured cross-ways on their backs.

The last horseman on his feet hesitated, then started to draw his sword. He suddenly fell forward with a dagger sticking out of his neck.

"A damn fine throw. That had to be over 60 feet," Brandon thought, admiring the aim of the lanky, sloppily dressed soldier.

The remaining horsemen, seeing nearly half their number depleted so rapidly, veered to the side and circled back into the woods near where they originally emerged.

"Stay put," General Darnon ordered calmly. "They'll return soon enough and we'd never make it to the trees."

Mike rose to his feet, staggering, still dazed from falling during his race down the hill. The cavalry officer reached his side and shouted at him in a foreign language. It was then Mike remembered the token, and he frantically shoved his hand into his pocket. As soon as his fingers touched the token, he understood the soldier was saying, "Hurry, they'll be coming!"

Still in a state of confusion, Mike felt the officer pulling him back down the hill. Without warning, the ground began shaking and the two men heard a massive explosion. Mike realized the sound had come from the platform.

He came abruptly to his senses, realizing for the first time that his friends were in danger. He stared intently up the hill toward the platform and saw soldiers standing between each chair. Among the chairs and soldiers, he could see Steve kneeling inside their protective circle. He seemed to be rummaging through something on the ground. He could see Brandon motioning frantically with his arms. Strangely out of place compared to the others was the heavyset cleric who had addressed them earlier, standing on the side of the platform gathering grass as calmly as if he were picking flowers.

Darnon's prediction that there was no time to escape the platform came true. The remaining 11 horsemen again left the woods, this time heading toward them in a controlled canter. Only they were not alone—seven more horseman had joined their ranks, and behind them came at least 36 foot soldiers.

During that first wave of the assault, Steve (in his typical thorough fashion) had begun rummaging through the supplies he grabbed on his way to the center of the chairs. In the first backpack, he found a small bag containing food, a coil of climbing rope, some repelling equipment, and a flashlight.

Steve dumped all but the repelling equipment onto the flagstone platform. He tossed the food bag near a chair and handed the coil of rope to Gloria. She was still shaken and didn't complain, but her doubt as to how this could be of any help showed plainly on her face.

Steve quickly removed his climbing harness and motioned for Brandon to do the same. He placed both harnesses in the bag with the repelling equipment. He then grabbed the nylon loop at the top of the bag and gave his makeshift mace a test swing. He picked up the flashlight and handed it to Brandon, knowing he would understand what to do with the heavy 3D-cell flashlight.

While Steve was busy with the backpack, Pattie slipped in beside him and retrieved a small bag that contained spare batteries for the flashlight. The bag held at least ten batteries and could be secured with its long nylon drawstring. Feeling empowered by the makeshift weapon, Pattie tested its weight, swinging it in a wide arc.

With their improvised weapons in hand, Steve and Brandon watched as, miraculously, the first wave was repelled. Pattie's attention had been drawn in another direction. The girl was mesmerized by the actions of the old cleric. He seemed to have lost his mind. He had walked off the side of the platform, waded into the knee-high grass that surrounded them, and started gathering handfuls of dry grass.

As the second wave of attackers started up the hill, Pattie continued to watch the old cleric twisting the grass into several long ropes. When finished, he doubled them, holding the loose ends in one hand. Walking back to the platform, he knelt at its edge. From his robes, he took flint and steel and began trying to ignite the looped grass ropes.

This second attack involved far more planning than the first. The attackers had divided their forces into three equal parts. Six horsemen and 12 foot soldiers were in each group. One unit moved up the center as before; both remaining groups circled around the hill, flanking the platform on each side.

One officer stood with General Darnon facing the center attackers. The other two moved to their right and Kail sidestepped to the left. As the attacking horsemen slowly increased their speed, the old cleric suddenly moved forward. He had managed to light the grass ropes and, to Pattie's surprise, began singing. The melody was much like a hard-driving classic piece. The words, though difficult to understand, seemed to invoke images of writhing snakes.

The old cleric released one end of each doubled flaming rope. As he did, the ropes twisted around like dancing serpents held tightly in his outstretched hand. Flames leapt from the ends of the ropes and stuck the grass at several places down the hillside. The flames danced from one spot to the next, instantly igniting the tall grass wherever it touched.

Two of the clerics began a song of their own. It seemed to Pattie this song was far more whimsical and light-hearted. The third cleric stood directly in front of the other two, whistling in harmony with the tune of their melody. From the mouth of the whistling cleric erupted a strong wind that he directed down the hill. The wind drove fire, smoke, and ash at the now-startled enemy and threatened to break their advance once again.

It seemed to the observers that the left flank would be spared by the fire; however, the lead horses began running harder, taking a more circuitous route instead of advancing on Kail. As this unit raced around the hill, Kail held his broadsword at its very end, gripping it by the pommel, and threw the weapon in an overhead motion as if he were cracking a whip. The sword sped through the air, end over end, sinking up to its cross guard into the chest of the last horseman. The force of the blow propelled the man off his panicked mount, dead before he hit the ground.

Kail reached for his belt and, in one fluid motion, pulled both his longsword and a dagger. He braced for the 12 soldiers who had doubled their speed to reach him and avenge their kinsman's death at the hands of the lanky warrior. Their enraged battle cries filled the air, portending Kail's almost-certain doom.

The soldiers on Kail's side of the platform assigned to guard the gaps in the chairs had already started using their bows to great affect: the two lead attackers had gone down in the first volley of arrows.

Just as General Darnon and his officer began to move toward Kail to aid in his defense, two riders and six foot soldiers broke through the fire and began racing up the hill. Instead of retreating, Darnon started down the slope toward his attackers.

Mike, now in full command of his senses, was resisting the cavalry officer's attempts to propel him down the hill behind Jeremy, Will, and Joshua. He was trying desperately amid the chaos to decide if he should return to the platform and help his other friends or obey the cavalry officer's pleas to continue on down the hill. Suddenly, the sounds of horses approaching at great speed filled the air, and Mike counted five riders bearing down on him and his protector. Realizing he would be of no help to his friends if he were dead, Mike made a split-second decision to follow the officer's lead.

"Run!" shouted the soldier protecting Mike, as he turned to face the first of the horsemen.

The seasoned cavalry officer assigned to protect the Summoned One waited until the last possible moment and leapt to one side. He just missed being run down by a large war horse. He let the momentum of the horse and rider carry them past as he reached up and dislodged the rider. The move was effective but came at a dear price—the horseman scored a glancing blow with his sword to the shoulder of Mike's protector. Both cavalrymen crashed to the ground in a twisted heap.

Mike did as directed and ran down the hill, trying to keep watch over his shoulder as the horrific scene unfolded. The group of soldiers sent to protect Mike slowed their race up the hill as they neared him and took aim with the short bows they carried on their backs. It seemed to Mike the arrows just missed him as they flew past and into the group of thundering horses directly behind. As he glanced back, five riderless mounts reared and turned to escape down the hill away from the fighting.

Additional movement near the trees caught Mike's eye. As his protectors approached and surrounded him, Mike recognized Will, Jeremy, and Josh disappearing into the woods. "How could that be Josh," he thought. "How can any of this be happening?"

The cleric and his guardian raced past the group and headed directly to the fallen soldier. With the aid of his protector, Balose pulled his comrade from under the enemy. From the odd angle of the man's head, Balose deduced that the enemy cavalryman had broken his neck in the fall. The protector of the Summoned One was unconscious.

Balose then began to sing, a song faint enough Mike could not make out the words, but a song nonetheless. Mike thought this might be some form of last rites, but no sooner had the thought crossed his mind than the soldier came to and stood up. His shoulder had stopped bleeding. As a matter of fact, the man looked as if he had never been injured.

Mike pulled himself away from the cleric and the now-healed soldier as his thoughts returned to his friends who were in danger. He looked up the hill toward the platform and the fighting and mayhem that surrounded it. Smoke and ash were lifting in the air from what had to be a sizable fire on the other side of the hill.

Mike started up the slope to help his friends on the platform as the soldier, the cleric, and the cleric's protector turned to rejoin the group heading down the hill. At that moment, however, the group saw a much larger enemy force break out from a shallow valley on around the hill, only 200 feet away. This force was heading straight for the area of the woods that Will, Jeremy, and Josh had just entered.

Mike's band froze and hunkered down, hoping against hope that the enemy did not see their vastly outnumbered force huddled on the hillside. Luck was with them. The enemy was concentrating on its attack upon the others and did not see the smaller group.

Mike turned again to head back up the hill, but another obstacle now stood in his way. A raging grass fire was sweeping around the hillside, cutting off their path to the summit and crawling rapidly over the ground toward them. It appeared that the routes to both groups of his friends were now out of the question.

"We can't go into the woods after the others and we can't go back up the hill, the only choice I see is there!" Mike pointed toward the valley from which the large enemy force had emerged. The fire had almost reached his small group, and they could feel its heat as ash and smoke swirled around them. It took no more prompting: Mike, Balose, Elisibrin, and the eight cavalry soldiers dashed for the cover of the shallow valley.

Looking between the chairs, Pattie kept her eyes on the general calmly striding down the hill to meet the first of their attackers, the two oncoming riders. The soldier guarding the gap had moved over, using one of the chairs to steady his bow. Pattie was sure General Darnon would sidestep the first charging horse and use his massive sword to cut its legs out from under it.

Instead, the general swung his six-foot great-sword in an arc away from the oncoming rider. Pattie watched in alarm, certain he was making a fatal error. His sword gathered speed as it sliced through the air. The horse and rider were almost upon him, yet he continued the circular swinging motion, anticipating the point in the loop where the sword would be aimed away from his attacker. At that exact instant, he used the momentum of the heavy weapon to pull himself out of the charging animal's path. As he was pulled aside, he somehow retained his footing and kept the deadly weapon on its circular path. The blade tip clipped the top of the knee-high grass then arced upward, propelled even higher as Darnon leaned back hard to prevent being pulled forward. The deadly blade just cleared the flank of the charging horse and slammed into the unprotected back of its rider. The force of the blow unseated the soldier, launching him over the horse's shoulder and under its thundering hooves.

At nearly the same instance that the general dispatched the first rider, the arrow of the soldier on the platform found its mark. The arrow struck the other horseman in the neck just above the open V-neck of his chainmail.

Pattie's attention shifted to the clang of steel on steel that rang out on either side of the raised platform. Kail and the two officers backed to the bottom of the steps, giving themselves more room to maneuver. They planned to use the stairs, as well as the protective fire provided by the guard at the top of the steps, to keep from being surrounded. The guard's arrows and daggers had taken their toll on the attackers, yet eight enemies still remained for Kail to battle; the officers would defend against five.

Meanwhile, the clerics had done their part to protect the Summoned Ones and now prepared to assume a background role. Moving to the rear edge of the platform, all four joined in a slightly different light tune, much like the one they had sung while blowing the fire toward the attackers.

A clear barrier appeared, defined by the smoke of the fire that now raged all around below the platform. The barrier, a clear partial dome about four feet off the ground, encircled the defenders below the platform. It then arched upward, tilting back just over the leading edge of the platform.

This barrier proved invaluable to Kail and his men as the arrows from the attackers bounced harmlessly away and fell on the ground. In addition, the barrier was above the ground just enough to allow the defenders space to shoot down the slope at the attackers.

Once the attackers started engaging the defenders with swords, the threat from arrows was all but eliminated. Only then did the clerics stop their song, and the barrier disintegrated at once. The clerics stumbled into the limited protection of the chairs and collapsed from exhaustion near the chair furthest from the conflict.

The fighting continued to rage all around the group of young friends. Despite the chaos, Brandon found himself captivated by Kail's skill. The fighter used his sword and dagger in a fluid motion, dancing back and forth, keeping his attackers off guard, never allowing more than two to engage him at a time. Within the first few minutes, all the lead attackers had suffered deep cuts that were affecting their ability to defend themselves.

Seeing the futility of devoting all their manpower to attacking Kail, several of the attackers in the rear started easing around the warrior to take on the soldiers defending the gaps in the chairs.

Suddenly there was a crash behind him, and Brandon tore his gaze from Kail's deadly dance. Spinning around, he found that four attackers had charged one of the soldiers while the man's companions were distracted in battle. The guard was quickly overwhelmed, and one of the attackers was charging through an opening.

Brandon was already moving in that direction when the attacker broke through the circle of chairs. His foe lowered his halberd, a menacing weapon with its spiked axe head set atop a six-foot-long wooden pole. Brandon did not hesitate or waver; drawing on his martial arts training, he met the attacker's charge in the center of the chairs.

When Brandon had fought competitively, his instructors praised him for his focus. But Brandon knew it went beyond that; it was more than the mere ability to focus. When the fighting was at its most intense, he achieved a sort of clarity, a preternatural understanding he was at a loss to explain. He had tried to describe the feeling to his instructors, his coaches, even his father, but they could not understand. Now, in this battle that meant death for him and his friends should he fail, he felt an overwhelming relief that his ability had not deserted him. If anything, his sense of clarity was greater than ever.

All of his senses were heightened. Everything around Brandon seemed to be occurring in slow motion, but he knew he was moving at normal speed. He could think through all the counters to his attackers' moves—it seemed as if he could replay a lifetime of training in his head, then choose the appropriate action in his own time.

Brandon was far more agile than his large frame suggested and he caught the attacker off-guard. Brandon darted to his right and grabbed the man's weapon with his left hand, just below the axe head, as it passed close by his temple. He struck at the man's head with the only weapon he possessed, his flashlight, hitting him hard in the shoulder when he dodged at the last second. Brandon pulled down hard on the attacker's weapon, forcing the spiked end into the flagstone floor. The tip bit in and held, but the man refused to release his grip. Brandon used this to his advantage. He was now lower than the man, having directed the end of the halberd into the ground. He stood up hard and fast, driving his flashlight into the man's stomach and lifting up with all his might.

The attacker was pole vaulted into the air from the combination of Brandon's brute force and the leverage of the weapon. His training did not permit him to release his weapon; as a result, the attacker flew upward with it in his hands. He hit a chair with the halberd under him and Brandon heard a loud crack.

Brandon rushed to him, hoping to find the man dazed from the landing. He found his opponent either dead or unconscious—Brandon didn't take the time to find out. The wooden handle of the halberd had broken off near the axe head, leaving two weapons: an awkwardly balanced blade and a long pole. Brandon did not hesitate. He threw down the flashlight and grabbed the nearly six-foot-long wooden pole. With the makeshift quarter staff in hand, a weapon he was quite familiar with from his martial arts training, he turned his attention to protecting his friends.

Steve and Pattie were swinging their makeshift weapons of weighted bags with all their might. They managed to keep their attacker off balance just enough to hold him at bay.

As Brandon charged across the 15 feet that separated him from his friends, he saw Gloria throw a coil of rope on one of two men attacking a defending soldier. The rope distracted the attacker just for moment, but that was all the time Brandon needed.

Lashing out with his newly acquired weapon, Brandon caught the enemy across the wrist of his sword hand with an audible crack. He dragged the pole through his left hand with his right hand until it rested at his hip and thrust the end of the pole hard into the man's throat. Just as the pole struck home, both Pattie and Steve hit the attacker in the head with their improvised weapons. The man slumped to the ground.

Brandon quickly turned to the aid of the nearest defender. His opponent's back was to him and Brandon thrust the end of the pole into the man's kidney with all his might. The man lunged forward; off-balance, he was quickly dealt with by the soldier.

Pattie and Steve turned to fend off another attacker, but their encounter did not end as well. The attacker turned unexpectedly and Steve was almost stabbed, dodging the blow at the last instant. Suddenly, he and Pattie saw a sword emerge from the man's chest. Their foe would never again make the mistake of leaving an armed opponent behind him.

As the friends looked around wildly for additional attackers, they found that all were fleeing. Simultaneously, a large force was moving at top speed up the hill. As a cheer rose up from the defenders, the friends realized that these oncoming men were the "good guys." Or so they hoped.

Brandon sat heavily in a chair. Five attackers were dead at Kail's feet, but the amazing swordsman suffered not a scratch. The other defenders had not fared so well; the officers sported deep cuts, but none serious. Of the soldiers, three lay dead and two others were severely wounded. Pattie was kneeling at the side of one soldier, working quickly to stop the bleeding, when the reserve force reached the platform.

General Darnon stepped forward. "Do what you must for the wounded, but I want everyone to the camp as quickly as possible. Captain, what caused such a delay in your arrival?" barked the general.

"Sir, we came with all haste as soon as we heard the call," came the man's apprehensive reply.

"It's of no matter," Darnon relented. "See to the wounded and the Summoned, we move out now."

The friends exchanged glances and silently acquiesced to the general's order. They began gathering their belongings, far too overwhelmed to begin asking the myriad of questions that begged to be answered.

CHAPTER 5

SPLIT

Pattie was awestruck. She had just witnessed men being completely cured of wounds that should have taken their lives, wounds she was certain would be far beyond the curative powers of this primitive people. The healing came not from medicines or devices, but seemingly from the mere singing of a song. The sensations were strange that came to Pattie through her translation token. The foreign lyrics, rather than being directly translated by the token into a language Pattie could understand, instead conveyed feelings that constantly faded in and out. These feelings were basic, primal, and almost elemental, conveying images of water, earth, fire. Pattie felt they actually spoke to her soul.

The cleric's song was beautiful, but one of the most complex she had ever heard. The texture of the song had several intricate layers. Complex rhythms, tempos, and tones were woven together in an arrangement that could easily have sounded cluttered, but miraculously was not. The pitch was well within Pattie's range, she realized, as she hummed along softly.

Pattie had sung in the church choir for as long as she could remember. She had studied music and was instrumental in the choir winning awards. At one time, she had even considered singing professionally. That was until Josh had invited her to perform with his band. The practices went great, and the band members and Pattie were excited about working together. Then, the night of the performance, the normally outgoing, outspoken girl stood before the microphone and the audience, unable to sing. Pattie was so humiliated, she never tried performing with Josh's band again, even though he tried over and over to coax her back.

When the cleric had moved to the next soldier to be healed, Pattie thought to put the translation token in a zippered pocket of her caving coveralls. Now, without the distraction of the feelings generated by the device, she could concentrate on the song itself. It came to her that this was not one complex song, but the blending of a few simpler songs into one.

Concentrating, she could pick out each melody as she practiced them in her mind as a means to isolate them. Once she understood the method, she mentally sang the song using the technique of the cleric. The songs were sung in succession; the changes from song to song were blended in a rhythm unique to each tune. Each independent song was sung for just a bit, then blended into a piece of another until the melody came back to the first song, picking up seamlessly where it had left off.

By concentrating on one song at a time, Pattie had figured out the biggest part of three of the four songs the cleric wove together. She was working out the last song and starting to get the rhythm of the weave when General Darnon ordered the group to move out.

Darnon's command interrupted Pattie's concentration, startling her, and she began fumbling for her belongings. Brandon gently grabbed her arm and led her down from the platform in the direction the last of the soldiers were heading.

Brandon said softly, "I know you are interested in healing of any kind, but we had better keep moving or I think they'll force us to move."

Pattie nodded agreement, still lost in her own thoughts. It had been a few years since she and her mom played what they called the song game. Pattie's mom started playing the game when Pattie was a little girl, just learning to play the piano. She would play a few notes when Pattie wasn't looking, and Pattie would replay the notes in her mind, then replicate them on the piano. Over the years, as Pattie's skill progressed, she could hear a song played once on the radio and after a time of concentration repeat the song perfectly on the piano. As complex as the healing song was, Pattie knew that with time to think it through she would be able to hum the tune.

Unnoticed, Varis stepped from behind a chair and fell in behind the pair. He had watched how intently Pattie studied the healing cleric. His own healing skills were limited, as healing required the most complex mixture of magic talent of any of the disciplines. The old cleric had devoted his life to studying all of the disciplines, but had not devoted the time required to master healing. Pattie's interest in their healing arts intrigued Varis, and he decided to remain near to study the girl.

Steve and Gloria were ahead of Pattie and Brandon in the small group. Steve had decided it best to get Gloria moving and distract her from dwelling on what had just happened. He observed that Gloria seemed to be quite calm now, almost eerily so. This new disposition concerned Steve almost as much as her hysterical screaming.

All four young people were in good physical condition, and Gloria's boots were finally broken in from all the walking over the last two days. None had a problem keeping up with the brisk pace set by General Darnon. After ten minutes of this rapid pace, the small group reached the remnants of a cold camp. Here, they joined the main body of the forces sent to protect the Summoned Ones on their journey.

The army numbered over 200. Of the 200, 30 were cavalry and the rest were foot soldiers. Ten horse-drawn supply carts were lined up near the troops. The carts were narrow, only three feet wide including their wheels, making the storage bed of the cart a little over two feet wide. The bed was 12 feet long, with the cargo area balanced between two large, spoked wheels. These wheels were seven feet tall, leaving a clearance under the bed of 40 inches. The sideboards of the bed were only a foot tall, but the oiled canvas cover was mounded in the center and tied securely. This design allowed the carts, which were pulled by one horse, to travel easily over uneven ground and fit through tight areas.

General Darnon shouted, "Primlas!"

A small man hurried over from one of the supply wagons on the other side of the line of troops. Primlas was not short, being 5 feet, 10 inches without his boots, but his narrow shoulders, spindly limbs, and the way he hunched over when he walked made him appear small. He was dressed in leather armor and had a dagger on his belt, but he would never be mistaken for a warrior.

Primlas carried in his hand a wooden writing table. The table consisted of a hinged wooden box large enough to store dozens of pieces of parchment. The box had brass rods, one across each end, which allowed several pieces of parchment to be held down to the top of the box. A small compartment was attached to the side of this clipboard that contained ink bottles, and a clip on the other side held two quill pens.

"Yes, General, you require my presence?" came the small man's formal reply as he approached.

"Is everything in order?" asked Darnon

"Yes sir, everything is in order. We are ready to move," answered Primlas, somewhat affronted by the question. He continued, "I took the liberty upon hearing the alarm to send out scouts and post guards around an outer perimeter. They were ordered to watch for our advance and match our movements."

The general seemed unaffected by his subordinate's comments and raised his voice to order, "I want the Summoned Ones and the supply carts in the middle, the rest flanking. You know your positions. Move out now, officers please join me!"

Kail and five other soldiers approached the four newcomers and led them toward the supply carts that had already begun moving. The brisk pace used to get to the camp was again deployed by the general, but with the entire army in tow this time.

The lanky warrior offered to the group with a shy grin, "Hello, my name is Kail. My colleagues and I will be your companions for the foreseeable future. Actually, we are your escorts. The general has asked that we ensure your safety."

The small army pushed on at the hard pace set by their commander.

CHAPTER 5 ✦ SPLIT

It was obvious that General Darnon wanted to put as much distance as humanly possible between his army and the forces that had attacked them earlier. The friends were beginning to feel the effects of their surreal experience. Steve, Pattie, and Gloria were tired from the walk through the cave, the adrenaline-filled excitement of the morning's battle, and finally the forced march of the last two hours. Brandon was the only one of the four not affected; he was in peak physical condition and had remained calm and focused during the fight on the platform.

Over the last few hours, Pattie, like Steve, had noticed Gloria's odd demeanor. The girl was moving along about ten feet ahead of the pair, seemingly unaware that Steve was not right by her side. She was walking at the same pace as the rest of the group, but she kept her head down, looking at the ground only a few feet in front of her. Her constant complaining of the last two days was gone, replaced by a trance-like walk.

Pattie spoke in hushed tones between raspy intakes of air, "Steve, I'm concerned for Gloria. She hasn't said a word since she stopped screaming on the platform."

"I've tried to talk to her a few times since we left the camp, but she acts as if she can't hear me," Steve replied. The concern on his face was mirrored in Pattie's.

Pattie said gravely, "We need to keep a close eye on her. I think she's suffering from a mild state of shock. Though we all could use a break, at least this march has given her something to do as her mind tries to digest what has happened."

Steve countered, "I don't know that any of us can digest this. We're in the middle of a medieval battle zone and we were almost killed moments after getting here." Pausing a moment in thought, he continued with a perplexed look, "And what about Josh? How could that be? He was right there talking to us."

Pattie was of course as mystified as Steve. "I don't know. I'm sure this isn't a dream. I never felt this sore and tired in a dream. I don't think this is the afterlife. I just know it would be different. That leaves only one explanation—magic."

Steve, astonished at her bizarre conclusion, blurted out, "Magic?"

Pattie tried to explain. "You saw the ground explode. The way that cleric caused the fire. The healing, that was amazing. It all seemed to be controlled by songs. Every time something strange happened, those clerics were singing."

"You really believe those events were caused by singing?"

Pattie was determined now to convince Steve and, more importantly, herself. "You saw it as well as I did, the clerics singing in the middle of battle and then something always happening as a result. Well, what I'm saying is, if it's magic, it might also explain us being here."

Steve responded, a little less sure this time, "It's just too hard to believe. But they do keep calling us the Summoned Ones." Pausing a moment, he continued, "Remember the chanting song when we first found ourselves on that hill?'

"Yes," Pattie replied.

The pair fell silent, both deep in contemplation and concentrating on putting one foot in front of the other as the march wore on.

The protective force led by Kail stayed close, but not so close as to intrude on the friends' privacy if they desired it. With his friends relatively safe for now, Brandon gravitated over to the gangly warrior.

"What you did up on the platform was truly amazing," Brandon offered with true admiration in his voice.

Kail was quick and sure in his response, "Me, you were the one facing armed men with no weapons. Jilliph here was one of the defenders of the chairs." Kail used his thumb to point toward another soldier walking just out of earshot and then continued, "He told me that the Summoned Ones would have been lost without you."

There was no pride or bragging in Brandon's somber reply, "There were two of them: the first one misjudged me, and the second my friends helped me with."

Kail studied the large man, somewhat concerned over the Summoned One's solemn mood. He decided that engaging the younger man in conversation would prove a good distraction. "Yes, I tell these men and myself all the time that no matter how good you think you are, never underestimate your opponent." He grinned lopsidedly in an effort to lighten the mood, "On the other hand, it's always good to be underestimated by an opponent."

Brandon found it was easier to continue talking with Kail than to plod on alone lost in thought. He was trying to come to grips with the fact that he had just killed a man. He had been in many tough fights. At times, his martial arts opponents would become so frustrated with themselves and their lack of success against him that they would strike at will, unable to land a solid blow. On occasion, these same opponents would even ignore their training and discipline and try to hurt him. But the fight on the mound was completely different. For the first time ever, Brandon had to fight for his very life. Even the knowledge that his attacker intended to kill him as well as his friends could not alleviate the empty feeling he had inside.

"As well as you fought, it was your first time," Kail realized with surprise, looking at Brandon in a new light.

Brandon was surprised by the warrior's comment, and felt as if Kail had just read his mind. "How did you know?"

Kail replied, sounding like an older brother, "I've seen that worried look too many times. Almost ten years I've been doing this. I've seen my share of raw recruits pressed into service. Most before they were ready, some that would never be ready."

At most, Kail looked to be only a few years older than Brandon. The boyish way he carried himself and his ever-present grin made him appear almost childlike to Brandon. He couldn't believe Kail had been fighting for ten years.

Kail continued, "I can say nothing that'll make that feeling go away. I'll say this, though. We fight and kill so that innocent people will not be slain or, worse, be made slaves of Zybaro."

Concerned, Brandon asked, "Who's Zybaro?"

Kail seemed truly surprised. "You're indeed from far away not to know that name. Zybaro's the overlord of Malabrim, the Western Realm, and our sworn enemy over the past ten years."

Kail paused a moment in his conversation and looked around. Brandon noticed that his quick pass took in everything. This was the third time in their brief conversation that Kail had assessed their environs. Brandon saw that it was a mistake to take this man with the seemingly carefree attitude for granted. He was keenly aware of his surroundings.

After his quick assessment, Kail continued, "We're currently deep in Malabrim, and our long journey will take us to Bericea, the Eastern Realm. That is where all of us are from. Bericea is made up of seven united city-states. This army was built from the best warriors and Reenones representing each of these city-states.

Brandon was struck by the use of yet another strange term, "Reenones, what are Reenones?"

Kail's amazement at the questions of this Summoned One was growing. "They're the wielders of magic, the clerics, of course. Surely, even in your land, clerics are the controllers of magic. Some of them were used to bring all of you here."

"Bring us here. You mean magic was used to bring us?" Brandon was becoming a bit overwhelmed by Kail's answers and growing somewhat skeptical.

Kail was incredulous at his big charge's lack of understanding. "I watched the clerics invoke the ancient magic of the summoning chairs. I saw you appear out of thin air. You are the Summoned of the prophecies. I assume you're the great warrior of the prophecies."

"Great warrior?" Brandon asked. He did not understand Kail's answers, but was curious to hear more.

Kail was convinced now that the Summoned One truly did not understand. "I'm no expert on the prophecies. Let me see if I can remember them all." He paused in thought, and then continued opening fingers of his closed hands to count off the answers. "The great warrior, the general, the ruler, the healer, the two builders, the great Reenone, and the betrayer."

Brandon suddenly had heard enough, needing to digest all the information the fighter had just divulged. Kail was content he had given the

Summoned One enough to occupy his thoughts so that he would not dwell on killing the enemy soldier. The two fell silent as they marched along, Kail scanning their surroundings and Brandon deep in thought.

The group pressed on until well after dark, though the pace of their march slowed considerably. Even Brandon was showing signs of fatigue by the time General Darnon called a halt. Primlas, the general's assistant, gave the friends bedding from the supply wagons and showed them to a flat area in the center of the makeshift camp. Steve made both his and Gloria's beds, then led Gloria over to hers. She fell asleep almost instantly without a word to him.

Steve sank down onto his bedding and said to his friends in a hushed voice, "I hope with rest she snaps out of this. I'm really worried about her."

Pattie was more concerned for Steve than Gloria, but still she did not want harm to come to the girl. In an attempt to comfort Steve, she said reassuringly, "I think with rest and a little time she'll be OK. She's much stronger than she seems. We'll help you keep an eye on her until she comes around."

Brandon shared what Kail had told him about Zybaro, clerics, magic, summoning, and prophecies. Steve and Pattie then related their thoughts regarding the acts of what could only be called magic. They all were reluctant to believe that such a force was really at play, but agreed that the increasing evidence was quite convincing.

Once the friends exhausted that topic, Steve said, "I've been thinking about Josh. It was so overwhelming at first that I couldn't even get my head around it. If magic is truly being used by these people, then maybe somehow their magic restored him. He was in the suit he was cremated in. The broken shards of the urn were at his feet and in his seat. If that was really Josh, I see no other explanation."

"It makes as much sense as any of this other stuff does," replied Pattie quietly. "It's just that seeing him for that brief time before the fight and then losing him again, it's tough."

The friends grew silent and crawled under the bedding. Even their heavy hearts and the surreal excitement of the day could not keep sleep from the weary group.

Pattie and Steve woke the next morning to the sound of the camp being broken down. Brandon was only a few feet away. He had his long-sleeved T-shirt hanging on the limb of a small sapling. His coveralls were unzipped to his waist where the arms were tied loosely, leaving his muscled torso bare. Despite the brisk cold of the fall morning, his chest glistened with sweat.

Brandon performed his morning ritual workout this day more to restore a sense of normalcy to life than from any physical need. His normal audience of campus girls had been replaced by soldiers that watched the performance as they worked to disassemble the camp. They would point from time to time and briefly speak to each other in tones too low for Brandon to hear.

"Where's Mike?" Will shouted as he ran, gasping for air.

Will was accustomed to long hikes and the rigors of caving, but his broad shoulders, large arms, and pot belly spoke of a man built for power, not endurance. More than he would like to admit, his lack of stamina was in part due to nights spent in various local bars listening to the Josh Stayton Band and drinking beer.

Commander Namir, running ahead of Will and showing no signs of being winded, ordered over his shoulder, "Just keep running. Don't worry about your friend. I sent some of my best men. They'll be along shortly."

The commander was being truthful with the exception of his statement about the others being along shortly. He knew that his group was far ahead of Mike and the other men now. The sound of the conflict was growing faint, but had been quite intense when they first entered the forest. He knew the other group's chances depended on pure luck and the skill of the men he had sent.

Commander Namir did not tell the Summoned Ones in his charge, but he had no plans to wait on the group he had left behind. The best they could hope for was a platoon of cavalrymen he would send back as soon as they reached the camp.

Namir and his group were running as fast as humanly possible through the dense forest. The first 100 yards had been brutal, with the undergrowth ripping at their exposed skin. However, after fighting their way deeper into the old forest, the undergrowth had all but disappeared, making their flight easier and faster.

"Horses are coming from ahead," shouted Jeremy.

Commander Namir was not concerned by this announcement. He knew his reserve platoon of 50 men would be responding to the alarm raised by General Darnon. He also knew his other men would be waiting at camp as ordered. They would be mounted with spare horses in tow and prepared to move as soon as Namir and his group arrived.

The horses Jeremy had heard came thundering into view. They quickly covered the ground between, pulling up hard in front of the group.

The commander had taken the lead and without slowing shouted his orders, "A Summoned One has fallen behind. Find him and protect him with your life."

The bewildered friends continued on, following the racing commander. They sped past the platoon of horsemen as they propelled their mounts in the opposite direction in hopes of reaching the abandoned Summoned One before the enemy.

Little did the platoon know that they would be plunging straight into an enemy force not long after leaving their commander, the same enemy forces that Mike had seen following his friends earlier. They would destroy this force with minimal losses, but would take another six days to wind their way past the enemy and track down the abandoned Summoned One.

Will was starting to show signs of his struggle to keep up with the fast pace, sweating profusely and breathing in jagged gasps. Jeremy, knowing that his brother would never complain, shouted to Namir, "Hey, enough, we need to slow down."

The commander was not going to bother with a response, but then decided differently. He started to chastise Jeremy for the comment, but stopped when he heard the clash of steel and the shouts of battle right behind them. The friends needed no further encouragement and continued their grueling pace.

A few minutes later, the sounds of the battle could still be heard but had faded; the camp came into the view of the exhausted group. Everything was as the commander expected: his troops were mounted, and additional horses were held in ready for the fleeing group.

As they drew within earshot of the waiting soldiers, Commander Namir shouted, "Eleven will not be joining us. Distribute their mounts evenly. We ride now."

"You can't leave Mike back there," demanded Josh angrily.

Namir reached his horse and swung into the saddle. "I've committed 60 of my men to his safety. That's the best I can offer. Your safety has been my priority from the beginning. So mount up gentlemen, I'm getting you out of here!"

The commander stated his final order in a way that left no room for interpretation. Josh, Will, and Jeremy reluctantly mounted the horses offered, but concern for their friend was plain on all their faces.

As planned, each mounted horse had the lead of a spare horse tied to its saddle. Now, with the 22 riderless horses spread among the ranks, most had two horses in tow. The plan had been for 35 to escort the Summoned Ones to the fortress, but now only 25 would make the journey. All but three of these were soldiers. The others were clerics, chosen for their riding ability as much as for other skills.

The friends had grown up in the heart of horse country, and under Pattie's instruction, they had all developed into capable horsemen. However, the pace that the seasoned cavalrymen set pushed their skills to the limit.

Thirty minutes outside of camp, they intersected an abandoned road and turned northeast. The friends were becoming accustomed to the swift pace and began to relax their tight grip on the reins.

CHAPTER 5 ◆ SPLIT

Will pulled his horse up closer to Josh's and spoke loudly to be heard over the pounding hooves, "Josh, I don't understand any of this, but I'm so glad to see you. At first I thought this might be a dream, but there's no way my butt could hurt this much in a dream."

Josh replied, "I thought I was in heaven. Things were so dreamlike and then this. I'm not sure what's happening either, but I don't think this is heaven or hell."

Josh was still trying to reconcile how he could have died and arrived here if it were not heaven or hell. Still, why were all his friends here?

After a few moments of thought, Josh added, "No matter where we are, there's no one I'd rather have with me than the Reinard brothers."

Commander Namir pulled close to the pair of riders. "We're retracing the trail we used to get to the summoning chairs. It won't be long before we reach the first of the rear guards. You'll get a brief rest. I suggest you take the time to grab a bite to eat. Supplies are in the saddle bags."

The commander then urged his horse forward, pulling up next to Jeremy.

Jeremy had separated himself from the others to sort things out. He tended to isolate himself when he had difficult problems to solve. Will knew his brother well enough to leave him alone during such times. When ready, he knew that Jeremy would talk through his thoughts.

After conveying his message to Jeremy about the impending stop, Namir drifted over to a pair of his men who were quite a bit smaller in stature than the others. "Gentlemen, please scout ahead and make sure all is well at the outpost."

Both men carried devices created by the priests of Phalmas. If the scouts saw trouble, they could use these instruments to send a clear warning. Each device was a wooden tube about seven inches long with a bailed stopper, much like the ceramic ale bottles their spare horses carried in the supply bags. When the stopper was opened, an invisible silent streamer would rush high into the air and explode, causing the sky to turn a dark crimson.

The dense forest started thinning, boulders and rock outcroppings appeared among the sparse trees. Finally, the trees were all but gone.

Only small, twisted ones and shrub remained. The pace of the flight slowed, as the previously straight road started to twist and wind through the ever-increasing boulders.

The group topped a rise and raced down a steep, wooded slope into a bowl-shaped valley. Several burnt-out buildings stood forlornly toward the left side of the valley. A mostly fallen split-rail fence lined the road. However, the friends had no time to inspect their surroundings more closely; now that they were on flat and open ground, Commander Namir had set an even faster pace than before.

One of the scouts the commander had sent ahead earlier came racing down a narrow, steep part of the road in front of them. The valley ended at a sheer cliff face, but the road turned sharply onto a narrow shelf wide enough for only a single cart. The road then climbed 20 feet and turned into a channeled pass carved directly into the cliff face.

Namir seemed unconcerned at the sight of the scout barreling towards them, and slowed the pace slightly as the rider approached.

"All's well, Commander," shouted the scout once he drew within earshot.

A brief nod was the commander's only response as he passed the rider. He slowed their pace once more and turned up the narrow shelf section of the road. At the top of the pass, they came to a stop on a flat plateau filled with scrub and rock. A troop of over 20 cavalrymen waited on the road before them.

"Lieutenant Wico, any enemy activity?" the commander asked as he quickly dismounted.

The lieutenant replied, "Sergeant Marlock had a team scouting on the other side of the valley and was able to catch an enemy reconnaissance party off guard. They were on foot; none escaped."

Commander Namir was carefully checking his horse's hooves in what appeared to be a well-practiced ritual. Not pausing in his task, he shouted, "We break for 15 minutes. Everyone make the most of it. When we leave, I want everyone on fresh horses!"

He added in a less commanding and strident tone, "Lieutenant, I will need to talk to you."

CHAPTER 5 ✦ SPLIT

Josh, Will, and Jeremy all took their time dismounting. They were sore enough they did not want to move, but the thought of one more second in the saddle was too much. Once on the ground, they started rummaging through their saddlebags. They had been in the saddle for three hours, and found themselves more thirsty than hungry.

What they found in their bags was even better than they had hoped for. Several earthen bottles with a cork held in place by a wire bail contained flat but hearty ale. One of the soldiers they had met up with saw the boys going through their supplies and brought over three canteens.

The soldier was one of the biggest men they had ever seen. He was several inches over six feet and, judging from his massive arms, shoulders, and barrel chest, he had to be weigh close to 300 pounds. He carried the three canteens in one hand by their leather straps; in the other, he balanced a massive war hammer topped with a wicked looking spike.

As the mountain of a man handed the canteens to Will, he said, "Tie these to your saddles. They'll come in handy to cut the dust of the trail."

Lieutenant Wico's call interrupted any further conversation. "Sergeant, you're needed over here."

The big man nodded in response to the thanks from the three young men and turned, walking back towards the lieutenant.

"That must be Sergeant Marlock," commented Josh.

After a quick drink from the canteens to slake their thirst, the friends took stock of the activity around them. Rather than eating, the soldiers were all tending their mounts. Following their lead, the three friends found fold-up leather buckets and carried water to their horses from a spring. Once their horses were taken care of and swapped out for fresh mounts, the three sat cross-legged on the ground and hurriedly ate a meal of hard cheese, dried fruit and nuts, and some hard tack, washing it down with the ale. It seemed the rest break had barely gotten under way when they heard Namir's voice.

"Mount up!" came the order from the commander.

The friends, especially Will, were hesitant to climb back into the saddle after the all too brief respite. However, it was obvious that if they didn't comply on their own, they would be forced to ride or left behind.

They rose from the ground awkwardly, nursing various aches and pains, and reluctantly took to the saddles of the fresh mounts.

"The rear guard is staying. They must be planning on Mike coming through soon," observed Jeremy. The troops started moving toward the narrow pass in the high-walled cliff at the far end of the plateau.

Will added, "Two narrow passes like these could be held for a long time. I guess they want the good guys doing the holding."

After a short uphill ride through the pass, the troops crossed a narrow bridge over a deep chasm. As the friends rode over the bridge, they could see a raging river below.

They traveled at a less taxing pace than earlier, yet one that still pushed the less experienced riders. The terrain they rode through was now one of rolling, grass-covered hills with occasional patches of woods. The wooded areas typically denoted a dry runoff valley or a spring-fed stream. The dirt-packed road they traveled looked as if it had been recently restored.

The commander maintained the brisk tempo for another two hours. He would have continued at the same pace, but dusk forced the tired group to slow their progress. The friends had just arrived at the conclusion that Namir planned to press on through the night when suddenly the commander took the lead and directed his troops off the road across the grass. He headed straight to a wooded area not far from the road.

The shallow valley into which Mike and the experienced soldiers escaped had begun to deepen. The ridges on both sides were becoming steeper and taller as they proceeded.

Carefully the group moved on; the conflict that they left behind had grown pitched shortly after they entered the valley, but now grew distant. The cleric and his ever-present protector trailed the others by 20 yards.

The members of Mike's group had fallen silent since escaping into the valley, and Mike was left alone with his thoughts. Something kept troubling him, but he couldn't pin it down. With the excitement and confusion lessening slightly as the sounds of the battle behind faded, it dawned on Mike why he was concerned. They were walking in the open bottom of the valley. He knew from years of experience with paintball tournaments that a position near the top of the ridge was easy to defend and over the ridge was a quick way to hide.

Mike could see these were seasoned warriors and suspected the omission was a result of their cavalry background. Cavalry training would direct these soldiers to seek the open valley so they could better maneuver their steeds should a conflict start. But these soldiers were not on horseback, they were on foot, and if they were not going to think like foot soldiers, he would have to think for them.

Because the enemy had come from this very valley only moments before they entered, Mike took no chances. He spoke just loudly enough for the furthest soldier to hear. "Stop for a second."

When the soldiers had stopped and gathered around, he continued even more quietly, "We're too vulnerable on the valley floor. We can be spotted from either ridge and, being lower, we're in a far less defensible position. I say we make for the ridge to the left. That's the side closest to our friends."

By the time Mike had finished, the cleric and his protector had also caught up with them and listened without comment. Mike finished laying out his strategy, and, receiving no opposition, started moving in the direction of the ridge. After taking only a few steps, he turned back to the group and added, "We don't want to go all the way to the top of the ridge. If we stay short of the top, we can't be seen by anyone in the next valley. We can have someone slip up to the top and scout every so often to make sure that no one occupies that next valley. We'll still want to stay slightly behind the ridge, but if someone comes, we can slip over the top to hide."

The cavalry soldiers, not used to these foot soldier tactics, seemed to welcome the young man's suggestions. They pressed on up the ridge as Mike had recommended.

A soldier obviously experienced at scouting soon broke from the group and slipped to the top of the ridge. He returned a short time later, reporting that the valley over the ridge was unoccupied. The terrain made travel slower, but Mike was more at ease knowing they were in a more defensible position and had a quick place to hide on the other side of the ridge.

As the group made their way as quickly as caution would allow, the soldier that had been injured earlier fell in beside Mike. He began speaking in hushed tones. "Summoned One, I've been assigned by my commander to protect you. My name is Millaro; I'm a captain in the 18th Regiment of the great city-state of Jerimassa. Our original plan was to move directly to waiting horses and, with spare horses in tow, make for the Pass of Karness and the city fortress there. Now I feel that the fighting is too intense for us to go that route, which is why I accepted your suggestion that we head down this valley."

Mike was heartened to hear that his friends might have escaped on horseback with the other cavalry soldier. They had enough of a lead, and their pursuers were on foot. This also explained the use of cavalry soldiers. Still, he had so many questions. He decided to try putting them to his self-proclaimed protector.

"I have a few questions."

"Yes, Summoned One, please ask whatever you like. I'll gladly answer all that I can," Millaro quickly replied.

"First off, why do you keep calling me Summoned One?"

The captain looked somewhat surprised. Realizing he was not answering, he hurried to reply. "I called you Summoned One, because you're one of the prophesied Summoned. I witnessed your summoning. You're not aware you've been chosen?" Millaro posed this last question hesitantly.

"I'm not sure what I'm aware of. I was exploring a cave with old friends. The next thing I know, I'm in a very foreign place, in what appears to be a medieval time, in the middle of a pitched battle. I know nothing of your prophecies or anything about a summoning."

This seemed to trouble Millaro quite a bit, but he remained quiet.

Mike continued, "I would prefer to be called Mike, not a 'Summoned One,' if that's all right."

"M-i-ke," tested Millaro, overemphasizing the "I" as if speaking a foreign language.

Then Mike remembered the strange coin he still held and realized it was a foreign language for him.

Millaro saw the coin that Mike now held out in his hand. He pulled a pair of leather riding gloves from his belt and said, "Summ…uh, Mike, you must not lose that language token, this will be difficult enough even with us able to understand each other."

He indicated that Mike should put on the gloves and gestured for the token. Mike took the thin gloves as he handed Millaro the coin. After pulling on the gloves, Millaro slipped the token inside the glove so that it rested on the back of his left hand. He then pulled a leather cord that secured the glove at Mike's wrist.

"That should do the trick," said Millaro, pleased with the result of his idea.

"What do you plan for us next?" Mike said, continuing his questioning as they walked ahead.

"Well, I don't think that going back the way we came would be a good idea. We had a number of forces in the area, but they all planned to move out quickly. Four of the Summoned were to go on the long northern route with foot soldiers, the rest were to come with us heading to the pass. I think we can assume that the others did exactly as planned, not risking the lives of their Summoned, which leaves us on our own, deep in enemy territory without horses."

Captain Millaro paused in his reply as he and Mike were forced to pass single-file through dense undergrowth. He then ordered one of his men to scout the ridge once again.

Resuming his thoughts on how to proceed, the captain continued. "Having so few troops, we must avoid any conflict if at all possible. That means we need to give a wide berth to the enemy troops we know to be behind us. The pass is northeast of our current position and we are traveling east. So, my plans are to continue east for a few miles before heading in a more northerly direction."

"Quick, over the ridge," Mike interrupted and started leading the way upwards. Mike was practiced at stalking adversaries in wooded areas from his paintball days. He obviously was better at it than the cavalrymen, who were more used to open-field combat.

Mike was several yards ahead of the cleric's very vigilant protector. His position had allowed him to see the enemy force proceeding down the valley only moments before she did. Her reaction was exactly the same as Mike's.

Mike's early warning and quick thinking in ordering everyone over the ridge saved the soldiers' lives. After scrambling over the top, they were able to spy on the troop of enemy soldiers. A quick count revealed that the enemy nearly tripled the number of their small group. Even from the distance of the ridge, Mike could tell by the way they traveled that this was a veteran troop of fighters. Mike and the cavalrymen slipped back out of sight and sat waiting for the enemy to pass.

After the sounds of the passing soldiers faded, Mike observed, "That was close. I think there must be a larger force up ahead, and they keep sending troops down this valley. If they send troops down this valley, they'll likely send messengers back up. We should stay on this side of the ridge and keep a close eye on the valley."

Millaro replied, "I agree. We may as well keep traveling in this direction. At least until we discover if there are any enemy troops ahead and their exact location."

Millaro ordered his men to continue on this side of the ridge as Mike had suggested. As they continued their trek, he ordered his men to scout the other side of the ridge more often. After about a mile, Mike's prediction came true. A messenger on horseback came up the valley they had just left and proceeded ahead of them.

The captain called a halt and ordered his best scout forward, hoping to determine the whereabouts of the enemy force before they stumbled into them.

Thirty nervous minutes passed before Mike heard a bird whistle that was answered in kind by Captain Millaro, soon after the scout rejoined the group.

The scout immediately began his report to his captain. "Sir, the enemy is about half a mile ahead. It's a large force of several hundred.

Judging from the camp, they've been there quite a while but have recently started preparing to move. I'd guess them to be ready to march in little more than an hour."

Millaro asked, "Is there any way around them to the north?"

Thinking only a moment, the experienced scout replied, "They're camped at a ford of a sizable river that flows southeast. I think we could skirt around them to the north, but we'll most likely encounter the river. I've no idea of the terrain or how far we'll have to follow the river for a place to cross."

"As unpredictable as that route may be, I think it's our only option. You did your job well, Keenabo. I'm sorry you'll not have time to rest, but we must move out now," the captain said with genuine regret.

CHAPTER 6

A RACE

Commander Namir's booming voice, honed from years of issuing orders from the saddle, rang out, "No fires! I want rotating guards through the night and four scouts out before the troops are settled."

The troops rode deep enough into the woods to hide their movement from any observers that might be lurking near the road and dismounted. The seasoned cavalrymen started their work without a word to the friends. Several went to gather the tall tundra grass for the horses while others unsaddled, rubbed down, and picketed their mounts. The friends followed suit and began seeing to their own animals. Jeremy went to collect grass while Josh set off with buckets to the stream in the middle of the valley. Will led their six horses to the picket and began removing tack and rubbing them down.

Once their horses were tended to, the friends saw that the troops were breaking into small groups and putting down bedrolls. Following suit, they retrieved bedrolls from the back of their saddles and found a place for themselves.

They placed the bedrolls in a semicircle around a large rock. Tired but too sore and keyed up to sleep, the three friends sat on the end of their bedding and spoke in hushed tones.

CHAPTER 6 ◆ A RACE

"Josh, what was it like?" asked Will.

"You mean death," Josh answered slowly. He paused to gather his thoughts. "It's all kind of sketchy. I can remember things clearly right up until the last. At least I think it was the last, at the hospital. Then my memories become much more dreamlike. That is, until we all end up on that platform in those chairs."

Will and Jeremy remained silent and still.

Josh saw their somber expressions and continued in a little less serious vein. "I feel healthy for the first time in months; in fact, I really feel great. Well, except for my sore butt. And even that screams I'm alive."

Josh looked beyond his friends at the others in camp. Like his small group, several small gatherings of soldiers seemed reluctant to turn in for the night and were discussing the day's events in hushed tones. Others set off to begin their turn at watch around the camp perimeter.

Josh found himself beginning to relax, both physically and mentally. Out of habit, he reached in his pocket, and his hand found what he subconsciously sought. The harmonica, his constant companion for so many years, was still there in the pocket of the ill-fitting suit. Josh pulled the instrument out and brought it to his lips.

A sudden nostalgia washed over him as he began to play one of his favorite songs. It seemed like a lifetime ago that he had discovered a Blackfoot record album in his father's collection. Based on its worn cover, Josh had always assumed it was one of his dad's favorites.

With a joy and passion stemming from his newfound lease on life, Josh began playing the harmonica introduction to Blackfoot's "Train, Train." Josh had come up with his own composition for the lick, making it much longer. It had always been a big hit in the bars where he and his band played.

As he was just getting into the riff, Josh felt chilled and wished he were warmer. The driving beat that sounded like a train gradually got faster and louder.

"Whoa, what the heck is that?" said Josh. He stopped playing and scrambled back from the rock they had placed their bedrolls around. His friends did the same, frantically putting some distance between themselves and the rock that was suddenly glowing red hot. Even from several feet away, the heat was just bearable. It felt like a bonfire.

"What do you think you're doing? I said no fires. That damn beacon of yours can be seen for miles." Commander Namir appeared as if from nowhere behind Josh, with two officers in tow.

"I…I…I didn't do that," stammered Josh.

One of Namir's officers broke in. "As I said commander, I saw the whole thing. He most certainly did deploy magic. The instrument he used is right there." The officer pointed to Josh's pocket where the end of the large harmonica jutted out.

"You deny this still?" Namir charged heatedly.

Josh pulled the harmonica from his pocket and stared at it intently. "I just played a tune I've played a thousand times."

Namir, still clearly upset, began to rant, "You disobeyed a direct…"

"Commander, I don't believe he knows what he did," a voice said calmly. Attracted by the commotion around the rock, the cleric who had interrupted Namir approached the small group, flanked by two others of his order. Two warriors came along behind the clerics.

Namir attempted to keep his anger in check and pointed to the still-glowing rock. "You mean to tell me he had no idea he did that?"

Beltaus, the lead cleric, turned to Josh and asked in a soothing tone, "Summoned One, what were you thinking as you played your song?"

"I don't know. I remember thinking about being cold…and how nice it would be to be warm," Josh recollected. The realization of what he just said sunk in slowly. He mumbled to himself, "Magic, there's no such thing as magic."

Jeremy and Will looked wonderingly at each other.

"Josh, we all saw what happened," said Will. "There was nothing heating that rock from the outside, and we were the only ones around. I wouldn't have thought it possible, but I don't see any other explanation."

Beltaus intervened. "Summoned One, we've little experience with Caleen. We shouldn't be instructing you. I suggest you refrain from using your instrument until you can be brought to our Order for training."

Josh was perplexed. "Caleen? What's that and what does my harmonica have to do with this?"

"You truly don't know the ways of magic. Caleen is the form of magic that affects objects. In Caleen, the magic is directed through music from an instrument," the cleric answered, discomfited. "Please, I shouldn't be training you. Just give us your word you won't use the magic of your instrument until we reach the Order."

"Ok, I won't," agreed Josh.

"Double the guard, and tell them to be extra vigilant," ordered Namir. "Goodnight, gentlemen, I think we've had enough excitement for one evening."

Commander Namir and his officers departed. The clerics also bid them goodnight and took their leave. The three friends settled down into their bedding and waited for sleep.

Before they drifted off, Will mused quietly, "Good thing you stopped playing when you did. I bet if that rock had gotten any hotter on this cold night, it would have exploded."

Lulled by the rock's warmth and exhausted from the extraordinary day, the three young men were asleep within minutes.

The next morning, Jeremy was first to rise. He immediately woke the others, as the camp was already in motion. The friends followed the lead of the soldiers, ate breakfast quickly, and were ready to mount up by the time Commander Namir gave the order.

The next six days passed in a similar fashion as the three friends settled into their mysterious journey. They stayed to themselves, isolated yet always surrounded. They rode at a fast pace, at times encountering rear guards protecting key passes, only to leave them after a brief exchange of information. The troops were careful to rotate the horses every two or three hours to keep them fit. Occasionally, it was necessary to exchange a lame mount for a fresh horse from the rear guards they encountered.

Namir was strict with his troops and his actions were well-disciplined. His subordinates did not seem to mind his authoritarian style; in fact, to a man, they seemed to have a great deal of respect for their commander.

Commander Namir used his smaller riders as scouts. Seated on smaller saddles and carrying minimal equipment, these men were very effective in carrying out their mission. They could push their horses in advance of the others to scout several miles ahead. Namir kept four of these scouts in the field at all times. They would report in at regular intervals. Will, who had been observing this routine, realized that the periodic reporting was intentional—if a scout didn't return on time, the commander would know something was wrong.

On the morning of the seventh day, Commander Namir approached the friends as they were breaking camp with the news that they were nearing their destination. If all went well, the Pass of Karness would be in sight toward the end of the day. They would reach the fortress by midmorning the day after. Will thanked the commander as he left to resume his duties, and exchanged glances with Jeremy and Josh. No one spoke, but all three were feeling the strain of the arduous travel and the uncertainty of what remained ahead.

Two hours into the day's ride, a scout missed his time to report back. Namir wasted no time in sending another in the direction the missing scout had taken. The group had been heading steadily northeast the entire journey. The man had been one of two sent forward to check for any unusual activity. He was to look to the east of the road ahead and the other scout was due back any moment north of the road.

The commander shouted out his orders, "Halt. You have five minutes. I want the horses tended quickly and everyone on fresh mounts."

Just as the group had completed their tasks and started climbing on fresh horses, two horsemen could be seen in the distance racing at top speed toward them. Namir held up his hand in a halt signal as the group waited for the men to approach. Two scouts soon slid their mounts to a stop in front of the commander.

"Bleck was safe when I last saw him, but we have a problem," the scout said before his horse had come to a complete stop. "Bleck caught my attention with his light-stick. He signaled the appearance of a large enemy force moving cross-country from the east. The force would intersect the road near where the plains narrow before the pass."

The scouts were using the Code of Klaphic, a closely guarded means of communication developed centuries earlier. The code itself was similar to Morse Code. With the use of a light-stick, the scouts could communicate over vast distances. The light-sticks were very powerful magical devices, similar to a flashlight. These sticks could direct a narrow beam of light, as bright as sunlight, over great distances.

Commander Namir assessed the situation rapidly and began issuing orders. "Grab fresh horses," he bade the scouts. To the remaining assembled men, he shouted, "Officers and the Summoned Ones with me. We ride now!" Before his words were uttered, he was kicking his mount into action.

Namir set their fastest pace yet. Enduring seven days of nonstop riding, the friends' horsemanship had improved greatly, and they were able to catch the hard-riding commander. Even so, as they pulled alongside him, he was already deep in conversation with his officers.

The commander shouted over the thundering hooves of their mounts, "We make for the pass with all haste. The time for caution has passed. If we don't make that pass before the enemy, we're doomed. Ride these horses till spent, then switch to the other mounts and cut these loose. The horses are fresh from the night's rest; we should be able to get within striking distance of the pass with them. All we need do is make the pass. Once there, we can hold any size army for some time."

After only 20 minutes of frantic riding at the pace the commander set, the group could see the plains narrowing. They had been gradually climbing for the last three days, but now the road was becoming quite steep. The gently rolling hills with wooded glens had given way to more rugged terrain. Temperatures had been cold at night yet almost pleasant during the day, but the washed-out grey horizon was a grim indicator of winter's imminent approach.

It was only now as the plains narrowed that they could see through the wintry haze and catch a glimpse of the mountains ahead. The narrowing of the plains as the scout had described was actually two long fingers of the mountain reaching out into the plains. These fingers started as low wooded hills in the distances, but grew in size as they rode toward the pass. The bases of these mountain ridges widened and encroached steadily into the grassland.

The road continued its path into the narrowing V-shape of these two wooded mountains. The riders were within roughly a mile of the road entering the woods that marked the long approach to the pass when they spotted a lone horseman racing at top speed along the wooded ridge to their right. Even at break-neck speed, the group could see he would not reach the point where the road entered the woods before they did.

Will's eyes were quite keen. He had spent a great deal of his young life in the wilderness and had developed the ability to spot items in the distance long before others. So it was no surprise to Josh or Jeremy that Will was the first to call out a warning.

"Commander, that's your scout Bleck, but he's being chased by some creature like nothing I've ever seen!"

"The creature, describe it Summoned One, quickly!" the lead cleric Beltaus said frantically.

Will answered rapidly, still staring at the creature as it bounded after the rider. "It's as big as a bear, but runs more like a cat, but it…it has features like a man. If it keeps gaining at the same pace, it'll overtake the scout before he can reach us."

The leader spoke quickly to the other clerics and their protectors. Within seconds, the two clerics and their warriors had split from the main group and took off at an angle to intercept Bleck and his pursuer.

Beltaus, still riding near Namir and the three friends, shouted, "Commander, send no others. That's a nollax. My colleagues from Whilanar are the most experienced at dealing with this. I just hope they get there before it catches your scout."

Nollax was a word originating from what the clerics referred to as the "ancient tongue." Translated, the word meant "altered." Even though the word came from a dead language, from their expressions, it held a grim meaning for the commander and his officers. The word was used to describe dangerous, twisted creatures of various types that often had command of powerful magic.

The predominant religious order in the city-state of Whilanar viewed the nollax as pure evil, as did most others. This order made it their life's work to eradicate the nollax. To this end, they were the best trained at magic-on-magic combat and were indeed the best equipped to handle the current situation.

Even though Namir had not slowed his group's pace towards the wooded portion of the road, the angle of the scout and his pursuer brought them closer with every passing moment. Will's keen eyes were no longer needed; all of them could see Bleck and the nollax clearly. It was evident that unless the clerics could work their magic from a distance, the nollax would reach the hapless scout before they could intercede.

Bleck, intent on his escape route, rode with his head so far forward it pressed against his horse's neck. Because of this, he only now noticed the approach of the clerics and turned his mount towards them. The angle would help close the gap between him and the clerics, but it also allowed a better angle for the pursuing nollax, and with that new angle, it would almost surely capture its prey.

Just as the creature was about to overtake him, Bleck was flung from his saddle, flying high into the air and sideways from the line of pursuit. Just as suddenly, he fell hard to the ground, rolling as he hit. The course of the nollax was simultaneously interrupted, as the creature halted in midstride as if it had run headlong into an invisible brick wall. Swiftly the creature was jerked, as if by an unseen force, high into the air. The nollax hung suspended, thrashing and bellowing, for only a few seconds before its invisible means of support abandoned it. Before the nollax had time to hit the ground, a protector buried a javelin in its shoulder. One of the clerics veered off toward the fallen scout as the two protectors and the other cleric charged on toward the collapsed beast. The lead protector leapt from his horse with his javelin in hand and, using the weight of his fall, impaled the creature. The other protector dismounted while pulling his sword, and both men began repeatedly hacking at the downed nollax.

The commander had slowed the pace during the exchange. Watching the protectors hack like madmen at the fallen creature, he muttered under his breath, "Zealots."

Ignoring the comment, Beltaus said, "Commander, your scout should be fine. The nollax could not have used magic running at top speed. The magic you witnessed had to have come from one of the clerics."

True to his word, Bleck was back on his feet and had nimbly jumped onto the back of the cleric's horse.

"Look out! Behind you!" Will shouted to the clerics as he pointed.

A large cloud of dust could be seen on the horizon, from the direction the scout and his pursuer had come. From the base of the dust cloud, figures appeared, small in the distance. Bleck and the cleric began racing toward the group; the protectors stopped their obsessive attack and ran to mount their steeds.

"All haste to the pass!" Commander Namir shouted as he spurred his horse forward.

The friends did the same, suddenly comprehending that the dust cloud was being generated by a large army. It was also clear that the army was aware of them and in full pursuit.

The scout that had returned earlier held back his mount and the two spare horses he had in tow, along with the other horse he had tied to his saddle. As the clerics and Bleck caught up to him, Bleck stood on the haunches of the cleric's horse and leapt to the lead horse being towed by his friend. The scout tossed the reins to him and Bleck charged forward. All of this was accomplished while everyone was racing at almost top speed.

The scout everyone had thought dead from his fall wasted no time reaching his commander. Bleck began his report as soon as he was within earshot.

"Commander, the portion of the army you see represents only the advanced units. I estimate these advanced units at only 200 hundred, but a few hours behind, the main body numbers well over 10,000. We're obviously not their objective; they mean to seize the city. They've a long supply train reaching back farther than I dared to scout, and I saw several engineering platoons."

Bleck fell silent for a moment as if considering carefully what he said next. When he finally spoke, apprehension was evident in his voice.

"Commander, there were dozens of nollax in and among the army." He paused again, forcing himself to continue.

"And they had at least one platoon of pallitors with them. They appeared to be under the direction of a nollax."

Beltaus, who had been riding nearby keenly listening to the men's conversation, burst in. The lead cleric vehemently voiced his opposition to the scout's observation.

"That can't be true. With the persecution of the nollax, there likely aren't that many left, nor would they be working so closely with humans. And it is well-known that the pallitors dwell solely in the realm of myth."

The commander calmly replied to the outburst, "Beltaus, the pallitors are most definitely not a myth. Both Bleck and I, along with most in this troop, have fought them. An experience I'd hoped never to repeat, and given what pursued my scout, I'd think your projections of the number of nollax may also be in doubt. Regardless, an army of that size is a force to be reckoned with."

Pallitors were men who fought as if possessed. They literally had no feelings, no fear, they never tired and could not feel pain. If an opponent were to slice off a limb, a pallitor would not even acknowledge the act of violence. It would continue fighting as if nothing had happened. The only way to defeat such an enemy was to destroy it, annihilate it to keep it from the battle.

Namir and his troops had learned over time that their main weakness was in functioning as a unit. Even though they fought hand-to-hand and were formidable fighters, they had difficulty with basic military tactics. Their weakness gave the oncoming cavalrymen a distinct advantage on the open field, making it paramount that the group reach the pass ahead of their enemy. The commander knew his men would prevail in the close fighting of a siege.

The commander and his group raced up a road that entered a deep forest. The friends pushed the horses as hard as they dared up the ever steeper terrain. The road had started a back-and-forth winding up the side of the eastern mountain ridge. The circuitous route through the woods meant that the pursuing force was lost from sight the moment they left the plains, but not forgotten.

It took 20 intense minutes for the group to gain the summit of the ridge. The road then turned and followed the crest of the ridge. The dense hardwoods forest at the base of the mountain had given way to less thick evergreens. The needles of these tall, straight trees carpeted the ground and choked out nearly all the undergrowth, allowing the trail to be seen from a much greater distance.

The ridge and road were heading back toward the northern mountain ridge where the two merged into one and continued up to the snow-covered peak of an incredibly steep mountain. The road in this area appeared to be better maintained than the one on the plains, and had the look of recent and frequent use.

The sweat of the mounted horses was lathering where the leather of the tack rubbed. They were laboring now to continue the grueling pace of the climb. The friends had never seen horses pushed this hard, and doubted they could maintain this pace for much longer. Yet the commander did not call for the mounts to be swapped.

"Bleck," shouted Commander Namir over his shoulder.

The small scout had drifted back to ride with two other scouts. Hearing his name, he bound effortlessly ahead despite the breakneck pace.

"Yes, Commander!"

Namir shouted back, "I want you to take two other scouts and ride ahead to warn the fortress. Have them send as many troops as they dare to the pass. The enemy must be held there to give them time to prepare for the assault.

"Yes, sir!"

"Wait, I'm coming with you." The lead cleric had ridden forward and overheard the exchange.

"Beltaus, I can't allow that, you'll slow them down and time is of the essence," Namir replied without hesitation.

Bleck had already fallen back to the other scouts, not waiting for the men's argument to be resolved.

Beltaus stated matter-of-factly, "Namir, your men will have trouble at the gates. I'll go. They don't need to wait for me, but I fear they'll still be at the gates when I catch up to them."

"Bureaucrats," spat out the commander in disgust.

Beltaus did not wait for a reply, spurring his lathered mount forward. He had a lead on the scouts. Bleck was still explaining Namir's orders to the others. It was a lead he would soon lose and never regain. Beltaus was small and carried no weapons to burden his mount. He and the others in the group had cut loose the bedrolls, saddlebags, and all other expendable items along the trail at the expense of speed, so his horse's condition was comparable to that of the scouts. Beltaus and the scouts disappeared out of sight rapidly, into the thinning trees.

The remaining members of the group pushed doggedly forward. After a few minutes, the road turned east and dropped over the side of the ridge opposite of the valley that led to the plains below. The trail then maintained a steady elevation as it skirted around the mountain.

"Change horses!" The commander finally shouted the order the friends had been waiting for.

The order was echoed up and down the line of soldiers. The men pulled their mounts up short, detached the leads, and quickly mounted the spare horses. The exchange was performed swiftly, and the horses that had carried them so far stood in the middle of the road, still in their tack, chests heaving, as the troop raced on.

Commander Namir had hoped to get a little more from the first horses, but some of the mounts had started to falter. He did not want to chance a bad stumble or total collapse. Persevering could have meant the loss of several horses and/or injury to his men on the narrow road. He only hoped their current mounts could make it to the fortress. He knew it would be a close race.

For almost two miles, the road continued to skirt the perimeter of the mountain. The elevation varied little over this distance. The road then entered a deep-cut valley, and the road became a shelf cut into an increasingly steeper hillside. Half of the road had been cut into the bank, where a 5-foot, dry-stacked stone wall held back the inner bank. An even taller stone wall held the outer bank that then dropped off to the steep terrain below.

Josh, Will, and Jeremy could hear a raging river below, but at their current pace, did not dare venture close to the edge to take a look. The low, foot-high stone curb they rode alongside offered little comfort to the friends as they sped along.

The road continued its trek around the mountain and began steadily rising. After a few minutes traversing the shelf road, the group rounded a bend, and the road straightened out before them. The friends saw a steep gorge on the right, and the silver ribbon of a river deep below. The mountain their road was on was joined by another mountain on the other side of the gorge.

The source of the river was at the intersection of the two mountains. Where the two mountains came together was a sheer cliff face over 500 feet tall. The river came from a waterfall that sprang from the face of the cliff about halfway up on the far right-hand side.

The road continued around the side of the mountain where it joined the cliff at the extreme left-hand side. The ribbon that defined the road could then be seen crisscrossing back and forth across the face of the cliff, gaining elevation with each pass. It took nine ever-higher passes to reach the summit above the spectacular waterfall.

"The Pass of Karness," shouted the commander to the friends.

It took the group a few minutes to reach the base of the cliff. The size of the landmark became clearer to the friends as they approached. The cliff was over 1,000 feet wide at the base and over twice as wide at the summit.

The enormity of the effort required to create the pass road was not lost on the friends. Half of the road had been cut into the sheer rock face of the cliff. The other half was held in place by buttressed supports of fine stonework.

The height of the outer stone curb wall had increased to over two feet, but that added little reassurance, as even at the base of the cliff the road dropped off into a very steep, rock-strewn, wooded valley that led to the river gorge.

Just before the group entered the pass itself, Commander Namir called a halt. As the group gathered around him, Namir began conveying his orders.

"I'll accompany the Summoned Ones to the fortress; I hope to persuade the king to hasten sending troops. The rest of you, I want gathering what you can for a defense. I want bushes and logs dragged up to the switchback of the third level and a barricade created. Scatter yourself along the level above the first pass and harass with anything you can gather to throw down. Keep moving so they don't gain the level you're on. If we don't return before you reach the barricade, you'll have to make your stand there."

Commander Namir then dropped his typical authoritarian voice and said plaintively, "Gentlemen, serve well."

He spurred his horse forward, with the three nonplussed friends right behind him.

Commander Namir raced up the Pass of Karness with Josh, Will, and Jeremy riding close behind. The closer they got to the top, the more Namir expected to see the support troops he had requested riding toward them across the open field to aid in the defense of the pass. Finally, the group reached the crest, and the concerned commander reined in, his eyes darting every which way looking for the troops that were not there. The scouts Namir sent ahead had already had ample time to raise the alarm, and troops should have been mustered. His concern immediately turned to anger when his eyes came to rest on these same scouts, still mounted, at the foot of the closed gates to Karness.

This was not the first time Namir's ire had been directed towards this city. The day Namir and Darnon brought the armies of the other six city-states to Karness, they had been welcomed with great fanfare. Citizens lined the streets offering cheers of encouragement, and the royal guards stood at attention in their dress uniforms all along the route to the royal palace. Upon reaching the palace of King Yarmis, the commanders were made welcome by his staff and ensured their troops would have the finest accommodations.

That was the last good opinion Namir remembered having of Karness. The king kept the commanders waiting for over 30 minutes in a small antechamber off the royal hall. When they were finally granted entrance, they were not greeted warmly as was the storied custom, but very formally. They were made to stand at the bottom of the steps that led to the royal throne. For several minutes, King Yarmis did not acknowledge their presence as he conversed with two clerks. When he finally did address the visiting commanders, it was very much in the manner of a monarch to his subjects.

King Yarmis had told Namir and Darnon that he appreciated them delivering the token army, but his commanders would be leading the Reenones to the summoning chairs. This order directly contradicted what had been decided a year earlier. A conference had been held in Whilanar, and a minor duke, not the king, had represented Karness. There, the joint command of Namir and Darnon had been voted on and approved. Now, Namir, though infuriated at the king's arrogance, stood silent, deferring to Darnon as had been arranged before the meeting. Darnon held his tongue as well, and, after a long and awkward pause, the king said, "Forgive me, you must be tired. Let me have the staff take you to your accommodations. We can discuss your positions in the army in the morning."

Without comment, both commanders allowed themselves to be led from the royal hall by one of the clerks. Once clear of the hall, Commander Darnon said, "We wish to see to our men before we retire. Please take us to them."

The clerk acquiesced with a slight nod and indicated they should follow. However, instead of leading them to the barracks within the city walls as the commanders expected, they were led to the rear gates of the city. Once outside the gates, they saw their army setting up camp on the grassy plains leading to the pass. Namir remembered being so angry, he could barely contain himself. Commander Darnon's only response was a sardonic grin as he said, "Thank your king, and inform him that we common soldiers would prefer to be with our troops." With that, he dismissed the clerk and proceeded to the command tent the men had already erected.

They left through the pass before first light, leaving a sealed letter for the king with the guard at the gate. The note read, "Thank you for your hospitality, King Yarmis. The army is proceeding to the summoning chairs as was agreed upon by the Council of Seven. If a Karnessian contingency wishes to accompany us, please bid them to make all haste. Respectfully, Darnon, Supreme Commander of the Army of the Seven."

An hour before they were to depart, the Reenones were told of the king's actions and the commanders' plan. They immediately dispatched some of their members into Karness to notify the Brotherhood of the Seekers. They relayed to the commanders that the petty politics of the Council of Seven was not their concern, but it was critical to have Reenones from the Brotherhood present at the summoning chairs.

Today, riding up to the gates, Namir could not believe that even King Yarmis could be so arrogant as to put his people and the entire city in jeopardy. The commander was heartened to see that only his scouts were at the gates. The Reenone Beltaus must have been granted entrance into the city. Reining in his horse, Namir asked a question that he already knew the answer to. "Bleck, what are you doing out here?"

"Commander, I was told that I wouldn't be granted access until an envoy of the king allowed it," Bleck said, clearly annoyed. He added, "Sir, I'm almost certain that no message was even sent to the king. They just laughed when I tried to tell them of the invasion force."

"Thank you, I'll take it from here. Our first goal is to get the Summoned Ones safely within the walls," Namir said, as Bleck seemed to see Josh and the Reinard brothers for the first time.

Commander Namir shouted up to the gates, "You in there!"

"Yes boy, what is it this time?" came the reply, amid a snort of laughter.

Namir's tone left no doubt of his contempt for the soldier in the gatehouse when he shouted, "I am Namir, High Commander of the Jerimassian Cavalry. My men are under attack by a vast Malabrim army. I invoke the Sanctuary Law of the Council of Seven Cities. I suggest you open the gates immediately, because if you fools are lucky enough to survive the 10,000 Malabrim troops that make their way up the pass at this very moment, you surely will not survive the siege from all of Bericea for not granting sanctuary."

Heated conversation erupted on the other side of the gate. After the melee died down, loud scraping and banging preceded the opening of the gates. The guards on the other side began to explain they would need to provide an escort for the group, but Namir did not wait for them to finish. He spurred his horse past their protests; Josh, Will, Jeremy, and the scouts followed suit.

The hard-charging group rounded the street corner in their trek to the palace, and the shouts from the guards were lost in the thundering of the hooves on the cobblestone streets. The city was vast, opening up from the narrow cliffs where the wall was set, and steadily rising and widening. The main streets were broad and well-tended, and the cross streets well-planned. All of the buildings they passed were of finely crafted stonework and slate roofs, and were at least two stories tall. Several on the main avenue were as high as four stories.

Their destination became clear to the group early: the spires of the palace were clearly visible above the other buildings. As they rounded yet another corner in their quest to reach the palace, the riders nearly bowled over a group of at least 25 clerics who were racing on foot for the gate. Leading this group was Beltaus. As the riders reigned in, the cleric said, "I'm glad to see you within the gates. You should reach the palace at about the same time as Eldest Brother Vableel. We're heading for the pass to delay the invasion force for as long as possible."

Namir quickly relayed to Beltaus the position of his men and the preparations they had made. With their brief exchange complete, both parties raced on in opposite directions.

Namir's group reached the palace gates only a few minutes after leaving Beltaus. They were met there by armed Royal Guard members and denied entrance. Yet again, Namir invoked the Sanctuary Law. This time, the commander was able to convince a member of the Royal Guard to send a messenger into the palace but no reaction came from within. Namir, seeing no hope of gaining entrance short of a fight they were sure to lose, decided to dismount. The others followed suit. They began walking their lathered horses in a circle in front of the gate in an attempt to cool them down. While walking the mounts, Namir called Bleck over. In a low voice, he said, "Bleck, old friend, I've a task for you and the other scouts. Take all the horses for spares." Namir reached into his saddle bag and produced a scroll of blank parchment and a small vial of ink and quill. He quickly penned a letter and handed it to Bleck.

Namir continued issuing orders. "Bleck, you and the other scouts slip out the front gates of the city. They should be open this time of day. You're to deliver this scroll directly into the hands of King Reskaen." Namir then reached into his tunic and produced a sizeable coin pouch. "Take this and buy anything you need. You must make all haste"

As Namir handed the coin pouch to Bleck, he said in a voice loud enough for all to hear, especially the guards, "You and the scouts use this to get the best accommodations for the horses that this city has to offer."

Under his breath, he added, "Bleck, yet again I ask too much, but it's needed if Bericea is to survive."

Josh, Jeremy, and Will did as the commander and handed over their horses to the scouts. No sooner had the animals disappeared around the corner, when a robed old man came toward them at a hurried gait from a side street. He walked with a severe limp and used a cane for support, and he was accompanied by two younger clerics.

"You must be Eldest Brother Vableel. Beltaus told me you would be coming to the palace," Namir said to the old man as he neared. Saying nothing, the old cleric walked past Namir and the friends and headed straight for the guarded gates. Once in front of the gates, he said in a strong, commanding voice that belied his age, "I am Eldest Brother Vableel of the Brotherhood of the Seekers. I demand immediate entrance for myself and for my friends, and I want an audience with your king at once."

Looking through the decorated iron gates of the palace, the three friends could see the ashen faces of the guards as they whispered among themselves. The Eldest Brother was the highest ranking cleric of the Brotherhood of the Seekers, the most powerful order in the city. From the time they were young children, these guards had heard stories about the power of the clerics in the Brotherhood and, in particular, the power of the Eldest Brother. Some of the stories were true, most were exaggerated, and some were complete fabrications. The Brotherhood had done nothing to stop the rumors or allay the fears of the townspeople, and it was on this fear that the Eldest Brother now counted.

After a few seconds of whispering among the guards, one headed off on a dead run toward the palace. It didn't take long for the others to open the gates at the command of this seemingly innocuous old man. The group, escorted by a member of the Royal Guard, then set out for the palace at a quick pace set by the Eldest Brother. The three friends and Namir brought up the rear of the procession. The guard took the group through the palace directly to the royal hall. The armed guards standing at attention at each entrance were evidence the king was present in the hall.

Upon reaching the guarded entrance, the Eldest Brother turned to Namir and whispered, "You should remain here. I'll call for you in a moment. Believe me, this is the best for our mutual cause." Namir nodded and backed to one side. The Eldest Brother and company of clerics disappeared into the royal hall.

Namir waited as patiently as he could, but he knew each moment of delay likely meant the death of one of his soldiers. He yearned to be there, to help where he could. However, he knew the best thing for his men in the long run would be to secure the help of the king. Ten long minutes passed. The friends could see the commander growing more agitated with each passing moment. Just when Namir's patience had reached its limit and he had decided to storm past the guards and suffer the consequences, the doors opened. Namir and the three friends were escorted into the Royal Hall to be presented to the king.

The friends had been impressed during their hurried, yet limited, tour of the castle. It was obvious they had entered through a service entrance but, even so, the stonework was exceptional. The vaulted ceilings were a full 20 feet high, with windows for natural light. Even this service hall with its flagstone floor was impressive; ten feet wide, it had alcoves where tapestries, statues, paintings, and trophies were decoratively placed.

The corridors they traveled, though well appointed, and did not prepare them for the grandeur of the royal hall. They entered through a side entrance, toward the end opposite the throne. The chamber itself was nearly 300 feet long and 70 feet wide. The vaulted ceiling peaked at 80 feet, with three levels of balconies lining the length of the chamber. The stone construction most resembled European cathedrals the friends had seen in movies, with ornate carvings, statuary, and tapestries filling every nook.

Namir and the friends were led by two flamboyantly dressed guards toward the throne, which sat over ten feet above the main floor. A great semicircle of stairs led up to the throne. The outermost flanks of the stairs stopped five steps shy of throne level, leaving room for several desks on both sides. These desks were occupied by clerical personnel shuffling papers. Two guards armed with long, ceremonial pikes and wearing the same garish uniforms as their escorts stood at the base of the stairs in front of the throne.

King Yarmis acted disinterested as the group approached. Vableel stood on the stairs in front of the throne, only a few steps down. The Eldest Brother was the first to speak as they approached.

"The king has agreed to send troops to the pass to relieve your men. They are already under way."

King Yarmis was obviously perturbed the Eldest Brother had upstaged him by starting the conversation. Quite tersely, he jumped in before the old man could speak again.

"A garrison of soldiers was sent, led by my Royal Guards as soon as my dear friend, Brother Vableel, brought me the news of this incursion."

The king then turned his attention to the three friends. "Are these the Summoned Ones? The prophecy said there would be eight. Where are the others?"

"I'm sure your delegate to the council relayed the decision to split the Summoned into two groups," Namir answered, leaving out any mention of Mike for the time being.

Before Yarmis could asked any further questions, he stated curtly, "My men may be in need. I wish to join them now. Thank you for your kindness, your Majesty."

Although he knew very well it was a complete breach of protocol, Namir didn't wait to be dismissed. He turned on his heel and exited the door through which he had entered. The king stood dumbfounded, while Vableel merely grinned.

Regaining his composure, King Yarmis told the friends, "Welcome, Summoned Ones. I'm sure you must be tired and dirty from your ordeal."

The king clapped his hands, which brought two gaudily dressed young men from an alcove behind one of the clerk's desks.

"See to their needs," the king said dismissively as he turned to sit on his throne.

CHAPTER 7

BATTLE FOR THE PASS

On their second day in the palace, Jeremy and Will awoke early with plans to explore the immediate grounds and the mechanics of the structure. Both brothers had already grown tired of the relentless opulence of the palace's public spaces. The day before, they had been advised, albeit diplomatically, by one of the king's senior guards that they wouldn't be playing a role in the city's defense. It was suggested to the pair that they keep themselves busy and stay out of everyone's way.

They learned at breakfast that Josh had already left the palace, returning to the Brotherhood of the Seekers after spending all of the previous day with them. The night before, Josh had complained to Will and Jeremy that the Seekers spent most of their time testing him and pressuring him to take vows. Their insistence made Josh leery of them, but his curiosity about their magic had pulled him back to the order this morning.

The first order of business for the two brothers was to discover where the wonderful breakfast they had just eaten originated. Servants directed them to a kitchen with enormous wood-fired ovens and spacious open fire pits, where whole carcasses turned slowly on spits. Obviously electrical appliances were absent, but the utensils and pans the numerous cooks were using would have been found in any kitchen back home.

After a comprehensive tour of the stores and an explanation by a wizened cook of the workings of the kitchen, Will and Jeremy decided to venture outside and explore the stables. The stables were well-run and meticulously maintained. Horses of all sizes, but primarily large draft horses, were housed in rows of stalls. The number and variety of carts, carriages, wagons, and sleighs the brothers found were amazing. These conveyances were stored in the stable's attached carriage house. They ranged from the utilitarian to the extremely ornate, each in their own divided bay, with matching tack hung neatly on the wall.

Curious as to how the palace stayed so comfortably warm, that afternoon they posed their question to the cooks and were directed to a nearby corridor. The corridor ended with a wide, torch-lit stairwell that led down over 40 feet. Once they passed through the door at the bottom, then a small antechamber, and finally another door, they found the source of the heat. Six workers carried wood from the bottom of a long chute that led to the outside. They used the wood to feed three large furnaces, their heavy iron doors swung open to provide access to raging fires.

Will successfully caught the attention of one of the workers who seemed to be in charge. "Excuse me, what is your name?"

The muscled worker stopped as sweat streaked through the dirt on his bare upper body. "My name is Himclese, sir."

"Himclese, do these three furnaces heat the entire palace?" asked Will.

The man flashed Will a friendly grin. "Yes, all but the kitchen, which is hot enough without our help."

"How does the heating system work so well?" Will asked.

Himclese hesitated a bit before answering. People from the elite class seldom talked to a worker unless giving an order. Here was an elite, not only addressing him but, more than that, seeking to learn from an "underling." Suddenly realizing that he was not answering the elite's direct question, he replied, "A series of catacombs are designed to evenly disperse the heat and smoke. Eventually, the heat makes its way throughout the palace to warm the stones of the corridor and room floors. It then travels up many small flues embedded in the walls, which eventually connect into larger flues in the roof, and is sent out the chimneys."

Will and Jeremy were impressed by the ingenuity, engineering, and planning required during the construction of the palace. From the looks of the fires, much wood had been added, though the pile at the bottom of the chute was still quite large.

Will noticed another man nearby, struggling to keep up and looking quite pale. Will said to Himclese before he could turn back to his work, "Your friend doesn't look well."

"He's been sick for three days. None of the priests in the city will heal him for what he can afford. If he can make it through this shift, he plans to see a countryside priest who's helped his family in the past," Himclese responded.

"Why didn't he just stay home today?"

"He would lose his job, of course. How would he feed his family then?" the stoker asked Will, raising an inquisitive eyebrow.

Will was taken aback by the comment, then remembered that this man was part of a different culture. This wasn't the first time he had observed workers being treated unfairly, if not cruelly, in the palace. Will began unbuttoning his shirt as he turned to Jeremy. "Time we earned our keep, little brother."

Jeremy had been listening attentively to the entire conversation and removed his shirt without hesitation.

"Sirs, please, you can't do that. This is a stoker's job!" Himclese said, alarmed at the two gentlemen stripping off their shirts.

"We insist. Have your friend sit on that large block over there, and we'll do his share of the work," said Will in a soothing tone. "No one need ever know."

Will and Jeremy weren't strangers to hard work; they started at a young age helping at the family-run metal fabrication business. As soon as they were strong enough, they emptied trashcans and swept floors. By the age of ten, they were unloading trucks, and bringing supplies and tools to the workers. By 14, they filled in for workers who needed a day off.

At first, the stokers were timid around the brothers, quick to get out of their road, even when the two were trying to help. But the energy and enthusiasm with which the brothers attacked the task proved contagious and, before long, the stokers and brothers began a friendly competition. In no time, the pile of wood was gone. The brothers stood panting, leaning over with their hands on their thighs trying to catch their breath. Jeremy was the first to recover. He began to laugh and, before long, all the men were laughing with him.

Renewed and able to speak again, they all began shaking hands, gripping one another's forearms, as was the Bericean custom. One of the stokers said, "That's the first time I've seen a highbrow work. Do all of you work so hard?"

The room fell deadly silent. Himclese paled and stepped forward to speak on the man's behalf. "Please be lenient, sir. He doesn't think before he speaks."

Will waited a moment before responding. Looking down at the billowy blue linen trousers, now soaked halfway to the knees with sweat, and the white silk shirt hanging on a peg, he began to understand. The workers of the palace must be treated like slaves or, at best, indentured servants.

He smiled at the tired men to dispel the tension in the room. "Don't let the clothes fool you. We're no highbrows. Our dad is a small-town metal smith, and so are we. Everyone keeps referring to us as the 'Summoned Ones,' and making us wear these silly clothes. You should've seen what they tried to make us wear before we got these."

Himclese remained ashen-faced and silent as he pondered this revelation. Finally, he said, "You're the Summoned Ones?" He knelt on one knee, bowing his head; the other stokers did the same.

Will looked at Jeremy, bewildered. Jeremy seemed just as shocked at the men's reaction. "Hey, stand up," Will implored the men, pulling on the arm of the closest stoker.

As Himclese acquiesced and stood, he begged forgiveness. "We're sorry, Summoned One, we had no idea."

"Please, everyone, stand up. We're just two men who are very uncomfortable in these silly clothes. I'm Will, and this is my brother Jeremy."

Jeremy grinned at the men. "If we're done here, what I want is a good ale, and not the watered-down stuff they serve us in the palace."

"I agree, and a good tavern without any stuffed shirts around would be great," added Will

Himclese considered. "Well, there's a tavern we go to occasionally after we're done here." He tried to keep a straight face, but broke into a grin as he finished. The other stokers grinned as well, and Will realized that the word "occasionally" was probably an understatement.

"There's no way you'll survive five minutes in those outfits. This is a tavern for commoners. I have a cousin in the chamber crew; I'll have her bring clothes to your rooms," the lead stoker concluded.

The brothers took a detour through the kitchen and grabbed a quick bite to eat. Back in their rooms, Will and Jeremy each found a set of clothes laid out on their beds. They sponged off as best they could from the room's water basin. Once dressed in the coarse linen shirt, wool pants, overcoat, and stocking hat left for each of them, the two set out into the city. They followed the directions provided by the stokers and, after a pleasant 15-minute walk through the neatly kept streets of Karness, found the tavern without incident.

The tavern was a large, two-story building with a first floor made of stone. However, unlike the buildings around the palace, its second floor, which overhung the first, was of a Tudor style, with large hand-hewn beams exposed in stucco. Also, unlike the slate roofs found in most of the city, the tavern's roof was thatched. The brothers had noticed as they approached the northern end of the city that the houses were constructed of less-expensive materials. The tavern was near the northern gate and was the most prosperous-looking structure in its immediate area.

They heard loud noises and laughter coming from inside, but the music they were used to hearing in the bars at home was missing. The weathered sign out front read, "The Golden Rooster." The brothers knew by the sign they had arrived at the right place.

Jeremy and Will couldn't help but smile at each other as they walked through the tavern's front door. The building's construction and the attire of the patrons may have been different, but a bar was a bar. The door they entered was in the center of the longest wall in the 70 by 40 foot structure.

The brothers were impressed that the stone they saw on the first floor exterior was not a veneer, but rather thick structural walls. The walls supported immense hand-hewn beams, which spanned the entire width of the building, holding the weight of the second floor without requiring any center support. To their right, the beams and the second floor they supported ended 20 feet before the end of the building. This feature served to showcase the building's gable end, which was made entirely of stonework rising from the hearth of the large fireplace to the peak of the roof. A bright and crackling fire burned merrily inside the impressive fireplace.

Several booths lined the outside walls, each with a small window and a curtain that could be drawn to shut the booth off from the common room. The rest of the room was filled with wooden tables of various sizes. To the left of the door, patrons stood packed tightly around an L-shaped bar. Behind the counter, kegs, barrels, and casks lay on their side on sturdy shelves, wooden taps protruding from their round faces. In the corner behind the bar was a wide door, closed tight. Will assumed it led to the cellar, with its stairs paralleling the angle of the stairs above that led to the second floor.

The stairs leading up ran along the outside wall opposite the entrance. The stairwell started several feet past the end of the bar. Just off the opposite end of the counter and directly to the brothers' left was a large, swinging double door. As they watched, a barmaid came hustling out carrying a tray of piping hot food, confirming that the doors led to the kitchen.

Scanning the common area, the brothers found the stokers sitting at a table near the center of the room. Will and Jeremy noted that the workmen wore the same clothes they had on earlier. The two also took in the impressive pyramid of empty mugs before the men; obviously, they all must have come straight to the tavern after leaving the palace.

Will and Jeremy didn't get far in their attempt to reach the table before they were spotted. All of the stokers surged to their feet, scattering the earthenware mugs and knocking over chairs in the process. The unruly group pushed toward the pair, careening into tables and patrons alike in their rush to greet the Summoned Ones.

"We're so glad you came, Summoned…," Himclese began.

"I thought you agreed not to call us that," Will said good-naturedly, cutting the lead stoker off.

Himclese lowered his voice so no one else could hear them.

"Sorry, Will, I wasn't thinking. We thought you might be a couple of young highbrows just having fun at our expense, but my cousin described the two of you to us. And now we see you in the clothes she put in your chamber. We're honored that you chose to join us."

Jeremy said loud enough for all nearby to hear, "Can we please dispense with formalities? I'm dying for some ale."

"My friends have arrived. Ales for all of us!" Himclese shouted to a serving girl three tables away. A brief nod was her only acknowledgement.

Will reached into the inside pocket of his overcoat and retrieved a pouch of coins. Earlier, Will and Jeremy had thought it best to inform Namir of where they were going. Namir had seemed pleased they were no longer hanging around the palace without purpose. He handed them the bag of coins and told them of the unsavory areas of the city to avoid. After a brief explanation as to the value of each coin, he bid them farewell.

Seeing Will reach for the coin bag, Himclese said, "Please, sir, this is our treat. We can't allow you to pay."

Considering the determined look on the proud man's face, Will decided that, even though these men had little to offer, it would dishonor them if he pushed the issue. He returned the pouch to his pocket. Heading toward the workmen's table, he slapped the lead stoker on the back and said, "Thank you, we're honored by your hospitality. Now, let's try some of this ale." Sometime during their exchange, the barmaid had brought along some helpers and cleared the old mugs from the table. Seven fresh mugs waited.

When it came to drinking, Will had a few advantages over his younger brother. First of all, he outweighed Jeremy by 50 pounds. Jeremy had been to a few college campus parties where he was able to drink despite being underage, but he had only been of legal drinking age for four months. Will, on the other hand, had three years on Jeremy. While his younger brother was in college, Will had spent most of his spare time in bars listening to Josh's band, and he often helped set up and break down the equipment. During those years, he had learned not only how to hold his drink, but his own limits.

After the third round of the tall mugs of ale, Will asked where the restrooms were. His question resulted in complete confusion. After explaining himself further and waiting for the raucous laughter over the term "restroom" to die down, the stokers directed him to the door near the stairwell leading outside. They explained that, once outside, the path would lead to one of three privies.

On Will's return from the privy, he was able to catch the eye of the barmaid. She made her way over to Will and looked at him expectantly. He said, "I'm not feeling well. Cut me out of any further rounds, unless I specifically ask." She nodded and resumed her duties.

Will returned to the table and saw that Jeremy was downing his ale at a pretty good pace. He thought several times about stopping his younger brother but knew it would do little good. Besides, he thought, the lesson Jeremy would learn the next morning would stick with him for a long while. As Will looked around the room, something struck him as being out of place. He zeroed in on a man drinking alone at one of the booths. The man seemed somewhat of a contradiction: his build seemed on the smaller side, yet his shoulders and arms reflected great size and strength. His hands were quite scarred and knotted, and belied the man's youth.

Will asked the men at the table who the stranger was and quickly learned his name was Phomel. All the stokers seemed well-acquainted with him. Apparently, Phomel was a blacksmith whose shop was near the palace. Will knew his blacksmith trade would place the man in a different hierarchy than his drinking companions. He couldn't help but ask, "Why is he drinking here?"

Himclese spoke up. "He isn't welcome among the highbrows. His father was a favorite of the king, but he married a commoner, a beautiful farm girl from the countryside. His father's smithy had been a favorite of the palace for five generations and, even with the breach in protocol, Phomel's father continued doing business with the royal family. Phomel's mother died giving birth to him, and he grew up in his father's shop. Most around here consider Phomel the best smith, not only in the city, but in the entire region, but when his father died last year, the palace cut off all contact with him. As a result, the only work he gets from the highbrows are small jobs he can do discretely."

Will was intrigued by the man's story; also, he was keenly interested in seeing the workings of a blacksmith's shop. He continued asking questions. "Why is he alone? Isn't he welcome here either?"

The lead stoker thought a bit before answering, then said, "Because he's a highbrow, some here will never accept him. But he has helped many people at very reasonable prices for the work, so many around town are thinking better of him. I understand in the countryside, among the farmers, his work is so highly thought of, he's welcome in many villages."

As the two talked, a man walked past the blacksmith, intentionally knocking over his mug of ale. The contents spilled onto the table, and the mug fell over the edge. The heavy earthen mug broke into pieces as it hit the wooden floor. Will automatically started to his feet in case he needed to help prevent any fisticuffs, but he moved slowly, curious as to how the blacksmith would handle the situation. Phomel said nothing, merely bending over to pick up the pieces. The man obviously wanted to fight, however, and kicked the pieces away from the blacksmith's large hands.

Will decided he didn't need to be in a bar fight on his first night out of the palace. He walked straight up to the blacksmith, ignoring the bully, and said, "Phomel, it's been too long. I'm so glad to see you here." Pointing back to the table of stokers, he continued, "And your friends, the palace stokers, say hello as well." Looking directly at his brother with a meaningful stare, he waved. Will had commanded the attention of all the stokers at the table as well, and they all returned the friendly gesture.

Phomel then stood, rising to his full height. He was two inches taller than Will, but even more impressive was his broad chest and muscled arms.

Will thought the bully would have likely gotten more than he bargained for if Phomel had taken him on. But that wouldn't be determined tonight. Between the two big men standing before him and the table full of muscle-bound stokers, the bully took only a second to decide on a different course of action. He met Will's eyes briefly then turned quickly, walked across the common room, and left by the front door.

Will extended his hand and smiled at the stunned blacksmith. "Hello, Phomel. My name is Will. We actually haven't met before, but I thought it the quickest way to back down the fool. My friends told me your name. I hope my intrusion didn't offend you."

"Quite the contrary, my dear man. Will, is it? I was in no mood for a fight tonight," Phomel said. Then, with genuine surprise, he asked, "Where are my manners? Please join me. The least I can do is buy you some ale."

Will accepted with a slight nod of his head and slid into the booth. Phomel remained standing till he caught the attention of a barmaid, signaling for two ales. As the blacksmith returned to his seat, Will offered, "I should be perfectly honest with you. I got involved for a selfish motive as well. You see, my brother over there and I are metalsmiths and when the stokers told me of your shop, I wanted to talk with you."

Phomel asked, "Metalsmiths? I haven't heard this term."

"Well, where we come from, it's called a metal fabrication shop. We cut, grind, forge, machine—in short, anything needed to get the metal the way our customers need it. More importantly, we invent, design, and build what's needed for the job." Phomel listened without interrupting. When he finished his explanation, Will felt he had done a fair job of summarizing his family's work.

Will's description of his family's fabrication shop intrigued Phomel. The two men swapped stories about various repair jobs and inventive solutions. Will was careful to keep his stories to what Phomel would understand without having to reveal his true identity. To that end, and because he found it interesting, he let Phomel do most of the talking.

Obviously passionate about his trade, the blacksmith spent most of the time talking about tools and equipment he had developed for the area's farmers. As Phomel put it, he loved to see his work put to practical use.

As the night wore on, Will not only forgot the time, he also forgot all about his brother. During a break in their discussions, Will noticed that he and Phomel had accumulated quite a stack of mugs at their booth. "So much for staying sober and helping Jeremy back to the palace," he thought ruefully.

Will noticed activity around the stokers' table as the men arose and made ready to depart. Circling around Will's brother, they approached Phomel's bench, aiding Jeremy considerably. Himclese said, "We have to be up early for the morning stoke. You'll have to tend your brother." As he finished, two other stokers poured Jeremy into the seat beside Will.

"Thanks for your hospitality. This was something we really needed. I'm sure after he recovers, we'll be back another night." Will nodded his head towards Jeremy. Each of the stokers politely acknowledged his thanks and made their way out of the tavern.

Phomel looked at Jeremy slumped against Will. "I think we've all had enough for one night. I can help with him. Where are you two staying?"

Will hadn't talked about being a Summoned One, or the fact that they were guests at the palace. After hearing Phomel's story from the stoker, he had thought it best not to bring up the subject. Now Will hesitated, trying to decide how to reply.

Phomel misinterpreted the delay, and said, "I see you don't have a place to stay tonight. This inn is likely full, and besides the noise won't die down until almost dawn. I have some stalls for the horses I shod, with plenty of fresh hay. That part of my business has been off lately. So, they're very clean. You two are welcome to use them tonight.

Will thought about the offer, contemplating whether he would have more explaining to do after carrying Jeremy into the palace this late, or explaining tomorrow morning where he had been all night. He decided that Namir and Josh were the only ones that would care and, with both of them so busy, if he got word to them first thing in the morning, it would be all right to stay with Phomel. His mind made up, Will simply replied, "That would be great, thank you."

Rising to help Jeremy to his feet, Will quickly realized that the ale had had more effect on him than he thought. With Phomel's help, they got Jeremy to his feet and headed into the cool night, toward Phomel's shop. Will had learned earlier that Phomel lived in a small house beside his blacksmith shop. He had been raised in a large house closer to the palace, but after his father's death, Phomel's business started to falter and he had sold the family home.

The walk required a sizable effort from all three men. Will was happy to hear that Phomel's shop was a short distance away, between the tavern and the palace. The blacksmith shop comprised two main buildings and a walled courtyard that took up half a block. The buildings were constructed of stone and each had a slate roof. Access to the courtyard was gained either through large double doors that fit neatly within a 12-foot-high stone arch or through a man-sized doorway in the middle of an eight-foot stone wall topped with wrought iron. The arched doors were obviously used to admit carriages and wagons.

The large double doors had no visible means by which to open them from the outside, so Will reasoned they must have been secured from within. Phomel produced a skeleton key and opened the side entrance door. Once inside, Will looked around the open courtyard and saw several smaller outbuildings, including the open-faced stalls that would shelter him and Jeremy till morning. Once the two men had Jeremy bedded down, Phomel bid Will a good night and headed off through another man-sized service door that Will reckoned must lead to his host's cottage.

Out of habit, Will woke before dawn. Thanks to some blankets he had found in a chest in one of the stalls, he had settled down to a decent night's sleep. He sat up slowly and rubbed his eyes and face with both hands. Keenly feeling the aftereffects of last night's ale, he staggered to his feet and dunked his head in the watering trough just outside the stables. His head clearer now as the shock of the cold water wore off, he decided to leave Jeremy to his sleep and head out for the palace. His plan was to get word to Josh and Namir of their whereabouts and then return for his brother.

Will made his way to the palace through the early morning light and entered without encountering anyone. As the door to their suite came into view, Josh emerged.

Will asked, "Are you off to study magic again this morning?"

Josh, deep in thought, was startled by his friend's sudden appearance. He looked at Will appraisingly.

"I should be asking where you've been, but I can guess pretty easily by your bloodshot eyes. Anyhow, Namir told me of your plans. Thanks for the invite."

"We decided you'd be worn out from all the training. Besides, you never get in until well after dark," Will explained.

"Oh, nevermind. I'm not so much worn out as frustrated. They're almost done with their testing. And I haven't had any training. They spend most of the day just showing me around the grounds and trying to talk me into taking lifelong vows. Actually, I'm getting pretty tired of it. A night at a tavern sounds like an excellent idea. Include me next time, would you?"

Josh grinned as he hurried past Will, calling over his shoulder, "See you later."

Will left word for Namir via the chambermaid. During the course of their conversation, Will discovered she was the lead stoker's cousin. She was familiar with Phomel's blacksmith shop and agreed to be discreet when informing Namir of Will and Jeremy's whereabouts. With his duty to Josh and Namir squared away, Will headed back to the shop.

He slipped into the courtyard and found Jeremy already up and inspecting the forge and tools. The forge was housed in a separate building a little ways away from the two main buildings. Jeremy saw Will just before he entered the open front of the forge building.

"What are you finding?" Will inquired eagerly.

In response, Jeremy groaned and put his hand on his forehead.

"Quiet, no need to be so loud," he pleaded in a low voice. "Most of the equipment is like Dad's. The biggest difference is this hand bellow instead of the foot-controlled motorized blower."

Will and Jeremy moved around the shop, inspecting the tools and noting the layout of the equipment around the forge. Other than the forge itself, the dominant piece of equipment was an enormous anvil. The anvil was surprisingly similar in design to their dad's, one end having the telltale elongated horn. The main difference was that the other end was actually Y-shaped, allowing more pritchel/hardy holes. A clever design, thought both brothers.

The hammers, sledges, chisels, wedges, punches, calipers, swages, tongs, and other tools were arranged neatly on the walls and work benches. Quenching tanks containing sand, water, and oil sat near the anvil on wooden stands.

"You two are early risers. I didn't expect to see either of you for hours," Phomel greeted them, standing in the entrance to the forge and smiling.

"Your tools and equipment are quite impressive. The envy of any metalworker," Jeremy replied admiringly.

Phomel looked the brothers over appraisingly. "I didn't see either of you eat last night. You must be hungry. I have my clerk cooking breakfast in the store. Come with me." Phomel turned, motioning for them to follow.

They entered the back door of a two-story main building. Neither brother had given much thought to eating, but the smell of bacon cooking quickly changed their minds. They crossed through a small foyer and passed an open door that led to a narrow pantry. Through the door, they could see a middle-aged woman with her sleeves rolled up, working in a small kitchen.

Phomel shouted to the clerk, "Claiphie, please add enough for two more." Without waiting for a response, they continued through the foyer and exited through a swinging double door into the store.

The store took up most of the bottom floor of the building. A series of shelves and booths contained every imaginable thing a blacksmith could manufacture. Phomel's collection ranged from items as simple as nails and horseshoes to intricate garden gates covered in beautiful iron leaves and flowers. Practical things such as hinges, garden tools, hardware for wagons, and various sizes of knives made up the majority of the stock.

"An impressive variety. And of the highest quality," commented Will as he looked around the store appreciatively.

Phomel seemed pleased. "Thank you. Some of this I restock every week, but several pieces have been in this store for as long as I can remember. My family has been at this same location for 115 years."

Phomel noticed Jeremy rubbing his forehead as Will moved off to peruse the objects on the closest shelf. The blacksmith reached into his pocket and withdrew a small ring of braided string. He offered it to Jeremy.

"Place this on your finger. It will relieve your head of the repercussions of last night's drink. It should take full effect before breakfast is over. But please return it to me. It is a very valuable gift from a priest in my mother's village."

Jeremy accepted the ring with heartfelt thanks. Immediately after he slipped the crudely made band on his finger, his head felt much better.

"If you would allow us the honor, we'd love to work off the accommodations and this fine breakfast," he offered as Claiphie served them heaps of steaming bacon and eggs, buttered toast, and coffee.

"Enjoy your meal first, then I'll show you the shop," agreed Phomel.

Will and Jeremy had always gotten along well enough as brothers, but they shared a special bond when working. They had worked together for many years, but their connection went deeper than this. While working, the two talked very little. If one needed a tool and the other was closer, a mere gesture was all that was required, and it was handed without a word. "Look out, coming through," was unnecessary—the other would already be clearing a path.

Will and Jeremy had caught the blacksmithing bug from their paternal grandfather, a retired factory worker. Grandpa Reinard taught their dad the skills he needed to open his shop, and had begun to share his hobby with his grandsons when they were mere boys. Grandpa Reinard loved to attend county fairs and summer festivals, and he often took a portable forge with him to introduce festival goers to blacksmithing. That's where the boys learned to make traditional items such as horseshoes and square nails.

After the brothers made short work of the delicious breakfast, Phomel asked them if they could use the smaller forge in a different outbuilding to make square nails. Thanks to Grandpa Reinard, they knew exactly what they needed to do and were eager to get started.

After Phomel showed them the forge and the two sizes of nails he needed, he had them choose the tools they required for the job. The pair passed his first test in choosing the correct tools. After watching them set up the forge, gather metal, and stoke the fire, Phomel was comfortable enough with their abilities to leave them on their own and return to his forge.

Phomel was working on a complex piece that required much concentration. As a result, it was early afternoon before the blacksmith realized he was quite hungry. Looking out at the sun high in the sky, he was taken aback that so much time had passed. Letting his forge fall silent, he could hear a steady rhythm coming from the other outbuilding.

Phomel stood at the entrance to the smaller forge where the two young men he had met only the night before worked seemingly as one. He was mesmerized by the efficiency of the pair's orchestrated movements. Not a single act was wasted: the younger brother heated the stock in the forge while his older brother hammered the nails.

Jeremy held the heated round stock, turning it with each blow, as Will's hammer squared the stock and drew it to a point. Jeremy then quickly moved the stock to a wedge-shaped hardy. With two sharp blows, Will nearly cut the nail from the stock. Will held the tool to form the head in his left hand, and Jeremy drove the point of the nail into the tool's tapered hole, both men twisting the stock and tool together before snapping the nail from the stock. Two more intense blows from Will formed the head before the cool iron of the tool drew all the redness out of the now fully formed nail.

Will twisted his wrist, turning the heading tool upside down. With a glancing blow on the side of the anvil, he knocked the nail to the ground. Jeremy was not idle while Will was forming the head. He replaced the now-cool stock back into the fire and grabbed another glowing rod, starting the process all over. Phomel watched them make a half dozen nails, then started to count the seconds require to produce one nail. Consistently the task took less than three seconds, which meant that the two young men were making nails more than twice as fast as he could, and they had been working for four hours straight.

Something suddenly struck Phomel as strange: he couldn't remember seeing the younger brother reach up to pull the bellows. Watching more closely now, he saw the bellows operating, but Jeremy had both hands on the stock. His curiosity got the better of him, and Phomel walked into the building to have a closer look. A long piece of metal, protruding nearly to the forge, was attached to a post in the back of the building. A leather cord ran from the rod up to a nail in a ceiling joist. It was bent, leaving a makeshift pulley. The cord then traveled back down to the lower handle of the bellows that, when pushed up, blew air, fanning the flames.

Each time the younger brother returned to the forge to grab new heated stock, he would step down sharply on the rod and the flames would respond. The rod then acted as a spring, resetting the device for the next blast of air. Phomel was no longer curious, he was impressed. This single, simple invention could save him countless hours at the forge. It was then that he saw the two piles of nails. He was amazed at the size of each pile near the anvil, and quickly estimated that each contained roughly 2,000 of each size nail. The brothers' output represented two days' work for Phomel.

"Stop…Stop, you two need a break!" Phomel shouted over the ringing of the anvil.

Phomel's shout startled Will and Jeremy. They had been so focused on the rhythm of their task, they hadn't seen him approach.

"We were just hitting our stride, but we could use some water," answered Will

"I'm sorry. I'm not much of a host, am I? I should have had a water-skin here for you before you began working," Phomel said.

"I'll make it up to you with a bountiful supper. Besides, you've already made enough nails to fill my order, and plenty for the store as well. I'm exceedingly grateful for your efforts. Come, let's wash up before we dine."

As the three men did justice to Claiphie's supper fare, tucking eagerly into the simple but delicious meats and vegetables, as well as her homemade bread, Phomel peppered the brothers with questions. He asked about the bellows, how they arrived at that particular solution, and offered to replace the crude, bent nail with a pulley from the store. Jeremy agreed that would help the leather cord to last longer, but told Phomel that what he really needed was a foot-cranked blower. Jeremy tried briefly to explain the design, but Phomel shook his head impatiently, holding up his hand to halt Jeremy's explanation. He called to Claiphie and had her bring paper, ink, and quill. Jeremy sketched the basic design as he covered the principals of the mechanics. Phomel quickly grasped the concept and leaned back in his chair, nodding approvingly. He was beyond impressed by the quick minds of these young men.

For the remainder of the evening and over the next two days, Phomel introduced the brothers to his inventions, all in various stages of design. They offered suggestions for improvements or identified flaws that would cause issues later. He found that Jeremy preferred to sketch designs and talk theory, whereas Will would rather set to and build the needed part.

The brothers had told Phomel after their first night at his place they had secured accommodations not far from the shop. This way, they could return to the palace for the evening and confer with Josh, then get back to the shop the next morning. Over the next few nights, Josh vented his frustration with the clerics of the Brotherhood. By the end of their second evening with Josh, he had decided it was a waste of time to return to the order. Josh asked if he could join the brothers when they set out for Phomel's shop in the morning. The brothers readily agreed, and arranged through the stoker's cousin to have work clothes delivered to Josh's room before he retired. Early the next morning, the three young men grabbed a quick breakfast and began to hurry out of the castle to cover the short distance to Phomel's shop.

Before they could make it out of the palace, however, they ran into Commander Namir.

"There you are. I was just on my way to find the three of you," Namir said. He seemed agitated, passing his hand over his eyes and looking past the young men as if he needed to see into the future.

"I want to make certain that each of you is ready to leave immediately upon my instruction, when I am certain of the need." He went on to inform them of the inevitable collapse of the defenses of the Pass of Karness, and of the dire outlook for the city's own defenses. This revelation startled the three friends, who had been distracted with their own pursuits in the city. After assuring Namir they would be ready to depart at a moment's notice, they decided to look into the city's defenses for themselves.

Before venturing to Phomel's shop, they walked quickly to the southern wall to scout the defenses. The brothers were less than impressed by the war machines they saw: undersized and crude catapults, and even cruder arrow launchers. There seemed to be precious few of these weapons, and they were placed in positions that made them almost useless. Josh pointed out that, through the clerics, he had learned that only members of the elite class were allowed to serve in the army. And of those, only children of lesser merchants and distant relatives of the royal family ever joined. This meant that a full three-fourths of the population would be excluded from helping in the defense of the city. The three turned back and headed to the blacksmith's shop.

The talk on the way back to Phomel's was of weapons that could be quickly constructed using the materials available.

Josh suddenly remembered something useful. "Why not make one of those flinger things, like you two got in trouble for back in high school? Only make it really big."

"Yes!" Will said excitedly. "A trebuchet. We could make two that were big enough to stay within the city, but launch projectiles over the walls."

Jeremy added eagerly, "And a few smaller ones for on top of the walls, they could be launched right up against the walls if needed. If we worked out the range and positioned them properly, they could cover the entire length of the wall."

The three raced to find Phomel. They knew without discussing it that they would get no help from the palace or the clerics. Their only hope was to somehow convince Phomel to help them build the trebuchets to defend the city.

Namir had debated telling the Summoned Ones about the likelihood of Karness falling. He judged them to be of strong character and ultimately decided that he owed them the explanation. It had been nearly a week since the securing of the Pass of Karness. Namir was furious to discover that three of his men had been killed before the clerics from the Brotherhood of the Seekers arrived. Two others had been hurt severely enough that, even with the healing powers of the clerics, they would never ride in battle again. Namir's anger upon hearing of the loss of his men couldn't compare to what he felt now.

Namir also learned that the Karnessians had completely shut him out of all defense planning for the pass and ultimately the city. He didn't expect to lead the defense, but he had at least expected to be included in the planning. The palace had not even acknowledged his or his men's role in giving them time to plan for an attack. Namir knew in his heart that it was not his pride making him angry. His ire stemmed from the fear that if Karness were to be overrun, all of Bericea would be open to the invaders. The council should never have allowed the king's arrogance to rule in this matter. If the Pass of Karness fell, it would be only a matter of time before all of Bericea fell.

Namir's men had lost two of the nine levels of the pass before help arrived. Once the clerics entered the scene, they had been able to block any further advances until the soldiers arrived. However, since that time, the defenders had steadily given ground to the overwhelming forces of the advancing army. As Namir surveyed the battle from the relative safety of the clifftop, the military man in him couldn't help but admire the skill and bravery of the Karnessian soldiers.

Unfortunately, everything the soldiers gained through bravery and hard-won fighting skills was completely offset by a total breakdown in their so-called leadership. All the way down to the unit level, coordination was nonexistent. And if that was not enough, the soldiers followed a twisted code of chivalry that prevented them from taking measures to help their cause. They refused to throw objects from their higher vantage point, insisting instead on engaging the enemy in hand-to-hand combat only. By doggedly following this path, they unwittingly negated their single greatest advantage in defending the switchback pass. The other major flaw was the way in which they used the Reenones. The clerics were relegated to a mere support role. The soldiers of Jerimassa were leery of the Reenones, even to the point of prejudice but, even so, it had been 200 years since they had treated the Reenones with so little respect in battle.

Namir had watched the battle unfold, and seeing enough had turned for the city to find the three young Summoned Ones. He had the answer he sought: the pass couldn't be held for more than two or three days. With no cavalry to speak of, the plains before the gates would be lost as well. "Another strategic advantage wasted," thought Namir. He watched impassively as three of his men rode out of the gate and headed east along the base of the massive city wall.

The wall his men followed ended seamlessly at the mountain cliffs that were hundreds of feet high. The city walls placed at the most narrow point in the two opposing cliffs meant that the plains before the wall widened sharply. All week long, three of Namir's men had been leaving the city on horseback and taking the same route. They followed the widening cliffs where the grassy plain gently sloped downward where it met a wooded area. Here, the source of a faint roar that could be heard from the city walls became apparent. A spectacular waterfall cascaded out of the cliffs, falling over 200 feet into a lake. The falls and lake were the source of the Karness River, which eventually flowed out of the falls beside the Pass of Karness.

The trail followed the edge of the lake and continued on along the river. The trio remained on the trail, almost all the way to the cliff overlooking the pass. A side trail led to a clearing that held 16 cavalrymen and their mounts. For the past week, three riders would leave the city but only two would return. The pair would wait until the litters of wounded or supply wagons made their return journey to the city, then slip back into its environs unnoticed.

Namir allowed himself a slight grin as he watched his men carry out their small part in the city's defense, in quiet defiance of its short-sighted king.

CHAPTER 8

ORGANIZED RETREAT

Gloria found her voice again. It happened near the end of the second day of walking, but to everyone's surprise, she directed her first remarks to Pattie, not Steve. Pattie was caught off-guard by her behavior, but also genuinely pleased to see the girl beginning to come around. Gloria spoke in an offhand manner, as though nothing unusual had happened, behaving as if she and Pattie were longtime friends. She asked in a conversational tone, "How far do you think they plan to take us?" Not waiting for a reply, she added, "I sure hope we can get a proper bath and a change of clothes."

The friends were still wearing the clothes they had worn into the cave. Their coveralls were holding up well, showing only soil stains from the trail. However, they could not disguise the body odors attaching to the garments underneath. Pattie, Brandon, Steve, and Gloria were all growing weary of their seemingly endless march. General Darnon had continued the hard pace of the first day, and had everyone up and moving before the light of dawn.

Darnon's command of his army was very efficient and thorough. He used the 25 cavalrymen at his disposal to great effect. Eight were scouting in the field at all times. One reported in every hour; if one did not return, his absence quickly became apparent. After eight hours in the saddle, each man benefited from 16 hours of rest, as did his horse.

The cavalry were not the only scouts used by Darnon. The General also availed himself of the talents of a group of woodsmen from Vylacrae. Of the seven united city-states that ruled Bericea, Vylacrae was the easternmost city and also considered the least civilized by the other six. Young by Bericean standards, Vylacrae was a mere 150 years old. It had grown from a frontier town in the shadow of the forbidden Trillosean Mountains and retained much of its distant outpost heritage.

The woodsmen of Vylacrae, each traveling with his trusted hound, were the finest trackers and scouts known to Bericea. Their abilities were the stuff of legend, even before the city evolved beyond its frontier-town status. No one knew exactly how the group came to be. It was widely speculated that its founding members were the scouts who led the first supply trains to the young outpost. Whatever the case, the stories that surrounded this group had grown to mythical proportions.

The dogs that aided the woodsmen were massive. Their shoulders and broad chests came roughly even with the waists of their masters. Their heads were wolf-like with sleek black fur. Their coats were almost solid black, interrupted only by small patches of brown. Their bodies were long and sleek, making it obvious to any onlooker that, despite their size, they could cover great distances quickly and effortlessly. These dogs required no sort of leash; they stayed near their master as if attached to his hip.

It was said that these teams could track a field mouse under the snow and could pass right near a man without being seen or leaving tracks. Whether any of this was remotely true, General Darnon was elated when he found out that eight of the finest had been sent to compose the Vylacraen contingency of his army. His only issue with the woodsmen was their quiet insistence on working independently of his army.

This fact he had discovered early on, when he had ordered Primlas to make a schedule for the group to follow. The efficient Primlas had the woodsmen coming in every six hours while leaving four in the field at all times. The group listened attentively to the aide's schedule, then waited patiently to be dismissed. However, once dismissed, they gathered their meager supplies and disappeared into the surrounding woods, one by one. None returned for three days as the army made its way to the summoning chairs, and then only one entered the camp, going straight to General Darnon with his report. This breach of protocol made Primlas furious, causing the general a bit of a struggle to hide his amusement behind a stone face at the aide's predicament.

The woodsmen were the first to report that the summoning chairs had been found. They also brought the news that an enemy force was several miles away but had not moved toward their position during the night. General Darnon had been caught unawares by the attack at the platform, and in the days after the attack, the scouting of the woodsmen proved quite valuable. The Vylacraens made themselves even more useful by blazing the trail the group now traveled.

The terrain the group moved through was primarily made up of heavily wooded rolling hills. The trees were quite old and large, limiting the amount of undergrowth. The sparse scrub allowed the small army to spread out, yet keep each other in sight. The Vylacraen woodsmen did their job well; never did the army have to backtrack to find a more suitable route.

As she trudged along with the group in the days that followed, Pattie found her thoughts returning to the songs the clerics used when they were healing others. On the fifth day of the march, her curiosity got the better of her and she sought out Varis. She didn't know why, but she felt very comfortable with the older cleric. His rumpled outward appearance and gruff demeanor reminded her of her grandfather. Just like Grandpa O'Keenan, she knew that Varis' rough exterior hid the true, warm-hearted person underneath.

As their journey wore on, Pattie found it comforting to keep the old cleric in her sights. One day, an opportunity presented itself that the inquisitive girl could not resist. Varis was walking alone behind a supply cart and seemed to be deep in thought. As Pattie came closer, she was struck by the fact that even though Varis was quite overweight, the burden of the march had little impact on him. In this too, he reminded her of her grandfather. Grandpa O'Keenan was in his late sixties, but on long hikes they had taken together, he seemed to have endless stamina. Her lips curved in a smile; despite his attitude, she couldn't help liking this crotchety old man.

"Hi, Varis," Pattie said as she pulled alongside him.

The cleric did not answer right away. After a long pause, he answered, never taking his eyes off a point in the distance. "I thought you would be along sooner with questions about magic."

Pattie was caught off-guard by his gentle rebuke, but determined to satisfy her curiosity. She pressed on, "Are religious leaders the only people who can do magic?"

Varis seemed genuinely amused. With a grin, he commented, "How refreshing. You are cutting straight to the heart of an ancient secret. No, my dear child, contrary to what those leaders might say, their belief is not what gives them the use of magic."

The old cleric hesitated, looking around to make sure they were not overheard. "There was a time, an unknown number of centuries ago, that magic was commonly used by nearly everyone. As with any ability, some were clearly more proficient than others. The best users of magic lived long ago; we now refer to them as the Ancients. They were the ones responsible for the summoning chairs that brought you to us."

Varis waited a moment to gauge the girl's reaction and give her a chance to respond. Pattie gazed steadily back at the old man but remained silent as she tried to suspend her disbelief and make sense of what she was hearing. Varis watched her closely in return for a negative reaction to his statements. As none seemed to be forthcoming, he proceeded.

"We have some text fragments from that time and some later writings thought to be translations from the oral descriptions passed down the generations. All point to a period of great unrest where magic was thought to be evil."

"I believe the issue that originated then continues today. Some practitioners who use magic begin to change; they take on the characteristics of animals. All of these poor souls are driven mad in time, but, more importantly, they lose their humanity. Remember I said some of them change, but not all. This is where the religious orders begin to play a part."

The girl continued to listen closely, so Varis continued his account.

"Even in the days of the Ancients, the most powerful users of magic belonged to the religious orders. It became apparent to the general populace that those who were devout were less affected by the changes. However, because of the evil caused by the changed magic users, the people turned, not only on them, but on the use of magic itself. Villages would hunt down and kill anyone showing signs of the change. Many nollax died during these hunts, but also so did many innocent people."

Pattie interrupted to gain some clarification on the strange new word, trying it out hesitantly. "Nollax?"

Varis interrupted his lecture to explain. "The word 'nollax' means "altered" in the language used by the Ancients. It is the name we still use today for those that have changed."

"As a result of the persecution of the nollax, the use of magic was driven underground, often the sole realm of the religious sects that practiced magic. As you have observed, music is the means by which magic is summoned and controlled. Consequently, all music, whether used for magic or not, is deemed evil by most people."

Varis fell silent as he and Pattie navigated around a large mud puddle in the trail. Pattie could see now why he chose to walk behind the cart. She hadn't really paid attention before, but forced to walk around the puddle, she noticed that they encountered far more undergrowth. Once they regained the path, the undergrowth was being all but eliminated by the horse and the large wheels of the narrow cart.

Falling in again behind the cart, Varis continued. "Now, if a young person shows signs of ability for magic, they're sought out and convinced that it's in their best interest to join one of the religious orders. And some people choose to hide their ability. Some in remote areas even practice magic to aid their neighbors; in return, their neighbors help keep their secret, but even so, they're never fully trusted."

Pattie was now very engaged in what Varis was imparting. She asked eagerly, "So, not all music causes magic?"

Varis was pleased the girl had begun to show such a keen interest. "Correct, but most people won't even hum to themselves for fear of being overheard. After centuries of this fear and persecution of magic users, the prejudice of the population is strong, even towards us clerics."

Pattie sensed that the old cleric was happy to have sparked her curiosity. She made up her mind not to appear too interested until she could work through the song she'd heard the healers use. She decided to cut her questioning short for the time being. "Thank you, Varis, you've given me a lot to contemplate," Pattie said politely as she began drifting back toward her friends. Without responding, the cleric trudged on alone, once again lost in thought.

On the seventh day of the forced march, a woodsman reported the find of a sheltered cove only a few miles ahead. After listening to the woodsman describe the cove's precise location, protected on all sides by hills where guards could be place at advantageous positions, General Darnon decided that a break for his beleaguered army was in order. It was just past midday when the army entered the cove, and the order to halt for the night was passed. Much to the relief of all, the General even allowed small smokeless campfires.

The friends made their camp near a stream. They quickly had a small fire going and gathered enough wood to sustain it through the night. While they were preparing their site, Primlas came by with some cooking supplies, food, fresh clothing, and (perhaps the most welcome item) soap. Seeing the homemade bars, Brandon and Steve quickly set to stringing rope between trees near the stream and used blankets to create a makeshift shelter for bathing.

They all bathed in turn and washed out their dusty, trail-worn clothes. The fresh garments that Primlas had left were well made and hand crafted, their heavy construction made to withstand the rigors of the trail. The attire consisted of linen undergarments and heavy wool outerwear. Pattie was quite disappointed to find that Primlas had brought long dresses for her and Gloria, a mistake she planned to remedy before the night was out.

The friends, refreshed by their baths and new clothes, set out preparing a meal from the supplies. Gloria pitched in as if she had helped them hundreds of time before. The foodstuffs were simple fare, consisting of fresh venison, dried pinto-like beans, and roots resembling small sweet potatoes that ended up tasting more like white potatoes. The able outdoorsmen turned the meager supplies into a hearty supper, made even better as it was their first hot meal in a week.

The friends worked together to square away the dirty dishes, then spread out their bedding and gathered around the fire. Each night of their journey, they had discussed their predicament. They had come to the conclusion that this was no dream, the only logical explanation being that they truly had been summoned to this place. Josh's presence was a little harder for the group to come to grips with. They decided that the Josh's ghost or soul must have been present at the chairs when they were summoned, and that his body had somehow been restored to him.

Steve was thinking again about how their family must be out of their minds with worry and how they were searching for them. Just as he was about to broach this subject, a group of soldiers led by Kail approached the small group.

"Greetings to the camp," was the formal announcement made by Kail.

"Greetings," answered Brandon, apparently the correct response as the soldier strode up to the fire.

"I've a request of you, my friend," Kail said, looking directly at Brandon. "The soldier and I saw you fight without weapons and have been quite curious as to how you handle yourself with a sword. So, I've come to challenge you to spar with practice weapons."

"I saw you fight on that platform as well. I think the odds are slightly in your favor," Brandon said in response to the challenge. He quickly added, "The sword isn't my most proficient weapon, and I'm not used to the long sword that you use, but I'm willing to spar if injuring one another is not your intent."

"Oh we're not out for blood, we use these for practice," Kail commented as he opened a finely embroidered cloth protecting a long bundle. Wrapped in the cloth were two finely crafted, wooden practice long swords.

Other than his battle weapons and armor, this finely crafted sparring kit was Kail's sole possession. He had won the kit from a foolish young nobleman who enjoyed goading the locals into sparring matches. The nobleman would then take advantage of his less fortunate opponents by using the training of his station to make them look foolish, and at times, even to cause them serious injury.

Kail had heard of the young man's exploits one night in a small-town tavern as he was settling in to swap tales with the regulars. When the nobleman entered that very establishment later that evening itching for a fight, Kail couldn't pass up the chance to teach the young braggart a lesson.

Kail had picked up his wages earlier that day. Because he had just arrived in town, he hadn't had time to squander his earnings as was too often the case. The soldier decided then and there to wager everything in his pocket against the nobleman's exquisite sparring kit. It didn't take the experienced fighter long to prevail over the untried youth. After defeating the insolent young tyrant in what amounted to a public humiliation, Kail knew it would be to his benefit to leave the area in a hurry, before word of the defeat spread. Because of his hasty departure, it wasn't until later that Kail learned the kit was a family heirloom presented to the young noble by his father, the duke of the region.

Kail handed one of the wooden sparring swords to Brandon and said, "Follow me."

A small crowd followed Brandon and Kail as they moved toward a clearing near the center of camp. Over the last seven days, stories of Brandon's heroics at the summoning chairs had passed among the soldiers, embellished with each telling. Brandon hadn't been nearby during these recounts to correct any misrepresentations. His mysterious early morning workouts only fueled the speculation about his abilities as the prophesied Summoned warrior.

Kail's exploits on the battlefield had been witnessed by most of the soldiers in the small army. Kail was quick to engage in battle to spare the lives of his companions. He seemed to have a knack for being where he was needed most. Nearly all the soldiers felt more than an abstract appreciation for the tall warrior, for he had saved the lives of many of his comrades several times over the years they had served together.

As the pair entered the clearing, Kail handed Brandon a pair of finely tooled leather bracers and a matching pair of shin guards. In an almost ritualized manner, Kail began to don his protective gear. Brandon noticed that where his gear was a light natural tan, Kail's had been dyed a chocolate brown. Both sets of gear were decorated with the same intricate designs as those on the practice swords.

"The match ends with a combination of three head or torso scores, or an "enough." An "enough" can be declared verbally or by signaling as such," Kail instructed, indicating the signal with his arm ending in a closed fist placed diagonally across his chest.

"I understand," was Brandon's only reply.

Brandon hefted the sword and set his feet in place. He had been cautiously swinging the blade as they walked to the clearing, trying to get the feel of the foreign weapon. He was quite surprised when he first took the sword in hand. The weapon was very well-balanced but heavy. He assumed its maker had attempted to approximate the weight and balance of a metal sword. He realized immediately that a blow from this weighty weapon, even with its blunted edges and rounded tip, could cause serious injury.

Kail made a formal bow to his opponent, ending in a sweep of his sword as he stood erect with the tip down in front of his feet. Brandon repeated the ritual bow, thinking how closely the formality of the process mirrored the sparring practices of the martial arts.

"Keeenooa," shouted Kail as he brought the tip of the long practice sword above his head, holding the hilt firmly with both hands near his right shoulder.

At the sound, Brandon drew his right foot back, holding the hilt of his sword in both hands near his left knee, the blade in front of him slightly crosswise to protect his chest. Both men began slowly circling one another, looking for an opening to strike.

Kail was first to attack, shouting his intent as he brought his sword down toward Brandon's left side, then changing direction at the last moment to land a blow on Brandon's right. Brandon moved almost effortlessly, and the report from the block of his blade against Kail's echoed across the clearing. The duel then began in earnest, both men attacking and countering, but neither ever quite getting the upper hand.

As the sparring progressed, rather than shouting encouragement or good-natured ribbings, the crowd fell silent. To the seasoned soldiers that ringed the pair, the exchange didn't seem humanly possible. The speed and power of the two men's blows were shocking, unlike anything the soldiers had witnessed, even in the fury of battle.

Brandon was experiencing a level of exhilaration and clarity during the duel that he had never felt before. He had always assumed that the clarity he achieved during matches came to him through a fierce competitiveness, whether he was fighting for a substantial prize or, back on the platform, for his life and those of his friends. And Kail was matching Brandon's speed and finesse blow for blow.

Kail knew far more moves with the sword. Brandon countered these moves with sheer athleticism and overpowering size. Both men were dripping with sweat, each pressing for an advantage. Though the two had very different physiques, each man was in his prime and at the peak of fitness. Even so, the fight began to take its toll on the two athletes, and both began to slow somewhat. As the duel wore on, the advantage was turning ever so slightly toward the older and more experienced swordsman.

Brandon realized that if he didn't do something soon, Kail would strike the first scoring blow. He had seen several openings during their swordplay where he could have landed shots with his fists or feet. He was reluctant to do so, as he understood this to be a contest of swords, not hand-to-hand combat. He was reassessing this, however, because Kail had just landed a blow with a backhand and at two other times had tried to kick Brandon's leading leg.

Brandon swiftly decided that to have any hope at winning this contest, he needed to call into play more than mere swordsmanship. Kail then tried a very aggressive move, it was all Brandon could do to block it. The young man ended up in an awkward stance, with all his weight on his bent left leg, his body and arms stretched out and his right leg cast back to balance himself.

Kail perceived this as a major mistake and quickly shifted his weight for a scoring blow. This was precisely what Brandon had hoped for. Pivoting on the ball of his left foot, he used the weight of his outstretched torso to whip his right leg in an arc. He caught the surprised Kail in the legs just above the feet. The effect was amplified, because Kail was shifting his weight for what he anticipated to be a scoring blow. Instead, the soldier's feet were swept out from under him. At the same time, Brandon continued the sweep of his leg, pulling Kail's feet up in front of him. The effect was just as Brandon had hoped; his surprised opponent landed hard on his back, winded. Brandon allowed the momentum to continue, then, twisting, he used the flat of his practice sword to strike Kail across his exposed chest.

Brandon sat down hard a few feet away from Kail, unsure of the protocol, but certain there would be at least a brief lull before they resumed their contest. Kail lay there unmoving, staring upward at the sky. Both men were breathing heavily and sweating profusely despite the cool air.

Kail had not been scored on in a sword contest since the third month of his training, while still a raw recruit. At 15, Kail had lied about his age and joined his city's army. His mother died when he was young, and his father had turned to drink to drown his sorrows. That left Kail and his sister, senior by only a year, to raise themselves in the fast-paced river port city of Boask. When his sister married and his father died, Kail was left on his own. Fighting was the only thing he felt he was good at, so it wasn't long before he enlisted as a new recruit in the Boask army.

Right from the beginning, Kail proved to be far better than the instructor had ever seen, better even than the graduating recruits. By his third month of training, he was consistently beating the army instructors. It was then that the camp's battle-hardened senior officer decided to put the recruit in his place, challenging Kail to a contest.

Kail was working hard to hold his own against the far better opponent when it happened.

The boy of 15 experienced what he would later refer to as the "Awareness." He became cognizant of himself, his surroundings, his abilities, his limitations, and even the limits of his opponent. This awareness intensified as the senior officer pressed for an advantage. It seemed to Kail as if the officer suddenly began moving in slow motion. Kail capitalized on this strange turn of events, scoring three unanswered points in quick succession to win the match.

From that day forward, the Awareness came more readily in contests and even more easily in actual combat. That was ten years ago. Until now, Kail had never been scored upon in a contest and had sustained only minor injuries in combat. The soldier remained prone in the clearing, stunned, but not because he had been scored upon. His thoughts were in turmoil. The Awareness was the most intense he had ever experienced. How could he have achieved so much clarity yet still have lost the point?

He continued lying there, searching for the answer, when it struck him. The Summoned warrior must also have the Awareness. No one could understand when he tried to describe the state of being. He began to think excitedly, now he had found someone who might actually be like him. As Kail's thoughts returned to the present, he saw Brandon standing over, extending a helping hand. Kail grasped the young man's forearm, and Brandon easily pulled the lanky warrior to his feet.

"What's going on here?" General Darnon shouted as he pushed his way to the center of the ring of soldiers. "I should have known you'd be at the bottom of this," the general said, looking directly at Kail. "I called this halt for rest, not for you two to kill each other. Break it up, gentlemen."

As the other soldiers turned to walk away, Darnon barked, "A little after dark, I expect both of you at the command campsite." Kail and Brandon were surprised to see the general wink and give them a quick smile before he turned and walked away.

Rather than being upset with the two men, the general was actually quite happy with their sparring. He had watched from a rise about 100 feet away and decided to let the duel play out. He was confident Kail would not hurt the Summoned One. Darnon also knew this was exactly what his men needed to break the tension of the last week. As he watched the match progress, he was astounded, as were all the other men; the display of swordsmanship he witnessed was like nothing he had seen in his 40 years of soldiering.

Kail whispered to Brandon as the general took his leave. "Meet me back here at dusk. I've a few things I'd like to talk to you about before our meeting with the general." A nod in response was good enough for Kail. He headed back toward his own campsite.

In addition to the ring of soldiers that witnessed the almost supernatural duel, Brandon's friends had also been awed by the performance. "That was truly amazing," Pattie said to Brandon as she and Steve approached.

"I agree. In all the sporting events I've watched, I've never seen its like," Steve said slowly. "It was like watching a movie in fast forward."

Brandon replied, "I'm a bit shocked myself. The faster his attacks, the faster my responses got. I knew I was moving fast, but it seemed like regular speed to me, if not slow motion. Let's get back to camp; I need to think this through."

Brandon stepped forward toward his friends and swept out his large muscular arms, corralling his friends and directing them toward their campsite. They responded to the gesture, each flanking him as they walked away from the scene of the contest. Silence fell among the friends, each lost in thought.

"Where is Gloria?" Brandon asked suddenly.

"She said she was tired and wouldn't come," Steve said. "She's been very nice to all of you, but at the same time she's grown quite distant towards me. I was worried at first, but I don't think she's still in shock."

Pattie spoke up, "Still, I think we should watch out for her."

When they reached their campsite, Gloria was nowhere to be found. Everything was as they had left it, and there was no sign of a struggle. They decided she couldn't have gone far. The three friends split up and searched the immediate area. When their search yielded nothing, they began to call out to the missing girl, and questioned the soldiers at the camps closest to theirs. No one had seen Gloria pass.

Reconvening at their campsite, Steve was now frantic. "I knew I shouldn't have left her alone!"

Pattie was quick to console him. "Don't blame yourself. She's probably just out exploring a bit, maybe she took a walk to clear her head."

Brandon helped them decide their next move. "I was supposed to meet Kail at dusk, then go see General Darnon at his campsite. It'll be dusk in less than an hour. Let's just head over to the general's camp now and see if we can get some soldiers to help look for her."

The friends started back toward the sparring ground and on to the command campsite. They had no sooner left the confines of their camp when they heard Gloria's voice. She seemed to be joking and laughing with someone. Through the trees, the friends could now see her walking with Primlas.

Steve didn't wait for the pair to reach them before he shouted, "Where have you been? We've been looking all over for you. We were worried about you!"

Gloria was quite flippant in her response. "Oh Steve, don't be silly. I just went to ask our new friend Primlas if he had any garments other than these dresses he gave Pattie and me."

Pattie had all but forgotten about wearing the long, cumbersome dress. She glanced at Primlas and saw he was carrying in each hand a bundle of clothing tied with a string.

"I told you they would be worried, my lady," Primlas said with the crooked grin he had been wearing since Gloria first approached him.

"Well, now that the excitement is over, I'm going on ahead," Brandon said as he brushed past Primlas and Gloria.

Primlas handed Gloria and Pattie each a bundle, bade them farewell with a last sideways look at Gloria, and followed in Brandon's wake. Steve and the two women returned to their campsite. Pattie was still taken aback by Gloria's lack of remorse for the concern she had caused them, but truly was grateful for the change of attire. She had already decided she would change back into her caving clothes in the morning rather than attempt a long journey in the bulky dress.

"I'm tired, I'm going to bed now. Good night," Gloria announced as soon as they entered the camp. She didn't wait for their reply, heading straight for her bedding. The other two exchanged glances, noticing that Gloria had moved her bedroll to the edge of the camp sometime while they were watching Brandon's duel with Kail.

Pattie and Steve walked on to their beds by the fire and sat down. It was dusk now, not even 6:00 pm. It seemed to both of them that Gloria had turned in early more from a desire to be alone than to sleep. There was little they could do, so they stoked the fire and sat quietly, enclosed in its warmth waiting for Brandon to return.

Brandon reached the sparring grounds just as dusk settled on the camp. Kail was already there waiting for him. "I'm glad you came. I wanted to talk a bit before we went to see General Darnon," Kail said as he rose from his seat on a fallen log and shook Brandon's hand.

Brandon waited for the soldier to continue.

Kail, seeing that Brandon wasn't going to respond, plowed ahead. "I'll get right to the point. I think we have something in common. An ability that I've been aware of for over ten years, but until now I've never found anyone else who had it. I've not been able to find anyone who even understood what I was describing. I call it the "Awareness."

Brandon remained silent, mulling over what the tall warrior had said. He was sure after the sparring match that his opponent had the same ability he had, but he was still taken aback at Kail speaking openly of it.

Finally, Brandon seemed to reach a decision. "I call it "clarity," and you're the first that I've known to have it."

The two went on to describe to each other the first time each experienced his gift. Kail related the sparring match when he was a recruit. Brandon told of an older boy from his class who had wanted to impress a girl. The older boy had forced Brandon into a fight just before the bell summoned them to class. Brandon was no match physically, and the boy was better trained in martial arts, but in the midst of his frantic defense, he experienced clarity for the first time. Despite his newfound advantage, he didn't cause any permanent damage to anything but the older boy's pride.

They talked about their earlier match and how their clarity was at the highest level either had ever experienced. Kail was curious about the fighting style Brandon used and asked many questions about his morning workouts. A mutual respect and admiration for one another developed between the two, and before long they agreed to share their respective fighting techniques, starting the next morning. They almost lost track of time and continued talking as they walked to meet General Darnon. They had just wrapped up their conversation as they approached the general's tent.

The new friends heard a roar of good-natured laughter coming from inside. Shortly afterwards, 12 officers left the command tent, brushing past the two waiting men. Kail made a feeble attempt at a salute, making a fist and holding his arm across his chest. Brandon found it ironic that the salute was almost identical to the symbol Kail had indicated for submission in the sparring match.

After making their presence known, the general granted the two permission to enter the tent. Only Darnon and Primlas waited inside.

General Darnon finished relaying orders to his aide. "Make sure the word is passed. We leave two hours after sunrise."

"Yes, General," Primlas said as he left the tent, the ever-present clipboard letterbox in his hand.

"Gentlemen, thank you for coming," Darnon said as he swept his hand toward two field chairs of canvas and wood. "Please be seated." The last was conveyed nicely, but was clearly an order.

"I saw most of your sparring match today. Word of the match has spread throughout the camp. I want no more of that, but I want both of you to learn from each other."

"We just talked about that very thing," Brandon said, after a quick look at Kail.

The General raised an eyebrow at the boy's comment. "I see you two have more in common than fighting skill." Darnon pushed on. "More to the point, I want you to choose several of the more receptive and promising soldiers to accompany you as you train. You already heard we will not be departing until well after daybreak. So, I suggest you get started early in the morning."

"I've a few things to attend to before I turn in, so good night, gentlemen," Darnon nodded to the two men, turned, and left the tent.

"Let's meet at dawn at the place we sparred," Kail said as he too rose and departed, leaving the bemused Brandon sitting alone in the command tent.

Back at the friends' campsite, Pattie and Steve sat in a companionable silence around the small campfire, both deep in their own thoughts. Pattie was going over the song she had heard on the platform that had healed the wounded soldier. She had worked out all the parts and even solved how the four separate songs rhythmically wove together. The only sticking point was the melody of the most complicated piece.

This piece comprised a very complex classical melody, energetic and fast-moving. The melody was interwoven throughout the overall song. Pattie had almost missed this melody, thinking it part of the other three pieces. It was only tonight in the silence of the camp that she understood her mistake.

Pattie found it easiest to mentally run through the separate songs; then, with her new understanding, she could weave these songs together using the rhythm she had discovered earlier. It was this newly discovered final piece that she mentally practiced now as she stared into the fire.

Pattie smiled as she completed the last puzzles of the piece. Content that she had it right, she began humming softly to herself, one last pass to lock it firmly into her mind. Just as the lively piece reached its peak, the small campfire flared up to several times its original size, sending Steve and Pattie scrambling for cover.

"What was that? It was as if someone threw gas on the fire," exclaimed Steve as he looked back to see the fire returning to its original size.

"I'm not sure, I think my humming might've done it," Pattie said as she looked away, trying to gain her composure.

Gloria closed her eyes before the pair could see she was not asleep.

From his vantage point behind an evergreen, Varis grinned at what he had just witnessed, his suspicions about Pattie confirmed. He turned to head back to his campsite, confident that the frightened girl wouldn't try that again this night.

CHAPTER 9

LESSONS LEARNED

Over the past week, the friends had become accustomed to the sounds of the camp coming to life around them before daybreak, the muted banter between the soldiers, utensils clinking around the reborn campfires. And although General Darnon had granted the group an extra two hours before embarking on the day's trek, Pattie and Steve found it difficult to take advantage of the delay to grab some much-needed rest. Nor was it a surprise to them that Brandon was having the same problem; after they were fully awake and packing away their bedrolls, they saw that he was already up and off somewhere. What did surprise them was the fact that Gloria was also up and nowhere in sight, her gear already stowed for travel.

"I don't know what's gotten into Gloria. She's like a different person," Steve said thoughtfully as he stoked the prior night's fire back to life.

Pattie nodded. "At first I thought she was in shock, but I don't believe that now. She's definitely distancing herself from us, especially from you. I just don't understand why."

Before the friends could continue their discussion, they heard Varis from a short distance declare, "Greetings in the camp."

Pattie remembered Brandon's reply to the same greeting the day before, and responded in kind: "Greetings."

Upon hearing Pattie's formal reply, Varis entered their camp. "I've come to see if you had more questions for me, young lady."

Pattie glanced at Steve. Seeing her quick look, Steve suggested, "You all have a good talk. There's something I've wanted to work on for a few days now. I'm going to see if I can find Brandon."

Steve stood up from the fire he had burning quite merrily now and walked past Varis towards the sparring area. Steve had been mulling over a way to use the language tokens to teach himself the actual language of their protectors. He had tried listening to the daily conversations of the soldiers, concentrating on their dialect while he had the token laced against his calf. In fact, all the friends had been wearing the tokens in this way to prevent losing them. For Steve, however, it proved so distracting having the mental translation of the words pop into his head, he found it impossible to study the language itself.

He decided he needed to listen to the soldiers without the aid of the token, then listen with it. He hoped this on-again off-again use would allow him to become familiar with the phonetics, and understand the more subtle meanings of their language as well.

Steve, now familiar with the route to the sparring area, reached his destination in no time. He was pleased to discover Brandon leading Kail and nine other soldiers in his morning exercise routine. This setting would give Steve the perfect opportunity to experiment.

Steve took the token from his boot and dropped it into the pocket of his pants. Settling himself on a log, he listened to Brandon calling out the routine. This method worked better than he had expected. Brandon was speaking English, and the soldiers were responding in their native tongue.

Brandon worked through a series of stretches, throwing in occasional push-ups or jumping jacks to get the men warmed up. Their young instructor would walk through each exercise, then call out the cadence as the group worked through a series. Occasionally, the soldiers would break the routine with questions, but all seemed genuinely interested in learning.

Brandon spent 20 minutes in warm-up before he began to demonstrate basic punching and blocking forms. Unfortunately, his new pupils were quick to let him know they were less than impressed with his simple techniques. Steve listened intently as Kail stepped in to remind them that learning the sword was no different, and that the basics were the foundation for all swordsmanship. Brandon agreed, and assured them that learning the foundation of martial arts was the same.

Steve sat quietly, learning much as the session progressed. He was very satisfied with his progress; after all, he had always been quick to learn new languages. The training continued for a little less than an hour, and the chit-chat during the break that followed helped Steve nearly as much as the exchanges that occurred during the training. He listened to Brandon and Kail discuss the second half of the session. It was soon decided that the session would be conducted with swords and Kail would lead. Steve was somewhat surprised when the two men finished their conversation to see Kail head in his direction.

"Don't just sit over here watching. I brought some extra swords. You can't go around swinging bags, it makes us all look bad," Kail said grinning as he handed Steve a sword.

Steve was secretly pleased to discover that he understood almost every word Kail spoke to him. And, what he didn't understand, he could fill in from the context.

"Thank you, I accept. I should know how to better defend myself." Steve stood as he took the sword from the lanky soldier.

Kail's keen powers of observation were in evidence. "I see you've learned our language and no longer use the token. Quite amazing in the short time we've been together." The warrior seemed genuinely impressed.

Steve now understood that the tokens must work in a similar fashion for those who listened to him speak English. He reckoned that the listener would understand his words depicted as mental images, just as images would appear to him when he had the token.

"I've only picked up a little," Steve said, struggling a bit to express the concept. "I look forward to learning more of your language."

Kail had moved back in front of the men, but continued to address

Steve, turning his attention back to the task at hand. "You may find these exercises a bit of a challenge. I plan on going over some advanced techniques. After your big friend's performance yesterday, I don't think he needs training on the basics. I'll leave swords for all four of you, and Brandon can instruct you while we're on the trail."

Steve had never mentioned it to his friends, but he had trained quite a bit in fencing back at Lexington Prep boarding school. His passion had always been competitive horse jumping, but it was just too much to continue while at Brown. To stay in shape, he had decided to try out for the fencing team. Steve was not the best swordsman and making the team was no small feat. His best event involved the épée, a small, heavy sword built for thrusting. Unlike the other types of fencing Steve learned at Brown involving foils or sabers, with the épée, the entire body was a valid target. This concept made more sense to him; he thought that a strike anywhere in a real fight would at least impede the opponent.

Steve took the sword in hand and tested its weight. Back at Brown, his épée was the heaviest of all his competitive weapons. He had heard the épée sometimes referred to as a smallsword, and upon researching the weapon, he learned that it was descended from the rapier. The sword he now held, however, was much heavier. As the morning's training commenced, he found the fighting styles to be vastly different. With his épée, the scoring only counted when the tip of the sword touched the opponent, making it a stabbing weapon. The long sword he now wielded was clearly intended for cutting and hacking.

Kail was impressed by his new recruit's ability with the blade. The weapon was clearly foreign to him, but his footwork was almost perfect each time. His balance was also quite good, even better than most of Kail's soldiers. With regard to the other young man, Kail noted that he was taking to the lessons that challenged the other soldiers with an ease and eagerness that was almost uncanny. Kail was still having trouble calling this Summoned One by his given name instead of a more formal address, but he had insisted.

As the hour-long session wound down, Steve's arm began to feel like rubber. Just as he was about to announce he wouldn't be able to duel much longer, he heard Kail shout, "Enough! We need to get ourselves bathed and ready to travel. You have half an hour." With that command, the soldiers dispersed quickly.

Brandon walked over to Steve to tell him how well he had done. Before he could speak, however, Steve interrupted him. "Hold on a minute. There's something I want to ask Kail."

Steve shouted after the gangly soldier, whose physique closely resembled his own. "Kail, please hold up. I've a quick question for you." Steve jogged up to Kail with Brandon close behind. "Is this the only type of sword you use?"

A look somewhere between surprise and confusion crossed Kail's face before the now-familiar grin appeared. He had realized the reason for the question. "You don't like the common soldier's Keamonose. You must prefer the Millek of the royalty."

Belatedly realizing that these were words he hadn't heard before, Steve dug in his pocket for the translation token. "Would you repeat what you just said?"

Kail repeated the references to the two types of swords. This time, the mental images that came to Steve were clear. He saw the weapon he had used during the training, a Keamonose, and a finely crafted rapier, the Millek.

Upon seeing the rapier in his mind's eye, Steve eagerly replied, "Yes, a Millek, that would be more comfortable."

"I understand. General Darnon should have some among his personal supplies. I'll see what I can arrange," Kail promised.

"The women should find those easier to use as well," Steve added.

"Very well, we must prepare for the journey. I'll see you on the trail." With this, Kail turned and headed toward his campsite.

Brandon and Steve fell in beside each other and headed back to their own site. Brandon wasted no time in peppering his friend with questions. Almost immediately, Brandon had noted his friend's skill with the blade during the impromptu training session. Steve mentioned off-handedly that he had decided to try out for Brown's fencing team merely to stay in shape. He downplayed his role on the team and quickly segued into an explanation of his training methods. What he didn't want to admit to his old friend was his reason for keeping this part of his life from Brandon and the others. Steve harbored a lifelong guilt that his family's wealth afforded him opportunities his friends would never have.

After Steve's departure from the friends' campsite, Varis took a seat on a log by the fire. He gazed at Pattie over the flames. After a brief pause, he began. "I don't want you to get the wrong impression, but I saw what you did to the fire last night. I think before you do any more magic, I should give you some formal instruction."

Varis waited for a moment, giving the young woman a chance to voice an objection. Hearing none, he continued. "Magic has two disciplines: Caleen, which means "object" in the ancient tongue, and Radece, which means "action." No practitioner has mastered both. Typically, though, they have the ability to dabble in the discipline they have not mastered."

Obviously familiar with the role of instructor, he proceeded. "You've shown me you have considerable power with Radece." Sliding off the log, he made himself comfortable on the ground, placing his feet closer to the fire. He leaned back against the log and settled in. Pattie could see he planned to be at this for a while, but her interest was keen and she didn't mind indulging Varis for a while if she could learn something.

"Before I tell you about Radece, let me first spend a little time on the subject of Caleen." Pattie could tell the old cleric was in his element.

"Caleen is the tool of an artisan; in particular, an artisan with extreme patience. This type of magic created the translation coin you have. By the way, if you've not guessed at the value of the talisman, let me just say, each one took almost three years of diligent work to create." Pattie listened without interrupting, surprised at the length of time required to create her token.

"Caleen, as the ancient name suggests, is the art of storing magic in an object," continued Varis. (He was reminding her of her nursing school instructors, she realized, smiling to herself.) "The magic can be stored in the object in layers. As a matter of fact, that is where the artistry comes in." Stretching and placing his hands behind his head, Varis continued. "This isn't my strong suit, but the practitioner can layer and weave the magic into the object."

"The key to Caleen is that it requires the playing of an instrument to deploy the magic. That's why it's not my strongest discipline." Varis paused.

"I may have assumed too much and gotten ahead of myself," he said, somewhat embarrassed. "I had assumed you'd already deduced that magic was summoned and controlled through music."

Pattie nodded. "I understood that magic was controlled by singing, but I didn't know that it extended to the playing of musical instruments. This kind of makes sense, I guess. This expression of magic through music doesn't occur in our world."

Pattie could see that Varis was listening attentively, but she could also see he was anxious to continue his instruction. She fell silent and waited for him to proceed. Varis took his cue with a sideways grin, and began anew.

"Both Caleen and Radece can be divided into four disciplines. These disciplines control the four basic elements of nature: earth, wind, water, and, as you found out last night, fire."

"It's these four basic elements that distinguish most denominations of churches. All of the denominations in Bericea tolerate one another, but each feels that theirs is superior. Some are more closely coupled than others. A few have even forged close relationships to achieve a single goal. The most famous of these is the relationship of the prominent orders of Whilanar, the river city from which our champion Kail originated."

He continued, "Almost two centuries ago, these two orders made it their chief goal to eradicate the nollax. One's primary element was air, the other earth. Long ago, they discovered that by combining their disciplines, they created a more powerful means of completing their mutual goal. However, only masters of their respective orders are allowed to cross-train."

Recollecting himself, Varis said, "I'm sorry. I didn't mean to spend the morning giving you a history lesson." Gathering his thoughts, he pressed on. "I tell you this about the different orders, because when they finally discover your talent, they'll all but force you to stop performing any magic. They'll want you to decide which of the orders you plan to join for your lifelong training."

Pattie began to feel the stirrings of alarm in the pit of her stomach. "Lifelong training, they can't make me do that!" The word "lifelong" seemed to echo in the very air around them.

Varis saw her reaction, and with concern etched on his face as well, he replied gently, "Of course, of this I'm not certain. You're a Summoned One, so this is new territory. If you were a native, they most certainly would force you."

"You seem like a free people, how could your society allow this?" Pattie asked.

"We are a free people, but because of the prejudice toward magic, a blind eye is turned. They try to make it appear as if the person has a choice, but, in reality, if they don't choose, an order will take the person to determine if they are showing signs of the nollax. No one that is taken to be studied ever decides not to join the order. They are persuaded even if it takes years of coercion."

"Please don't get me wrong, these people are convinced they are doing right. They actually do this in the name of good."

What Pattie had been hearing did not help to alleviate her concerns. She asked, "If that's the case, why are you telling me all of this? Are you here to recruit me to your order?"

Varis chuckled while he said, "No my dear, I'm not here to recruit you to my order. As a matter of fact, I'm a bit of an exception. I have no specific order, or maybe better said, I'm the last of my order.

Varis' countenance turned more serious as he went on. "I was only eight years of age when I first used magic. I lived in a remote village, so my mother and father tried to hide the fact. My mother forbade me to use magic ever again. But one day, my father asked my mother to go into town and get supplies so he could continue working the fields. Going into town was always a cause for excitement, and I begged to go along. Finally, she relented and allowed me to accompany her."

"We had just entered the town when a man appeared from an alleyway and attacked my mother. It enraged me so much, I lashed out at him with magic. I had no training, and the song that came to me happened to be a song of fire. I literally boiled the skin off his back. Unfortunately, he lived just long enough to tell others what I had done."

Varis took a moment to gain his composure. Pattie could tell that this story had been told very few times. He cleared his throat and pressed on.

"The villagers became very afraid of me and my mother. That fear caused them to lash out, and they decided that I would be put to death. They locked my struggling mother in a storage shed and prepared a bonfire in the village square. They gagged me, placed me on the stack of wood, and lit the fire."

Pattie was astounded by the tale. She could not imagine the terror the young boy must have felt. After a brief hesitation, Varis continued.

"Just as the heat started to become unbearable, a wall of water rose out of a nearby water trough, knocking the nearest villagers from their feet and drenching the fire. A lone cleric stood in the street behind the soaked villagers. They knew him as Lynar. He was quite old and lived in a monastery several miles away. He came to the village every few months for supplies. He never spoke, merely passing vendors handwritten notes and paying in gold."

"In all the excitement, the villagers had forgotten Lynar was in town that day for supplies. When he heard of the villagers' intent, he was on the other side of town and ready to take his leave. To this day I am grateful to the old man who hurried to my rescue. Once he reached the gathering and doused the fire, he stepped forward from the crowd and simply pointed to me. The villagers cut me loose without a protest and I left with Lynar. I didn't see my family or the village again until I was a grown man."

"He didn't even let you see or speak to your mother?" Pattie was incredulous. Varis shook his head.

"The monastery was an ancient order; it was made up of only men that had taken a vow of celibacy. When I arrived at the monastery, there were only four clerics, all of them old. Their teachings were unique in Bericea. They studied all forms of magic, both Caleen and Radece, as well as all the basic elements. Other orders devote themselves solely to healing. They study all four of the elements, but only enough for the purposes of healing, and only within the discipline of Caleen."

"I was 20 when the last of my instructors passed. Let's just say at that age I was not as devoted to their pledge of celibacy as they were. So I left the monastery to the support staff and went on my way. I visited my family; they had thought me dead all those years. They tried to make me feel at home, but the tension from having a magic user in the house was palpable. I left after only a week. I would return and visit the monastery every decade or two. I watched several generations of the Keepers, as they came to call themselves, grow up in the monastery. I also saw as many generations of my nieces and nephews populate the valley."

"Several generations—you can't be that old!" Pattie exclaimed.

Varis responded with an academic curiosity, "That's right, you don't have magic the way we do. You wouldn't know."

"Know what?"

"How old would you guess me to be?" Varis said as he adjusted himself and tilted his head in an attempt to put his face in the best light.

After a brief study of the grandfatherly figure, Pattie answered, "I don't know, probably late fifties or early sixties."

Varis laughed, "You would be right. I turned 161 this last spring."

Pattie was speechless. After staring at Varis for a few moments, she asked, "How can that be?"

The old cleric said with a grin, "Magic, my dear child, magic. The use of magic to satisfy one's animal instinct can change a person into a nollax, but use that pays homage to your human nature comes with changes as well. In this case, an improved constitution and a longer life."

After a pause, Varis added in a more serious tone, "I must admit, I'm a bit of an exception. It has to do with when you start using magic, and I started at a very young age. It also I think has to do with the amount and variety of magic. Living on my own, I've had to rely on my magic far too many times. You see, I've outlived what was thought to be the oldest magic user by 30 years."

Varis ended with a bit of concern in his voice, "There're only a few that know my true age. I hope you'll keep that to yourself."

Varis' mood and tone turned upbeat and he said, "Look at me talking about myself. I want to understand how you came to know the song you used yesterday, and why you chose it."

Pattie thought for a moment on how best to begin her story. She decided to start with her ability to memorize music. She went on to describe how she had figured out the song the clerics used for healing, the four separate songs all woven together in a specific rhythm. She concluded with how she had isolated and memorized each song, then figured out the cadence of the weave.

When the young girl finished speaking, Varis remained silent. He couldn't believe what he was hearing and wasn't quite sure how to proceed with this Summoned One. He finally spoke.

"I don't doubt you, my child, but what you have said is beyond belief. The cleric you saw probably trained with his order for over 20 years before he advanced far enough to even attempt that song."

Now it was Pattie's turn to be amazed. Varis said, "You may have deduced this already, but the words are not important. It is the feelings you convey in the music and what you are thinking that matters."

"Let's try just one of the songs. Why don't we try the water portion of the healing song," Varis said, hoping to test Pattie's ability with a discipline other than the fire she had used the night before. At her blank look, he added, "That's the song with the lively tempo."

Pattie quickly responded, "Oh, the light jazz song."

The translation token didn't understand the word "jazz." As a result, Varis heard it just as Pattie said it, and he repeated it back to her to make sure it was right.

"Wait, let me get some water." Varis stood up and walked over to a small crock that had been used to store the beans for last night's meal. He filled it in the small stream and returned. Placing the crock at Pattie's feet, he said, "Now, sing or hum your song, and concentrate on the water in the crock."

Pattie started the song softly, but as the tune progressed, she lost her apprehension and increased the intensity. Varis backed away from the girl and just a moment later, the small crock exploded into a massive shower of water.

Pattie stood quickly, drenched from head to toe. The wood that remained in the fire pit was steaming. Her bedding was soaked, with small rivulets making their way back to the nearby stream.

Varis, who had not quite escaped the effects of the small explosion, stood shaking water from his hair and clothing. As he wiped his face, he grinned at Pattie. She couldn't help herself and began laughing.

Varis chuckled as well, then asked as seriously as he could, "I want you to explain what you were thinking from start to finish."

Pattie tried to compose herself. "Well I started out just concentrating on the song. I was translating what I had memorized mentally into a gentle humming. As I progressed, the song seemed wrong to be only represented by humming. So, I started singing in a wordless way, but with more volume. About that same time, I shifted my thoughts from the song to the water. I was surprised when nothing happened, but then I saw, from the corner of my eye, you backing up. I thought you were leaving, that you were disappointed in me, and I wanted to do something. It was then that I thought of a fountain I saw as a young girl. That's when it exploded."

Varis responded, back in the role of instructor, "The music calls and gathers the magic, but the thoughts control it. Thinking of the fountain focused the magic you had gathered, and your urgency to please me caused it to be released all at once."

As the cleric spoke, he walked over to a thumb-sized smoking stick that had been knocked away from the fire, but somehow not soaked. He blew on the end of the smoldering brand and quickly produced a glowing red ember. He started a song that wove the strong beat of a fire song with the whimsical beat of a wind song. Holding the ember in front of him, he directed a steady, warm, almost hot breeze toward the bedding and then toward Pattie. In no time, both were dry.

"We need to get ready for travel. So, as we end this lesson, let me leave you with this thought. The song you sang was for healing a human body. What do you think would have happened if you would have unleashed that kind of power on the fluids of a person's body?"

With that statement, Varis walked out of the camp, leaving Pattie to contemplate the answer.

At the edge of the nearby forest, Gloria moved deeper into the woods to remain out of the old man's sight. She had approached the campsite just as Pattie started her song. Gloria was, to say the least, intrigued by the performance. She heard the old man refer to this as a lesson. Gloria vowed then and there that she would hear the entire lesson in the future. She was certain that if this stupid tomboy could learn magic, so could she.

Lost in thought, Pattie rolled up the bedding and began preparing for the day's march. Before she had completed these tasks, Brandon and Steve returned from their training. They quickly bathed in the makeshift shelter and helped Pattie finish packing up. Gloria remained in the trees, waiting until they were all busy. She then slipped out of her hiding place and walked nonchalantly into the camp.

"Where have you been? You were up early this morning," Steve asked in the most casual tone he could muster.

"I went to see Primlas. I didn't thank him properly for the pants, and I needed to return the dresses," Gloria answered without her usual defiance. Unbidden, she began to help carry the gear to be stowed in the supply carts. The friends exchanged a look, finding Gloria's new demeanor more peculiar with each passing moment.

Kail and the other soldiers arrived soon after. As promised at the morning's training, Kail brought four swords. One was a long sword or Keamonose much like the one Kail himself used. He handed this, in its belt and scabbard, to Brandon. The other three were Milleks, or rapiers, that Steve had said would serve him and the women better. All the weapons were exquisitely made, including matching daggers, whose scabbards were secured on the opposite side of the belt from the sword. Both women felt very uncomfortable with the weight of the weapons hanging from their hips, but given the events of the last few days, Brandon and Steve found them a relief.

Marching for the rest of the day and well into dusk proved to the friends that the all-too-brief rest they had was not nearly enough. If anything, their new pace was more brutal than ever before.

Pattie was amazed at their stamina when, after the evening meal, Brandon and Steve slipped off for more training with Kail and the other soldiers. Gloria had disappeared while the others were still finishing their meals. Left to her own devices, Pattie was torn. She wanted to continue training with Varis but she was so tired, she actually dreaded the thought of him showing up. She had felt tired right from the start of the day's journey, and it was all she could do to keep from climbing onto the back of a supply wagon and going to sleep. Pattie's internal struggle between going to sleep and training with Varis was settled for her when she nodded off into a restless oblivion.

Pattie woke the next morning with Brandon gently shaking her, saying, "Wake up sleepyhead. You're going to miss a beautiful walk."

Pattie sat up rubbing her eyes and saw that the others had broken camp and were ready to move. All but her bedding had been stowed by her friends. She slowly realized that she felt much better than the day before. Her sleep had been sound and uninterrupted. Last night's rest was more refreshing than any she could ever remember.

"I saved you some breakfast," Brandon said, handing her a cloth-bound bundle after pulling her to her feet.

"Thanks. It looks like I'll have to eat this on the trail."

Before the words were out of Pattie's mouth, the lead columns began the march. Brandon quickly rolled up her bedding and, with that no sooner done, it was their turn to fall in and move out.

CHAPTER 9 ✦ LESSONS LEARNED

The terrain had become more rugged than it was the day before. The trees were still large and the undergrowth limited, but the rolling hills had given way to more pronounced valleys. The valleys ran primarily east and west; however, the route the army took had been almost due north from the very beginning. The trail wound up and down ever steeper ravines, and, in some cases, they were forced to make their way downstream to find a suitable crossing or to avoid hillsides too steep to traverse.

The streams and dry ravines always flowed east to west, and at near midday the friends found out why. They had negotiated a particularly difficult hillside that forced them to make a few switch-backed passes to gain its summit. The top of the hill was a rocky knoll where no trees grew. This was the first time since the journey began that the group had escaped the large ancient trees of the forest. At the high point of the clearing, the group could clearly see a vast mountain range to the east.

In late afternoon, to find a suitable place to ford a particularly deep and fast-moving creek, the army was forced downstream. This stream cut deep into a steep-sided valley, leaving only ever-narrowing banks to travel upon. The banks narrowed so much at one point that the supply wagons had to proceed with extreme caution to keep from rolling into the water. It was immediately after this most narrow part of bank that the trail widened considerably, because a valley containing a tributary brook joined theirs at this point. Thick undergrowth blocked the entrance to the side valley. At the intersection of the two waterways, the larger stream widened and the scouts had determined this was the point where it would be safe for the army to cross.

The troops behind the friends had dropped back. Only the four Summoned and four of their protectors were on the landing, the thick undergrowth behind them. The procession of soldiers was just starting onto the narrow ledge leading to the landing. The horse-drawn supply carts in front of the friends were having a difficult time crossing the cold, fast-moving, mountain-fed stream. This left a considerable gap between the supply carts and the soldiers that had crossed before them, as they had moved ahead rapidly on the much easier terrain found on the other side of the stream.

Suddenly, a scream tore through the air. It came from one of the soldiers assigned to protect the Summoned Ones. The friends turned in horror to see large blisters appearing on every inch of the soldier's exposed skin. His agonized scream ended as he slumped to the ground. From the shelter of the bushes, armed soldiers emerged and rushed toward the group in an obviously well-planned attack. Two of the new enemies went straight away to block the narrow pass so that aid would not come easily.

Kail was the first to react, his sword and dagger drawn in a blur. He charged headlong into the lead, attacking the enemy. As he charged, he shouted, "Nollax!"

Kail blocked the first attack, meant to sever Brandon's head from his shoulders. The blow would not have been effective as Brandon was already moving, but the distraction did buy Brandon time to draw his weapons. Kail had looked into the eyes of his opponent, and what he saw there caused him to be filled with both fear and rage, two emotions he seldom allowed himself in battle.

Kail once again stepped between Brandon and another opponent, only this time it was not to parry. Using his longsword, with one vicious blow, he lopped off the attacker's head. As he moved to a more defensive position trying to guard all the Summoned at once, he shouted, "These foes are called pallitors, they're after the Summoned Ones."

Kail and Brandon were fighting like crazed men just to keep the pallitors at bay. As the pair worked to keep the attackers from the others, Kail shouted to be heard over the crashing metal, "This is no time to be timid, my large friend. These pallitors are seasoned warriors controlled by magic."

Kail hesitated as he parried a particularly vicious coordinated attack by two of the pallitors. In all his previous encounters with these foes, they had lacked the ability to coordinate attacks. Unfortunately, that was the only advantage to be gained. Kail was quite concerned now.

Successfully defending another attack, Kail shouted again at Brandon, "They have no fear, feel no pain, and won't stop until all of us are dead. You must either sever their head, or hold them off long enough for them to bleed out."

Gloria, Pattie, and Steve were standing in the water at the edge of the stream. From their vantage point, they could see the battle unfolding. Steve and Pattie had their swords drawn, but saw no immediate opening to help Kail, Brandon, or the other two soldiers. Two of the enemy soldiers were successfully holding off any help by way of the narrow trail. The two had even pushed well up the trail itself, and were fighting standing on the bodies of the friends' potential rescuers.

Kail and Brandon had their hands full with three of the enemy. Three other pallitors were engaging the other two soldiers assigned to be the friends' guard. It was here that Steve saw the most potential for the first threat. The enemy fought with such reckless abandon that it was taking a toll even on the well-trained soldiers. All five fighters, both enemy and protector alike, were covered in bleeding cuts, but the pallitors took no notice of their wounds.

Pattie found the nollax enemies to be the most terrifying. She knew the nollax at first sight; it was a grotesque representation of a human. Covered in dark curly hair, the nollax had a large, broad chest and powerful arms and legs. The head of the beast was a blend of a human and a bull; the face was slightly elongated, but ended with a human mouth and chin. Its horns and ears were like those of a western steer, and it had a mane that started on the top of its head and flowed down its back.

The sight of the nollax was not what frightened Pattie the most, it was the fact that it was singing in a beautiful baritone voice. The song and the tune were like none she had ever heard, dark and menacing. The closest thing she had ever heard to this was an opera her aunt had taken her to when Pattie was in her early teens. The opera was so dark, the music had scared her, but this was far worse. It represented something positively evil.

Pattie wasn't sure why the nollax was singing, but she knew it had something to do with magic directed at the enemy fighters. She sensed that the only hope she and her friends had was to stop its magic. As Pattie stood transfixed in the water, frantically thinking, Gloria began screaming and bolted further into the water, away from the fighting. The slick rocks and swift current quickly overcame her, and she toppled headlong into the cold, rushing waters.

Steve watched the scene unfold in a mental agony. It was only a matter of time before an enemy broke loose, and then Pattie would be at its mercy, but Gloria's need was immediate. It didn't take long to make his decision. The trail across the river made its way downstream. He would take the chance that they could fish Gloria out later, unharmed. Steve had no sooner reached this conclusion than one of the protecting soldiers fell, and two of the enemy began charging toward him and Pattie.

Pattie was so consumed in thought, she didn't even notice this new threat. She had made up her mind. She would do what she had sworn she wouldn't—she was going to use her newfound talent on another living being.

She had just started her song when a large column of water shot skyward from the center of the stream. The column took with it so much water that an area over 50 feet long and as wide as the stream suddenly dried up. The column of water rose to over 50 feet, then arcing, fell full force onto the nollax. The weight of so much water was devastating; the creature never rose again. Pattie glanced across the stream and saw Varis, obviously the source of the column of water.

With the nollax gone, the enemy soldiers seemed to hesitate slightly. This was all Kail needed to dispatch another pallitor in the same manner as before. Brandon took advantage of the enemy's uncertainty and stuck a hard blow deep into the shoulder at the collarbone. This blow opened a major artery, but still the possessed fighter did not slow.

Pattie watched in horror as two of the maniac fighters charged Steve. Steve was faster and better with the long, thin-bladed rapier than she could have ever hoped, but it was clear that it was only a matter of time before he was overwhelmed. Steve landed blow after blow to the extremities of the assailants, but the cuts seemed to have no effect at all.

Then it happened.

Steve was just a millisecond too slow in parrying a vicious slash aimed at his side. Barely deflecting the potentially deadly blow from his midsection, Steve felt it cut deep into his thigh.

Pattie did not even stop to consider her actions: the man she had loved most of her life was in mortal danger. She acted out of instinct, and a song came quickly to her lips. It was in part the song from the healing weave, and the rest came from someplace deep inside. The water at the feet of the attackers instantly began to boil, and their flesh turned a bright red. Large boils appeared on their skin and cracked open, releasing steam and pus. The thing that nearly broke Pattie and caused her to retch was the look on the faces of both enemies just before they collapsed and were swept away by the water. The look was not of pain, or terror, but of relief. One of the assailants smiled at her before being carried away.

When Pattie was able to look up again, she saw that the other pallitor had been eliminated, and the fight was over almost as quickly as it had started.

Realizing the full extent of what she had done, the young woman began to weep. When Steve reached her and folded her into his arms, she began sobbing uncontrollably into his shoulder. The two stood in the middle of the fast-moving stream, Steve holding her tight and wishing futilely he could help her in some way.

CHAPTER 10

LITTLE HEALING

Pattie sobbed into Steve's shoulder. The pair stood with Varis in the middle of the stream, oblivious to the cool water channeling around them. Steve had only seen Pattie's strong persona, her "I can handle anything" front. Now he held in his arms a fragile, vulnerable young woman. He wanted to comfort her, but the words wouldn't come.

As he held Pattie, Steve replayed the battle in his mind, trying to come to grips with what he had just been through. The two pallitors would surely have killed him if they hadn't been … "What did happen to them?" Steve forced his mind clear of thoughts of what might have been.

"It couldn't be helped, my child," Varis said gently as he placed a comforting hand on Pattie's shoulder.

"It couldn't be helped," thought Steve. What couldn't be helped, the battle? No, Varis was referring to Pattie's actions. How could she have… The singing? He remembered her singing just before it happened.

In a flash, it came to him—Pattie had just caused the horrible death of those two men. This was such a contradiction from the girl he had known back home. Many times, she had stopped others from stepping on insects or spiders, then carried her small charges to safety. She had been inconsolable for more than a week after the death of a patient at the home. Steve understood that the men dying by her hand had to be killing her inside. He pulled her tighter, caressing her hair and rubbing her back. Pattie's crying subsided and she began to relax against his chest.

Steve knew this wasn't the time or place, but he couldn't help thinking how good it felt to have her in his arms. For a moment, the pair was closer than they had ever been, but that moment was short-lived as soldiers began to pour into the ford and landing. Pattie forgot her sorrow as she felt the warm blood from the wound in Steve's thigh soak into her pant leg. She looked down and, seeing the dark stain spreading outward from the wound, immediately pulled out of his embrace. "Steve, your leg! We need to get the bleeding stopped." At once, she reverted to the girl Steve knew from home, the take-charge caregiver.

Grabbing his arm and placing it over her shoulder, Pattie guided Steve to the bank. Varis had already moved away and was tending to the soldiers who had been injured defending the narrow ledge. He stabilized the last of the wounded and stood, looking around till he found them. Varis slowly made his way toward the pair.

Pattie was helping Steve to the ground as the magician approached. She looked up at Varis and was momentarily distracted from Steve's plight when she saw how frail and wan the older man was. "Are you all right?" Pattie asked apprehensively.

Varis shook his head slightly. "I've pushed myself almost to my limit. I knew the nollax controlled the pallitors and had to be stopped. That column of water took nearly all my strength." Varis lowered himself to the ground beside Steve. "Most of the Reenones were toward the front of the column. It will be a while before they reach us, even if they've received word. We need to stop his bleeding at once."

Pattie removed her scarf and used it to apply pressure to the wound, but that only managed to slow down the ominous dark flow. She knew Varis was right. The magician looked directly into the young girl's eyes. Not without empathy, he was still insistent.

"I know you've been through a lot, but I'm too weak. I must have your help."

Steve watched the exchange between the two. He saw the conflicting emotions dance across Pattie's features. He knew that the thought of using magic on a human so soon after the battle was abhorrent to Pattie. He wanted to tell her not to worry, he would be fine, but already he was becoming lightheaded. He feared he would pass out soon if the two didn't come to a quick resolution.

Pattie felt so helpless. She had vowed right after the death of the pallitors never to perform magic again, and suddenly Varis wanted her to use it on the man she loved. She hesitated for what seemed to her like an eternity, but she knew from her medical training that Steve desperately needed her help. Looking appraisingly at the magician in front of her, who looked 20 years older than he had an hour earlier, it was obvious Varis was in no condition to complete the task on his own. Pattie relented with a sigh. "All right, how can I help you?"

"You know the healing tunes. I just want you to hum along, lending me your magic. I'll be the one guiding the magic," Varis said encouragingly.

Seeing the young girl's look of resignation, Varis pressed on. "Before you begin, I want you to clear your mind. You know that music calls and concentrates magic, but your thoughts initiate and focus it. You'll experience new feelings during this. It is critical that you not act on any new thought."

Pattie couldn't hide her concern at this last instruction, but remained resolute. "I understand."

Before she could change her mind, Pattie began to hum the tune she had practiced so many times in her head. Soft and low she hummed at the perfect pitch she had mastered playing the game with her mother. After so many mental runs of the song, she found it almost effortless. Varis started to sing along, his voice weak and raspy. Pattie's humming faltered, then stopped. A look of wonder passed over her face.

Varis nodded as if expecting just this reaction. "I had to let you experience it on your own, my child. Nothing I could have said would prepare you. Take a brief moment to gather yourself, but soon you must start again. Explore with your mind only, don't take action."

The overwhelming feeling Pattie had just experienced was of being inside Steve's leg. She had been looking and thinking about the bone-deep gash under her hands. That became the entry point to the sensation. Vividly, she saw his thigh as she felt the flesh around the gash. Within her mind, she looked deeper into the wound. She could see past the blood, past the flesh to the bone, and further still to the nick on the bone from the enemy's blade.

A gentle touch on the arm from Varis brought Pattie back. Realizing more than ever the gravity of the situation and the need for urgency, she began humming again from the beginning. This time when Varis started to sing, she was more prepared. Even so, she still had to fight against being overpowered by the sensation.

Pattie did as Varis suggested and used her mind to explore. She found she could mentally peel back layers of tissue, as if it were pages of velum in an anatomy study guide. This allowed her to explore each of the body's systems separately. Seeing something strange in a blood vessel, she pushed deeper with her mind. She was astounded to discover the phantasm expanding as if she were looking through a magnifying glass.

Pattie was fascinated, and she pushed deeper and deeper. Mental pictures appeared as if she were turning different magnifications on a microscope. The images were already near the cellular level, and yet she felt she could push further. Then abruptly the images stopped.

She looked around and saw Varis passed out, lying next to Steve. Steve's wound, though still gaping, had scabbed over somewhat. Blood had dried and caked around the opening. To her great relief, Pattie saw the end result of their efforts—the bleeding had stopped. Varis must have completed the task before he lost consciousness.

She quickly checked both men. Their vital signs were fine, and they both appeared to be in a deep sleep. Suddenly, Pattie's heart leapt into her throat as people began crashing through the undergrowth near the landing. Kail and Brandon appeared, followed by several soldiers. They seemed to be scouting to make sure additional enemy were not in hiding.

Pattie waved at Brandon and Kail till they saw her. The two men made their way over to the pale girl and her prone companions. Pattie took in their condition at a glance and made both men sit on the ground near Steve and Varis. Using water from the stream and supplies from her small first aid kit, she cleaned and dressed the many minor wounds on them both with practiced skill and efficiency.

The landing was soon swarming with Reenones who finished the healing work Pattie and Varis had started. She observed them as they sang songs similar to the one she had memorized, closing wounds until they were undetectable. She listened closely to the nuances each cleric gave to their particular song's tune. She also concentrated on the lyrics. These varied greatly from cleric to cleric, even for the same task. She concluded that the words themselves did not determine the result; instead, the catalyst must be the additional emotion conveyed by those words.

General Darnon ordered a few of his men to prepare makeshift beds in the supply carts for Steve and Varis, along with two wounded soldiers. Once the wounded were settled, Darnon shouted orders for the march to continue. He then motioned for Kail, Brandon, and Pattie to accompany him to the front of the column.

"The Summoned One you call Gloria is fine," he began as they assumed the lead position.

"Despite her belligerence to her rescuers, she was fished out of the fast-moving water by soldiers near the front of the column. Primlas has proven to be the only one capable of calming her."

The general quickly moved on to the real reason he required their presence at the front of the column. Darnon wanted every detail of the attack. He questioned each of the friends separately, saving Pattie for last. She went over the attack thoroughly, but when it came to her part, without telling an outright lie, she allowed the general to believe that Varis had killed the two pallitors. She was relieved to learn later that Steve had also allowed Darnon to assume Varis had ended the attack.

"We were lucky this time. Now I will double the guards, and at least two Reenones in addition to Varis will be with you at all times." The three friends exchanged glances. From Darnon's tone, they knew this more restrictive arrangement was non-negotiable.

Not long after the general issued this order, a Vylacraen scout stepped out of the woods near him and fell in alongside. After the earlier attack, the man's sudden appearance startled everyone, including Darnon. Both the scout and his dog bore several wounds, which were hurriedly field-dressed as the column pressed on. In all the previous meetings with the scouts, they would speak only with Darnon, in private. This scout either felt his information was too important to wait or he trusted Pattie, Brandon, and Kail, because he began his report right away.

He began, "Sir, please do not condemn us for this attack. The enemy has been using nollax to hide their tracks. It goes beyond repairing damage to the forest floor; they've actively used magic to shield things from us. This means they know of our existence and have been tracking us."

Darnon had not slowed the brisk pace, and the strain to keep up was taking its toll on the injured scout. Darnon saw the man struggle and used hand signals to slow the pace of the column. The scout acknowledged the gesture with a slight head nod and continued.

"We always work independently, using sophisticated techniques to communicate. After the attack on the knoll, we suspected the use of magic. So we broke with the long-standing tradition of scouting solo and started working in pairs. We never worked far enough apart that we were out of sight of one another. I have excellent vision in the forest because of my experience and trained eye."

The scout caught his breath, holding his side where blood was beginning to seep through the makeshift bandages. Swallowing hard, he pushed on.

"At some point, I realized I could no longer see my colleague. I headed in the last direction I'd seen him to investigate. Halfway to my destination, I came into a small clearing and saw my friend and his dog high in the air, pinned against a tree. The nollax must have been distracted, and I saw a faint outline of the creature silhouetted against the limp body of my friend."

The scout closed his eyes as he remembered, wincing in pain, and walked on in silence for nearly a minute before he continued his narrative. "As soon as I saw the silhouette, I tackled the beast, driving my dagger deep into its body. As I did, the hideous creature revealed itself. It turned on me and pulled itself up to its full height, three feet taller than I stood. It stayed far enough away that I could not attack and began singing its magic. I surely would have perished if not for Jacrob, my faithful friend," the scout said, patting the injured dog limping beside him.

Grimacing from the pain that petting his dog caused, the scout continued. "This brave boy leapt with his full weight, landing on the nollax's chest. By instinct, Jacrob ripped at its throat and with luck beyond belief, managed to leave it unable to sing. Even still, it took all our trained teamwork to defeat it."

Bowing his head with eyes closed, the scout gave closure to his grim tale. "My friend and his companion didn't make it."

They moved along in silence for several seconds before Darnon spoke. "I'm sorry for your loss. Now, you must make haste and find the healing cleric near the center of the column."

"I'm sorry for the delay, sir. I need just a moment more of your time. I've more to tell you," the scout said, now obviously in a great deal of pain.

Darnon signaled for the pace to slow even further. He would have called for a halt, but it was vital the group attain a more defensible position as quickly as possible. They were still vulnerable, moving through the narrow valley of the stream.

When the scout finally spoke, he rushed to finish while his strength lasted. "I started tending my dog's wounds and then my own. As I finished, I began to see faint signs that I swear weren't there before the fight. That is when I realized something critical—the nollax was using magic to mask the trail. The magic shield must have faded with the nollax's death."

The scout paused again, his breathing ragged and his face pale. Pattie was concerned for him and moved to his side. She gently took hold of his arm. Following Pattie's lead, Brandon did the same on the other side. Their aid was not refused; it seemed to boost the scout's constitution.

"I followed the trail. Even this had been repaired using magic, but we're trained to look through such measures. The trail led me to within sight of the ambush. I reached that point as the last of the battle played out." The scout turned to Pattie, and as their eyes locked, she knew her magic use was no longer a secret.

With his tale finally told, the scout collapsed into unconsciousness as Brandon and Pattie struggled to hold him upright. They moved the injured scout off to the side of the trail and the column moved past them and waited for the healing cleric. The scout's faithful companion sat beside the trio, poised to protect if required. The healing cleric soon made the young man whole again. Once healed, the scout made it clear that his dog should receive healing as well. Even though he was exhausted from the battle, and his energy had been depleted during the healing process, the scout insisted on departing immediately to find the other scouts.

As the scout prepared to leave, Darnon appeared, back-tracking through the column. "I've a message for you and your brethren. I'd like for you to break yet another tradition, and have two Reenones from Whilanar travel with you. They're trained to detect magic use and are best equipped to handle the nollax. I don't need an answer now, but I'd appreciate word soon." With a nod, the scout disappeared into the forest undergrowth, the dog close by his side.

The rest of the day passed without incident. Steve and Varis slept until the army was ready to move out the following morning. Both were groggy but seemed none the worse for what they had been through. Steve went to inquire about Gloria, even though she had made no effort to see about him or the others. She had taken to staying as far away from the friends as the protective guards assigned by Darnon would allow. Steve didn't think it possible, but her cold-shoulder treatment of them was worse than ever. He didn't even try to explain there was nothing he could have done to help her.

Pattie remained isolated as much as possible. The look of relief on the faces of the two pallitors when anguish and pain should have register disturbed her almost as much as the action she was forced to take. Immediately follow her use of magic to take the life of the pallitor she had vowed to never use magic again, but even then she knew she was lying to herself. The good she could do through healing was too great of a lure for her to ignore. All of this coupled with her feeling about Steve she thought long since buried had her emotions too raw to tolerate the company of others for long.

Darnon ordered Kail to keep his company of protectors in the presence of the Summoned Ones at all times. Kail had every intention of fulfilling that order, but thinking back all those years ago to the first time combat had forced him to kill, a memory that he would never forget, he felt a tremendous amount of sympathy for the plight of the woman he had sworn to protect. So, he had made the decision to allow Pattie to move ahead of the group far enough to be by herself, but close enough to be reached quickly should another attack occur.

Pattie walked forward mechanically. Her physical actions occurred involuntarily as she fought through the emotions that dominated her thoughts. She had moved far enough ahead of her friends and protectors that she wouldn't be disturbed by them. She trailed the supply cart far enough that the teamsters didn't intrude on her privacy either. Time passed for her in this way until a commotion ahead drew her from her walking trance.

Pattie looked up and saw the teamster who was assigned to the supply wagon shouting at a horse that was stubbornly refusing to take another step. The man's tirade quickly escalated till he grabbed a fallen branch and began striking the unwilling draft horse on its rear flank. Without thinking, Pattie raced across the distance that separated them, her only intent to stop the assault.

Pattie reached the man just as he pulled his hand back for yet another blow. With the force of her running momentum and the aggressiveness with which she grabbed his wrist, she almost caused the two of them to tumble to the ground. However, the man was able to right himself and, with a violent tug, he wrenched his arm free of her grasp.

With the branch now above his head, the teamster was just about to redirect his wrath towards his new aggravation. At the last moment before he brought the blow down on Pattie, he happened to look into her eyes. He saw a wild-eyed woman, her face twisted in rage.

The man turned white and immediately dropped his makeshift switch. He was one of the teamsters who had crossed the stream just when the fight broke out with the nollax and pallitor. He had witnessed the entire exchange, including what Pattie had done to the pallitor.

The teamster stood motionless. After a moment, he hung his head and said softly, "Forgive me, Summoned One."

Pattie ignored the man, focusing all her attention on the horse. She did not hesitate moving around to its front right foot and leaned her shoulder into the large draft mare. Her father had taught her the technique. She wasn't capable of offering much support to such a large animal, but the contact helped to reassure the creature that it would not fall. With the mare comforted by the contact, she responded easily to Pattie when she lifted her hoof for inspection.

The reason the horse had stopped was immediately evident. The mare's frog was swollen to nearly twice its original size. The reason for the swelling was clear. A thorn protruded from the center of the inflamed mass. The embarrassed teamster looked on, amazed that Pattie was able to go directly to the source of the issue, unaware of her extensive equine background.

Pattie needed no prompting for her next course of action. Quickly, she yanked the thorn free. In the past, she would have extracted the pus and packed the wound with a poultice, but instead, almost as naturally as using the methods she had been taught by her father, she began to sing softly, drawing the magic required for healing. The superstitious man charged with the care of the horse slowly backed away from the woman and her song. He had always considered magic an abomination.

Pattie made quick work of the healing that was becoming easier for her. As she finished the last verse, making the final seal of the wound, Kail and Brandon raced on to the scene.

Kail could see all along that Pattie was not in danger, but having her race away from him so quickly made him rethink his decision to allow her space to think. This was a decision he rectified as they got under way again. But this time, the space wasn't necessary. Pattie had finally come to terms with her use of magic. The look on the pallitor's face would stay with her for the rest of her life, but she knew she must continue to use this newly acquired gift.

Varis sensed that Pattie needed time to deal with the consequences of her actions, so he had kept his distance from the group of friends all day. As they made camp that evening, he finally approached to speak with Pattie. He was silent at first, and began helping her gather evergreen boughs for bedding. After a few minutes, he spoke.

"I won't try to tell you I know what you are going through, or even that it will get better soon. After all these years, and as young as I was, I remember like it was yesterday. The look of horror on the face of the man who attacked my mother just before he died is etched in my mind forever."

Pattie listened quietly and completed arranging her bedding for the night. She sat down, and Varis moved over to sit beside her.

"Magic is part of you, and you can't escape it. What I've been trying to convey to you is that the effective use of magic demands mental discipline. Deployed in its raw form, guided only by the fight-or-flight instinct, it can be devastating, not only to those it is used against, but also to the wielder of the power."

Pattie interrupted before the old man could continue. "Let me tell you my thoughts. I've been trying all day to come to grips with what I've done. I see now that if I'd been thinking clearly, I had several options. I could have knocked the men down with water or, like you did on the platform, erected a shield with wind."

Pattie gathered her thoughts, for she had anguished over the decision she was about to share with Varis.

"Watching Brandon train over the years, I've realized that the mental aspect of the discipline is more important than the physical. His training gives him the mental discipline under stress to make the correct choice from any number of alternatives available to him. I need the same ability with magic. Only then can I hope to better control the outcome."

Varis looked into her eyes, then slowly broke into a grin. He put his arm round her shoulders and squeezed briefly, planting a light kiss on her forehead. "Well then." He labored to his feet. "We're both too tired to start tonight. Seek me out first thing in the morning before we break camp. We can get started then."

Pattie awoke early the next morning. Frost was still on the ground, and dawn had pushed back the darkness just enough that she could pick her way through the camp. She found Varis waiting for her, ready and as eager as she was to get started.

Varis laid out his training plans for his young apprentice. He intended for Pattie to progress quickly through the variations and nuances of the songs of each discipline. But, more importantly, he had mental exercises in store that had been developed to focus one's thoughts. The concept involved concentrating deeply on a subject, all the while being aware of and interacting with her environment.

Varis began to work with Pattie on specific songs, letting her use magic in a controlled manner. They did their hands-on training in the early morning and after the marching halted at the end of the day. During each day's march, he had Pattie do mental exercises. On the first day he instructed her to build a wall block by block, giving her the dimensions of the building by the number of blocks, both wide and long. Pattie had to think through mortaring and setting each block. Varis had her stop every 30 mental blocks and walk around the structure, inspecting the results. He also encouraged her to interact with others while she continued her mental exercises.

Unbeknownst to Varis and his new student, another individual in their midst was also keenly interested in their sessions. Gloria had used the attack at the stream as an excuse to completely separate herself from the group. In truth, she was now completely uninterested in the others or their welfare and began making her nightly camps out of sight of her "friends." The real reason for this separation (other than her contempt for the others) was that it allowed her to spy more easily on Pattie's training sessions. Gloria could hear most of Varis' instructions, but couldn't benefit from the mental exercises. Varis typically didn't give those to Pattie until they were on the trail.

Gloria found that she could match or, in her opinion, best most of Pattie's performances of the various songs. Gloria had the added luxury of being able to practice a particular song at her isolated evening campsite without Varis restraining her. The times that Varis had to restrain Pattie, he did not do so to limit her potential. He did so to teach her control and how to focus, a lesson she took to uncommonly well, unlike a former student of his who remained always on his mind.

Varis had found himself reluctant at first to instruct Pattie after his experience with this particular student. On the other hand, he couldn't bear thinking of a talent like Pattie's wasted with years of pointless, mind-numbing exercises that every one of the sects would have imposed on her. These times called for bold measures if the wrong Varis felt he had played a part in would ever be righted. And now, he couldn't be more pleased with the character and discipline of his new pupil.

While Pattie's days were filled with morning and evening lessons, as well as ever more difficult mental exercises, Brandon and Kail were inundated with soldiers who wanted training. After the attack at the stream, the reputations of Kail, Brandon, and Steve as valiant fighters who had defeated multiple pallitors spread through the camp. Twice the number of soldiers showed up at their first morning training session after the battle. After this session, Darnon had instructed the three to split the class into two groups and hold two shorter sessions instead to prevent so many of his men being occupied at the same time. He was secretly pleased, however, with the increased participation and the affect the brawny Summoned One was having on Kail, who could be quite a pain-in-the-behind to Darnon when he chose.

The next several days passed without incident. The Vylacraen scouts began reporting in more often. They also allowed the two Reenones from Whilanar to accompany them as they scouted. The Reenones didn't return to the camp with the reporting scout, though, preferring to remain constantly in the field. The evening of the eighth day, while Pattie was forming a shield of air during a training session, she spooked a bird from its roost in a bush. It flew out of the bush and headlong into the trunk of a tree. Pattie rushed over and picked up the tiny, frightened creature. It was still breathing, but laboring to do so.

Varis approached and looked over her shoulder. "Go ahead and see what you can do to help. Judging from the progress you've made this last week, I think you're more than ready. I warn you, though, its injuries are extensive."

Pattie hated to see any living thing suffer and didn't hesitate. Cradling the bird in her hands, she started her song. She wasn't familiar with the anatomy of birds, but right away the song gave her vision, and she could see that the bird's lungs were filling with blood. She was quickly able to isolate the tears in the vessels that allowed the blood to flow into the lungs. Not only did Pattie repair them, she forced the blood out of the lungs and back into the vessels before she made the repairs. She was pleased when the bird's breathing began to improve dramatically.

Pattie didn't release the bird immediately. She used her magical vision to probe for any other damage. She found various injuries ranging from minor bruising to broken bone and cartilage damage. She wove the song of the four disciplines for each one in turn and repaired the damage down to the cellular level. When her probing moved to the bird's head, Pattie was shocked to discover that she could understand the bird, though she was receiving sketchy impressions at best. She couldn't read each thought, but she could gauge its overall feeling of terror. Pattie was still inspecting the bird's head when she felt Varis put his hand on her shoulder.

"You and the bird have had enough. You know healing takes energy from both you and the patient. You can push your patient too far if the injuries are too great. The bird needs rest, and I believe you do as well."

Pattie was a little tired, and the bird she held was now fast asleep, its breathing steady.

"You're right." She gently placed the bird in a wicker food basket for protection and bid the cleric good night. She fell into her bedding exhausted and was asleep before her head hit the ground. The next morning when Varis woke her, the bird was chirping loudly in its basket. Pattie raised the lid, let it go, and watched in wonder as the bird flew swiftly away from them as if it had never been injured. Pattie smiled up at Varis, who nodded approvingly at his young protégé.

CHAPTER 11

REBELS SHOWN

The tenth day after the battle at the stream, a scout uncharacteristically came rushing into the midst of the column as they were marching. Seeking out his commander, he stumbled to a halt in front of Darnon.

"Commander," he gasped as he saluted. "We're in a trap, there's a sizable force in front of us. They're well dug in. We would have never seen them without the Reenones."

Darnon interrupted the scout's frantic report as he came to a stop and signaled the column to a halt. "Can we get around them?"

"No, not without a four-day march away from the mountains, deeper into enemy territory, and that's not the worst of it, sir. There's an army half your size behind you. They're primarily foot soldiers, with less than ten mounts used primarily by the scouts. On your command, these scouts could be eliminated. This rear force is maybe two hours behind, and advances at a pace to match yours."

Darnon quickly assessed his options. He knew that, even if he could rush the entrenched forces and hope for victory, the rear forces would have them in a vise before they could break through. He settled on his only viable option.

"About 30 minutes behind us, we came through a glen that ended in a narrow pass. If we set an ambush there, could your scouts ensure that the enemy wouldn't become aware of our plans?"

A confident "Yes, sir!" was the scout's reply.

"We could use as many of the enemy's horses as you can capture from their scouts. Also, I'll need as much information about the entrenched forces as you can gather," Darnon ordered and began using hand signals to gather his officers.

Not waiting to be dismissed, the scout faded quickly back into the surrounding forest. Darnon wasted no time in getting the column turned around and headed back the way they had just come. His plan was simple: he would use a small portion of his army to bottle up the enemy at the narrow pass on his side of the glen. He would separate his remaining forces and, using his superior numbers, hit his foe in the open glen, striking them on both flanks simultaneously.

En route, his mind racing through various scenarios, Darnon refined his plan slightly. Upon arriving back at the glen, he placed his best archers in the treeline where the trail from the glen entered the pass. The horses he had planned early on in their march for the scouts to use had not been needed for some time. The Vylacraen scouts preferred the horses not accompany them in the field, viewing them as a disruption. Darnon would therefore be able to commit all the mounts to battle. He would divide up the 20 among the two flanking units. He hoped that his flanking army would force the enemy within range of the waiting bowmen.

Darnon ordered Kail and ten handpicked soldiers to form an elite reserve to be used in case of a pallitor attack. He was taken aback when he saw Brandon moving among their ranks and made his way over to the Summoned One to dissuade him from joining this potentially ill-fated group. He countered Brandon's protests briefly but soon realized that the young man could not be dissuaded. Darnon reluctantly consented and moved on to direct his men. He ordered the Reenones evenly dispersed throughout his forces. He knew that for the trail to have been hidden from the scouts, nollax had to be in the area. Finally, he ordered the carts hidden well off the road, in a separate location along the trail leading to the pass. Two soldiers would be all he could spare to guard each cart. The

Summoned Ones (minus Brandon) and Varis would remain hidden with one of the carts.

Darnon's army settled into their positions, hiding well within the trees and waiting for their prey to enter the trap. After an interminable hour, Darnon saw two scouts appear out of thin air, leading a total of five horses. He quickly ordered the five mounts to be added to the ten already on his side of the glen, and was heartened to hear that five horses were already being delivered to the forces on the other side. "They secured all ten. Amazing," thought Darnon. The scouts informed their commander that the enemy was only ten minutes from the glen before they slipped effortlessly back out of sight.

As the scouts had faithfully reported, the enemy appeared within minutes. When they approached the pass, Darnon's group delayed their assault, allowing many to enter unmolested. By so doing, several of the enemy were soon bunched up outside the entrance to the narrow pass. Darnon gave the signal, and his men sprung their trap. The hidden archers made quick work of the closest enemy soldiers. Soldiers on horseback next entered the scene, striking sweeping blows then rapidly retreating. In the midst of this chaos, the disoriented enemy was set upon from both sides of the glen by Darnon's flanking forces.

In short order, Darnon realized the battle was progressing far better than he had hoped. From the corner of his eye, he saw a scout and his dog racing across the glen at full speed. Because the scout had abandoned any attempt at stealth, Darnon knew the message he carried was an urgent one. He began running toward the scout to make up the ground between them. The scout began shouting across the distance, trying to make himself heard through the melee.

"The entrenched forces have moved on this position! They're only five minutes away, sir!" The scout, upon delivering this grim news, turned before reaching Darnon and sprinted away with his dog toward the shelter of the trees.

Darnon halted and muttered an oath under his breath. He knew what he must do. Without hesitating, he called for the reserve forces, including Kail and his handpicked cadre. The commander was upset with himself for leaving the Summoned Ones on the other side of the narrow pass leading into the glen with so few guards to protect them. No pallitors were present here near the rear troops, and the two nollax that had presented themselves early had been dispatched quickly by the Reenones.

Kail and his men soon reported in, panting and covered in grime. Darnon quickly covered the scout's report and his concern for the Summoned Ones, then ordered Kail and his group to lead a charge into the heart of the remaining enemy. Darnon would follow immediately thereafter, leading the small reserve force.

Kail ordered his small force into a box formation. He and Brandon took up positions at the front. They drove straight for the narrow pass, leaving a path of death and destruction in their wake. Darnon didn't wait for the void created by Kail and his men to fill in before he followed, striking at the stunned foe with his massive sword. He began shouting to his men, "To me, to the pass," all the while swinging his two-handed sword through the enemy's ranks, yet somehow keeping pace with Kail's team.

The seasoned soldiers, hearing the cry of their beloved commander, rallied and forced themselves toward the sound of his voice. Within seconds, the enemy was broken, running in the only direction available to them, toward the archers in the woods. The Reenones that accompanied the archers quickly erected magical barriers only two feet high. Unseen by the retreating enemy who were hell-bent on overwhelming the archers, the barriers stopped the foes short as they slammed into and toppled over the short wall of wind. The effect gave the archers the time they needed to find their targets and the time Darnon's pursuing soldiers needed to reach the battle.

The commander breathed an oath of relief when he reached the pass and saw a welcome sight. The carts and the Summoned Ones were racing back down the trail towards him. The scouts must have understood the danger and sent them back to the safety of the army. Darnon knew he still had only moments to clean up the battle behind him and prepare for a new force, the full strength of which was maddeningly unknown to him.

As if reading his mind, a scout suddenly emerged from the woods onto the trail, racing full-tilt towards Darnon.

The scout gasped with his hands on his knees, "Sir, the initial force numbers a little over 200. The first to reach you will be 20 pallitors, led by two nollax. The others are strung out somewhat, but they won't be long. We've caught glimpses of a reserve force, roughly half the size of this one, only 10 to 15 minutes behind." The exhausted man fell to his knees on the side of the trail, trying to catch his breath.

Upon hearing this news, Darnon's heart sank. They hadn't even finished this fight and now to encounter a force of that size, with no time to rest and regroup. He suddenly understood how unlikely it was that any of them would survive. Then, determined to prevail, he decided to abandon his dark thoughts. Undaunted, Darnon began ordering his soldiers into position to meet this new threat.

He had all the archers reposition themselves along the trail leading to the pass. He planned to use Kail and his team as bait for the pallitors. The archers would cut down as many as they could before the enemy reached Kail's elite team. The two Whilanar Reenones who were not in the field with the scouts prepared to deal with the nollax. The other Reenones, including Varis, moved among the troops, healing as many minor injuries as they could that would disable soldiers from fighting. The healers merely stabilized the more severely wounded, preserving their energy for the fight ahead.

With the glen now taken, his army was in a very defensible position, but Darnon knew the coming battle against 300 plus troops would take its toll. As the scout had foretold, the smaller enemy force of nollax and pallitors soon appeared. Fortunately for Darnon and his men, the trap they had set for the creatures worked perfectly. The Whilanar Reenones engaged the nollax in magical combat. Once the nollax were distracted in battle, their immediate control over the pallitors disappeared. Apparently, their last direct order had been to attack Kail's forces in the middle of the path. They methodically marched toward the small group, never changing their pace. The hidden archers attacked the moment the enemy came within range. Each archer aimed at an individual pallitor. To the defenders' amazement, the pallitors continued their same measured march, even after several of their number were struck down with multiple arrows. Kail had his men back up slowly, giving the archers time to continue their deadly barrage. As the remaining pallitors moved steadily beyond the range of their arrows, the archers left cover and continued sending volley after volley. The pallitors did not turn on them, nor did they change pace. On they marched, even as the deadly shafts thinned their ranks. Rather than risk injury to his men, Kail ordered a retreat that matched the pace of the pallitors as they advanced. Kail's men continued their retreat into the glade until the last creature fell.

With the pallitors and nollax destroyed, Darnon rallied his troops and prepared for the next phase of the attack. The archers quickly retrieved a new supply of arrows from the supply wagons and readied themselves, trying to ignore their quivering forearms and aching muscles. Once again they would play a key role in Darnon's plans. Each man knew this battle would be a grind. Hold the pass and wear them down. Darnon anticipated it would be a bloody affair on both sides, but he also knew it was the best plan left to him if he hoped to save the Summoned Ones.

The next wave hit them just as their preparations were getting under way. This wave was led by two more nollax. The clerics from Whilanar, exhausted from their one-on-one fight against the first nollax, were in no shape to help win this battle. Darnon could only hope the other Reenones together could limit the damage. The nollax approached almost within range to begin their magic, each great beast standing over nine feet tall, one with the head of a ram, the other a reptile. The twisted blend of human and animal facial features only enhanced their hideous appearance.

Each nollax in turn laid back its head and let out a roar, then started singing in a beautiful voice. Their songs were cut short before the magic manifested. They became frozen, standing like statues in the middle of the trail. Two Vylacraen scouts burst from the forest, knives raised. The two scouts and their dogs made quick work of the nollax. The two Whilanar clerics embedded with the scouts emerged from the forest, running all-out toward the safety of the army. The scouts and their faithful companions were close on their heels.

The enemy troops, stunned at first, sprinted after them, enraged by what they had seen. Kail, Brandon, and the hand-selected soldiers waited patiently in the opening of the narrow pass. Kail knew the others still needed time to prepare their defense of the pass. Not awaiting orders from Darnon, he had stepped forward to ensure the others received the time they needed.

The clerics and scouts passed through the waiting formation of soldiers, with Kail and Brandon standing side by side in the lead positions. Just a few seconds later, the advance elements of the charging enemy slammed into the same formation. However, the results were quite different, as the enemy did not pass through unhindered as the allies had. Instead, they ran into the equivalent of a buzz saw. Kail and Brandon took down the first four soldiers before they realized the gravity of their tactical error. Brandon then leaped into the air and landed with both feet square on the chest of the next attacker. The stunned assailant flew back into the ranks of his charging comrades, knocking several of them down as well. The enemy troops surging from behind quickly fell over the men on the ground, creating a domino effect. Kail, Brandon, and the others wasted no time wading into the pile of thrashing men. Here was the barrier they needed to keep the advancing enemy at bay, a barrier of fallen, twisted bodies.

Over the clash of battle, the elite troops suddenly heard Darnon bellow "All is ready!"

As they had practiced several times in their morning training sessions, the team began an organized retreat. They began to peel off in pairs, only to be replaced by the pair behind, allowing fresh troops to engage the adversaries, yet all the while slowly giving ground. They even took advantage of the transitions to strike effective blows. The technique was Kail's contribution to the training. He was far more experienced in group-on-group fighting than Brandon.

The technique was quite effective, and the team "escaped" into the waiting trap set by Darnon. They were the bait used to lure the enemy deep within the gauntlet of bowmen positioned in and among the trees, and foot soldiers wielding long, spear-tipped pikes. With devastating impact, the trap closed shut, causing the enemy to falter and retreat back down the trail.

One of the Vylacraen scouts who had dealt with the nollax stepped forward to speak with Darnon. "We were wrong about the larger enemy force held in reserve. This force has begun attacking the rear contingency of the enemy you now fight. It's only a matter of time before this group gets word of the attack!"

Darnon never dreamed it possible they would find an ally here, deep in enemy territory. His joy was short lived, however, when it dawned on him just who this ally must be. The only logical explanation had to be Carsanicean rebels. He had encountered these rebels before. He admired their bravery, but in all truth they were an undisciplined rabble. They seemed to have a knack for dealing the enemy a devastating blow before escaping relatively unharmed, though Darnon surmised this was due more to good fortune than skill.

The battle-weary commander turned to watch the fighting, just in time to see Brandon struck down. Darnon cursed himself for letting the Summoned One persuade him to join Kail. Together, the two men presented a dominant force. Their prowess had lulled Darnon into a false sense of security. Watching the two in practice sessions had made him believe that if they fought together, nothing could touch them. Brandon had moved to step over a seemingly fallen soldier, but his adversary was merely lying in wait. He struck savagely at Brandon's exposed left leg with a blade, bringing the big man down.

Darnon quickly signaled for reinforcements, hoping his men could reach the two before both were lost. He watched intently, praying that the Summoned One would be spared. To the commander's relief, Kail quickly had Brandon back on his feet, all the while fending off opponents after swiftly dispatching Brandon's assailant. The two fighters were now standing back to back, Brandon still fighting mightily though he could place weight on only one leg, blood soaking his clothing from the injured thigh down. Slowly but steadily, the two backed toward the safety of the approaching reserves. Even with Brandon dragging his left leg, opponents continued to fall dead around him. To Darnon's amazement, with Kail protecting the left side that Brandon could not effectively defend, the two made it to the safety of the reserve force without further injury.

Once out of harm's way, Kail slipped Bandon's arm over his tall frame and together they made their way into the glen. Pattie was helping triage the wounded from the first battle when she saw the two men moving slowly towards her. She signaled for a soldier with a minor injury to hold pressure on his friend's wound and ran to Brandon's side. Steve followed quickly. He had been helping where he could, but primarily he had been sticking close to Pattie to offer his protection.

Kail helped Brandon down into the tall grass of the glen. Pattie reached the pair just as a healing cleric arrived. Without a word, Pattie sank to the ground beside her friend. She gently shoved Brandon back into the grass and over onto his belly. Brandon's cut was deep, running diagonally from the left inner thigh, across the back of the knee, and down into the calf. Pattie soon ascertained that his injury was not life-threatening, but the damage to the function of the knee was extensive.

The cleric knelt next to Brandon's injured leg and wasted no time starting a healing song. Pattie began to hum under her breath as she gently held her friend's thigh. She concentrated inward, using her magic to probe the injury. The tendon that attached the hamstring to the back of the knee was completely severed; the muscle pulled way back into the thigh, forming a knot near his buttocks.

Pattie's mental exploration was suddenly interrupted as the cleric began to close Brandon's wound, oblivious to the injuries the muscle and tendon had sustained.

"Stop! You can't close the wound until his knee is healed."

The startled cleric sat back and watched as Pattie began singing aloud her healing song. Her tempo, pitch, and rhythm was considerably better than her counterpart's right from the beginning. Her first act was to locate the severed end of the hamstring. Using primarily wind spells, she pulled the detached end back into place. Then, using fire, earth, and water, she stitched the severed tendon back together at the molecular level.

Pattie and the cleric had now exchanged roles. He was humming, all the while probing to see what this unschooled Summoned One was doing. He was amazed by her performance as he watched her pull pieces of the anatomy together that he didn't understand, but once completed, he knew it was correct. The girl worked at such a detailed level, not content to simply line the two layers of flesh together so the healed area didn't scar. She used the same precision with every weave. She knitted together the smallest blood vessels and, using wind and water, forced the blood out of the muscles and back into the vessels before she sealed them.

The knee finished, the cleric watched her move on to heal the remaining minor wounds of the warrior Summoned One. She finished by curing a small blister on the young man's big toe before she finally stopped singing. As her beautiful melody faded into the air, the abashed cleric tried to regain control of the situation.

"Who taught you the healing song? You can't use magic without declaring allegiance to a denomination."

Pattie glanced up at the cleric with a bemused expression. She wasn't sure how to respond. It was obvious he was agitated and demanding a response, but she was apprehensive about revealing the identity of her tutor. As she hesitated, Varis, who had witnessed most of Brandon's healing, stepped forward.

"She is a follower of the Monastery of Hinloose."

The cleric was taken aback by the odd man's comment. It was one thing to tolerate this rogue cleric on account of his knowledge, but a mere student? He was certain his order's leaders would object to this. Hinloose was no true denomination; it had died out over 100 years ago, and had been considered a fringe order even at its inception. There was nothing he could do now, but as soon as he could make his way back to the order, he would inform the leaders of this aberration. Also, despite her impertinence, he was certain they would want to recruit such an unmistakable talent for themselves.

Meanwhile, Brandon had bounded to his feet. He felt better than he had in days. Even his soreness and muscle fatigue were nearly gone, as Pattie had identified and fixed the many microscopic muscle tears caused by overexertion. He caught Pattie's eye and nodded his thanks, then clasped Kail by the shoulder. Without a word, the two men turned as one and headed back to the pass. Pattie smiled and shook her head slightly before returning her attention to Varis and the disgruntled cleric.

The battle for the pass raged on for several minutes, with Darnon's troops never giving nor taking ground. Finally, their enemy became desperate at the stalemate and began throwing themselves at the entrenched lines of soldiers. The faint sound of another conflict could now be heard. Their adversaries became more frantic and began to ignore the cries of their leaders. Small pockets at first, then all the remaining troops turned on their superiors. After dispatching them, they laid down their weapons, knelt on the ground, and placed their hands behind their heads in surrender.

Just like that, the battle was over. Cheering rose among Darnon's troops, and shouts of triumph could also be heard not too far down the trail. A minute later, a flamboyantly dressed young man strolled into view, making his way through the kneeling enemy. He wore a bright-red, fur-lined cape that nearly touched the ground. By his side was a stunningly beautiful young woman, dressed nearly as ostentatiously. Both were armed to the teeth and moved with a cat-like stealthiness. The rabble that followed close behind them was a ragtag group, dressed in everything from near-rags to well-kept armor nearly as polished as Darnon's. They were securing weapons and gathering prisoners as they proceeded.

Darnon stepped forward to greet the pair. "Rayde and Jasheal, it's been a long time. How's your father?"

"He is well, I suppose. What are you doing so far from home, Darnon? I'd have thought someone of your advancing years would have retired by now," the young man Rayde replied with a mischievous grin.

Jasheal eyed Brandon appreciatively, as if she were choosing a prime cut of meat. Rayde smiled at her impishly and continued. "If you've no objections, we'll take care of the prisoners and their weapons. We've found that, once back in Carsanic, with minimal persuasion, these poor blokes see the errors of their ways and fight for the cause of freedom." He waved his hand as if to put an end to their exchange.

"Enough talk for now, let's clean up this mess. Then we can make camp together, your men can rest, and we'll have a drink or two while we talk of old times."

The commander knew better than to argue with this unruly lot. Besides, the young rebel was right about one thing—Darnon's beleaguered army needed a rest. He ordered the wounded tended, weapons and arrows gathered, the dead buried, and camp made in the glen.

Meanwhile, the audacious Rayde turned his attention to a young woman he had just glimpsed across the way. He stared openly and admiringly at the caregiver as she moved among the wounded, stopping to attend the most severely injured.

Following the rogue's eye, Steve realized he didn't care one bit for the way this man was looking at Pattie.

CHAPTER 12

MIKE'S ESCAPE

Captain Millaro pushed the group rapidly along a hard due north route. Mike could see the swift pace taking its toll on the soldiers around him, but no one complained. The men were obviously in excellent physical condition, but they bore the additional burden of leather armor, weapons, and heavy packs. Mike had been a cross-country runner in high school. To stay in shape, he still ran daily on various jogging paths around the Ohio State campus. Because of his workouts and the light weight of the caving pack he still carried, the pace set by the captain was not difficult for him.

The cleric Balose seemed to struggle the most. His protector, the tall woman warrior they called Elisibrin, seemed completely unaffected by the fast tempo, but the cleric was beginning to falter and fall behind. At several points, Elisibrin caught his arm to keep him from tumbling to the ground.

Mike was about to mention the cleric's condition to Millaro when a change in the terrain slowed the group's progress. As the small band approached a ridge top, the forest opened on to a wide grassy valley with sparse small trees and shrub. The captain called a halt just inside the forest line, sending his scout ahead. Mike stepped forward to have a look from the shelter of the trees. Behind him, he could hear the winded cleric panting as he finally caught up with the others.

Mike knew from his paintball days that if you moved slowly and then stood still, it was difficult to be spotted from any distance. He also knew that the boughs of the large trees behind him and the low hanging limbs in front would further obscure his silhouette. He scanned the valley, standing only 30 feet from the scout who was doing the same, and found no sign of the enemy.

The river would cross the group's path, just as the scout had foreseen. About 400 yards away across the open grass and down a gradual slope, the river was slow-moving and over 100 feet across. Mike knew that slow-moving water meant deep water. The forest picked back up again on the far bank after 200 or 300 yards of similar grassy slope.

The scout returned and reported to his captain what he had seen, and Mike nodded his agreement. Millaro quickly made up his mind.

"We can't afford to be caught in the open and we can't cross here. We'll stick to the trees and parallel the river heading upstream."

The captain added to his men, "I think this might be the river we crossed yesterday morning. If so, we might be lucky enough to find some rear guard members that Commander Namir left behind to aid us." To himself, Millaro thought, "I only hope we find them before the enemy finds us."

The news that help might soon be at hand had the intended effect, as the tired men's spirits rose instantly. They pushed onward, pursuing a northwest path along the river. Their progress was slow, as they often encountered steep valleys carved into the landscape by tributaries seeking the larger river, cutting across their path. The group covered only five more miles before night fell and Captain Millaro called an end to the day's trek.

The group made a cold camp in a shallow basin, making use of the topography that sheltered them from the chill night breeze. The temperature had dropped sharply since sundown. The members shared a cold meal of dried meat, cheese, and hard tack they'd retrieved from their packs. Once again, Balose and Elisibrin stayed apart from Mike and the soldiers, choosing to share their rations with one another.

Mike watched the odd pair as he ate, idly wondering why they continued to distance themselves from the group. He shivered involuntarily. He would get very little rest tonight if it got much colder. The caving coverall he still wore had offered ample warmth when he was up and moving, but since they had stopped for the night, Mike had grown steadily colder. One of Millaro's men noticed the young man's reaction to the night air and tossed him a blanket. Mike accepted the man's offering gratefully.

The captain ordered two guards to remain on watch throughout the night. The soldiers moved on to the other side of the camp to work out their guard rotation. Mike took advantage of the momentary quiet to continue his questions to Millaro.

"Captain, what's the deal with the cleric? He saved your life, yet either by his choosing or yours, he stays removed."

Captain Millaro considered the question a moment. When he answered, it seemed to Mike as if he were truly saddened by what he was about to relate.

"Well, it won't be easy for an outsider such as yourself to understand. Those who practice magic are not trusted in our culture, an attitude ingrained in most of our citizens. However, Balose is a person I've come to appreciate, even learned to trust. I don't hold as others to the old prejudices built up by years of misinformation. Sadly, though, I'm in the minority."

Mike merely nodded in response. Privately, he believed that Balose had revived the captain with some sort of powder or something similar to smelling salts, and that Millaro, ignorant of this fact, assumed it was magic. He knew from his studies that people of medieval times would often blame things they didn't understand on magic or the occult. He still couldn't reason away how the cleric stopped Millaro's bleeding so quickly, but he was sure a logical explanation would present itself in time.

The captain arranged his bedding and removed his weapons, placing them on the ground nearby, within arm's reach. He settled into the blankets still wearing his armor, finally relaxing despite his odd nocturnal attire. After a moment, Millaro continued.

"I think Balose removes himself more from habit than from any mistrust shown by me or my men. His protector is a bit intimidating though. I'm rather glad she stays away," he added with a wink.

Mike chuckled, but he wasn't entirely sure the captain was joking. Though tired from the excitement of the day, he was too full of unanswered questions not to push the captain further.

"Who is this enemy and why would they attack us without provocation?"

Captain Millaro was taken aback—how could a Summoned One not know of Zybaro?

Unable to conceal his surprise, he responded, "They're Zybaro's men."

"Zybaro?" Mike questioned, sounding out the strange name, unsure if he was pronouncing it properly.

"You know nothing of Zybaro?" the captain asked incredulously.

Mike only shook his head and shrugged.

The captain began explaining in earnest. "Zybaro took over Malabrim and has set his sights on Bericea. He took control using his guile and magic to either subjugate or enslave Malabrim's people. We are sure the same fate is in store for Bericea."

Mike, again testing the words, said, "Malabrim, Bericea, I'm not familiar with these places."

Captain Millaro stared at the young man in silence, his mouth slightly agape. Recovering somewhat, he went on, "Malabrim is the country we're currently in, it's sometimes referred to as the "Western Realm." Bericea is the country that we're trying to get you to. It's my home, the country you've been summoned to save. Where are you from that you don't know of Malabrim and Bericea?"

"I'm from a country called the United States of America, but I think I should also say I'm from the planet named Earth. I'm not even sure we're actually on Earth, because in all my studies, I've never heard of Malabrim or Bericea. Even the plants here are different from any I've seen. That tree there has leaves like an oak, but the smooth bark of a beech. That tree looks like a pine, but has a shag bark. I'm not sure how we got here, but Toto, we aren't in Kansas anymore," Mike ended with a rueful grin.

"Who is Toto? These names, America, Kansas, Earth...they mean nothing to me. You are indeed from a strange and different place."

Mike replied, as much to himself as to the captain, "You can say that again, you don't know the half of it."

In the silence that followed, both men pulled their blankets closer around their shoulders, contemplating what they had just learned.

Mike thought, "How in the world could our old Camp Wyanet gang possibly help these people?" He felt confident he wasn't experiencing a dream, but he wasn't sure what to believe. As he fell into an uneasy slumber, he wondered what had become of his friends.

The next morning, the group started their day in the cold camp with breakfast, which consisted of the same fare as supper the night before. After breaking camp, they began travelling in the same manner as yesterday. The soldiers spread out around Mike and Captain Millaro, separated by 15 or 20 feet. Balose and his protector trailed the others but remained within shouting distance.

The group continued to follow the river, staying just inside the shelter of the forest's edge. For most of the morning, the terrain remained the same. They crossed several more valleys cut by tributaries to the river. In some cases, the steeper valleys forced the group to backtrack upstream, away from the water at times, to find a place suitable for crossing. This made their progress slow; nevertheless, they advanced steadily.

By late morning, the terrain began changing and the group found themselves higher and higher above the river. At this point, the only access to the river was down a 20-foot cliff. Captain Millaro was certain now this was the river his army had crossed two days earlier. He recalled that their crossing had taken half a day, his army's progress slowed by a narrow bridge over a deep chasm and even narrower passes.

The group's steady progress finally ended when they came upon a large tributary with an impassable gorge leading to the river. They stopped to take stock of the situation. After some discussion between Mike and Millaro, and taking into account the information gained by advance scouting, the group began walking upstream. About a mile further and they would reach the point where the ground gradually sloped downward. Once they reached this juncture, they could ford the stream and begin their journey back toward the river.

It was nearly noon by the time they made the crossing. Once they reached the other side, Millaro called a halt to the morning's march. After a brief rest and a quick meal, the group refilled their canteens and resumed their journey.

The terrain didn't permit heading straight back to the river. The captain surveyed the landscape and chose a path at an angle that he thought would lead back to the water. An hour after their brief break, they came across a sizable trail that looked to be a trade road that once had been well-maintained, but recent neglect had allowed it to become overgrown.

"This is what I've been hoping to find. This is the road we took to the summoning chairs," the captain confided to Mike.

They began walking northeast on the trail that seemed bound to cross the river eventually. They were able to pick up their pace on the mostly cleared and straight abandoned road, even though they traveled with great caution. Each member remained ready to dash into the surrounding forest at a moment's notice should they spot anything or anyone on the trail.

"This road just three or four years ago was a major trading route between the Eastern and Western Realms. That was before Zybaro became strong enough to make raids this deep into our allies' territories," Captain Millaro reflected.

Mike noticed improvements on the well-packed dirt road, such as flagstone set in low, wet spots and retaining walls. He noted that although not a well-built Roman road, it would serve wagons well. Judging from the fading ruts, he thought it must have been a while since it had seen heavily laden wagons.

The trail began to climb as they made their way closer to the river. The deep forest began giving way to a rocky landscape of sparse trees and shrubs, and the path started to wind its way through larger boulders and rock outcroppings.

Suddenly, the lead soldier stopped and, using hand signals, indicated that they should stop. Mike noticed the signals used by the soldier were similar to the ones used in his own paintball games. As they came to a halt, the faint sounds of battle emerged from a distance. Several of the soldiers pulled bows from their backs and nocked arrows.

They proceeded cautiously, Captain Millaro fearing that the rear guard he had mentioned to his men earlier was now under attack. He knew if this rear guard fell, his group's one chance to traverse the river at this particular crossing would be gone.

As the small band traveled along the road, yet another steep hill appeared before them. Almost simultaneously, they heard the thundering of hooves. Five horsemen swiftly topped the rise. The soldiers with bows fired their readied arrows as everyone dove off the road—everyone, that is, except for the cleric's tall protector. Elisibrin gripped a large mace in her left hand and a smaller in her right. Four of the soldiers' arrows hit their mark; unfortunately, only two riders went down, one felled by two arrows and another struck in the neck. A third rider kept his mount despite a projectile sunk deep into his thigh.

The female warrior had a bit longer to prepare, being further back the road. With the grace of a dancer and the quickness of a cat, she threw the smaller mace, striking the lead rider square in the chest and sending him over the back of his horse.

She wielded the large mace with both hands and stood her ground as the next horse charged straight at her. In a graceful display of agility, at the last moment, Elisibrin leapt up and to one side, spinning as she went, bringing the mace around into the steel breastplate of the rider with a thunderous crash that left no doubt he would be dead before he hit the ground.

The remaining wounded rider road hard past the battling warrior, his only goal escape. Just as it looked as though he may escape with only the injury to his leg, an arrow, shot from maximum range for the cavalry short bow, found its mark, striking the rider in the shoulder. Miraculously, he was able to keep his seat and rode around a boulder and out of sight.

The warrior collected her throwing mace, and the cleric quickly checked each fallen enemy. Mike thought his intent might be to aid them, but the cleric shook his head slightly and moved away. Apparently, these men were either all dead or beyond his ability.

Captain Millaro quickly brought his group back in order, and they all started forward again as the sounds of battle continued. After a few moments, he nodded toward Mike and gestured that they should move ahead of the group. Mike and the captain crept forward to look over the rise in the road and found themselves spying down onto an open, bowl-shaped valley. The side of the valley was steep and tree-lined. The opposite side of the valley was defined by sheer cliffs, 30 to 40 feet high.

The road continued down the wooded slope and cut across the middle of the level, grassy valley floor. It continued all the way to the cliff side of the valley, where it turned sharply right and moved up a steep grade cut into the cliff itself. The grade ended 15 feet from the top of the cliff, where the road again turned sharply into a narrow pass and disappeared from sight.

The valley had obviously been used as a trading outpost, and from what Mike could surmise, also served as a place for the horses that pulled the cargo wagons to rest or even be replaced. On both sides of the road, the remnants of a split-rail fence were visible through the overgrowth. All that was left of the outpost's buildings were grown-over, burnt-out structures. The wooden roof of the main building had collapsed within its four stone walls. Several beams of the roof had also fallen down in the stone structure and were sticking out of the open top like straws in a drinking glass.

From the stone structure emanated the source of all the noise. A fierce battle raged as a superior force attempted to dislodge a group of soldiers from the stone walls of the former building. Mike could see from the leather clothing that the embattled defenders were cavalry of the same regiment as the captain beside him.

Defense of the structure seemed to be led by a mountain of a man wielding a long-handled battle hammer tipped with a wicked spike. The attackers were being kept at bay by the soldier and his enormous hammer. Mike saw several dead and wounded scattered around the burnt-out porch, a testament to failed attempts to dislodge the big man.

This main building must have had a porch that once stretched across its entire front. Now burnt away, it left an opening three feet in the air where the front door once stood. At least a portion of the floor remained in the structure, because the defender was standing just inside the doorway, and Mike could see archers at the windows flanking the doors.

There was another manned opening where a window had once been on the side exposed to the road from which they watched. Two snipers had climbed the fallen roof beams and were using their bows to great effect to keep the bulk of the enemy at bay.

The big man would attack any target that foolishly presented itself, then duck back under the cover of the doorway. The fighting was all but at a standstill now, as the larger force had pulled out of bow range and was conferring on the best approach for their next attack.

Mike pointed to a place to their right, across the road from the main structure. Through the trees, his keen eyes had spotted dozens of horses picketed where the wooded slope met the meadow.

With a tap on the shoulder, the captain motioned for Mike to follow him back to the group, now waiting expectantly for the two men to return with a report.

"What did you see?" the captain urged as they turned away from the ridge.

Mike didn't respond immediately, going over the scene in his mind. He gave the captain his assessment as they reached the others. "I saw three things. The pass that we need for our escape is unguarded, but several enemies are between us and that pass. The enemy has at least 40 horses picketed away from the battle and guarded by only a few men. Finally, I see a group of your men engaged in a desperate battle that they cannot hope to win."

Captain Millaro thought for a moment, then quickly conveyed his plan to the group. "We make our way through the wooded area to the picketed horses. Dispose of the guards. Take the horses we need, scatter the rest, and head for the unguarded pass. The Summoned One remains our first priority."

"You're just going to leave those men behind?" Mike asked, disturbed by the turn of events.

The captain answered abruptly—he was not used to being questioned, even by a Summoned One. "They've been ordered here for the very purpose of giving you enough time to escape. Sergeant Marlock knew what he was getting into when he volunteered for this assignment."

As usual, Mike kept his composure in the heat of the moment and answered in a measured tone, "Those enemy horsemen we encountered were racing away from the fight for a reason, and the only reason I can see would be to give warning to a larger force. The man that escaped was injured but kept his saddle, so we have to assume he'll reach his destination. That means we have only a short time to get ahead of them."

Mike continued, "If we leave this group behind, they can keep those soldiers bottled up with far fewer men than are down there and use the others to pursue us. In this enclosed valley, it won't take them long to gather the scattered horses. All they'll need to do is harass us just enough to slow us down until the larger force can catch up."

Gaining the captain's attention with his logic, Mike pressed his advantage. "I saw at least five men in that structure and I'd bet more are lurking unseen. We only number 11; additional numbers would be welcome if we had to fight. Those men attacking are disorganized, and I think leaderless thanks to the sergeant. I've seen your men fight and they're a far superior fighting force than that muddled bunch and, unless I'm mistaken, I've not seen the half of it once you're all on horseback."

Mike finished confidently, buoyed by the plan he had just developed while he was speaking, "I think we can take all the horses, rescue most, if not all, of the soldiers, and scatter the enemy."

Mike quickly laid out the details of his plan. After listening quietly, the captain reluctantly decided the young man's idea had merit. He agreed to try it only because the plan left Mike out of harm's way during the battle

Initiating Mike's plan, the group slipped over the edge of the valley and into the wooded strip to the right of the road. As they made their way into the wooded area, Mike saw that the enemy was just beginning their new attack on the structure. If Mike's luck held, they would be preoccupied long enough for his plan to take shape.

Captain Millaro ordered his four best archers forward, though he could not tell how many men would be guarding the picketed horses. As it turned out, there were only three guards, and they were foolishly watching the battle of their comrades. The archers dispatched the hapless guards quietly and efficiently.

Keeping to Mike's plan, the seasoned cavalrymen chose the best of the mounts for each person in the group, plus five extra animals, and tied the rest into three strings. In all, there were 43 war horses and eight pack animals. Mike calculated silently that with the three dead guards and the six bodies around the structure, that should leave 36 adversaries.

"Things will have to go very well for us," he thought grimly.

All was in order; four of the soldiers leading the five extra mounts proceeded into the trees back toward the road. The rest of the group mounted and Mike, Balose, and his protector each took the reins of the lead horse of their respective string of horses. The group then moved out at a light canter so as not to draw attention and started for the winding pass at the other side of the open field.

They were halfway to their goal when a shout rose up from the enemy attacking the structure. Well over half the enemy broke away from the attack and gave chase. A satisfied smile crossed Mike's face, and they quickened their pace to a light run.

"Wait just a bit longer," shouted the commander to his men over the pounding hooves.

"Now!"

Mike had read many stories about the Mongols' success with this very tactic, feigning retreat to draw out the enemy. However, Mike had to admit to himself that, in most of those cases, the Mongols were not outnumbered two to one.

His plan depended on two theories, each based on pure speculation:

(1) the enemy was leaderless, based on their disorganized attack on the structure, and, (2) Sergeant Marlock had more men than Mike could see. Mike was also counting on the fact that their enemies were cavalrymen like his new friends and would not be as experienced fighting from the ground.

At Millaro's command, he and the other three cavalrymen in the group turned and charged straight at the shocked and now strung-out enemy. The three soldiers flanking the leading captain were standing in their stirrups, short bows in hand. The front three enemy soldiers went down before Millaro even came near them.

Mike reached the winding road cut into the cliffside. From this vantage point, he could see that the four horsemen who made their way through the woods earlier were also starting their charge. To Mike's relief, they made it even closer to the structure than he had hoped for and quickly overwhelmed the few enemy soldiers who were nearby. Mike saw the big sergeant and his men rush from the structure to aid them. The extra mounts the four horsemen had brought were quickly put to use by the men that followed the sergeant from the burnt-out building.

Now the tide was turning just as Mike had anticipated: 13 mounted, experienced cavalrymen against 30 leaderless, horseless cavalrymen. Not the greatest odds, he thought, but much better than before. Suddenly, exceeding Mike's wildest hopes, six additional soldiers came running out of the building shell.

The hulking sergeant with his huge hammer was a frightening sight before, but on horseback standing in the stirrups with the massive weapon clutched in both hands, he inspired sheer terror. He artfully guided his steed with his knees and unleashed his weapon in long, sweeping arcs that no mortal could defend against. The sergeant and the captain fought like men possessed, carving deeply into the enemy as they worked their way toward each other.

Mike's original plan was to disrupt and frighten the enemy just long enough for the trapped men to escape. As he watched the battle unfold, it now seemed as if the enemy would be routed. Then, just as success seemed certain, Mike watched in horror as Captain Millaro went down.

The leader was knocked from his saddle by the arrow of an enemy archer who had kept his wits and took aim at what was obviously an important target.

The battle-hardened soldiers did not hesitate upon seeing their leader fall; they continued to execute the battle plan as he had ordered. A few brief moments after wounding the captain, the enemy broke and headed for the same road Mike's group had used earlier to enter the valley.

Mike had intended to leave the road open for the enemy to use in their escape, reasoning that there was no need to place his small group in any more jeopardy than absolutely necessary. He couldn't have guessed that only ten of the enemy would escape, nor that most of those would suffer serious injury during the brief but intense battle.

As soon as Balose saw the captain fall, he handed his stringer of horses to Mike and galloped as fast as his limited horsemanship would allow toward Millaro. Balose's protector Elisibrin did the same and chased after him, quickly pulling even with the inexperienced rider.

Their abrupt departure left Mike at the start of the ramp leading to the pass with three stings of horses numbering over 30 in all. Mike new his best bet was to keep them moving but, rather than continue up the ramp as planned, he turned and headed back toward the others.

As Mike approached, a few of the cavalrymen came over and relieved him of the strings of spare horses. He rode quickly to where Balose was working over Millaro. The captain was bleeding badly from two wounds. An arrow was protruding from his left shoulder and another had passed through his right side, just below the floating rib.

Balose was singing as he had when he tended the captain the day before. He had no bags of ointments or powders as Mike thought he would. Then, right before Mike's eyes, the wound in the captain's side knitted itself together. The cleric broke off the arrow in the captain's shoulder, causing him to shudder with pain. Suddenly, just like the wound in his side, the shoulder wound closed up.

"Well, old friend, I've lost count of all the times you've healed me over the years. This time, though, I can feel that my injuries are beyond even your talents," the captain said weakly. His face was deathly pale and blood trickled from the corner of his mouth.

"Old friend?" thought Mike. The cleric looked closer to 20, Mike's age, and the captain had to be well into his forties.

"You've been a pain in my backside since you were a raw recruit all those years ago," Balose replied gently. "But this time you are correct. If I had you back at the abbey, maybe the outcome would be different, but considering the trek that lies ahead..." Balose fell silent.

A moan came from a short distance away and Balose reluctantly stood to make his way toward another fallen cavalryman. The man appeared to have been pulled from his horse and was unconscious. His arm had a very severe break, judging from its abrupt angle. After the cleric's ministrations, in only a few minutes, the cavalryman was up and helping his fellow soldiers prepare to move out.

Sergeant Marlock approached and guided the cleric to the burnt-out structure. A few minutes later, Balose and the sergeant emerged, accompanied by four additional soldiers. Two more had to be helped from the building, but they were up and walking.

The captain was back on his feet but not looking much better. He called the big sergeant over, and they talked in hushed tones. When their conversation ended, Marlock ordered the group to mount and started for the cliffside shelf that led to the pass. Mike very quickly grasped that Marlock intended to leave the captain and the two injured soldiers behind.

Mike rode quickly to the sergeant's side and said in an impassioned tone, "Sergeant, what are you doing?"

Marlock replied in an even voice, "I'm leaving behind two good men and the only officer I've ever trusted. They'll have a chance to die with dignity. Don't get in the way, boy; they were here for you, after all."

Mike shot back much more fervently than he intended, "Sergeant, I know full well that you all are here on my account. I also know that they're injured beyond the ability of your healer. Leaving them here in the open is doing no one any good, especially them."

Mike struggled to gain control of his emotions and continued, "If we help them to the top of the pass and help them prepare just a bit, they'll be in a far more defensible position. From there, they could defend the pass for as long as their strength would hold out and give us a longer head start. That would be far more noble and dignified than just waiting for death here."

The sergeant reined in his horse sharply and Mike did the same. Marlock stared into Mike's eyes, each man holding the other's gaze as they sized one another up. After a moment, the sergeant wheeled his mount and began shouting orders to have litters made to haul the wounded. Mike released his pent-up breath, his shoulders sagging in relief. Marlock ordered ten men to ride forward with Mike and make whatever preparations he requested. Finally, the sergeant rode back to the captain and began earnestly explaining the change in plans.

Mike first ordered three of the men to gather bows, arrows, cross bows, throwing knives, basically any projectile they could gather from the dead enemy. He told the men to take the weapons to the top of the pass, then headed in that direction with the other soldiers.

The top of the pass was a flat area that gradually rose until it ended in a rock wall. The road continued through this area and entered into a canyon carved into the wall's face. The plateau was a poor, rocky field covered with thorn bushes and shrub. Without the hard-packed road that was reluctantly giving ground to the vegetation, the path to the canyon would have been very difficult. The level ground extended right up to the cliffs that overlooked that valley they had just left.

This topography was better than Mike could have hoped for. He ordered three men to gather rocks of varying sizes and drag large logs to the cliff's edge overlooking the valley. Two men were sent to gather dried brush that he ordered piled to the side of the road where it left the pass and entered the plateau.

Mike helped the remaining men build protection using arm-sized sticks lashed together with rope and propped up by two long poles fashioned like a lean-to. Mike and the men placed two shelters along the cliffside overlooking the path below; they built the third one on the other side of the pass near where it entered the plateau.

Using the logs and larger stones, Mike rigged two slides that could be triggered by pulling a rope and causing an avalanche of debris onto the path below. The smaller rocks he had piled at the shelters.

The men who had gathered weapons made their way up the pass just as the others completed their work. They split the stash into equal parts and piled them at the shelters. The rest of the men and horses arrived soon after, pulling the wounded on litters.

When everyone was on the plateau with the litters, Mike walked over to Millaro and said, "Captain, I think with some luck you should be able to keep the enemy at bay for quite some time."

"We might even hurt them badly enough they'll think twice before following," said the captain, with a forced laugh that left him wincing in pain.

Captain Millaro took the position near the end of the pass. The other two wounded manned the shelters overlooking the pass. The rest of the group began to take their leave, moving down the road. Mike had the piles of dried brush pulled into the middle of the pass at the top where it could not be seen from the valley below. The captain could fire the brush with a torch when the enemy could be held back no longer.

Sergeant Marlock ordered some of his men to retrieve the horses they had picketed in a makeshift corral made from brambles. The men disappeared down a small trail and were out of sight of the main road for a few minutes. When they returned, they were leading 20 horses.

And so it was that the company, now composed of Mike, Balose, Elisibrin, and 23 cavalrymen, set out for the Pass of Karness. They had extra horses and ample supplies, including the enemy stores they had captured and fresh supplies brought by the troops.

As the group moved on, Mike's thoughts turned inward. He was relieved that his plan had worked better than expected, but his relief was short lived. He thought about all the enemies they had killed, then the three men they left to certain death. Finally, he worried about his friends and wondered if they had escaped. He hoped they were faring better than he was.

CHAPTER 13

WHO'S THE LEADER

Mike, Balose and his protector Elisibrin, Sergeant Marlock, and 22 cavalry soldiers made their way through a second pass, away from the dead enemy and the three wounded soldiers left to certain death. Mike was thankful to be leaving the valley behind, but certain the images of the battle there would not fade as easily as the miles.

The troops had entered the pass through an opening at the bottom of the cliff face. Proceeding uphill, they quickly came upon a chasm and saw a fast-moving river far below. The lead soldiers didn't hesitate in crossing the bridge, and the others followed on their heels. Once on the other side, Mike urged his horse to hasten its pace till he caught up with the burly sergeant.

Pulling his horse alongside the sergeant's mount, Mike pressed, "Why not fire the bridge? That would buy us a couple of days. They'd have to backtrack to the ford downriver."

"An excellent observation," answered Marlock, continuing to push his horse forward. "But it wouldn't do any good. That bridge was built by the Ancients using powerful magic. It has stood for all of recorded history, well over 1,000 years. Many attempts have been made to bring it down, both magical and mundane. It doesn't even bear the marks of the attempts."

Shortly after gaining the other side of the bridge, the group could see that the terrain opened into vast grasslands. Only small patches of wooded areas broke up the horizon. The far distance was filled with rolling hills. Only a quarter-mile into the grasslands, Marlock, who had continued to ride beside the Summoned One, said in a voice loud enough for only Mike to hear, "We've no officer. These soldiers need leadership if we're to survive the days to come. I'm a disciplinarian and one of the best squad leaders, but I'm no officer."

Mike interrupted after a pause, "You aren't thinking of me?"

"Of course I am," answered the sergeant. "Cap told me what you've done in just two days. From what he said, every one of these men, including me, owes his life to you."

"I wouldn't go that far. Captain Millaro was their leader," responded Mike to the unwanted admiration.

"It doesn't matter what the truth is. It only matters what these troops think," stated Marlock matter-of-factly. "You're a born leader. That was obvious to Cap and it's becoming obvious to me. We need you if we're to survive."

Mike rode silently beside the big sergeant as he mulled over the proposal. He had never thought of himself as a leader, but as he looked back it began to dawn on him that throughout his life, people had looked to him for guidance. As his thoughts drifted back through the years, he saw a pattern emerging: from school group projects, quickly assembled paintball teams, even the Camp Wyanet campouts. People always looked to him for answers. Back then, he had assumed they just wanted advice. Thinking about it in a new light, he could see now that they had wanted his leadership.

Mike always took time to think things through and choose the most logical path; this time was no different. He remained quiet as he considered the merit of Sergeant Marlock's request. Reaching a decision, Mike said, "I'll do it, but I'll need help."

The sergeant gave a quick grin, then laid out his thoughts. "I won't second-guess you in front of the men unless I think you are about to get us all killed. So, I suggest that we talk through decisions in private. That way I can give you my advice without affecting the troops' perception of you."

Mike nodded. Deciding he might as well assume his new role right away, he began, "I do have a few ideas. First, we need scouts in the field as soon as possible. In this terrain, a large force could be just over the next ridge and you wouldn't realize it. Second, Balose's healing ability is too valuable to leave him in a vulnerable position, trailing the troops. The men will have to get over their prejudices and put him in a more defensible one."

Mike's instructions were interrupted by a particularly difficult stretch of trail as they approached the first wooded area. Apparently, a new spring had developed that had flooded the road and left a five-foot-wide (and just as deep) washout in their path. Mike took firm control of his mount and easily jumped the relatively short distance. By urging his mount to leap a few feet early, he landed well past the edge on the other side, hoping to avoid any loose earth that might give way.

Marlock smiled at Mike's jump as he made his own. He was pleased to see that the Summoned One was an able horseman. Upon landing, he asked Mike, "Is that all?"

"Not quite," Marlock's new leader replied. "I don't know if the Captain told you about the sizeable force we encountered downriver. Your scout, Keenabo, said they numbered several hundred. He also said they were preparing to depart. That was yesterday afternoon, and we saw scouts arriving from the direction of the chairs to report. So they must've known of your commander's escape. I'd bet anything that same force is on this side of the river."

Mike rode in silence for a while, letting Marlock digest this information. He continued, "You know as well as I do that if we run into that force, we don't stand a chance. This road leads northeast and the force would be coming from the southeast and likely be covering the road. I say we head due north and stay in the valleys, away from the top of the knolls as much as possible. Once we're far enough from the road that we can't be seen, we ride parallel with it, remaining within easy riding distance back to it if need be. This way, the scouts can watch the road yet stay out of sight, and we can quickly make our way to the next group of rear guards."

Marlock was impressed by the young man's logic; he had thought of the scouts but had planned to use the road and make haste. He realized that the Summoned One's plan would cost them little time and prove far safer. The sergeant nodded. "I agree. If there's nothing else, I'll make the arrangements with the scouts and we can leave the road." Waiting only a moment for a reply, Marlock urged his mount into a gallop and headed in the direction of the scouts.

In just a few minutes, the scouts had been dispatched and the group was heading north. Mike, Balose, and Elisibrin were in the center, surrounded by the remaining troops and accompanied by the ever-vigilant Marlock.

The scouts were soon able to make contact with the rear guard assigned to a bridge over a fast-moving stream. The new troops followed the scouts upstream and met up with Mike.

To Mike's amazement, after a brief discussion with Sergeant Marlock, the lieutenant that led the group did not take charge. Instead, the newcomer waited for Mike's orders. Mike sent more scouts into the field and, at Marlock's urging, established specific intervals for them to report back. Mike was busy working out a strategy with Marlock and the lieutenant for guarding their growing force after nightfall when a scout reported in early. The man brought news that contact had been made with a second group of rear guards.

This newest group brought the ranks of the cavalrymen to over 60. Mike's biggest concern was how to keep a force of this size hidden. He decided that splitting the force in two, with messengers to maintain contact, would be most effective.

"Divided, each half is still a sizeable force, but our greatest ally is surprise. If we're spotted as a whole, we have only two choices: a head-on fight or escape. Separated, if one force is spotted, the other force can attack in the place of their choosing with the element of surprise," Mike explained to Marlock and the lieutenant.

When the two offered no resistance to his plan, Mike ordered, "Lieutenant, choose five soldiers. Sergeant Marlock and I will take the remaining forces to the northern edge of the wooded area up ahead. When the new troops arrive, lead them to the southern edge of the same area and enter deep enough to be well out of sight. It will be dark soon, and we can't afford to stumble into trouble. We'll rest the men and horses in the protection of the woods; it's large enough that we'll remain sufficiently separated."

The lieutenant started to leave, but halted as Mike continued. "A couple more things, Lieutenant. I'll have a scout sent to your location in the woods. Have the officer of the new troops join Sergeant Marlock and me. I want the troops ready and moving at first light. We'll stay about 20 minutes apart. You follow the road as we have all day. We'll be 20 minutes further from the road traveling a parallel course."

"Yes sir," was the lieutenant's only reply. He turned his horse, barking out the names of five soldiers as he galloped away.

Marlock wasted no time in gathering the troops and starting the journey to the large, wooded ravine just over a mile ahead. As the troops got under way, Marlock circled back to ride alongside Mike. He commented, "You're doing very well with the leadership of the troops. The lieutenant's acceptance of you as his superior will go a long way, not only with his men, but the others as well. I'll warn you though, Lieutenant Caosor, who leads these newest men, will be another story."

Marlock paused, judging the reaction of the young Summoned One. He didn't seem to be bothered by the comment, the sergeant noted with approval. Marlock proceeded, "If Caosor agrees to leave his men where you asked and join us, it will be a good sign, but be careful. He's a young, brash officer from a wealthy family. He's been hand-picked to rise up the ranks quickly. You'll have to be bold and decisive if you're to gain his loyalty."

"Why not just have him lead the troops if he's such a skilled officer?" asked Mike.

"I never said he was a skilled officer," Marlock replied as he drew closer to prevent the others from hearing his comments. "He has little experience and too much confidence. He'd have us all killed or scattered within days. You must remain in charge if we're to have any hope of survival."

Mike rode on, choosing not to respond to Marlock's comment, but mulling over what he had said as they made their way to the far side of the ravine. They reached their designated area of the woods, and Marlock wasted no time in placing pairs of guards on the three surrounding hills, as well as the immediate perimeter of the camp. He went about his way to ensure that all horses were properly tended and saw to it that all in the fireless camp was in order.

Mike busied himself with the needs of his own horse and prepared his bedding. He had everything squared away and was rubbing down his horse a second time just to keep busy when a ruckus erupted on the edge of camp. Mike looked up from his task and was surprised to see a very young, ostentatiously dressed officer boldly crossing the camp towards him. His first thought was that Caosor looked to be even younger than him. Even in the faded light filtering through the woods, it was clear that the quality of his armor was on par with that worn by the commanders on the platform, but this individual wore his armor with an added flair. Caosor (or a hapless aide) had tied bright red and yellow silk sashes around his waist and looped them from his left hip across his right shoulder.

Moments before the flamboyant officer reached his campsite, Mike felt more than he saw Marlock approach and stand a pace behind and to the right. Caosor made no formal request for permission to enter camp, nor did he offer any greeting. Instead, he started addressing Marlock straight away, purposely ignoring Mike. "Who has ordered me here as if I were a common soldier? My men need a strict hand, and I daresay the men in this camp could also use some leadership."

Caosor achieved his intended result, commanding the undivided attention of most within earshot. The soldiers who were not already tracking the approaching officer turned to watch the exchange. Marlock's reaction, however, was not quite what Caosor expected. There was a tension in the big man but he said nothing, standing still in the subordinate position behind the man who was the true target of the comments. Mike remained as silent as Marlock, his eyes boring into the side of the young officer's face. The long, awkward silence wasn't broken until Caosor finally took his eyes from the stony expression of the big sergeant and turned to look at Mike.

Caosor wasn't prepared for what he saw in the young stranger's eyes. The steely gaze he encountered did not waver; instead, it cut into his very soul, and Caosor felt his confidence falter. Mike, on the other hand, was accustomed to this scenario and had played it out before. Over the years, his average build and quiet demeanor had convinced bullies that he would be an easy target. Then, as now, Mike was confident in his ability to defend himself and he knew that, in most cases, just calling the bluff of an aggressor was usually enough to back them down. Besides, with a man the size of a large bear standing near him and leaning on a war hammer large enough to knock down a tree, Mike knew he was in no danger of physical harm.

Once Mike saw the brash officer's confidence falling away from him, he wasted no time in pressing his advantage. He pointed to a nearby fallen log and commanded in a strong, clear voice, "Sit down, Caosor. We've much to discuss. I'm the Summoned One who ordered you here."

Mike's penetrating gaze had remained steadfast upon Caosor since he first locked eyes with him. The pretentious officer remained standing, glaring at the odd young man and trying to maintain the pretense that he was still in charge. Only a few seconds into the standoff, however, Caosor's confidence deserted him, his shoulders slumped, and he dropped his gaze. He paused, looking at the ground, then walked to the log and took a seat, watching Mike and waiting for him to proceed.

Mike had stared down bullies many times before. He saw before him not an impudent officer but a vulnerable young man. He knew he had won the battle and that he now needed to restore some of the young man's spirit. He chose his words carefully. "Caosor, I need the help of every officer if we're to survive long enough to reach the pass. I especially need you—these men around us trust me, but your men don't know me yet."

When Caosor remained silent but attentive, Mike went on to describe what he wanted: squads of 25 to 30 men that would stay 20 minutes apart and use messengers to communicate. He detailed the plans for the night guards, and the schedule and pattern of the scouts both night and day. When Mike was satisfied that Caosor understood what was required of him, he concluded, "Thank you for your attention, Lieutenant. I'm sure you're anxious to get back to your men and get started. That will be all."

Caosor was somewhat stunned when he realized he was being dismissed, but recovered quickly. Rising to his feet, he hesitated for only a moment before replying, "If that is all." Caosor turned and quickly left the campsite in the direction he had entered.

Waiting until the newly subjugated officer was well out of sight, Marlock grinned like a proud uncle and clasped Mike's shoulder with his enormous hand. "You did better than I could have ever hoped, my young friend. Let's get some rest."

The next morning, as the sun peeked over the horizon, both squads were in place and making their way parallel to the road as planned. Mike and Marlock had worked out a plan to have four messengers in constant rotation between the two forces. If one of the forces was attacked, the other would be notified within minutes.

The day passed without incident, with two new groups of rear guard added to the growing army. These new troops brought their number to 93, and Mike was required to create a new squad. The squads were forced to bed down in the open, choosing deep valleys as wooded ravines were not available.

At first light, Mike had the squads move out in a triangle formation. One squad was led by the new lieutenant riding closest to the road. Mike and Marlock's squad moved slightly ahead of that squad, but further from the road. Caosor's squad brought up the rear.

The next three days went by in the same manner. Rear guards were added as they traveled along, the army now consisting of eight squads.

In addition to the cavalrymen, six magic users, including Balose, were scattered among the squads. Mike was particularly happy to have these new Reenones after hearing Marlock's description of the nollax and pallitors. A captain named Brealnack had even joined their ranks and, much to Mike's relief after their introduction, the officer had delegated command, ending the exchange with a resounding "Yes, sir."

On the sixth day since Mike had been summoned into this strange world, hours before dawn, he received a report from his scouts of a group of riders approaching from the south. They were following the same path Mike's newly formed army had traveled the day before. According to the scouts, this band consisted of somewhere around 20 riders, and each had at least one extra horse in tow. Mike decided to err on the side of caution and immediately ordered the camp made ready to ride and the number of scouts doubled.

Once everything was in order for their departure, Mike commanded the squads to proceed at a walk into the darkness. He had Marlock send the best scouts off to observe this new threat. He cursed the lack of better cover—an ambush was an ever-present threat. The last thing Mike wanted was to be spotted by advance scouts of a larger force. They journeyed on through the dark hours of the early morning, maintaining a steady gap between themselves and those who followed.

Shortly after dawn broke, two scouts appeared and raced to Mike. "The soldiers are our own, sir. They're from the 18th Division."

Hearing the news, Mike called for a halt. Still dubious, he maintained the doubled scouts.

"Who could these soldiers be?" Mike asked Marlock.

"I'm not certain. We scouted thoroughly enough that we couldn't have missed a group of rear guard numbering that many," Marlock responded. "I can only guess that they were sent by Commander Namir for your protection."

An hour later, Marlock was proven correct when Captain Dreaklin joined the main group. His soldiers were battle-weary, and several had been seriously injured. Balose immediately began their healing, and Mike ordered two more clerics brought from other squads to aid in the effort.

Captain Dreaklin had a deep cut on his arm but refused healing until he could talk to the officer in charge. After getting over the initial shock of having the very Summoned One he was sent to protect appear before him as the leader, he began his report.

"Right after the attack at the summoning chairs, Commander Namir ordered that we find and protect you. However, within minutes of receiving that order, we encountered a sizable enemy force. Both groups were surprised, but we had the advantage of being mounted. That advantage was negated by the wooded terrain, a fact that ended up costing us ten men."

The captain grimaced when he described the losses. Mike could tell he cared deeply for those he commanded.

After only a brief pause the captain continued his report. "The loss of the men was bad enough, but the loss of time was even more devastating. By the time we wrapped up the fight and tended to the wounded, we were over an hour behind you. It also took us nearly another hour to find your trail. Following you up the valley we encountered a small scouting party that was dealt with quickly, but that delayed us even further.

When our advanced scouts found the tail end of the large force moving northwest we feared the worst. However, just before nightfall we found your trail paralleling the river. Afraid to move after dark with so many enemies, I ordered camp made. Heading out at first light we were certain we would catch up with you the very next day. We nearly did just that. Dogging your trail we pressed on through the morning, all the while the scouts reported fresher and fresher tracks. We gained confidence when your tracks led to the road. I was certain I would reach you within the hour, but my hopes were dashed a short time later when we heard the unmistakable sound of battle.

As we rushed forward the first thing we encountered was fallen enemy soldier lying along the road. Then topping the rise we saw an army that easily outnumbered us two-to-one. They were in a pitched battle attempting to gain the summit of the cliff pass leading out of the far end of the valley. Many of their dead lay at the base of the cliff where the road sloped upward toward the pass.

A fire raged in the pass itself, the heat and flames temporarily holding back any attempt to gain the summit. However, with the flames dying an all-out assault was imminent. I knew my men's hopes lay in that very pass. If those troops took the pass we could never hope to dislodge so many. Besides my orders were clear; to find and protect you at all cost.

So, I quickly made the decision to attack while the enemy was distracted. The majority of them were cavalrymen, but they were dismounted realizing it was no advantage on the cliff to place their horses in jeopardy. So, my first priority was to scatter those horses. That was one advantage I intended to keep.

With a handful of men assigned to scatter their horses, the rest of us charged into their exposed rear flank. We were nearly on top of them before the shouts rang out, leaving them no time for an organized defense. We struck deep into their ranks before losing momentum and calling a pullback. We went back to the burnt-out buildings and rested our horses. The attack had gone better than expected, decimating over half of their ranks with only five casualties. We also had wounded, but to a man they insisted they could continue to fight.

Without horses they would not challenge us in the open field. So, they pulled back to the pass, awaiting the last of the fire to burn itself out. They had placed all of their troops on the switchback road, above the field itself. This completely negated our advantage, we would need to attack them up the narrow road or exchange bow fire from the field.

Deciding that there was no alternative I ordered the charge. Halfway across the open field, even above the horse's hooves, we heard screams and curses. The whole lot of them was pushing their way back down the elevated road and pouring back out onto the field and into our charge. In the heat of battle they had forgotten completely about those on the cliffside defending the pass. Those on top had wisely held their fire until we had begun our charge, and as a result the enemy had unwittingly placed themselves in the range of their deadly projectiles.

This time with the enemy bunched at the bottom of the road, our charge was even more effective. After the full weight of our charge slammed into them and our momentum waned, I didn't call a retreat. This time we fought it out until the last enemy fell. That decision cost us in casualties and the injuries you see, but I think more would have been lost if we pulled back yet again.

By the time the fight was over the pass' fire had died down enough for us to make our way to the summit. We were astounded to see only three soldiers had defended the pass, and at that only Captain Millaro was alive. As I approached it was clear that he was in bad shape. He had taken an arrow in the shoulder, but even worse he was coughing up blood.

I shouted for the medic and Millaro said, "There's no need for that Dreaklin. I've fought in my last fight. A good one I must say." He then looked at his shoulder. The white feathers of the fletching stained with his blood, and said, "Damn, same shoulder as this morning."

Those were the last words he said, dying only a moment later. By this time darkness was coming. I had several wounded that needed rest before they could be moved. So, I ordered camp made in the very defendable area between the two narrow passes. I had the three heroes of the battle buried where they fought so bravely. After that I was forced to slow our pace for the wounded, which is why it has taken so long to reach you.

Captain Dreaklin had been shifting his eyes around as he told of his ordeal, but now he looked directly into Mike's eyes, and said, "You seem to have things well in hand. Our meager numbers can't make a big difference, but our swords are yours till the end."

Mike guided his horse along-side of the captain's, shaking his hand he looked him directly in the eyes and said, "Captain, it is a great honor to be joined by a squad as brave and loyal as yours. You have already done us a great service in destroying an enemy that would be harassing us from behind. I believe this will prove invaluable. That single act will change how we proceed, allowing us to scout more aggressively forward rather than being so concerned with what follows." Shaking his hand, Mike added, "Thank you. You and your men have my gratitude."

CHAPTER 14

DAVID HARASSES GOLIATH

Two more days passed without the addition of troops. In answer to Mike's thorough questioning, Captain Brealnack, the officer who had joined the group just before Captain Dreaklin, explained that the rear guards had been placed at easily defensible locations only, places the enemy could use as ambush points. The terrain over the last few days had consisted solely of rolling hills that seemed to go on without end. If all went as planned, according to the captain, they should come upon two more groups toward the middle of the following day, one early on the third day, and a final large force led by a Colonel Melrue.

Mike also learned that all the rear guards were from the same outfit, the 18th Division, led by a commander named Namir. Captain Dreaklin stated matter of factly, without bragging, that the 18th was the most decorated and respected division of Jerimassa, the proud central plains city-state known for its fine horses and exceptional cavalrymen.

Early on the third day, after picking up the additional squads just as Brealnack had foretold, Mike started to allow himself the hope that they could complete the trip to the Pass of Karness without incident. His hope, however, was short-lived. By midmorning of the following day, scouts and messengers reported seeing a large enemy force using the road heading towards the pass. Mike knew this couldn't bode well for Colonel Melrue.

Mike and Marlock accompanied the scouts to their lookout; Mike wanted to see the enemy forces for himself. He had a plan in mind, but the configuration of the enemy army and how it traveled would be critical. According to the scouts, comparing all their accounts, this was the same force they had seen over a week ago at the river, which would place the total number at several hundred bodies. A force of that size, made up primarily of foot soldiers, would require vast amounts of supplies. Mike knew this meant heavy supply wagons were traveling nearby. He also knew from reading about countless historical battles: cut the supply lines and a large army cannot sustain an attack. This knowledge helped Mike form his battle plan.

The two men and their scouts soon reached a large knoll, some distance from the road, which offered an unobstructed view for at least a mile in both directions. Just before they crawled the last few yards to the scouts' hidden vantage point, Marlock put his arm out to stop Mike. Reaching into a pouch that hung by a cord around his neck, Marlock produced a velvet pouch, its opening pulled tight together by a golden tasseled cord. Opening the pouch, Marlock pulled out a clear glass sphere the size of a golf ball. As he handed the sphere to Mike, he whispered, "Look through this, it will give you much clearer vision."

Mike accepted the sphere with a nod, and crawled with the others to the peak of the ridge. Pushing back the tall grass just slightly, he was able to see the road clearly in both directions, yet remain virtually invisible. To his dismay, to his right and left, the force stretched along the road as far as he could see.

Mike brought the sphere to his eye and peered through. To his amazement, the experience was much like looking through a powerful pair of binoculars. The image he saw was clear and undistorted. Even more astounding was this discovery: as Mike concentrated on one aspect of the force—the caravan of well-guarded supply wagons—the sphere zoomed in even further on the image. Taking advantage of this feature, Mike concentrated even harder. This time, he was able to see the design on the pommel of the sword carried by the driver of the furthest wagon.

Mike pulled back with his mind, and the image followed suit, zooming out all the way to a scene he could have observed with his naked eye. He continued to experiment until his curiosity surrounding the device wore off. Mike then began to use it in earnest to make an initial assessment of the enemy force. He was able to get more accurate counts, as well as the make-up of the troops. The enemy force seemed to consist primarily of foot soldiers, with a small contingency of cavalry.

Mike was most interested in the supply wagons and how well they were guarded. The wagons carried heavy loads that required four horses each. They had more guards than he had anticipated, but the soldiers seemed less disciplined than the troops toward the front of the column. One thing he was encouraged by was the rear location of the supply wagons; better yet, the cavalry was on the opposite end of the column, over a mile away.

Suddenly, Mike's attention was drawn to a horrific sight. It took him a moment to process what he was seeing, creatures straight out of a "B" horror movie, human-like beings blended with animal parts. Eight of these creatures surrounded an extremely disciplined group of 20 soldiers. The group walked with a mechanical precision that made the hair stand up on the back of Mike's neck.

"Marlock, you need to see this," Mike whispered as he handed the sphere over. "The fourth group back from the cavalry."

Marlock took the magical device and quickly confirmed Mike's fears. "Nollax and pallitors." Marlock had gone into great detail during their evening camp talks describing these dreadful creatures that, to Mike's ears, sounded like the stuff of myth. Seeing them in the flesh made the young man shudder.

After a quick scan of the entire column, Marlock handed back the sphere. Mike thought he had seen enough, but on second thought decided to take one last look at the column. Starting at the back and working his way methodically to the front, he saw nothing that yielded additional information.

Just as he was about to return the looking sphere to the sergeant, Mike saw movement at the front of the column. Focusing the magical orb, he saw what he assumed to be a scout charging on horseback up to the lead cavalry unit. Moments later, riders were dispatched to other army units, and the cavalry units raced ahead till they were out of sight. Mike nudged Marlock and handed the looking sphere to him, gesturing for the sergeant to take a look. By the time Marlock began using the device, Mike could already see the front columns of foot soldiers advancing into the distance at double time. He watched the riders reach the rear guard assigned to protect the supply wagons. To his amazement and relief, almost half raced ahead to the destination the rest of the army was pursuing. This left the remaining guard and supply wagons to follow as best they could.

Mike tapped Marlock and the scout who had led them to the knoll, and they began crawling back down the hill toward the horses held by the second scout. Without speaking, all four men quickly mounted and raced back to the troops. Mike wanted to confer with Marlock on the way, but their breakneck speed prevented it. Mike was glad he had sent messengers before he left, directing the leaders of each squad to meet at the lead squad's position. It was to the lead squad that they now raced.

They quickly reached the squad's position. Reigning in their horses, Mike and Marlock slid to within feet of the waiting leaders. Wasting no time, Mike shouted as he dismounted, "They've found Colonel Melrue's position. We must be cautious but proceed with all haste. They've made the mistake of leaving their supplies poorly guarded, and in the rear. Squads five, seven, and eight will hit them using oil to burn the supplies they can't capture, and secure or drive off all the horses. Squads nine and ten will wait just out of sight in reserve.

Mike's tone changed from one of complete authority to concern. "Gentlemen, you're only after the supplies, no heroes. Make it quick, and leave before any of their lead soldiers can make it back to help. This attack is meant only to slow them down and confuse them. We'll need every possible soldier in the days to come. All of you will meet up with us at the first outcropping of the western mountain range leading to the pass. Stay well wide of the road and avoid conflicts at all cost."

In conclusion, Mike shouted, "Gentlemen, you have your orders, now move!"

The leaders of the affected squads turned their horses and hurried off to convey Mike's instructions to their men. The young man immediately turned his attention to the remaining leaders. "The rest of us will ride as hard as we dare push our horses to aid Colonel Melrue. We'll rest the animals a little over halfway there, and again just shy of the colonel's position."

Mike paused, looking around as he gathered his thoughts. He continued, "I want the same formations as before, but close the distance between them by half. All but four scouts out front, I want the squads stopped out of sight of the conflict, and I want all but four of the lead scouts waiting to report the details."

Mike swept up the reins of his mount and leapt into the saddle. He nudged his horse past all the scrabbling leaders, including Marlock, and raced to get his squad moving. He and Marlock pushed their men as fast as they dared, at a pace that fell somewhere between a light run and a fast gallop, depending on the terrain. As Mike and his horse tore through the countryside, he thought with gratitude of the time Marlock had spent painstakingly describing the surrounding landscape to him; in particular, the topography of the land between them and the pass. Mike knew that Colonel Melrue's position was in a heavily wooded area and easily defendable. Not far into the woods, there was a deep crevasse, forcing anyone wanting to pass to go miles around in either direction, or go over the bridge built by the Ancients.

Just past the halfway point, Mike sent messengers to the other squads with instructions to have them walk the horses for a mile, then rest them for 15 minutes. They were to gradually return to speed when they resumed their journey, taking one mile to regain full speed. Mike knew that, in all likelihood, the squad leaders and their soldiers already knew of these techniques for cooling down the horses without letting them chill on this cold autumn day. Still, he felt compelled to ensure the horses were sound enough for an attack and retreat.

"Marlock, my plan is simple," Mike confided soon after they had stopped. "I hold no hope that we can reach the colonel before their cavalry. But I'm hoping to get there long before the foot soldiers arrive." Pointing back the way they had come, he added, "And that should serve to divide and confuse most of them." A large black plume of smoke was rising from the burning supply wagons.

"You continue to impress me with your thinking," replied Marlock. "Quick, bold, logical decisions that not only save lives but better our position. Your talent isn't lost on the other men either, including the officers." The sergeant nodded approvingly as he completed his ritual inspection of his horse's hooves and used grass to wipe the lathered sweat from its flanks.

Mike found that the interval spent giving the horses their all-too-brief rest was agonizing. On the one hand, it seemed like hours, but when the time came to ride, it seemed as if mere seconds had passed. Each squad led spare horses, so any mount struggling with the pace was swapped out with a horse that had been traveling unencumbered. This tradeoff allowed the tired horse to rest as much as possible while on the move, without the weight of rider or saddle.

As planned, Mike gradually brought his squad up to speed, then traveled as quickly as the terrain would allow. He knew they couldn't match the pace of the enemy cavalry, which had used the road, but he was determined to reach Colonel Melrue long before the foot soldiers. Mike wasn't sure if it was the excitement of the chase, or if the scouts had misjudged the halfway point; whatever the case, it seemed that, in no time, his squad was being met by several scouts.

In his eagerness, the lead scout began his report before Mike could come to a complete stop. "They're two ridges away, sir. Colonel Melrue has established a perimeter in the woods ahead of the bridge, and they're successfully defending that perimeter. The enemy seems content with minimal engagement."

"That makes sense, they only want to hold him long enough for the foot soldiers to arrive. Were you able to see all the cavalry?" Mike asked.

"Yes, the bulk of them are in the road, maybe the range of two arrows away from the perimeter. Two groups of around 20 have dismounted on either side of the road. They're making their way through the woods in an effort to use the trees to flank the colonel's position."

Mike's mind was racing. "Are there any scouts or messengers about?"

"No sir, none that we've been able to see."

Mike could now hear the sounds of battle. He knew the enemy was pushing the colonel to keep him busy and engaged until the foot soldiers arrived. Mike fell silent, waiting for the approaching squads to gather around him to set his plan in motion.

It didn't take long for the closer squads to arrive. Their leaders quickly converged on Mike. He conveyed the information the lead scout had reported and began his orders. "We will proceed back down the road and attack from the enemy's rear. I want squad one to attack the main force and sweep through. Try to divide their force in two. Almost immediately after that, I want squad two to hit their left flank, and squad three their right. We want to push them close to the woods. Unless I'm wrong about your colonel, he'll take care of the dismounted enemy and push out from his position to force the enemy into a vise."

Mike surveyed the leaders for their reactions. All he saw on their faces was determination, which gave him comfort that the orders were to their liking. "Squads four and six will be held in reserve, and ensure that no stragglers reach the foot soldiers with information on our numbers."

"Gentlemen, this will be a bloody battle, and not one enemy soldier can be left alive to report. Once the fight is over, I want as many of the enemy horses driven across the bridge as possible. Then, we'll fell trees on both sides of the bridge to slow any pursuers while we rest the horses and meet up with the others. Questions?"

No one spoke, but Marlock stepped forward. Mike said, "Before you say anything Marlock, I'll remain with squad six, in reserve, and you'll lead squad one. Captain Brealnack, you're leading the attack, it's your command. If there's nothing else, any further delay is only to the enemies' advantage. Prepare yourselves and your men. We head out in one minute."

The officers, Marlock, and Mike dispersed to their assigned squads. Mounted and ready, all but the squad that was to attack the left flank paralleled back down the road to a point out of sight of the enemy. The squad would then be sent to the left flank. Timing and surprise would be crucial.

Captain Brealnack elected to stay with Marlock and squad one, leading the center attack. The plan was for this center squad to proceed down the road until the enemy was in sight. At that point, they would break into a run using a wedge formation. The flanking squads would wait just out of sight and begin their charge as soon as they heard the onslaught of the center squad.

Captain Brealnack waited patiently to give the right flanking squad time to get into position and then moved the group forward at a light canter. Mike ordered the reserve units to spread out in two semicircles 100 yards apart. If any of the enemy broke through the first line, the second was the last line to bar their escape.

Marlock and Brealnack were in the vanguard of the now hard-charging V-formation. Marlock's horse was noticeably larger than all those around him and, standing in the stirrups with his huge war hammer held above his head, the big man and his steed were an ominous sight. The captain wisely had the V-formation split into two and did not use the road as they approached. The knee-high grass they rode in, as well as the sounds of the battle, muffled the sound of the approaching squad until they were almost on top of their quarry.

The entire squad cried, "Jerimassa" as they slammed headlong into the rear of the surprised enemy. Mike soon realized he had but a small glimpse of the cavalry's capabilities in the valley of the outpost. Here, they were in their element: an open field, a spread-out enemy, their charging horses versus stationary ones. The effect was devastating.

Long before the cavalrymen reached the conflict, they tied the reins of their horses loosely to their saddles. The entire squad then stood in the stirrups, masterfully guiding their mounts with their knees. They passed through the enemy like a swift, wicked blade and into the field directly in front, losing only two men in the process. Upon their passage, a full third of the enemy lay dead, dismounted, or wounded.

The enemy force was in disarray, horses rearing and out of control, the troops seemingly lacking any structured leadership. Those fit to do battle were just starting to gather themselves to face the menacing threat before them when the flanking squads slammed into them from both sides like a hammer meeting an anvil. The effect was so violent and one-sided that Mike felt a flicker of remorse for the men they were routing.

Mike watched Colonel Melrue's troops pour out of their positions and quickly overwhelm the dismounted enemy forces in the woods. As quickly as it had begun, the battle was over. Only a handful of troops had an opportunity to attempt escape, and they were dealt with quickly but mercifully. Mike ordered the reserve troops to round up the remaining enemy horses. The clerics tended to the wounded, and Marlock reported back that only eight men had been lost.

Mike surveyed the carnage and destruction, then forced himself to assess their next move. "Squads two and three, collect as many weapons and armor from the fallen as possible before the trees are readied to fall. Then get across that bridge. Get everyone else and the horses on the other side of the bridge, and start working on felling the trees," Mike instructed as he began to herd the horses towards the bridge.

Once the enemy horses were safely over the span and well out of harm's way, they were corralled, calmed, and made ready to be led as spares. Mike had the soldiers secure the collected weapons and armor to the backs of the horses. He also had as many men as possible take a brief rest while the others felled the trees.

Mike and Marlock were tending their own horses when an older man with short, gray hair and a thick white moustache approached on foot, leading his horse. Mike didn't notice his arrival until Marlock snapped off a sharp salute. The old cavalryman ignored the salute and inquired genially, "Well, what have we here, Sergeant Marlock?"

Marlock dispensed with the formalities. "This is the Summoned One, name's Mike. He's the one who's led us since the outpost where we lost Millaro and Wico. He's also the one who orchestrated this latest attack."

It seemed to Mike that the two veterans knew each other well.

"I'm sorry to hear about Captain Millaro and Lieutenant Wico. They were both good men and will be missed," Colonel Melrue said sincerely as he rested his hand on the big man's shoulder. The older man bent his head near Marlock's and said softly but firmly, "I'd like to talk to the Summoned One alone, my old friend."

Mike was certain he knew the reason the colonel wanted to talk with him in private. He had mixed emotions about the outcome of this conversation. On one hand, he was relieved to finally be out from under the constant pressure of being responsible for the lives of so many people. On the other hand, the past week and a half had been the most exciting and rewarding days of his life. As Mike waited for the others to leave, he realized he had grown to love the challenges of leadership. He knew he had been lucky, and that wouldn't always be the case, but he also knew his actions had saved many lives. This filled him with a strong sense of pride and a yearning for more.

"Greetings Summoned One, I'm Colonel Melrue," the officer said as he gave Mike the now familiar salute: a fist across the chest, then an extended hand for a shake.

Mike returned the salute, then reached past the colonel's extended hand to grasp Melrue's forearm, as he had observed was their custom. As the colonel returned the gesture, Mike said, "Greetings, Colonel Melrue. I hope you and your men are doing well, or as well as can be expected."

The colonel replied, "We're doing far better than I'd ever expected, thanks to you." Melrue started to say more, but was interrupted as the first tree on the far side of the crevasse came crashing down across the road. Its large, bushy top branches shivered and came to rest, covering the entrance to the bridge. Both men looked appraisingly at the destruction, satisfied that the enemy's pursuit would be slowed considerably.

While crimson leaves of the felled tree were still floating down from the forest canopy, the colonel continued. "I can't remember a time when I wasn't a student of the prophecies. My career has afforded me the opportunity to study them all over Bericea. I'm convinced you are the Summoned general mentioned in so many of the writings and oral lore.

I never dared hope of still being alive at the time of the summoning, let alone serving under the general."

"What are you saying? You think I'm the general?" Mike asked in disbelief. He started to say more but thought better of it.

Before either man could say more, they heard a second tree crash to the ground, its tops overlapping the first. The men who felled the two trees made their way through the tangle of branches. After they made their way clear of the mess, they came running across the bridge, shouting for the other cutters to finish.

Mike and Colonel Melrue remained silent, watching the events unfold at the bridge, neither sure what to say next. The woodcutters on Mike's side of the bridge had prepared the trees, and all they need do now was finish the job. As a result, the third tree fell less than a minute after the other cutters had cleared the bridge. Two more trees then fell in rapid succession.

Mike made up his mind. "I'm not sure about being a Summoned general, but I'm willing to lead for a while longer. I'll need your help, though."

Melrue's only response was a smile, and he placed his foot in the stirrup, pulling himself into the saddle. Mike quickly looked around, and seeing the woodcutters reaching their horses, he climbed up as well.

From the saddle, Mike shouted, "Gentlemen, mount up, we need to catch up to the others."

Mike accurately assessed that the men and horses had been through too much already, and the threat posed by the enemy was not pressing. The pace he set for the rendezvous was merely a fast walk. The slower paced journey allowed all a much-deserved rest and time for he and Colonel Melrue to talk.

The two rode beside each other in a companionable silence for some time until the colonel asked, "What are your plans when we reach the others?"

Mike didn't answer right away, his mind elsewhere. Melrue's question finally registered, and the preoccupied young man replied, "The pass has always been our goal. I hope to keep the enemy behind us as we head there."

Mike fell silent again, deep in thought. Melrue prodded, "I think there's more on your mind."

"I've been thinking about the army we encountered. I don't think they were looking for me, or even expected to engage you. They had enough supplies to be in the field for a very long time." Mike paused, then added almost to himself, "Or to supply others. Why would an army that size be heading toward the pass, if not searching for us?"

Both men fell into a brooding silence, contemplating Mike's last question. After several minutes had passed filled only the sounds of hooves and occasional snorts from the horses, Mike asked, "Could an army of that size hope to storm the gates of the city at the top of the pass?"

Colonel Melrue didn't hesitate with his answer. "Ten times their number would be hard-pressed to enter those gates, even with nollax and pallitors among their forces."

"So why travel with so many and so well-supplied?" Not really expecting an answer, Mike went on. "They're either advanced troops or the trailing reserves of a larger force."

Mike had come to this conclusion soon after leaving the bridge, dread consuming his thoughts. He was very anxious about the well-being of his friends. If this were a reserve force, the others very likely had traveled straight into the main force. He was also concerned for the army for which he was now responsible.

"Our dilemma, colonel, is this. If this is the advance troop of a larger army, our only hope is to reach the pass ahead of them. However, if we race for the pass and encounter a much larger force, we may find ourselves in a position from which escape is impossible." If there were any doubts in the colonel's mind that this young man could be the Summoned general, Mike's astute observation cast them away.

The colonel remembered an event he had witnessed earlier. "So, the scouts you sent racing ahead on fresh mounts soon after the fight?"

"Yes, they were to scout the pass and report their findings as soon as possible," Mike said before the colonel could finish his question. "Still, that may not give us enough advance notice to avoid being caught between two forces. That's also why we're setting a relaxed pace; I want the men and horses rested for what might be ahead, and the scouts need time to report back."

The remainder of the ride to the rendezvous with the troops that attacked the supply wagons was uneventful. Mike was pleased when he saw the troops in the distance. Not only were they already at the rendezvous point, but most, if not all, the men were there, and they had two of the smaller supply wagons in tow.

Mike shouted as they approached, "Lieutenant Caosor, I see the hunting went well!"

Now that he was closer, he saw that not only did they have the two supply wagons, but all the spare horses carried supplies, and most of the men had additional stores as well. Mike had made up his mind as to the possible purposes for the enemy force shortly after seeing them for the first time. He had hoped the loss of supplies might slow the enemy's invasion and, if they could make the pass before the assault, the captured supplies might well be needed.

The lieutenant replied, "A good hunt indeed, Summoned One. We routed the guards and destroyed all that we did not take. We were able to secure ten horses in addition to the eight draft horses on the wagons. One of the wagons contains weapons, the other foodstuffs, and several of the men grabbed what they could from the other wagons before setting them to flame."

"Well done, lieutenant. Have runners gather all the officers. I want a quick meeting before we proceed." Mike wanted to set the order of the squads before proceeding but, more importantly, he wanted the scouts to have more time.

Mike was still concerned they might be heading into the grip of the enemy, a grip so tight, they may not have the numbers to fight their way out. He chose a spot for the meeting with the officers, where the trees of the forested western mountain spur had encroached very little into the plains. This meant that the beginning of the mountain base's steep grade could easily be seen just inside the tree line.

The last officer rode up to the waiting group. Mike was still reluctant to begin, but knew there would be precious little daylight left to reach the pass. If he stalled much longer, the known enemy behind him would be regrouped and on their trail. Just when Mike was about to begin, a clear shout rang out from the somewhere on the wooded ridge behind them, "Hail, Melrue. What's a boy like you doing so far from home?" The shout was followed by booming laughter.

"I know that voice, but it can't be," said Colonel Melrue. "That sounds like Commander Porack. He was a commander when I was a captain."

Lieutenant Caosor said, "That can't be, sir. Commander Porack's been dead for more than ten years."

"Correction lad, he has been missing and assumed dead for ten years."

Melrue told Mike and the others of Commander Porack's retirement and how he disappeared while riding only a few days later, never to be seen again. Just as the colonel was wrapping up his story, a tall, thin, white-haired man appeared from the woods that all of the officers had trained their eyes upon.

"Well, it is you, boy, and those fools have gone and made you a colonel," the spry old man barked loudly with a wide grin.

Melrue jabbed back, "I see the years have been kind to you, old man." Laughing, he added, "What brings you here in these dangerous times?"

"This is my home, boy," Porack said. "And as far as what I'm doing, why, I'm planning to pull your butt out of the ringer like I've always done."

"What do you mean, Porack?" the colonel demanded, his tone now sober and curt.

"You're getting ready to ride into a world of trouble. There must be at least 10,000 of those Malabrim dogs in the pass, and with those following you, I'd say you'd be in more trouble than I could help you out of," Porack said. Then thinking on it, he added, "Well, that might not be true." Porack pointed a long, bony finger at Mike and burst out laughing. "That young man you have there is full of all kinds of surprises. He might just find a way to defeat them all by himself."

Melrue said, "Excuse me, Commander, this is the Summoned general. He calls himself Mike."

"You don't say," said Porack, eyeing Mike closer. "And don't call me that, boy. I gave up that title with my commission."

Mike started to dismount to introduce himself, but Porack stopped him. "No time for that now, lad. We need to get moving."

With that said, he put his fingers to his lips and produced a loud, shrill whistle. On his signal, men pulling pack mules started emerging all along the tree line of the ridge. Porack's demeanor became serious for the first time since his appearance. Speaking in a voice that no doubt of his ability to command, he instructed, "The wagons will be unloaded onto the pack animals, and they will be left here. What the pack animals can't carry can be distributed to the horses you're riding. About two miles along the tree line, we'll enter a trailhead. After that, it'll be all those horses can do to get themselves through where we're going."

Porack waited as if expecting something. Finally, he said, "Well, general, don't you think you should let your men know what is about to happen?"

Mike hesitated for just a second, then said, "Lieutenants, inform the men and make the preparations. We'll be on foot for a while."

"Good job, boy," Porack said with a grin. "A few more things before we get started. Don't worry about the scouts. They're being intercepted and will travel a different route. They'll meet up with us late tomorrow. Also, I'll need the help of your Reenones to cover our trail from here and well into the trailhead. We sure don't need to be followed."

Porack turned and headed back into the forest where he had emerged earlier. A few minutes later, he reappeared 50 yards away from the group. He had two pack mules in tow and was heading towards one of the wagons.

CHAPTER 15

BUILD DEFENSES

Will and Jeremy rushed with Josh through the well-maintained streets of Karness toward the center of the city. The three had just finished a surreptitious inspection of the city's wall defenses. The two brothers still couldn't believe that Josh was the one who had come up with the perfect weapon for defending the walls—a trebuchet. It wasn't that they doubted Josh's intelligence, but he rarely paid attention to anything mechanical unless musical instruments were involved. Although a little annoyed at not coming up with the idea themselves, Will and Jeremy were happy for it now and eager to get back to Phomel and his forges. The two needed to go over their initial plans with the older and experienced blacksmith. His cooperation would be vital to the city's defense.

The brothers were glad Josh was with them now. Just days ago, they had believed him to be gone from them forever. Since their arrival in the city, Josh had been spending most of his time with the Brotherhood of the Seekers, and Will and Jeremy had seen little of their friend. Fortunately for them, he had decided not to return to the Brotherhood. Although he desperately wanted to learn more about his newfound magical talent, Josh could never agree to the lifetime commitment the Seekers demanded.

After seeing the dismal condition of the defenses for the walls, the young men felt there was no time to waste. Jeremy had already mentally calculated the scale required to launch a 50-pound stone from the ground over the wall. Will was working out the materials needed, the best way to transport and assemble the trebuchet, and was even contemplating the joints, knowing that wood would have to be the primary material used in the weapon's construction.

Jeremy's thoughts shifted to the release mechanism. When he and Will built their trebuchet in high school, it could launch a golf ball nearly the length of a football field. This small feat had eventually earned them both a three-day suspension; however, that miniature version had shown them a most critical design consideration. In the construction of this massive trebuchet, the ability to tune the release point and have it remain consistent would be essential to the successful defense of the city's walls.

The brothers' mental calculations were disrupted by a dust devil appearing out of nowhere. A cyclone, 15 feet high, was picking up small debris in the street, and forced the trio to seek shelter in a business's doorway. The whirlwind ended as quickly as it began, and the three returned to the street, wiping dust from their eyes.

Red-faced with embarrassment, Josh said, "Sorry, guys. I was bored and started whistling. I need to get control of my new powers, but I'm not going to become a priest!"

The brothers burst out laughing at Josh's declaration just as Will opened the door to Phomel's inner courtyard. The smith was walking out of his shop as they entered. Seeing the young men laughing, Phomel couldn't help but smile. In the short time he had known the pair, he had grown quite fond of them.

Noticing Phomel, Will and Jeremy rushed to him, eager to tell what they had heard from Namir and to share their ideas. If Phomel wondered how they knew Namir, he didn't show it. As he listened, he became gravely concerned.

"Most of the City Guard is at the pass. If the pass falls, they'll lose the wall soon after. If that happens, the city and countryside have nothing that can stop them."

As the full weight of his words hung in the air, Phomel fell silent.

Will blurted out, "Exactly! That's why we're so eager to get your help. We have some ideas for the wall's defense, but we need you to make it work."

The brothers went on to describe the trebuchet. Phomel had a hard time understanding the concept, a confusion that was greatly compounded by the two talking over each other in their excitement.

In response to the blacksmith's perplexed look, they blurted out simultaneously, "We'll build a prototype."

Finally, the two stopped talking over each other, to Phomel's relief.

Will said, "We can have a scaled-down, crude prototype mocked up in less than 20 minutes."

As Phomel went to collect the tools Will asked for, the brothers began gathering all the materials required. True to Will's word, the prototype was completed almost exactly 20 minutes later. It consisted of two tripod towers about midthigh in height. These were mounted far enough apart that a board, turned on edge and used as the throwing arm, would clear the towers as it rotated on an axle made from a wooden dowel. The construction looked like a see-saw, but one that was too tall for its size and greatly off-center.

On the short end of the lever arm, they tied a fist-sized rock as a counterweight. Into the other end, they drove a headless nail. Jeremy tied a short string to a rock the size of a golf ball and, on the other end, a small washer.

They had worked out this simple but effective release mechanism when they built the trebuchet that got them into so much trouble in high school. Gravity and centrifugal force held the washer on the nail until the projectile gained enough momentum to fly away from the arm. At that point, the washer, still attached to the projectile, simply slipped off the nail.

With everything in place, the brothers aimed the contraption toward the center of the compound, set the projectile in place, lifted the large rock counterweight, and let it fall. The golf-ball-sized rock flew over 30 feet in the air but landed only ten feet from the prototype. The trebuchet's performance disappointed Will and Jeremy, but amazed Phomel.

Will explained, "We were thinking of towers 30 feet tall. That puts this model at a scale of 20 to 1. So, this poor first attempt would scale to a rock almost two feet in diameter going over 200 feet. And with just a little work, we could get five or six times that distance."

Phomel was truly at a loss for words. Amazed, he walked over for a closer inspection. As Phomel looked the device over, Jeremy posed a question to the group at large.

"What if we rigged up a basket filled with rocks the size of apples? They'd impact far more soldiers than a single boulder."

Josh, who had remained on the sidelines throughout the brothers' demonstration, had a sudden inspiration.

"Hey! What about using lawn darts? Remember when we were little and your uncle let us play with his set? Our parents were all so angry. They said darts had been outlawed because they were dangerous. Something as big as you're talking about could throw 100 or more at a time."

It took a moment for Will to digest the full implication of Josh's suggestion. Then, a smile began to spread across his face.

"You know, you're on to something. We can work with this," he said enthusiastically, nodding to his friend as he spoke.

Will turned to Phomel and began an earnest explanation of lawn darts. He began with its physical description, that a lawn dart consisted of a heavy weight and a long, sharp point attached to a shaft with fins. The weight of the point, coupled with the way the wind caught the fins, forced the dart to always land point down when thrown. Because lawn darts were well over 12 inches long, they weighed enough to be thrown a good distance by hand, and land with significant force. Phomel seemed to understand the description of a lawn dart, but still failed to see its true potential. Once again, the brothers decided a quick prototype was the best way to demonstrate the weapon's true capability.

The two went straight to work on the prototype, leaving Josh to his own devices once again. To stave off boredom, he explored all of the blacksmith's outbuildings and eventually made a new friend by helping Phomel's assistant Claiphie prepare lunch.

Jeremy, Will, and Phomel made quick work of the full-scale weaponized lawn dart. The dart was as long as a man's arm. A square iron shaft accounted for two-thirds of the length, with a sharpened point on one end and a flared hollow receptacle on the other. The brothers inserted a wooden shaft into the hollow end, and Phomel held the shaft in place by crimping metal around it. They used flat pieces of wood for the fins, and placed the fins in notches cut into the shaft. Finally, they used string to bind the fins into place.

Will and Jeremy were pleased with their work. This weaponized version was larger and heavier than the ones they had played with as kids, and the sharpened tip was terrifying. They accomplished another goal in that their design was extremely simple, which would allow the darts to be mass-produced with lesser skilled labor.

Leaving the forge, Will threw the large dart only 20 feet in the air before it landed in the hard-packed soil in front of the stables. The dart took the characteristic flightpath the brothers had hoped for, wobbling as it made its way to the apex of its trajectory. Then the weight of the tip pivoted downward as the wind buffeted the fins of the dart, forcing it into a straight downward path until it stuck in the soil.

Phomel was first to reach the dart and crouched down to inspect the point of impact. For the first time, he truly understood the potential of this weapon. After its simple, low-key flight, the dart had driven itself nearly eight inches into the dense dirt, compacted by decades of horse traffic. Phomel turned and stared at the brothers as they joined him, hardly believing his eyes.

He said, "Jeremy, help me get something from the shop."

The two emerged with a large plate of iron and carried it into the center of the compound. The plate was easily twice as thick as any iron used for a helmet. They placed the plate on the ground and walked back to where Will was standing. Phomel hefted the dart and threw it much higher this time. To his amazement, the dart not only penetrated the iron, but sank another four inches into the ground below it.

Phomel was now as enthusiastic as the young men. Josh joined them and they wolfed down an early lunch, then Phomel and the brothers dove into building a scaled-down version of the trebuchet. Josh, left on his own again, set out to explore the neighborhood.

This time, Phomel and the pair concentrated on making far more accurate parts than the crude version they had built earlier. They worked off drawings Jeremy created on the spot. Later, they would put Phomel's formidable blacksmithing skills to good use. After a brief discussion to verify dimensions, Will joined the act by bringing his woodworking ability to bear on the components that would represent large timbers in the full-scale version.

The brothers had to increase the model to a size that would allow the metal parts to be created on the forge, which made the prototype a full six feet tall. Completing the scaled-down version in the late afternoon, they settled on an apple as the projectile of choice for the first test. Their launch sent the apple impressively high in the air but straight up, forcing its builders to scramble for cover.

Jeremy made a slight modification to the adjustable release mechanism he had designed.

"Ok, try it now," he directed.

Will cocked the arm, but this time he allowed Phomel to pull the release lever. On the second flight, the apple sailed high over the compound wall, cleared all the rooftops in sight, and landed with a crash four houses away. Although pleased with their success, they all agreed it best to wait until they had more room before attempting any further experiments. They couldn't wait to see the full-scale version.

The men began disassembling the small trebuchet. They planned to measure each piece painstakingly and modify Jeremy's drawings accordingly. Both Phomel and Will had made small alterations as they created their pieces, and they made further modifications during assembly. These inaccuracies bothered Jeremy as they always did, but Phomel had never seen such exactitude in a hand-sketched design, and one done on the fly at that, just ahead of the assembly.

They had the main structure on the ground and were working to dissemble the larger pieces into manageable components when Commander Namir entered the compound through the store's back door.

Josh followed close behind.

Dispensing with any formalities, Namir began.

"The battle at the pass is going worse than I expected. I want all three of you out of the city and into the countryside. I've tried for the last time to get a council with the king. I'm going now to see if I can persuade Eldest Brother Vableel to lend aid. Regardless, my men and I will do what we can to prevent a complete rout of the guard once the summit is breeched. If that happens, the city walls won't hold an hour."

Namir paused, surveying his small audience's reaction. Just beyond his three young charges, he saw Phomel, standing still and wide-eyed with shock at the news. He had the blacksmith thoroughly investigated when he found out the brothers were spending long days at his compound. It didn't take long to discover here was a man of honor, albeit on the outs with the kingship, and somewhat of a hero around the countryside. Just the man he needed now.

Namir turned squarely toward Phomel.

"I am Commander Namir, High Commander of the Jerimassian Cavalry. These three young men are my charges and are the Summoned Ones of prophecy. I know of you, Phomel. You're a good and honorable man. I am charging you, in the event the city gates should fall, with this task. You are to muster as many able-bodied countrymen as you can and race for Jerimassa with the Summoned Ones."

Phomel was stunned. He kept looking into the faces of the four men before him, as if searching for something that could help him make sense of Namir's startling news. And now he saw these young men in a whole new light.

"Well, man, do you accept the charge or not?"

Namir's harsh question jarred Phomel to his senses.

Weakly, he stammered out an assent. Then, regaining his composure, he forced himself to speak clearly.

"Yes. I accept your charge. They'll make it safely to Jerimassa."

Namir relaxed, smiling at the worried smith.

"Don't be so glum, Phomel. Unlike politically appointed positions here in Karness, we must earn ours in Jerimassa. I've a few tricks that might save enough of the City Guard to hold the walls. And if the walls hold the initial invasion, I doubt there'll be a need for you to leave any time soon. The enemy will set camp, grow their numbers, and slowly probe for weaknesses. All the while, they'll be gathering materials and building siege weapons. So, if we can save enough of the guard to hold that first surge, it will be as long as two weeks before the siege begins in earnest."

Seeing a glimmer of hope in the blacksmith's eyes, Namir turned to the friends before departing.

"I must hurry and make my preparations. You must leave now and don't stop at the palace for any of your things. Go straight through the north gates, and wait for news in the countryside."

Namir sprinted away, leaving the compound the way he had come.

The men looked at one another. Josh was the first to speak.

"Well, let's get this apple thrower ready to travel. I suggest you grab all of your notes and that big lawn dart."

Phomel came to life. "Saddle up five horses. You'll find the tack in the stables. I need to warn Claiphie. She can catch up with us in my mother's village. She'll quietly spread the word among the country folk working in the city.

Phomel started towards the store, shouting over his shoulder, "If the king can't protect them, they'll have to protect themselves."

Josh headed straight for the stables and began readying the horses for travel. Will and Jeremy started breaking down the trebuchet—the goal now was to get subassemblies small enough to be carried on horseback. By the time Phomel returned to the compound, the three friends were mounted. Josh held the reins of Phomel's horse. Claiphie's horse was tethered to a post just outside the rear entrance to the store.

As they rode through the city, they weren't sure if the noise of the fighting was getting louder or if they were just more aware of it. They purposely controlled the pace of their ride and luckily no resistance was offered at the north gate. In no time, they were on the eastward road, heading to the village of Phomel's mother.

As they rode along, Will pulled up beside the blacksmith.

"Why didn't we bring some of your tools, Phomel? With luck, the walls will hold, and we can continue to work on the weapons."

"I have a shop in the village that in many regards is better equipped than the one in the city. This is especially true for the large-scale work we need to do on a full-sized launcher."

Falling silent, Phomel rode on for several minutes. Finally, he felt ready to ask the question that had been bothering him since Namir's revelation about the young men.

Staring ahead, he asked, "Why didn't you tell me?"

Will took a moment to reply, answering with a question of his own. "Would you have allowed us to work alongside you?"

Neither man said anything more as they rode along. In time, they turned off the flagstone-paved road onto a narrower, hard-packed dirt road. Will broke the awkward silence.

"We're still what we said we are, sons of a man that runs a fabrication shop. It wasn't magic or prophecy that allowed us to operate your forge. It was countless hours spent working with our grandfather at his forge."

Will paused as they reached a portion of the road where springs had made the ground soft, leaving deep wagon ruts in the dirt road. Once he navigated this area safely and no longer had to concentrate so hard on his riding, he continued.

"We were brought here by magic from a world very different from yours, yet in many ways quite similar. The people, animals, and plants are almost the same with only subtle differences. The cultures are where we're most dissimilar. We have little or no magic, but we have more advances in technology."

The young man waited for a response. Though Phomel was listening intently, he didn't ask any questions. Will pressed on.

"I've been thinking about this quite a bit. With magic aiding your people, the need for technology hasn't been as great. For example, I've seen your clerics' amazing ability to heal using magic alone. We have similar abilities to heal, but they're based on science and technology. Our technologies allow us to talk over great distances, travel quickly between places, and even fly, but we've made most of these advancements only in the last 100 years."

"Jeremy and I are exceptions in our world. We were taught the old ways of doing things, as well as how to use technology. Very few people have horses, and even fewer would know how to use a forge."

"I'm sorry we didn't tell you earlier. I hope we can still be friends."

Phomel rode on in silence. The trail turned into a wood-lined dry wash. As they climbed out the other side, they began to make their way towards a village in the distance. Finally the blacksmith answered.

"I'm not upset. Not telling everyone you meet is understandable. It's just that it's still a bit overwhelming to me. I'm not sure I ever believed in the prophecies, and I certainly didn't imagine I would meet a Summoned One. Now I find that the High Commander of the greatest cavalry the world has ever known has made me promise to be the protector of three Summoned Ones. And to top it off, these Summoned Ones are people I consider my friends."

Hesitating a moment, he added, "I just need some time. This day has offered a bit more than I can take in right now."

As the small group neared the village, they heard the sound of clanging hammers ringing clearly through the brisk, late-autumn afternoon air. On the edge of town stood a complex of buildings that spanned both sides of the street. The first, a large barn, was surrounded on three sides by corrals. The other four main buildings were forges where all the smiths and their assistants were busily working on various projects. The first forge was obviously a farrier's shop devoted to shodding horses, based on its proximity to the livery stable and the large open-faced lean-to where three horses were leisurely munching on hay.

As they approached the buildings, they slowed their mounts, and the friends eagerly took in the sights. One other forge was located on the same side of the street as the farrier. Judging from the contents hanging from the posts and rafters, it was set up for the manufacture of day-to-day items such as nails, hooks, harnesses, and small hand tools. This forge had two smiths working at a massive forge, each with their own bellows. This setup allowed both men to work independently with their own level of heat, but they had the ability to share resources for projects. Both smiths had two apprenticed helpers, and all were in constant motion.

Directly across the street was a forge designed for farm equipment. The single forge was even larger than its neighboring double forge. The enormous scale of the single forge could easily accommodate plows, wagon parts, scythes, and the metal rims for wheels of any size. Attached to the building housing the forge was a large, timber-framed structure with pulleys and ropes hanging overhead. This, coupled with the four assistants helping the blacksmith, suggested it was a place where large equipment was made and repaired.

The final forge was set up specifically for blades. Everything from kitchen knives to large meat cleavers were at various stages of completion. Those appeared to be well-crafted, but what caught the eye of the brothers were the swords. Everything from small daggers to large, two-handed swords hung from the rafters, representing every step of their processing. A man worked one side of the back-to-back split forge making the utilitarian blades. Based on his attire, he was clearly not a full smith yet, but he was more than an apprentice. This man had a single assistant. The smith on the other side was pulling a glowing ingot from his side of the forge. The smith called out the cadence in a baritone voice as his two assistants hammered away at the glowing red bar, sending sparks in all directions.

As the riders drew near the weapons forge, the smith calling the cadence looked up from his work. The gray-haired man carefully placed the ingot back into the flames and hurried to Phomel's side. The large chest and muscled arms, exposed in an armless vest, seemed out of place on the leathery-faced old man.

"Phomel, we're glad to see you. But we didn't expect you for three days," the master smith said, failing to hide his concern behind a forced smile.

Phomel got right to the point, and his sense of urgency could not be mistaken. "Klaris, I must see the village council at once. I want both of your forges making weapons. No swords or daggers, they take too long. Concentrate on polearms, axes, and hammers. We're looking for quantity, not quality. Get Frond's forge doing the same thing. We won't be shodding horses for a while."

Remembering the young brothers in his charge, he pointed in their direction. "These are my companions, Will and Jeremy. They'll direct the efforts of the other forges. I need to hurry on. They can explain the situation better than I."

Leaving master smith Klaris dumbfounded, Phomel turned to Josh.

"You need to follow me. There's someone here you should meet."

Nudging his horse into a quick trot, Phomel headed towards the center of town. Josh nudged his mount forward to catch up and pulled alongside the blacksmith. Before he could ask, Phomel began to explain.

"I want you to meet an old and dear friend of mine. Will told me of your frustration with the Brotherhood. My friend is the village cleric. He's loosely affiliated with the Brotherhood, but he takes a less structured approach to training his apprentices."

Halfway between the forges and the center of town, Phomel pulled up to a small cottage. A knee-high, white picket fence separated the dirt road from a well-manicured lawn. A small gate gave access to a meandering flagstone walkway that led to a stoop. Vibrant fall flowers were planted along the walkway and encircled the entire house.

Phomel dismounted and tied his horse on a metal ring attached to an intricately designed wrought-iron post. Josh followed his lead and joined him on the stoop. Phomel knocked sharply on the cottage door. The knock was quickly met with a reply.

"Hold your horses! I'll be there in a minute. Give an old man a chance."

Despite the circumstances, a smile crossed Phomel's lips when he heard the occupant grumbling. Then the door opened abruptly and before them stood a white-haired man Josh guessed to be easily in his eighties. It took only a moment for the man to recognize Phomel. He forgot all about his hobbled walk, his cane, and his hands gnarled with age, hands that were almost useless to him now. He reached out to his younger friend and gave him a warm and lasting embrace.

The robed old cleric steadied himself on his cane. Phomel stepped back and smiled warmly at his friend. He gestured towards his companion.

"This is my new friend Josh. He finds himself heavily recruited by the Brotherhood."

Before Phomel could complete his introductions and take his leave, the cleric completed them for him.

"And he's not keen about making a lifetime vow without knowing the commitments or benefits. Come in, young man, let's talk. I am Elinack. Phomel, it seems as if you're in a hurry, as usual. Your friend is in good hands here, as you know. Why don't you run along?"

Phomel had known Elinack his entire life and knew better than to argue with the willful cleric. Besides, he was in a hurry. He nodded at the two and turned to mount his horse, gathered the reins, and headed for the center of town. Turning around in the saddle, Phomel saw the two shake hands before Josh followed Elinack into the cottage. Now that he had Josh taken care of, he began to concentrate his efforts on gathering the elders for an emergency council meeting.

The last High Council had been called 11 years earlier when nomads from the wild country southeast of Karness made armed raids into the villages. When no help was forthcoming from the Karnessian City Guard, the villages formed a militia. After finally repelling the invaders, the decision was made to form wards with eight villages in each, where each ward was responsible for the outfitting and training of 50-man squads. Once a year, a festival was held where the squads of all 12 wards competed to determine the best overall squad.

Each man of the village was required to serve three years in a squad. The region was known throughout all of Bericea for producing the most lethal archers. As soon as they could walk, the village boys and girls were given toy bows by their parents. By nine or ten, they would be aiding families by providing meat for the table with their skills. The bo-staff was used by these same children for personal protection. This weapon could be used to keep wild animals at bay or, as in the case of a few, save their lives from bandit attacks.

An ancient village tradition dictated that teenage boys were taught swordplay by their fathers. By the time the young men were of age to serve in the squads, they were already proficient in the use of a variety of weapons. The primary training they received was fighting from horseback and, more importantly, fighting as a unit. Despite their extensive training, however, rarely did the men serve more than their required years. Therefore, the High Council could typically rely on a regular complement of 600 active squad members. Luckily for the council, many veteran squad members were also available, including over 100 men who had served in the original battles against the wild country nomads.

Six years earlier, Phomel had been given a seat on the council. Not only had he been the youngest person named to the council of elders in this village, he was the youngest anyone could remember in all of Karness. The success of his forges and the wealth it had brought to the village was the original reason for his appointment, but Phomel had strengthened his position with his insightful suggestions and creative solutions.

Phomel conveyed such urgency in his call for an immediate council that most of the elders literally ran to the tavern common room where their meetings were held. Once they were all assembled, the blacksmith wasted no time in relating to his attentive audience the dismal status of the battle for the pass. To impress upon them the accuracy of his information, Phomel decided to reveal the source of his information.

"I cannot doubt the veracity of this news. The scouting report came directly from Commander Namir, High Commander of the Jerimassian Cavalry."

The council erupted. It took some time before Phomel could regain control of the meeting. Namir was a legend throughout Bericea, distinguishing himself in combat long before he was named high commander. Since being named to that office, he had been credited on three different occasions for critical blows to the enemy, blows that prevented them from staging an attack like the one currently being waged.

"Please, calm yourselves. I have good news as well," Phomel shouted over the din. After giving the council members a moment to collect themselves, he continued.

"I have met three promising young men who can help us defeat our enemies. They are brilliant and travel with Commander Namir." At the mention of Namir, an excited murmur ran through the assemblage. "Two are brothers, named Jeremy and Will. The third is called Josh."

"They have shown me the most amazing designs for weaponry. So amazing, I have instructed that my own forges be devoted to the manufacture of their machines. And I have vowed to Namir to protect his young friends should the walls fall. He places much importance on their safety."

Phomel purposely left out the fact that Namir had referred to the young men as "Summoned Ones."

The council wasted no time in making several decisions. First, they agreed to send scouts into the city to observe the battle's progress. To convey any developments regarding the battle, Phomel suggested that a series of riders be placed no further apart than the distance a horse could sprint at full speed without tiring. This way, a written message could reach the villagers quickly, giving them as much advance warning as possible.

Second, the council, with no prompting from Phomel, unanimously agreed to press the entire village into preparing for the village's defense or building the brothers' weapons.

Third, the council's final decision was to straightaway call to order the High Council. Each village was governed by a Council of Elders, and the villages would typically help their neighboring villages in times of need. The High Council was reserved only for dire times that affected all villages.

Pleased with the decisive progress made by the council, Phomel bid them all good evening and took his leave. He was anxious to get back to his charges. As he drew near the complex on the edge of town, he noticed some differences near his forges. Intrigued, he urged his mount forward.

Phomel walked slowly around the open structures and observed the men working, pleasantly surprised by the newfound efficiency of his forges under the brothers' direction. The two had shifted the workmen around in such a manner that Phomel would have expected confusion. Instead, production was moving along at a smart pace.

In the nail and small-tools forge, only apprentices were working, but there were six of them at just this one forge. Instead of the chaos he anticipated, Phomel saw men working in an orderly fashion, either individually or in pairs. Upon closer examination, he was taken aback by the order of operations. Rather than working on a single item till it was completed, the men were working on only one task involved in the manufacturing of each large dart. If a task took longer to accomplish, two men had been assigned to it. They would complete their task and hand the dart off to the person or persons working on the next step. As he watched, the technique made sense to him: the workers didn't need to change tools, and the pieces never had time to cool. This method also pushed the apprentices at the slower tasks to keep up and prevent delay of the next step. To top it off, they had the young boys who typically hung around the shops now helping with menial tasks: fetching coal for the fires, water for the workers, and any other nuisance task that would otherwise have slowed the operation.

The brothers had the men at the large-equipment forge occupied with the full-scale throwing machine. At this forge, Phomel found his smithies hard at work. Detailed drawings with precise measurements were nailed to posts, and pairs of master smiths were diligently pounding out their assigned components. Phomel noticed immediately that these were men he had purposely separated to work different forges because of their constant bickering. The brothers must have done their job in explaining the urgency and importance of the smithies' new role, because the men seemed to have set aside their petty rivalries.

Phomel looked around but saw no sign of the pair. Just as he was about to enquire as to their whereabouts, Will and Jeremy emerged from behind the building that housed the forge. They were pushing a hand cart filled with bricks. Phomel saw they had found his pile of fire brick that he used for repairs. Looking in the direction they were heading, he noticed for the first time a newly constructed forge in the middle of the compound.

Catching sight of Phomel, Will waved and called out, "This one will be exposed to the elements, but it will give us another forge. Besides, with it out in the open, we can use it for final fittings on the larger pieces." The experienced blacksmith nodded his approval and began rolling up his sleeves.

As the morning wore on, the entire village began trickling in to the complex, ready to help. The woodcutters already had enough logs to build half of the first trebuchet. The farmers and teamsters brought these logs to the forges, while Will explained Jeremy's drawings of the joints required for the large timbers to the village carpenters. The wheelwrights began construction of the huge wagon wheels that would support the weight of the trebuchet. These wheels would allow the trebuchet to be transported and maneuvered into new positions for aiming. The villagers who didn't help at the forges gathered farm tools that could easily be turned into weapons and continually ferried materials to the others.

The work continued nonstop until well after dark. Finally, Phomel called everyone together in the street between the buildings of the complex. He waited until he had their complete attention before he began.

"The weapons we're preparing now will be of little use if the wall falls in the next few days. Our only hope in that case will be to gather what we can and flee. In fact, the thrower and darts would have to be destroyed to keep them from the enemy. But do not despair—Commander Namir gave me hope that the walls can hold the initial attack. If so, those walls can be defended for days with only a handful of soldiers. What I'm trying to say is we'll be working on these weapons for some time. We don't want to wear ourselves out on the first day. We'll reassemble at first light."

The tired villagers murmured their agreement and disbanded, heading back toward town to their late suppers and waiting pillows. Phomel and the brothers helped the smithies bank the forge fires. While they were finishing up, Jeremy broached a question to Phomel that had been bothering him all day.

"Why don't the villagers help with the defense of the walls? They were so willing to come help us here, it doesn't make sense."

Phomel shook his head slowly. "Our aid is not welcome. The king and City Guard would never allow it. It would violate their completely twisted sense of honor."

Phomel turned and motioned to the brothers to follow. He led them to a modestly sized but well-appointed house just down the street from the forges.

"We'll spend the night here. Make yourselves comfortable."

Jeremy asked, "Where's Josh? Is he staying here too?

"No, Josh is staying at the home of a dear friend of mine, the village cleric. If anyone can help Josh with his understanding of magic, it will be Elinack."

The brothers woke early to the delicious smell of breakfast cooking. Claiphie, whom they hadn't seen since they left the city, was setting the table in Phomel's large eat-in kitchen. An ornate contraption resembling a pot-belly stove with several metal boxes hanging off it was sitting at the far end of the kitchen. Two frying pans sat on one box, apparently containing sizzling meat, the aroma that woke both of them. A steaming kettle sat atop another box.

Claiphie bid them a cheery good morning and hurried back to the stove. She opened a door on yet another metal box and pulled out a tray full of fluffy biscuits. The stove was well-constructed, its design similar to a combination of commercial kitchen appliances. Phomel walked in as the brothers were admiring the stove.

"The round part my father built for a customer when I was 12. The customer never came for the stove. I bothered him nearly every day for a week with ideas on how to improve it for cooking. Finally, out of frustration, he told me to take it and do whatever I wanted. This is the result."

Phomel waved a hand at the appliance with a grin. In a more serious tone, he added, "It took me all summer to make it. As was my father's way, he never said a word, but he moved it into the house. Claiphie has used it ever since. It makes her cooking taste good." Phomel said the last as he kissed Claiphie on the cheek. Will realized she must have been with the family since Phomel was a boy.

Will said appreciatively, "This is amazing workmanship at any age, let alone at 12."

After breakfast, Phomel, Will, and Jeremy left for the forges. All three were eager to get started again on the one thing they felt would help the defenses the most. As they neared the street, Will and Jeremy saw a very strange carriage. To their great surprise, sitting atop the driver's bench was Josh.

Through the clear, cool late autumn morning air, Will called out, "Morning, Josh. Where are you off to?"

Waving to all three, Josh replied with a grin, "I'm not quite sure. A picnic, I think."

That comment brought a chuckle from Phomel. As they entered the street and headed in the opposite direction of the carriage, toward the forges, he explained.

"Elinack is going to test Josh. He always takes his potential apprentices to a place where no one can get hurt and gives them a challenge to push the limits of their ability. Tasks like digging the largest, deepest hole they can, or stopping the water of a small stream to see how big of a pool they can create."

Upon arriving at the forges, they discovered three apprentices and two master smiths already hard at work readying the fires banked the night before. They already had all but one of the forges roaring with fresh coal. The three wasted no time donning leather aprons and joining the others in the morning preparations.

The sun had just peeked over the horizon as the crew, now at full strength, began hammering away at their respective projects. The brothers were no exception, returning to work on the pieces they had left unfinished the night before. With the hammers ringing out their chaotic rhythms, the villagers began emerging from their houses, eager to help again in some way.

Phomel knew he had only a few hours at the forges before he would have to begin preparations for the High Council. And although he longed to spend the entire day at the forges and lend his skill with a hammer, he knew his first responsibility was to organize the villagers. He called for messengers and had them send word to all the outlying farms. The messengers were to carry news of the battle, and tell the farmers and their families to gather as much food as possible and any weapons or tools that could be converted into weapons. They were to bring their wagons, carts, and draft animals into the village. Phomel set others to preparing meals and drinks, and some to building fences around the fields on the outskirts of town. His plan was to gather all the people together in the village. If flight was their only hope, going en masse would give them their greatest chance. Phomel returned to the forge and hefted his hammer.

At 10:00 a.m., Phomel stopped working and took off his leather apron. He gathered a handful of villagers to assist him, and they left the forges to erect the tent where the High Council would meet. Because it was their village that called the High Council, they would host the event. Even before the tent was up, the first of the representatives from the neighboring villages began to arrive. They stood in awe, watching as an entire village marshaled to serve an unknown cause. Not surprisingly, Phomel saw concern etched on their faces, but he steadfastly refused to answer questions until the full High Council was assembled.

Finally, the last of the village elders arrived, just in time for the 11:00 a.m. start of the High Council meeting. Phomel was relieved that all the members were now accounted for. He realized that those from the outlying villages must have started their journeys within an hour of receiving the invite. That meant some of them had been traveling since 3:00 or 4:00 in the morning. Phomel believed this was a good sign—it meant they were taking this meeting seriously.

The elders of the village had appointed Phomel their spokesman and because his was the host village, he would be the one to start the proceedings. The meetings began with formal protocol, which Phomel rushed through as quickly as he dared. Finishing the roll call, the last event of the formal opening, Phomel jumped straight into describing the dismal situation of the City Guard.

"The plight of the City Guard is a dismal one. They are in grave danger of losing the pass and if that happens, soon after, the city of Karness."

A lone voice challenged, "And just how did you come by this information?"

"It came directly from Commander Namir. He told me himself."

A hush fell over the meeting. Phomel quickly pressed on to describe the lookouts they had posted since, and the relays using multiple horses to transfer information quickly. Phomel sensed that he now had their full attention, and he intended to take full advantage of it. He wasted no time launching into the plans already approved by his council.

Phomel started with the evacuation plan. They would establish fully supplied camps, each separated by a strong day's march. The camps would be guarded by teenagers and aging veterans. These sentinels would wait as long as possible before ordering evacuation. Then, a reserve force of cavalrymen would harass the enemy to slow them. All the while, the people not burdened with supplies would be evacuating as swiftly as possible.

Phomel paused to let the idea of a full-scale evacuation of all the villages sink in. The leaders began talking amongst themselves in hushed tones. Phomel let the internal debates go on for nearly a minute before he resumed.

"But we have no intention of ordering that evacuation. If the walls hold the initial attack after the fall of the pass, we intend to aid in their defense. Together, we can muster a force of over 1,200 soldiers. All well-trained soldiers and capable archers, and many seasoned veterans of conflicts. And we have other ways to aid the defense."

Phomel introduced the brothers, but merely as acquaintances of Namir, leaving out their true identity and his role as their protector. He had asked the two young men to attend, but not merely as a courtesy. Phomel had a specific plan in mind. Earlier in the morning, they had set up the scale-model throwing machine near the meeting tent and covered it with a tarp.

Will demonstrated the trebuchet and Jeremy the militarized darts. From the gasps and whispered comments of the assembly, Phomel could see the display had the effect he had hoped. Back in the meeting tent he spelled out the plan from beginning to end, from calling up the militia with all its reserves, to the full-out effort to build the war machines, to supplying the road in case a retreat was needed. He even went so far as to ask that messengers be sent beyond Karness to ask for aid. He knew they could not go to neighboring cities without the king's permission, but some of the adjoining villages might send help. If nothing else, they could be more cooperative in allowing and protecting the supply lines during the retreat.

After answering questions and accepting some ideas regarding the plan's implementation, Phomel formally called for a vote of the council. Typically, these votes would last for days as debate raged back and forth, and Phomel expected this vote to be very hard to bring to a resolution. This would be the most significant mobilization in the history of the High Council. However, to his surprise and relief, the vote took only minutes and enjoyed unanimous support.

The council members were working out the details and timing of their decision when a lone rider suddenly came racing into the village at breakneck speed. The rider leaned back on the reins, and his horse nearly sat down as it skidded to a stop. The man was flung from the saddle, the momentum of the sudden stop throwing him off balance. He quickly picked himself up and headed straight for Phomel with a crudely rolled parchment clasped tightly in his left hand.

CHAPTER 16

SAVE THE GUARD

Phomel stepped off the wooden platform he had been speaking from and extended his hand to the gasping rider. He quickly scanned the document, a look of resignation settling on his features. He turned to address the council.

"What we feared has come to pass much sooner than we anticipated. The Pass of Karness has been lost, but the walls of the city have held."

Phomel waited for the furor over the announcement to die down. He shared their mixed emotions—the pass had fallen for the first time in history, but the walls had withstood the onslaught of the enemy force. Those assembled fell silent one by one as all eyes turned to Phomel and the document. Taking his cue, the blacksmith continued.

"This is a firsthand account by a scout who witnessed the battle. Bear with me, as it has been written in haste. I will read it to you now."

Phomel nodded his thanks to the rider and stepped back up onto the platform. After reading ahead quickly to himself, he began the scout's narrative.

The sounds of battle intensified greatly this morning, and for the first time I could see the enemy from the vantage point of the city walls. The guards had a slight advantage as they had all been pushed back onto the plateau. This allowed the City Guard more room, while the enemy was bottled into a small area at the top of the pass.

The battle raged on for over an hour, with the enemy making no real progress, even losing some ground to the motivated guard. Then, as suddenly as they appeared on the plateau, the enemy fell back. They were not pushed back but rather methodically fell back. Only moments later I could see them again, this time surging onto the plateau, forming a bulge, allowing more of their numbers to gain the summit. I could clearly see that this surge was led by pallitors and nollax.

Upon hearing the names of creatures thought by most to be myths, those gathered could not contain their emotions and began whispering nervously among themselves. Phomel paused, waiting for order to return, then continued.

As the ranks of the enemy swelled on the plateau, the order among the City Guard began to break down. I watched in horror as I realized any hope for an organized retreat had long passed. As if all the guard came to the same conclusion, small pockets of men broke for the city gates. This seemed to incense the enemy, and they fought with a renewed savagery.

The meeting tent went deathly quiet as Phomel read on.

I realized I was witnessing what could only be considered a complete rout of the City Guard. Glancing back over the wall upon which I sat, only a token number of guards were present, and they were new, unseasoned recruits. I began to pen a quick note for the riders: "All is lost, escape if you can."

But as I finished the words, a most unexpected sight appeared on the plateau. From the shelter of the trees surrounding the falls and river, men on horseback, encircling a half dozen wagons, charged at full speed toward the mass of fighting soldiers.

Phomel paused to catch his breath, as excited as all the others in the tent. Eager to proceed, he plunged ahead.

The wagons were filled with clerics, and the horsemen were the handful of Jerimassian cavalrymen that had been visiting the city. As the newcomers approached the fight, the enemy began to separate from the guards. Both groups looked shocked and frantically tried to reach each other through an impenetrable invisible barrier. The cavalrymen broke out in front of the wagons, forming a V. They made straight for the heart of the enemy as the wagons veered behind the guard.

The cavalrymen were vastly outnumbered; nevertheless, they charged straight into the exposed flank of the enemy, racing their horses parallel to the cliffside, only ten feet from the edge. The effect was devastating—caught completely off guard, the enemy soldiers didn't have time to defend themselves. Many were trampled underfoot or slashed down by the longswords and pikes of the cavalrymen. But by far the most overwhelming tactic was forcing soldiers over the cliff as their comrades scrambled to avoid the onslaught.

The courageous and skilled cavalrymen cut a path clear through the ranks of the enemy and emerged out the other side, losing only one man. Watching the amazing feat unfold, I almost didn't see the nollax that had reached the summit. One by one they flew into the air, only to disappear over the precipice. It had to be the work of the clerics, who were now 50 feet beyond the guards, their wagons pointing toward the gates.

The cavalrymen wheeled around in the open plain beyond the fight and regrouped for another charge. In a booming voice that could be heard easily from the walls, the leader of the cavalrymen shouted, 'Race to the gates, you fools.' No further prompting was needed. The City Guard broke as one. They ran at full speed, racing frantically for the safety of the gates.

The wagons of the clerics didn't advance as the guard raced past and, surprisingly, neither did the enemy. They seemed to be throwing themselves against an unseen barrier. Arrows began to fly from their midst toward the cleric-filled wagons. Just in the nick of time, earth exploded directly behind the wagons, arching up in the air and deflecting nearly all the arrows. Unfortunately, either a few arrows found their mark or the explosion caused some sort of disruption in the clerics' protective spell. Suddenly, the invisible barrier dissolved and the enemy rushed forward in a massive wave.

The wagon drivers didn't react quickly enough and despite moving forward as fast as they could coax the horses to move, it seemed as if they could not avoid being overrun. The horde gained quickly on the heavily loaded, lumbering wagons. The first of the enemy forces were nearly within striking distance and all seemed lost when, seemingly as one, their front ranks tripped and fell headlong to the ground. Others coming behind fell over them, piling atop one another, and I realized that the clerics' unseen barriers were obviously in play again.

The enemy still on the switchback road of the pass gained room when some of their numbers surged forward. More and more were now pouring onto the plateau, and that surge was a tide that could not be contained. The fallen soldiers didn't have a chance, as wave after wave of their fellow soldiers swept over them. However, this brief delay just wasn't enough; the horde would still catch the clerics before they could get their wagons up to speed.

Just when I thought that all was lost, the forgotten cavalrymen once again slammed into the ranks of the lead soldiers. However, this time they didn't cut deep into their rank but rather dealt them a glancing blow. Their intent this time was to slow the advance, not to cause any serious damage. As the cavalrymen pulled away from the enemy, who had bunched up while reeling from the attack, the ground exploded in their midst, sending bodies and debris flying, and leaving men screaming in agony. This surprise coordinated attack gave the wagon drivers just enough time to get their rigs moving at full speed and slowly build distance between themselves and the growing enemy army that spilled onto the plateau.

The battle continued in this fashion, allowing the exhausted City Guard to reach the safety of the gates. The clerics lobbed a continual barrage of fire, earth, and wind at the advancing throng. They did this even as they slowed to pick up the straggling wounded guard. The cavalry had made four more passes on the enemy, each one just preventing the capture of a clerics' wagon. The last of these happened just as the lead wagon entered the gates.

The last of the wagons finally moved within the protective barrier of the walls. The cavalrymen charged at the gates, having just cleared a final pass at the enemy. But, as they did, the gates began closing. I could see that if any cavalrymen made it through at the rate the gates were closing, it would be a precious few. The lead horsemen, seeing what was unfolding, began to hold up their mounts. It was clear they had decided to die with their countrymen. However, when the heavy, iron-clad wooden doors got to within the width of a horse, the doors froze. They shuddered and creaked under the strain, but miraculously remained open until the last cavalryman passed, none other than Commander Namir himself. The moment he cleared the gates, they slammed shut with an echoing boom.

Some of the more-seasoned City Guard members, first to arrive, had recovered enough to race to the top of the walls. Hurling javelins and firing arrows from bows, they quickly repelled the gathering enemy, who was forced to pull out of range. I returned my attention to the chaos of the parade ground just inside the gates. I saw that it must have been Eldest Brother Vableel who held the doors open. He had collapsed from the strain into the arms of the clerics surrounding him.

Some of the guard were congratulating the still-mounted cavalrymen when an order rang out.

"Arrest those men!"

Those gathered turned in unison to see the king, fully decked out in his gaudy, gold-trimmed armor, sitting astride his white stallion. The king had positioned himself on the main road leading from the parade grounds and up into the city. Looking down on everyone below and pointing toward the cavalrymen, the king shouted again.

"I said arrest those men! They violated my direct order to stay out of our fight."

No one moved, all stunned by the absurdity of the command.

The king, red-faced with rage, shouted almost hysterically at his men.

"Are you violating a direct order as well? I said arrest them. Now!"

Some of the guards reluctantly turned toward the cavalrymen. Then, before they could react to the king's demand, a booming voice, far more loud and forceful than the king's, filled the air.

"No arrests will be made today."

Recovering his strength, Vableel added in disgust, "Thanks to these brave men, you have a wall to defend and soldiers with which to defend it. I suggest you get to it."

With that, Vableel and his clerics marched out of the parade grounds, followed by the cavalrymen. They moved past the outraged king without a glance. Although simmering with anger, the king held his tongue, unwilling to challenge the powerful cleric.

Phomel stood quietly, as moved by the story as his audience. Then he carefully rerolled the parchment.

"I think we could all use some time to digest these developments. Refreshments are waiting at the tavern."

Typically, this remark would have caused a stampede, but this day certainly wasn't typical. All assembled remained in their seats trying to absorb the scout's news. Finally, a few stirred, but rather than getting up and making for the tavern, they began talking quietly amongst themselves. Phomel was about to formally call for a recess to the proceedings when he saw, through a gap in the back of the tent, a group of riders approaching. They stopped at the forges but soon continued towards the council tent. As they came closer, Phomel could see it was the Jerimassian cavalrymen with Commander Namir in the lead.

The horses were close enough now that the hoofs hitting the packed earth of the street could be heard over the discussion. The entire assembly turned as one and soon recognized the riders. Spontaneous cheers rang out of "Namir" and "Jerimassa." The cavalry was startled at first but proceeded until they were just outside the tent. Dismounting, the seasoned soldiers stood stoically holding the reins of their horses as their commander approached the tent.

Namir walked through the cheering crowd and right up to Phomel.

The cheering gradually quieted.

"I see you already have news of the battle. Just outside the parade grounds, the clerics insisted on healing our wounds. They were in such a hurry we were still mounted and in the middle of the street. While that was happening, I saw a horseman racing through the back streets of the city at top speed. After the healings, I decided we should see where the rider headed. It didn't take long to discover the line of exhausted horses, which eventually led us here. That was quite a clever approach for a non-cavalryman. I see I entrusted my friends to the right man."

Phomel smiled, filled with pride at the comment. Extending his hand to Namir, the two shook hands. Cheers erupted again from the crowd.

When the cheers died down, Namir commented, "There seems to be a lot going on in this small village. What is happening here?"

Phomel quickly covered the decision of the High Council to aid in the city's defense. When Phomel related the number of troops that could be brought to bear, Namir was encouraged. Once he had heard all the details of the plan, or at least all they had formulated so far, he asked for a demonstration of the brothers' throwing device. The two were more than eager to show Namir its capabilities.

Namir had been nearly hopeless when he left the city. He second-guessed his decision that had cost four good men, a decision that had merely served to postpone the inevitable. Even if Bleck, the rider he had sent for help the day he arrived in the city, made it to Jerimassa, it would be several weeks before the first troops would arrive. Now he felt there was a slight chance and some hope where none existed before.

The council took very little time to decide that Namir should lead the defense, and he agreed only because of their unanimous support. After Namir accepted the appointment, Phomel addressed Namir in front of the council.

"Thanks to you, we now have time for planning and preparation. I had just called for a refreshment break. I think we're ready for that now," Phomel said, smiling and gesturing in the direction of the tavern.

The response to Phomel's request this time was immediate and enthusiastic. Cheers rang out, and the entire council headed towards the tavern. Phomel quickly made arrangements for the cavalrymen's horses to be properly tended. On his way to the tavern, Namir fell in beside Phomel.

"I've seen the brothers, but where is Josh?"

Phomel pointed into the distance, and said, "He's with a close cleric friend of mine, receiving training. They're at a glen just over that rise."

No sooner had the words left his mouth than a huge column of water produced a massive fountain, far taller than the trees. It was in the same direction Phomel was pointing. Namir didn't hesitate—he raced to catch the man leading his horse to the stables.

Josh woke to the sound of pans clanging. He had spent the night on the floor of the small cottage, in the front room that took up half the dwelling. The other half consisted of the kitchen and the cleric's bedroom. The pleasant smell of breakfast fare permeated the air. Josh roused himself and moved to a small washstand in the corner, near the bedroom door. He poured half the pitcher of water into the ceramic pan and began splashing his face.

Josh needed the bracing effect of the cool water on his skin. It had been a long night, and he and the cleric had talked well into the early morning hours. He lit the sole lamp in the room. It was so early that the first light of dawn had not yet come. Elinack had finally sent Josh off to bed and warned it was going to be an early morning, but Josh had never expected it to be this early. Still, after the long night's talk, Josh was excited about the prospects of the day ahead.

He had learned more about magic in one night than he had in the last three weeks dealing with the brotherhood. He learned of the two types of magic, the four disciplines, the morphing of some magic users into nollax, and of most people's fears and prejudices toward the use of magic. Some of these things had been hinted at but never discussed in the detail provided by Elinack, and definitely not with his enthusiasm and vigor.

Yet this newfound knowledge was not the reason for Josh's excitement, especially after so little sleep. It was because of the challenge Elinack had issued him. They had been sitting at the kitchen table, but near the end of their talk, Elinack stood and made a surprise announcement.

"Well, young man, it's high time we see just where your talents lie. Follow me."

Using his ever-present cane, Elinack shuffled off into the front room. Josh placed their coffee cups in the dry sink and followed. As he entered the room, Elinack turned and handed him a small stringed instrument. Josh took it gingerly, wondering what Elinack expected of him. He turned it over in his hands, examining it carefully. It had seven strings and a hollow body that ran nearly its entire length, much like a dulcimer, but its wooden-topped base was nearly perfectly round like a banjo.

Out of habit, Josh thumbed each string one at a time, checking the tuning. He was surprised at just how out of tune it was. Elinack moved over to the fireplace and spoke softly to his new pupil.

"I'd restart this fire, but my kindling has run out. Why don't you put the heat from those hot coals into the end of this poker? We'll then see if it can be used to start a fire."

Josh remembered that magic could be amplified with a catalyst. The hot coals would be the catalyst he needed. Josh mentally walked through the evening's discussion with Elinack. He had always been good at memorization. Although not the smartest kid in school by any means, Josh had always managed to get decent grades by memorizing the lessons. He had a way of purging some things he learned while retaining others. For example, he had thousands of songs committed to memory. In the case of the cleric's lessons, he was quite determined to remember all of them.

Josh found that he had changed since coming to this new world. In addition to his excellent memory, he now had a mental acuity he never had before. It wasn't that he thought he had become more intelligent, not at all. It just seemed as if worries that had plagued his mind in the past were gone. To himself, he thought of it as living in the present, and his goals were simple and clear.

Thinking through the songs he could use for the task set before him, he decided on an old blues song his dad had played on a 78-rpm record. It had the strong beat needed to draw the magic required for the discipline of fire. The other reason he chose the tune was the instrument. It was tuned most closely to the open E-note. The song he was thinking of had originally been recorded on a guitar open-tuned to E, using a slide.

Josh brushed the white ash off the coals and blew them into red-hot embers. He quickly tuned the instrument to his satisfaction and laid the poker on the hearth, with the end extending into the fireplace near the coals. He decided to sit on the edge of the hearth and settled the small but bulky instrument on his lap. Finally, he broke off a finger-long piece of a stick that was bark-free to use as a slide.

Now that he had everything ready, Josh cleared his mind of all but the song and began. The long acoustic introduction built slowly in tempo. He felt it would be perfect to draw the magic, as Elinack had instructed. Josh knew he had been given a task for Caleen, the magic invoked using instruments only. However, by the time he reached the point in the song where the vocals began, he was already feeling the tingle from the drawn magic throughout his body. So he began to sing. It just felt right.

Elinack took a step back, unsure what to expect when the large amount of magic gathered by his new apprentice would be released. He had owned that instrument for over 50 years, with dozens of apprentices playing it, but never had it been played in this fashion, or so well. Elinack was startled when Josh started singing, but the vocals blended seamlessly with the instrument and seemed a natural fit.

The song built to a crescendo, then ended abruptly. The sudden silence startled Elinack. Looking into the fireplace, he saw the poker's original position unchanged, but the glowing coals of a moment ago had been reduced to piles of ash.

Anxious to see the results, Elinack gathered some larger pieces of wood and placed them in the fireplace. Retrieving the poker, he laid the end against the log. Where it touched the log, it instantly burst into flames as if oil had been used. Touching the logs in areas that had yet to ignite, they too burst into flames. Elinack stood holding the poker in front of him, unsure what he had just witnessed. He used the poker five times, each time with the same result.

"Did I do what you expected of me?"

Elinack looked at Josh, still a bit bewildered.

"Not exactly."

Seeing the dejected look on Josh's face, Elinack explained, "I would have expected an apprentice, with what little the brotherhood taught you and our one night's conversation, to either accomplish nothing or to produce little more than a puff of smoke. Not only have you gone far beyond that, you've exceeded what I would expect from someone who had spent their entire life using Caleen."

"But how?"

"I think it was the result of combining voice and instrument. Typically, the methods are kept separate. I myself have experimented with combining them, but it always resulted in an instant release of the Radece magic, and each time I destroyed the object my magic was focused on. I made a handful of additional attempts with similar results, and everyone I have spoken with related similar experiences," explained Elinack.

"If an accomplished magician were to produce the same object as you just did, it would have taken weeks. He would have had to produce large fires and then transfer the heat from those into the object. He would have layered each use one at a time into the poker."

"Ancient magical artifacts are almost always more powerful than the modern versions. Also, from the markings, it appeared that one individual made several of the objects. We always thought that was impossible, because it would take a lifetime to produce objects of that power. So, the symbols had to represent an entire religious sect. Your first use of magic for me has shattered those beliefs."

Elinack suddenly seemed to remember the lateness of the hour and decided to halt his instructions for the evening.

"Well, we should both be plenty warm tonight. Let's get to bed. I can hardly wait for you to try using only your voice tomorrow on a more challenging task. I imagine you'll be tired enough to sleep well after what you've achieved tonight."

Elinack smiled at the bemused young man and moved off towards his small bedroom, closing the door quietly behind him.

The two men sat down to breakfast and began eating quickly, eager to start the day. Although the meal was a brief affair, Elinack didn't pass up the opportunity to impart a few more instructions to Josh. His approach had always been to overload each pupil, to feed as much information at an apprentice as possible, until they cried for mercy. Their capitulation typically came within the first hour. It was different with this one. Josh not only listened but seemed to understand, and eagerly awaited more.

After breakfast, Elinack made Josh leave the dishes and directed him out the back door. Josh found himself on a flower-lined path to a small building that served as both a carriage house and stable. The stable consisted of a single stall that opened into a little paddock, and a carriage house closed off by double doors. It was just large enough to house the strangest carriage Josh had ever seen.

The carriage could best be described as a stage coach, but a completely open one. The driver's long bench was suspended high in the air, while the passenger area consisted of a single overstuffed chair slung low between the axles, suspended by heavy leather straps. The chair was also mounted on springs, as if the swinging straps were not enough, and the carriage itself was affixed to an elaborate and complex suspension system. It was obvious the entire purpose of the carriage was to afford the occupant of that chair the most comfortable ride possible.

Elinack explained, "This ugly contraption is the brainchild of that worthless blacksmith who brought you here."

Josh understood the comment was made with great affection. The old man's voice always filled with pride when he spoke of Phomel, and this time was no exception. Elinack instructed Josh on hitching the carriage.

"I'll leave you to it. When you're done, bring it round front," the cleric ordered. Elinack turned back towards the cottage and headed up the picturesque path.

As he hitched up Elinack's sturdy horse to the carriage, Josh thought of how glad he was to have Pattie as a close friend. One summer, her father had decided to buy eight young draft horses to train and sell. One day at school, Pattie confided to Josh and the others that the care and training of the horses had become too much for the family to handle. They had begun arguing constantly, which was rare for the close-knit clan. Without hesitation, all the friends offered their help. Steve cancelled one trip and would have postponed another if Pattie hadn't insisted that he go. Using the knowledge he gained that summer, it took Josh only a few minutes to get the carriage ready.

Josh settled himself on the driver's bench and coaxed the horse around to the front of the cottage. He waited for Elinack to emerge and thought about his friends. He worried about them at times, but he always felt in his heart that they were safe. He sensed that he would know somehow if they were ever in trouble. As if his thoughts had invoked them, he saw Jeremy and Will with Phomel, emerging from a house up the street. Will spied Josh atop the carriage and the two had a brief exchange before he hurried off with his brother and the blacksmith toward the forges.

Josh thought they seemed to be in a terrible hurry, or maybe they were just not very curious about his plans for the day. Phomel had seemed amused at the mention of a picnic. Only a moment after the men had departed, Josh heard Elinack coming out of the cottage. He was struggling with a large basket. Josh quickly set the brake, tied off the reins, and rushed to help his new instructor.

Josh helped the cleric into the strange seat and waited for his instructions.

"Drive the carriage down the main street and out of town."

It didn't take long for them to reach their destination. Elinack directed him to a beautiful, secluded glen, a little over a mile from the village. The view back was blocked by a rise, and heavy woods completely surrounded the glen. Despite the coming of fall, enough leaves clung stubbornly to the trees, such that the glen seemed cut off from the rest of the world.

A brook cut diagonally across the glen. It was fast-moving, less than a foot deep and just narrow enough to jump across, except in two places, where larger pools formed and the water slowed. The glen was dotted with massive trees that offered intermittent shade, but not too much that would stunt the grass that dominated the tranquil setting.

Elinack instructed Josh to drive the carriage toward the middle of the glen and stop near one of the large trees, an easy walking distance from the water. Josh brought the carriage to a halt only a few feet from an area of well-manicured grass. A well-worn path led from this small oasis where they parked to the stream.

Elinack opened a panel directly in front of him. The lid was hinged at the top and slid up and under Josh's seat, like the doors of a barrister bookcase. The opened panel revealed a set of finely crafted drawers, from which Elinack removed blankets and canvas chairs.

Once the chairs and blankets were unloaded and arranged to Elinack's satisfaction, the training started in earnest. He had decided to renew his efforts to reach the breaking point of his new pupil. However, after an hour of poring through excruciating details of complex tempos, rhythms, and the subtleties of various types of magic, the typically inexhaustible instructor found that he was the one in need of a break. Not only had his pupil retained most of what Elinack had thrown at him, judging from the small tests administered along the way, Josh had all but mastered each concept.

Elinack produced some wine from his large basket. While the two were enjoying their drinks, Elinack posed the question that had been puzzling him since the night before.

"If you've never performed magic until now, how is it you know so much about music?"

Josh could hardly conceal his embarrassment at the question. Elinack could tell the young man was struggling over his answer, but he soon seemed to reach a decision.

"There's something about me that you should know."

Elinack nodded encouragingly.

"Namir instructed us to keep this to ourselves, but I believe you need this knowledge to help you with my instruction."

Elinack waited patiently, his eyes never leaving the young man's face, and continued sipping his wine.

"This is going to sound very strange to you, but I'm not from this world. Namir and his men, they're calling me a Summoned One."

The old man sputtered and spilled wine down his front. Josh waited while he scrambled to contain the mess. After he had cleaned the wine up as best he could, Elinack sat back in silence and regarded his pupil with wide eyes. When Josh realized no response was forthcoming, he continued.

"On my world, music doesn't invoke magic. In fact, magic is regarded by many as merely an illusion, mere tricks or sleight of hand. It's also true that many people on my world devote their entire lives to music. I'm one of those, a musician. So, I understand and can perform music that is far more complex than what you have shown me. What I still don't understand is which music is linked to the different aspects of magic, and what impact the magic has on me."

Elinack had regained some of his composure. Refilling his glass, he spoke carefully, as if he were weighing his words.

"A Summoned One. I'm not sure I would have taken you on as a pupil if I'd have known. This is a tremendous responsibility. The prophecy clearly calls out only two Summoned Ones as magic users. One is a healer, the other is as great as the best of the ancients. How could I possibly be qualified to be your instructor?"

"You've taught me more in the few hours we've been together than in the weeks I spent with the Brotherhood. I'm sure that, even if I took their vows, the training would not progress any faster. If not you, who could I turn to, or trust for that matter?" Josh said this with a determination that left no doubt he wanted Elinack's instruction to continue.

Pondering Josh's forceful response, the old cleric finally came to a decision.

"I'll help you as much as I can. But you must promise me that when my instruction no longer aids you, you'll seek another's counsel."

Josh nodded his agreement, and Elinack turned his instruction to the conservation of energy.

"Even the best magic users have a limited amount of energy to devote to magic use. At some point, every magic user must rest before they can continue. The key is to be smart about how you use the limited energy available to you. Pushing hard into your reserves will leave you feeling as if you've run a long distance. If you push too far, you could pass out. It is even possible you could die."

"The trick is to be clever about how you use magic to accomplish your goal. For example, if you wanted to create a bridge over a fast-moving stream, you might create a bridge of air. However, on a breezeless day, that would prove far more taxing than using the earth from the banks."

Listening to this explanation, Josh offered an alternative.

"If it were a small party, maybe you wouldn't need a bridge at all. All you would need to do is hold back the water enough for them to ford the stream."

This observation brought a brief smile to Elinack's normally placid face. He pressed on, describing mundane items for aid.

"Drawing heat from the air for fire is daunting, but just a small ember makes it far easier. And the larger the source that aids you, the more that can be done with less of your own energy."

Elinack spent the rest of the morning on demonstrations that he purposely kept small in scope. The cleric explained to Josh that keeping them small served two purposes: to introduce many of the basic songs from each of the disciplines without tiring Josh out, and to teach the art of control. To that end, each exercise had very specific parameters, such as enlarging a flame to a certain height but no higher. Elinack did the demonstrations one a time, asking Josh to repeat each one before moving on to the next. Josh struggled at first to understand the magnitude of his newfound powers, but as the morning wore on, he began to perform each exercise flawlessly.

Elinack grew more impressed with each challenge his new pupil conquered, as Josh eagerly tackled one exercise after another. Unfortunately, caught up in the excitement of the moment and eager to discover the boundaries of the young man's talent, Elinack neglected to conserve Josh's energy. Even though these small challenges required Josh to rest only briefly in between, Elinack knew his pupil would need a thorough respite to recover his full strength. Well, it couldn't be helped now, Elinack thought. He motioned to Josh to take a seat and began to demonstrate drawing water from a pitcher.

After the display, during which a column of water rose ten feet into the air before arcing over into the nearby grass, Josh offered an observation.

"You used a combination of both water and air songs. They were interwoven, but each one was unmistakably used."

"Very impressive," replied Elinack. "Some students take years to understand that concept."

Josh couldn't believe Elinack's admission. Having composed music for years, these concepts were very basic, almost second nature, to him. Josh realized that the extremely restrictive way in which music was treated on this world would hold back even the most naturally talented musicians.

The long morning and water fountain display had also fatigued Elinack, but he was reluctant to interrupt their activities just yet. He wanted to gauge the true boundaries of his remarkable pupil's abilities.

"We've covered quite a bit, Josh, but do you think you can complete one test more before lunch? One that should reveal your limits. Go to the stream and copy what I've just done. Create the largest water fountain you can and make it rise as high as you can."

Josh at last seemed reluctant. "Won't that be dangerous for me?"

Elinack replied with a chuckle, "Don't worry. People who died from using too much energy did so by doggedly forcing themselves way past reasonable limits. The worst that could happen to you is fainting, and even that is very unlikely."

Such a possibility hadn't even occurred to Josh. He was more worried about the weight of the water crashing down over him. He nodded his assent, already deep in thought. He considered his approach as he covered the distance to the stream. Elinack began setting up their lunch. He was convinced this exercise would result in the total exhaustion of his new apprentice. A lunch and a nap would be needed before any more instruction.

Josh stood at the bank, his plan finalized. He now composed the tune he would use. He used tunes he was familiar with, but that closely resembled the basic tunes of the morning's lessons. The most complicated part of the composition was interweaving the tune fragments into a coherent song. After a few minutes, he felt ready. It helped that he seemed to know instinctively that the exact words were not as important as the feelings behind them.

Josh had learned to draw the magic needed and then use his mind to focus that energy. The secret was to make your mind a blank slate as you called the energy. He found that keeping his mind clear and focusing his thoughts was much easier since arriving in this new world.

Josh began slowly testing his composition, concentrating solely on the song itself. He felt energy begin to surge into him. His confidence bolstered, he increased the volume and tempo of the tune. He continued building the energy, wanting badly to impress the old cleric. An impressive accomplishment here would go far towards proving that Elinack's instruction had been worthwhile and should continue.

The hair on Josh's arms stood straight up, and he could feel the energy of the magic as it spiraled around, literally coursing through him. Once he had collected all the magic he thought would need, Josh concentrated on his predetermined plan. His thoughts were in laser focus—not even the thought of failure interfered now.

Elinack had had the picnic laid out for a while now. He decided to walk over and see why Josh was having trouble. It was taking considerably longer than he thought it should. From everything he had accomplished thus far, surely the boy could produce a fountain that could be seen from this distance. Shaking his head, Elinack started walking toward the stream. He had taken only a few steps when suddenly the ground shook beneath his feet, and the entire stream in front of Josh shot skyward!

The stream had changed course and was now flowing straight up into the air, already well above the trees and still climbing. At nearly 200 feet, the fountain abruptly ceased its ascent and began fanning out in all directions. The vast amount of water soaked everything within a large radius. It even reached Elinack and the carriage, though at that distance it merely had the effect of a light shower.

The magnificent display lasted a full minute, until finally the column of water came crashing back to the earth, filling the void between the banks once again. Elinack was too dumbfounded to react, recovering only once he realized that the bulk of the enormous column had landed directly on Josh. The horror he felt was almost immediately replaced by amazement. He could hardly believe his eyes, but he was sure he saw a clear dome over Josh, just large enough to protect him. Water was still dripping from it, but the boy's clothes were dry, which meant the dome had to have been in place from the beginning.

Elinack knew he had just witnessed the single largest expenditure ever of magic by an individual. And, as if that were not enough, the boy was walking back towards him unharmed. By all rights, he should be dead or, at the very least, unconscious. Elinack stood staring at the young man as he approached, trying to comprehend what he had just seen. Josh finally reached the clearing. He looked at the old cleric expectantly.

"How did I do? I know I expanded the volume of the water too much in the air tube. I didn't plan on that much pressure, sorry about that."

CHAPTER 17

CROSS EXAMINED

Pattie was healing a soldier with an arm badly broken at the elbow, oblivious to the stir she was causing across camp. No longer did she hide her healing powers from the others. All pretense was gone now that Varis had stood up for her, and her beautiful voice carried easily across the short distance to Rayde. The rebel leader could scarcely believe his eyes. A female Reenone was rare enough in Carsanic, but a female healer was unheard of since ancient times. The brazen young man wasted no more time before pursuing his latest conquest and strode purposefully toward the girl.

Rayde stopped just behind Pattie, who was kneeling beside her patient. In a playful tone, he asked no one in particular, "What will the Bericeans think of next! They send what has to be their most beautiful woman into enemy territory to perform healing?"

Pattie completed her ministrations and turned to see a handsome young man with his hands on his hips smiling down at her. Caught completely off-guard, she could feel her face burning and was too discomfited to reply. Rayde extended his hand to help her to her feet.

"My name is Rayde," the tall miscreant said as he pulled her to her feet quickly enough to make her stumble. She fell into his waiting arms, blushing furiously, and quickly pulled away. Rayde threw back his head and barked an infectious laugh.

Steve watched the entire exchange, agitated and conflicted. Upon first observing Commander Darnon's lukewarm reaction to Rayde, he had made up his mind to bring the two together in some sort of alliance. Steve understood that an ally in command of so many men and familiar with the territory would be invaluable. Plus, his initial gut feeling had been to trust the outgoing rebel leader, even to like him.

Rayde's laughter ceased abruptly when he saw Pattie's patient stand and pull his sword with his bad arm. The man took a few tentative swings and smiled gratefully in Pattie's direction. He then began testing his newly healed limb in earnest, each swing more aggressive than the last. Rayde was speechless as he watched the display. The best Carsanicean healer would never have been able to restore an arm that badly broken.

Seeing Rayde distracted by the soldier, Steve decided it was the perfect opportunity to inject himself into the situation. As he walked toward Pattie, a sudden realization hit him—he cared deeply for her and was downright jealous of this Rayde fellow. He was also ashamed of himself. It had taken this brash stranger to force Steve to finally admit something he had known for some time. His thoughts drifted back to holding Pattie as they stood in the river. The circumstances hadn't been ideal considering his physical wound and her mental ones, but holding her and comforting her felt perfectly right, as if he had come home.

As Steve approached, he heard Pattie recover and defuse the awkward situation. He was relieved to see Pattie putting a quick end to the rebel's advances.

"Nice to meet you Rayde but, as you can see, I'm quite busy."

She didn't wait for a reply, turning away and moving on to the next injured soldier. She was flattered by the tall, handsome man's attention. He was nice to look at, Pattie had to admit, but he wasn't someone she would ever be interested in. She sighed, suddenly feeling exhausted, and went on about her work.

Pattie was tiring quickly now. Varis watched her, concerned that her healing energies would be consumed before her work at the camp was done. He and the other clerics were astounded by the number of patients she had already healed. Varis had aided her with a few healings, partly so she could conserve her energy and partly so he could use his mind to journey into the patient and see exactly what Pattie was doing. He didn't begin to understand all she was accomplishing, and he couldn't believe the exhaustive level of detail at which she worked. He concluded that her stamina could only be derived, at least in part, from taking the time to attend to each microscopic part of a wound in excruciating detail. Pattie would start at the deepest part of an injury and methodically work her way out, going over a tiny section and healing it before she moved on. The other clerics healed large portions of a wound all at once.

Regardless of the reason for her stamina, it was noticeably failing her now. Four seriously injured soldiers still awaited treatment, and Varis was certain Pattie wouldn't last long enough to heal them all. Unfortunately, if any of the other clerics healed them, there was a good chance these men would never fight again. He himself no longer had the strength to lend her, so Varis decided the best course of action would be to encourage the other clerics to assist. As he expected, they all jumped at the chance, hoping to learn how the young woman could be so effective in her healing while conserving her powers.

Steve strode up to the rebel as the clerics surrounded Pattie. The tall young man was still grinning in Pattie's direction, and turned to look at the newcomer who was offering his hand.

"Hello. My name is Steve. Thanks for the help back there."

Rayde gripped Steve's hand firmly, fixing the newcomer with a curious expression.

Steve had stopped using the language token altogether. Not only had he mastered most of the common words and phrases, but he had taken to using the same dialect as Darnon. His use of the Bericean accent wasn't missed by Rayde.

"I am Rayde, and any enemy of Zybaro is an ally of ours. You must be from Bericea, but I've never heard the name 'Steve' used before."

"You're very perceptive. Actually my friends and I have just traveled from a remote area of Bericea," Steve lied. He nodded in Pattie's direction. "Pattie you've just met, Brandon is over there talking to your sister, and also Gloria, who's around here somewhere."

Steve added, "You see, I study languages. Bericean isn't my native tongue, but I've used my skill with language to pick up the Carsanicean dialect." Steve had switched over as he spoke, mimicking Rayde's strong accent nearly perfectly.

Rayde laughed as he heard his own speech being echoed back to him. "I wager in no time you would be speaking Carsanicean. It's an ancient and beautiful language."

Steve responded eagerly, "I'd love the opportunity to learn your language. Maybe after the camps are set, I could stop by and hear some of the dialect."

"On one condition. You bring your friends. I've some business I must attend to. I'll see you in a few hours," said Rayde and left without waiting for Steve's reply.

The next few hours passed uneventfully. Pattie and the clerics tended to the remaining four soldiers with success as Varis looked on approvingly. Eventually, the four friends gathered to set up camp.

To Steve's surprise, Gloria was unusually excited when he told the group they had all been invited to the rebels' camp for the evening. Gloria had come out of her hiding place too late to be introduced to Rayde when he first arrived. Evidently, when she finally did spot him, she had spent much time and energy trying to find out who he was. She was attracted to his good looks, but more so by the number of troops the young man led.

The preparations for the night's camp went smoothly. Pattie, exhausted from the day's healing, slept straight through the noisy activity surrounding her. Gloria moved her campsite near the others and actually pitched in to cover Pattie's share of the work. After the camp was in order, the friends also rested, in part to let Pattie sleep and to give the rebels time to set up their own camps for the night.

Later that evening, after Pattie had awakened and washed up, the four began picking their way through the camp in the direction of the rebels. Kail and a few of his men stepped out of a campsite as the group passed and joined them.

"We caught word of your visit to the rebels. Darnon wants to know if any among you disclosed that you are the Summoned Ones." Each friend indicated they had not.

"Well, Darnon thinks it best to keep it that way, and he's ordered us to accompany you tonight to ensure your safety."

The now larger group made their way out of the Bericean camp and into the rebels' environs. Their invitation must have been communicated, as their presence hardly caused a second look. It was easy to spot their destination: three brightly colored tents marked the center of the camp. A large deep-red tent was flanked by smaller turquoise and emerald-green ones.

They could hear raucous laughter coming from the large tent. The tent was closed but, as the group approached, Rayde threw open the largest flap and greeted them warmly. His sister peered over his shoulder at them, smiling, and looking beyond the pair, the friends could see dozens of men and women sitting on cushions upon the rug-covered floor of the tent.

"Come in, new friends! I'm pleased to see you've brought others to join in our festivities. It's our custom to celebrate after every victory, and today has certainly brought us all great success." Rayde ushered the small group into the warm tent, flashing a white smile at Pattie. The merrymakers brought mead and wine to the friends and their escorts. Kail and the soldiers declined their offerings. When pressed, Kail explained briefly that they were on duty, and the friends were in their charge. This seemed to intrigue Rayde and Jasheal, and Steve noticed they exchanged quizzical looks.

After two drinks, Steve asked the whereabouts of the latrine and was directed to the wooded edge of the glen. Pattie overheard and gestured to Steve that she would accompany him.

Once outside, Steve said, "I'm certain they're trying to get us drunk. They're milking their drinks and filling ours. I've seen the same thing done at frat parties."

Pattie laughed. "You've seen it? Oh, I bet." She stopped in front of him, putting her hand gently on his chest. "But I agree with you. I've got an idea. Let me try something on you."

She looked into his eyes and began a soft, pleasant song. She was attempting to force Steve's internal organs into a sort of overdrive; this would force the alcohol in his system to be processed very rapidly. Steve didn't know what Pattie was up to, but he knew he was beginning to feel light-headed. Just as he was about to protest, the sensation passed and he suddenly felt completely sober.

Steve wondered anew at her talent and smiled. "It worked! That's amazing. Can you do that to yourself?"

"I think so. I'll stay here and try. When you go back inside, send Brandon to me. And if you can pry Gloria from Rayde's side, send her a bit later."

When Gloria came outside, she was at first reluctant to cooperate with any plan of Pattie's. Once she had experienced her first "healing," however, she seemed very pleased with the results. Pattie was relieved that Gloria acquiesced, but she couldn't help feeling disturbed by something the difficult young woman said over her shoulder as she returned to the festivities. "I wonder what other influences your magic could have on someone's mind."

All evening, the four friends repeated their routine of drinking with the others, then excusing themselves to slip outside and heal through Pattie's song. The foursome had agreed to act more and more affected by the drinks to try and get to bottom of why they had really been invited to the rebel camp. At first, their plan worked beautifully. As the evening progressed, however, the rebels began accompanying them outside to the latrine. This made it difficult for Pattie to work her healing magic, so the friends unobtrusively slowed their drinking.

Steve was quiet as the party went on, seemingly content to let Brandon, Pattie, and Gloria do most of the talking. He engaged in conversation only when asked a direct question, or when he wanted something repeated. He was concentrating on the speech patterns of the rebels, who had realized early in the evening that some sort of magic was in play. An elder member of the rebels stopped the conversation and stated as much. After producing the language tokens and explaining their function, Steve was able to diffuse the tension in the tent. Relieved that no foul play was involved, the rebels relaxed and the atmosphere in the tent returned to normal. Steve relied on his technique of intermittent use. He would wear the token for a while, then take it off. Towards the end of the evening, he was able to engage in simple conversation without the language token. He also memorized several complicated words and phrases for later use.

Eventually, the reason they were being plied with liquor surfaced. Rayde, Jasheal, and the other rebels began questioning their guests.

Rayde asked casually, "Where are you from, and what is your purpose here?"

The four gave the answer they had agreed to on the way over to the camp: they were all representatives of the newest city in Bericea called Kentucky. Rayde permitted their vague responses to his more pointed questions as he played the role of the polite host. As the festivities wore down, though, Jasheal and the other rebels joined in and began a more specific and insistent line of questioning.

They wanted to know why a Bericean army of this size was in Malabrim, and what the army's final destination was. The friends continued to offer as little information and as much useless speculation as possible while doing a little probing of their own. At times, the frustrated rebels adopted a more aggressive style of questioning. More than once Kail started to rise, on the verge of stepping in to halt the inquisition, but sank back down when he saw his charges holding their own.

To distract their hosts, Pattie brought up the subject of Kail and Brandon, and how they would sometimes work out together before breaking camp. This odd pairing and their workouts intrigued both Rayde and Jasheal.

Rayde asked eagerly, "When will the next session take place? Would it be possible for me and Jasheal to participate?"

Kail quickly jumped into the conversation before the friends could comply with his request. "That would be up to Commander Darnon, of course, but the next workout will be the morning after next."

As the evening waned, the rebels seemed to sense that their opportunity to glean information was almost lost and began to demand answers from their recalcitrant guests. For their part, the friends realized they had extracted all the information they could from the rebels and, after a brief glance at the others, Steve took matters into his own hands.

"Although we've enjoyed your company tonight, I believe we've exhausted your hospitality." Steve stood to put an end to the exchange.

To smooth things over, Pattie rose and moved toward Rayde. She extended her hand to the scowling rebel and smiled warmly.

"Thank you all for this evening. It was a welcome diversion. But I'm sure you can understand. We're exhausted and must get some rest before we continue our journey tomorrow." Rayde seemed to remember his manners and again assumed the role of host, accepting the others' proffered excuses, albeit reluctantly.

The friends and their escorts prepared to take their leave when Steve noticed Gloria, still sitting with the rebels. He motioned for her to accompany them.

Gloria stared back at Steve defiantly. "I'm not going yet. I'll leave when I'm ready." Her chin was thrust out, and Steve knew it would be useless to argue. Despite Gloria's protests, Steve remained steadfast that Kail and two of his men would remain with her.

Darnon met the group at the edge of the camp and led them to his command tent where they briefed him on the evening. He seemed pleased to hear of Pattie's resourcefulness. However, he was somewhat concerned at their discovery that the rebels planned to accompany his group over the next few days. Darnon couldn't refuse the extra troops, but he knew he would need to keep his men separated from the independent rebels to keep the peace. He was also dismayed that Gloria had remained behind, but merely commented they would have to hope for the best and trust Kail to handle any problems caused by the wayward girl.

The friends didn't see Gloria until the next day. The army was nearly ready to march. Once on the trail, Kail confided to them that Gloria had spent the night in Rayde's tent. The soldiers spent the night outside at a discreet distance, as far away as duty would allow.

Surprisingly, the day's march, though brisk, seemed easy for Gloria. The others took for granted that she had lost the benefit of Pattie's healing after their departure from the party. They assumed she must have stopped drinking. However, unbeknownst to Pattie, Gloria had listened carefully to her song and, during one healing, hummed along ever so softly, probing the exact locations of Pattie's healing. She was even pleasant to the others, pleased with herself for snagging the handsome and powerful rebel. But as the day wore on and Rayde did not come around to see her, Gloria's mood turned bitter.

That evening, the two armies camped within a short distance of one another but clearly segregated. Shortly after they had eaten, Gloria departed without any notice and walked off toward the rebel camp. She didn't show up again until the following morning, arriving as the friends were heading out of camp with Kail. They were off to the morning workout, the one Rayde and Jasheal had said they would attend. They invited her along, but Gloria wanted nothing but the bed she had made up the night before.

Brandon had chosen the workout grounds, an area located between the camps. The brother and sister rebel leaders walked out of their encampment as Kail and Brandon's early morning workout team finished their preparation of the grounds.

Rayde greeted them heartily, "This is far earlier than we're accustomed to. This is the hour we're usually just getting to bed!"

Brandon smiled in response and got down to business. "We may as well get started. We usually begin by stretching and doing a few warmup exercises." Seeing the siblings exchange baffled looks, he added, "Just follow along and you'll get the hang of it."

Brandon conducted the session in his normal fashion, starting slowly with stretches and adding progressively more difficult calisthenics. In just ten minutes, despite the coolness of the late autumn morning, the participants could feel their hair sticking to their scalps. Brandon was pleased to see that the undisciplined newcomers, though struggling with the unfamiliar exercises, were in better shape than he expected.

"All right, now that we're warmed up, let's walk through a few standard forms. Kail, if you'll lead these, I'll help the new folks." Brandon approached Rayde and Jasheal. "These forms will be strange to you at first but they can be very useful, as you'll see later."

As the group walked through the forms, Brandon worked with the pair, showing them the proper techniques. They learned quickly—both were athletic, but Jasheal in particular had amazing balance and grace, seeming to glide through the forms.

Satisfied the two were catching on, Brandon called out to the rest of the group. "All right, form up in pairs. Kail, how about you with Rayde? We're going to work on the attacks from behind that we worked on last time. And remember: use your opponent's momentum."

After a brief explanation to his new student, Brandon had Jasheal attack him from behind, grabbing him around his neck and feigning a stab to the chest. He grabbed her arm and rolled her over his hip, his intention to flip her and have her land on her back in front of him. Jasheal had other ideas. He was amazed as the girl somehow twisted her body in midair to land on her feet. Small daggers appeared out of nowhere in each of her hands. She crouched in front of Brandon like a wildcat ready to pounce.

"Easy now," Brandon said. "This is just an exercise to teach hand-to-hand combat." He held up his hands in a placating gesture.

Jasheal stood upright, flashing a dazzling smile in response, and the daggers disappeared as mysteriously as they appeared. She met his eyes with a steady gaze, confidently awaiting his next set of instructions. Brandon made a mental note to mull over her natural instincts later when he had more time to think.

A few minutes more of the exercises and it was Kail's turn to lead the session. He announced they would now work on sword exercises. Brandon noticed that Rayde's interest in the session intensified. Jasheal, on the other hand, seemed completely indifferent to the study of sword fighting. It was her utter lack of response that made Brandon realize she carried no sword. Instead, she wore two long daggers, one at each hip. She also wore a crisscross harness, like a bandoleer worn in an old western, filled with rows of small daggers. Brandon assumed these daggers were for throwing, as their only hilt was the metal that eventually formed the blade.

Rayde had kept up with each of the routines, which involved fighting against imaginary opponents. When Kail finished the exercises, Rayde announced in a voice loud enough for all to hear, "That was a nice little workout, but none of those imagined scenarios would help in actual combat."

Jasheal chimed in. "I agree. You men and your swords have never been very effective."

Kail responded evenly, "Well, we have a nonlethal way to resolve this." He walked over and picked up the cloth-wrapped bundle containing his wooden practice swords. "Brandon, I think you should have the honor."

Brandon nodded at Rayde. "I'm game if you are."

The soldiers formed a large ring around the two men. Kail said, "Three strikes to the torso wins the match."

After Rayde took a few short swings to gauge the weight and feel of the nonlethal weapon, the two men squared off and made the ceremonial bows. In an unsportsmanlike move, Rayde rushed at Brandon before he had a chance to straighten. Fortunately, the clarity saved him from being scored on immediately.

Kail had told Brandon after their first fight that hand-to-hand fighting was acceptable in a challenge and, short of trying to permanently hurt your opponent, just about anything was acceptable. With this in mind, Brandon decided that knocking the overconfident rebel down a few notches was in order. Brandon found Rayde's style to be very different from Kail's and the other soldiers. At first it seemed chaotic and totally random but, as he dodged or blocked blow after blow, a pattern began to emerge. This allowed Brandon to anticipate the exact moment the rebel leader would be lunging forward.

It was during one of these lunges that Brandon made his move. He waited until he had deflected the blow, and he knew Rayde would have to pull his front foot back to keep from being overextended. The moment Rayde raised his foot, Brandon struck. He used a move all too familiar to Kail. Only this time, he was facing a good, but not nearly as talented, opponent and Brandon was not off-balance. The result was a textbook leg sweep, with Rayde's legs flying into the air, higher than his shoulders. Before the stunned rebel hit the ground, Brandon had already landed a scoring blow across his chest.

As soon as Rayde hit the ground, Brandon was up and moving a safe distance away. He waited for his prone opponent to catch his breath and gain his footing. Seeing that Brandon wasn't going to force the issue, Rayde started to rise slowly, keeping his eye on Brandon's every move. Much like a boxer with a standing eight count, he allowed himself time to recover from the stunning blow.

The moment Rayde was upright, he launched into a vicious attack, driving Brandon back as he fended off blow after blow. Sensing he was near the ring of soldiers, Brandon threw himself headfirst to one side. Just before hitting the ground, he tucked his shoulder and somersaulted, springing back to his feet and into a defensive posture over ten feet away. The move was so quick and unexpected that Rayde stumbled headlong into the ring of soldiers, all of whom were distracted by the unexpected intensity of the exchange before them.

Rayde was far more cautious now as he approached his hulking adversary. Brandon held his defensive stance as the rebel advanced, making up his mind to take the offensive. Brandon waited patiently for his challenger to extract himself from the soldiers he had fallen into; this slight delay might give him the breathing room he needed to execute his strategy.

With a swiftness Rayde never dreamed possible from a man so large, Brandon rained down blow after blow upon him. Reeling from the onslaught, the renegade was just able to block the powerful hits. Kail wasn't sure his beloved practice swords would survive, even with their magical enhancement. But he certainly didn't believe the young brash leader had any chance against Brandon's deliberate attack.

Just when Rayde thought the blows couldn't come any faster, Brandon somehow managed to land a left hook to his jaw. Shaking his head to clear the fog and clearly dazed, Rayde looked down at his empty hands.

Brandon had stripped him of his weapon. Resting his sword on Rayde's shoulder, Brandon pressed the blade firmly against Rayde's neck. A devilish grin began to spread over the Rayde's face, and he reached into his robe. Anticipating a counterattack, Brandon instantly increased the pressure of the blunted practice blade against Rayde's neck. Laughing softly, enjoying the exchange immensely despite his dilemma, Rayde pulled his empty hand back out of his robe and held it up in a gesture of surrender. Gingerly pinching the blade, he slowly lifted Brandon's sword from his shoulder. As he did, he brought his other hand up to his mouth in a closed fist and coughed.

Brandon, breathing hard from the furious exchange, never took his eyes off Rayde. Nonetheless, a moment too late, he saw an almost-transparent cloud bursting from Rayde's fist. Inadvertently, Brandon breathed it into his lungs. Within seconds, the mist took effect: his vision blurred and his mind fogged. He could see and react to his surroundings, but all his reactions were slower and initiated without his customary awareness. In less than a minute, Rayde had scored the three blows he needed to end the match.

Jasheal threw a cold look at her brother as menacing as the row of daggers she wore. If her look could have caused physical harm, Rayde wouldn't have been left standing. Pattie, seeing Jasheal's expression, knew something was wrong and ran to Brandon's side. Wasting no time, she held his face gently in her hands and began her song. She could sense right away he had been poisoned with a mild sedative. Just as she did with the alcohol, Pattie was able to use Brandon's body and accelerate the process, eliminating the drug's effect.

As soon as she completed her ministrations, Pattie wheeled round to Rayde and demanded, "How could you?"

Kail was already squared off in front of the young rebel, who was making a feeble attempt to look innocent. It was Brandon who defused the tense standoff. Standing, he addressed the warrior.

"You yourself told me there were no rules to a challenge, Kail. Besides, there are no long-term effects. I say we see a demonstration of what Rayde's daggers can do."

As an afterthought, he added, "I did, however, learn my lesson. If there is a next time, I'll be more specific about the rules."

Steve was relieved Brandon chose to defuse the conflict between Kail and Rayde, but he wasn't surprised. Steve hadn't been around Brandon as much as the others. He had only seen him in the one fight when they were 12, the fight where they first met, and had only heard of him being involved in one other. During that fight, evidently Brandon had tried repeatedly to back the other guy down. Even though his friend ultimately administered a thorough beating, Steve had been told that Brandon stopped the instant his opponent capitulated.

Desperate to change the subject, Rayde said quickly, "If it's daggers you want, then it's Jasheal you'll need. She's the best in our clan, some say the best in all of Carsanic."

Jasheal said nothing, instead walking toward the forested edge of the clearing. The others followed to within 40 feet of the trees, where she stopped and turned to face them. "That's far enough. I'll only be a minute."

With that said, she walked directly to the nearest tree and removed from the pocket of her overcoat a white rock the size of an egg. Using the caulk-like stone, she made a clearly visible circle, head high, about the size of an apple. She repeated the effort until seven trees had similar markings and walked back towards the waiting group.

Stopping halfway between the trees and her audience, she asked, "Brother, would you be so kind as to signal me?"

Rayde responded by reaching into his robe and producing a bright-red silk handkerchief. He held it slightly above his head with an outstretched arm. With mock innocence, he asked, "Ready, little sister?"

At the nod from Jasheal, whose back was still to the trees, Rayde released the handkerchief. As soon as he did, Jasheal spun toward the closest tree in a low crouch. Her hands were a blur as dagger after dagger flew toward their targets. Before the last weapon reached its target, she turned quickly back around, still in the low crouch. She had both of her long daggers drawn, a triumphant grin on her face, as the handkerchief fluttered gently to rest on the ground.

Jasheal's silent audience was awestruck. Each dagger was buried deep in its respective tree. The two that were not in the center of their circle were clearly within the circle's bounds. Brandon was the first to break the spell of her impressive feat. He began clapping, slowly at first, and then stronger and faster. Pattie and Steve added their applause. Apparently, this was not a custom in Bericea because no one else joined in, and the three received sideways glances from several of the others.

Brandon walked up to the petite, yet obviously dangerous, rebel woman. "That was amazing," he said appreciatively.

Jasheal shook her head slightly. "Nothing compared to your sparring. Now that age has slowed our father, Rayde's the best swordsman in our clan. And if my brother hadn't used tarellis root, you would've defeated him easily."

Brandon grinned, extending his hand, and Jasheal accepted it with a smile and a hearty shake. Soon the two were joined by the others, all offering their admiration and praise.

CHAPTER 18

TRAITOR AMONG US

Three days passed. The rebels remained with Darnon's army, never giving any indication how much longer they intended to travel with his group. The rebel siblings attended each morning session, though sparring wasn't mentioned again. They brought ten of their soldiers with them to each session, rotating those who attended. This aroused Darnon's suspicions, but Steve talked the commander into allowing the exchange of fighting techniques.

On the evening of the third day, Kail formally asked permission to enter the friends' camp. Brandon, Pattie and Steve were sitting near their bedding. Absent as usual was Gloria, who hadn't missed an evening visiting the rebel camp. Sitting heavily on a log near the friends, Kail sighed. The three waited expectantly, as something was obviously weighing on his mind.

"I need to ask a favor of all of you. What I'm about to say would likely be considered insubordination. So I ask that you keep this between us."

The three friends quickly assented to his wish.

Kail proceeded, "I'm becoming more and more convinced there's a traitor among the army. The placement of the ambushes is far too strategic to be mere coincidence." Kail paused to let the significance of his words sink in and to gauge their reactions.

"I agree," said Steve without prompting.

Brandon and Pattie both nodded. Brandon said, "Makes sense. I've been so wrapped up in the newness of all this, I never stopped to think about it."

Kail continued. "Darnon is the last person I can go to with this. The very thing that makes his men devoted to him would be my undoing. He trusts them, especially his officers, explicitly. And unfortunately, it makes the most sense that the traitor is one of the officers. It has to be someone in his inner circle who knows the troop movements. He never tells any of us soldiers the plans far enough in advance."

Pattie exclaimed, "Then we have to get proof!" Catching herself, she finished more quietly, "That's the only way Darnon will listen."

"That's exactly what I hoped you'd say," Kail said, relieved.

He listed each of the ranking officers, the ones that sat in direct council with Darnon. The three friends started dividing the list. Suddenly, Pattie sat back. "I think we should also recruit Varis to help. He's a very reasonable man, and he may have access that we wouldn't."

Kail thought about her comment for a moment before consenting. "I don't hold the malice that other soldiers do toward magic users. Besides, I owe him my life after the stream."

So it was that the three friends and Varis started a careful observation of Darnon's most trusted officers. During this time, Kail and Brandon continued to hold their morning workouts. Steve didn't miss any of the sessions. He was glad to see that one or two of the rebel soldiers in each session used the smaller millek sword. The rebels would spend a portion of the workout training with Steve; in doing so, they could exchange moves specific to that type of weapon. As an added bonus, Steve got to converse directly with the rebels in their native tongue, a skill that impressed the rebel leaders.

Jasheal even led a few sessions on throwing daggers. Brandon was particularly interested in this, partly because he wanted an effective weapon at range, and partly because of his beautiful and intriguing instructor.

Pattie renewed her magic training with Varis. He made their sessions far more intense now that they didn't have to hide their activity. He also solicited the aid of a few of the more open-minded clerics. Both Varis and Pattie knew that their real motivation was to learn Pattie's healing technique, but the arrangement still worked to Pattie's advantage. The clerics had a lot to offer her in addition to Varis' ability in certain disciplines. Besides, she didn't mind in the least sharing her knowledge with them in return.

The two clerics were quite surprised by Pattie, and didn't expect the kind of training the young woman shared with them. All of her lessons were related to human anatomy. She in turn was shocked at how little they knew, though Pattie kept it to herself. She had to start with the basics, beginning with the high-level systems. Only after they achieved this fundamental level of understanding could she delve into the detail needed to analyze injuries and determine what was required to repair the damage.

Pattie passed the word throughout the camp that she wanted even minor injuries sent to her for healing. Every evening after camp was set, a small parade of sprained ankles, minor cuts, dislocated shoulders, blisters, and migraine headaches would form and make its way to Pattie's camp. The clerics would take turns during these healing sessions to hum, lending magic and, more importantly, exploring what Pattie did during the healing process as she sang out the names of the anatomy that she affected.

Despite her impressive talents, Pattie continued to struggle with the act of healing headaches. As she probed a patient's brain for the cause, she would be overwhelmed by his thoughts. And on more than one occasion, before she learned to block out all but the most forceful ones, she became very embarrassed. Most of the thoughts were predictable, coming from soldiers who had been away from home for months and found themselves with a beautiful young woman gently holding their heads as she sang mesmerizing songs. She would often pull back when she realized what they were thinking, but she never disclosed to them what she had just heard: their innermost thoughts.

At some point over the course of the training, Pattie decided she needed anatomy diagrams to add to her lessons, so she asked Steve to lend a hand. Given an excuse to spend more time with Pattie, he eagerly accepted. Besides, he loved technical drawing, and it also forced him to do something he knew was necessary—learn a new language. The tokens were only able to translate spoken language. However, with help from Varis, he quickly learned the letters of their alphabet, as well as their sounds and the sounds of the basic letter combinations. Using this knowledge, he was able to label the diagrams in both English and phonetically spelled-out Bericean.

Steve would spend the day's march talking with Pattie about the next system to be diagrammed. He would take quick notes and make crude drawings during the march. At camp that evening, he would create clean diagrams to be given to the training clerics the next morning. Pattie and Steve walked with each other most of each day, which gave them plenty of time to talk about more than just human anatomy. As the days passed, they learned more and more about one another, inevitably growing closer and more comfortable together.

It was now late October. As the winter solstice drew near, the nights started getting longer. To the friends' surprise, it seemed to be turning warmer, however, not colder. Varis explained that they were indeed approaching winter and that would mean cold weather and snow for most of Bericea but, because they were moving north, the temperatures would become warmer. Eventually, if they continued far enough northward, they would reach a massive desert where the daytime temperatures seldom dropped low enough to bear for more than a few hours at a time.

The friends did not let the long nights go to waste. They used them to find out as much as they could about the officers Kail suspected. The officer camps were open to them and, at one point or another along the journey, they had already spoken to all of the officers for one reason or another. The random visit from a Summoned One to an officer camp was therefore not at all suspicious.

Varis, who had instantly agreed to help, proved to be the most valuable. He had a knack for getting people to offer information during casual conversation that they would never have divulged if asked directly.

Varis would linger around Pattie's healing sessions and talk with the waiting soldiers and low-ranking officers alike. Unbeknownst to them, he was also gleaning valuable intelligence.

Each morning after the workout and training, the four investigators would meet with Kail and discuss the prior day's findings. After two weeks, they were able to narrow their list of suspects to three. Casual observation was not enough now. Without laying a trap, there was little hope of catching their spy red-handed. The friends suggested enlisting Darnon at this point, but Kail assured them that the leader would never condone such a scheme. They decided that constant surveillance was their only alternative. They began to work out a rotation where all three suspects could be observed at all times. As they discussed the schedule, Steve brought up Darnon again.

"Kail, are you sure Darnon wouldn't cooperate with us? The easiest and fastest way to catch this traitor is to lay a trap."

"You would be foolish going to him without hard facts. Darnon's greatest quality is his loyalty to his men, to his officers. I'm certain that his reaction to all of you wouldn't be pleasant, and I'm pretty sure he would hang me from the nearest tree." Watching Kail's face closely, Steve knew he wasn't joking.

For four days, the friends kept their vigil on the suspects. Pattie was able to use her magic to limit the impact of fatigue on their watches. Even so, they were all beginning to tire easily. On the fourth evening, Pattie was looking for Steve to relieve him. She found him beside a supply wagon, trying to look busy. She smiled and started to greet him, but stopped when Steve held up a finger.

"Wait a minute, Pattie. Something's happening," he whispered as she approached.

Pattie and Steve stayed together beside the wagon and Pattie acted busy too, as if she were looking for something. Camp had been called for about an hour earlier. The nearly full moon provided ample light for the two to keep tabs on the officer they were watching. The officer was whispering to one of his subordinates. The subordinate listened intently, then suddenly walked off in the opposite direction from Steve and Pattie.

Steve said softly, "This may be what we've been watching for. It's too bad he went that way. It would be too suspicious for us to follow now. Let's just wait here and see what the officer does."

Only a few minutes later, the two had their answer. Commander Darnon walked up behind them, the subordinate in tow. As the pair turned and saw Darnon's expression, they knew the jig was up.

"What do you two think you are doing? Some of my officers said they were being watched, but I had a hard time believing them."

Before they could explain, Darnon held up his hand to stop them and gestured for them to follow along to his command tent. He had already sent word to round up the other two would-be spies. As Pattie and Steve approached the tent, they saw Brandon and Varis being led from the other direction.

When the three friends, Varis, and the three suspected officers were in the command tent, Darnon looked around at them slowly as if taking each person's measure. In a quiet voice, he then asked what they had been up to. Caught literally in the act, they were forced to confess; however, they all purposely left Kail from their stories. As Kail had predicted, Darnon became enraged. The longer the friends and Varis spoke, the angrier he became. Finally, Darnon, normally calm under even the toughest circumstances, balled his hands into fists, as if he could strike the very persons he had sworn to protect.

He roared, "These men have served under me since they were raw recruits! I trust them implicitly! We each would give our lives for the other."

Pausing to regain his composure before he lost it completely, Darnon drew a deep breath and turned his attention to Varis.

"I may come to forgive these newcomers, but you! You've known some of these men since they were babies."

Darnon didn't give them a chance to speak a word in their defense. In a booming voice, he barked out one word.

"Primlas!"

The clerk took mere seconds to respond, throwing open the tent flap as if on cue. The hunched-up man shuffled into the room, carrying his ever-present clipboard.

"Yes, sir?"

Even Darnon seemed startled by the quickness of his clerk's response. He recovered quickly and pointed towards Varis.

"He is to be returned to his camp and placed under guard until I can determine what to do with him. See that two of the Whilanar clerics are among the watch. These three are to be returned to their camp. Ensure they don't leave it."

Primlas dutifully left the tent to make the arrangements. In less than a minute, two soldiers and a cleric entered the tent to escort Varis.

Varis was on the opposite side of the tent, but Pattie could see his lips move ever so slightly. She was startled to hear him whisper clearly to her, "Primlas."

"Primlas, of course! Primlas! How could we have been so blind," thought Pattie.

She said to Steve and Brandon, "I think it best we start for our camp now."

If the others thought her comment odd, they didn't show it. They headed out of the tent without further prompting. Luckily, as she exited, she caught just a glimpse of Primlas as he disappeared between some trees. Although she was taking a chance that Darnon or one of his officers might leave the tent and see that she was not heading in the direction of her camp, Pattie quickly turned to follow Darnon's clerk.

Steve and Brandon caught up with her a bit beyond the command tent. Steve caught Pattie's arm and hissed, "What's going on?"

Pattie jerked her arm away and kept moving. In a low tone, over her shoulder, she explained "It's Primlas, Varis magically whispered 'Primlas' to me. It makes sense now; he has to be the spy."

The three determined friends rushed to catch up to the traitor who had cost so many lives. The narrow path led through thick undergrowth. They pulled up just in time to keep from being discovered. Primlas was crouched in a small clearing, working frantically with his clipboard. He disassembled the object, essentially turning it inside out. He then began urgently writing on the new surface that had been the inside of the tablet.

Pattie sensed that he must be stopped and acted quickly. She decided on a song of wind; her intention was to weave the wind similar to the shields used on the platform, but this time the wind would be concentrated. She would use it to handcuff the clerk. Pattie started her song and approached Primlas, who had stopped writing to stare at the girl in disbelief. Steve and Brandon flanked her as she moved toward the clerk, whose expression had changed to one of hatred and resolve.

For some reason Pattie couldn't understand, Primlas seemed unaffected by her spell. As they reached him, the clerk suddenly pulled a dagger from his boot. With a violent upward movement, he thrust the dagger at Pattie's abdomen. His only thought was to bring an end to the life of one of the Summoned prophesied to destroy his master.

Only Brandon's clarity saved Pattie's life. His training kicked in and without thought, he quickly grabbed Primlas' wrist and stayed the blade a mere inch from Pattie's flesh. Holding tightly to his wrist, Brandon jerked the crazed man away from his friend. Primlas rose to his full height, nearly as tall as Brandon. He was no longer a meek, slouching clerk but a menacing and dangerous opponent.

Taking no chances, Brandon yanked on the wrist of the hand still clutching the dagger, pulling his opponent downward and away from his body. At the same time, Brandon brought his free forearm down on Primlas' exposed elbow with an audible crack. Primlas let out a loud, primal scream, as much of frustration as of pain, and dropped the dagger. Brandon released the now-useless wrist and pulled back slightly. This gave him room to land a ferocious right hook that landed on Primlas' jaw, instantly rendering him unconscious.

It took less than a minute for Darnon and his three officers to appear in response to the scream. Brandon was just finishing securing the hands and feet of the obviously injured and unconscious Primlas. Furious at seeing his trusted assistant being man-handled, Darnon demanded an explanation. Steve held out the tablet Primlas had written on, the tablet that was obviously a component of the now-familiar clipboard.

The writing on this tablet was not on the parchment, as were all of Primlas' other documents. Instead, it was written in a thin layer of smooth clay set in a wooden frame. Etched deep into the clay was the frantic handwriting of Primlas. Steve had noticed that the writing was not Bericean, but used most of the letters of the same alphabet.

Darnon snatched up the tablet and quickly read aloud, "They suspect a spy. The ambush must be sooner than planned. We'll be to the pass of Karlibus in one day. I can delay them only until the following day."

The shock and horror in Darnon's voice was reflected on his face. The writing disappeared before their very eyes and was replaced by writing that appeared as if by magic. Continuing to read aloud, Darnon relayed the message, "We can be in place as you command."

Reaching to the ground, Steve picked up the strange, pointed writing utensil that Primlas had used. Looking at the clay residue, not only on the tip but also on the sharp edge running its length, Steve realized something.

"Commander, I think they would expect him to clear the message after it was read."

Darnon offered no resistance, so Steve stepped forward and gently took the tablet from Darnon's hands. Using the sharp edge, he wiped the tablet smooth.

"Major, go get Varis and bring him to my command tent," ordered Darnon, who seemed to be recovering from the shock of his clerk's betrayal.

Brandon added, "You should get Kail as well. Without him, we would never have started looking for a traitor."

With a raised eyebrow, Darnon assented with a slight nod. "Bring Kail also."

The command tent was soon filled with Darnon's top officers, but now the friends and Kail were included among the commander's council. Later they surmised this was Darnon's way of apologizing. The tablet had been sent to the clerics for inspection, with strict orders not to make any markings in the clay.

Primlas was left bound and held with six guards. After Pattie had explained to Darnon that her magic had no effect on the clerk, he had been searched thoroughly. They found an amulet that the clerics determined was an ancient artifact that would cancel out any magic used directly against the wearer. They also discovered his dagger to be an extremely dangerous and effective weapon. It was an ancient and rare heart-seeker. Once the blade entered the body, a small sliver would detach and travel directly to the victim's heart.

It was evident to everyone that, given not just one, but three, priceless magical artifacts, Primlas was no ordinary spy. Darnon had met him almost ten years ago. He had started reporting directly to Darnon three years ago, after his long-time assistant died in a fall from a horse. Given Primlas' high ranking within enemy forces, execution, though warranted, was out of the question. Regardless of the difficulty, Darnon and all those present decided that Primlas had to be taken back to Bericea.

The group also decided that the ambush described in the magical tablet was a perfect opportunity to turn the tables on the enemy. Darnon suggested that the Vylcrean scouts be used to find a way to flank the enemy and attack simultaneously from both sides of the pass. The three friends and Varis had remained silent throughout the discussions, but Steve was compelled to speak up.

"Commander, you've overlooked a valuable asset."

The interruption silenced the discussion, and all eyes were on Steve. Gaining the attention he had hoped for, he pressed on.

"If we have any hope of getting this trap in place by the second day as Primlas arranged, we won't have time for scouts to find the way. From what I understand, we've been traveling in the Carsanicean home territory for more than a week. If anyone would know an alternate route through the pass, the Carsaniceans would. I say you should have Rayde and Jasheal involved in this planning."

Steve knew that Darnon didn't like or trust the Carsaniceans, especially Rayde, but he felt strongly that this alliance was important. Not just for this battle, but for the longer term. Working with the brother and sister every morning with Kail and Brandon, he had grown fond of the pair. He only hoped the logic of using their aid was not wasted on

Darnon.

Darnon took his time responding. He seemed conflicted, but finally reached a decision.

"Kail, please invite the two…leaders to the command tent."

As Kail turned to leave, Darnon made it clear to everyone that the brother and sister were not to know about Primlas. Also, he was to do the talking when they arrived.

When Kail returned with the pair, Darnon brought them quickly up to speed, imparting as little information as he could get away with. The discussions then continued as to their plan of attack. As Steve had hoped, Rayde and Jasheal knew the Carsanicean territory like the backs of their hands, and he was relieved to learn there was indeed a way to flank the enemy in time. Better yet, not only could they hit them from the front and rear, but a small force of archers could slip through a steep, narrow trail that led along the edge of Karlibus Canyon.

The plans finalized, the officers wasted no time making preparations. Each of the three forces were chosen from a mixture of Darnon's men and Carsaniceans. The slightly smaller flanking force, as well as the elite hand-picked archery team, left that very night. They planned to press hard, then rest within striking distance. Clerics were well-represented among the groups, in hopes that their magic would ensure the parties were not found out.

The bulk of the forces left the next morning and made camp only a few hours march from the pass. The plan was to strike out early and start the attack around midday. The Vylcrean scouts were notified. Their role was to alert Darnon if there were any signs of the enemy moving, or if they had become aware of the other troops.

The same night the flanking forces left, Gloria made a rare return to camp, clearly upset. Not only had she been unceremoniously kicked out of Rayde's camp, but she also found out that the only friend she had made on this awful journey was now being held prisoner. The lack of sympathy she received from the others didn't improve her demeanor.

In the early afternoon, as planned, the main force walked headlong toward the ambush. Just as they drew near to bow range, a Vylcrean scout rushed out of the woods between the two forces, shouting warnings. This was part of their plan, intended to make the enemy believe the readiness of their army was due solely to this advance warning.

As the main force advanced, clerics erected the invisible wind barriers. Seeing their arrows falling harmlessly and believing their numbers superior, the enemy began to leave the protective shelter of the trees to attack directly. Darnon waited till a large portion of the enemy was committed, then ordered the other two forces to be signaled using magical flares. Arrows rained from the woods where the scout had emerged, as the enemy now raced across the open trail. At the same time, Darnon pulled back his lead forces and used his archers to great effect. The enemy wavered, then began a full retreat, hoping to gain the shelter of the trees. Instead, they found the flanking forces, led by Rayde, screaming a war cry and running out of the very trees they had hoped to reach.

The tables turned, the ambushers found themselves being ambushed. Chaos reigned for the enemy as all discipline dissolved. Towards the end, only a small group of pallitors remained, frantically attempting to guard three nollax. The troops were pulled back and archers were used. Whilanar clerics and their protectors came forward to guard against any countermeasure the exhausted nollax might attempt.

Darnon had ordered the Summoned Ones to remain in the rear of the main force. However, as he had the troops pull back for the archers, they found themselves forward enough to witness the battle with the pallitors and nollax. Once the last of them had fallen, the zealot protectors of the clerics rushed in to begin systematically finishing the wounded survivors.

Seeing the carnage, Pattie rushed across the field before anyone could stop her. She began screaming "no" at her top of her lungs. Once within range to use her magic, Pattie began singing a whimsical song of wind. A protector ready to deliver a death blow to one of the pallitors froze like a statue, his sword held high above his head. The pallitor, shot with several arrows, still thrashed frantically trying to reach the now helpless protector.

The pallitor froze as well, and Pattie rushed to his side. Placing herself between the cleric's protector and the pallitor, she released the protector but continued her hold on the pallitor. The other clerics shouted at her to get away, but instead she used her song to amplify her voice, commanding the clerics to hold the pallitor without hurting him. She could feel their magic around her own, and she released her magical grip.

Now able to concentrate her magic solely on healing, she began stopping the worst of the bleeding. After healing several wounds, she began to heal a deep head wound. Just as she started the healing there, her song faltered and she went silent.

Varis was worried; no one had ever attempted to heal a pallitor. He thought to himself, "Why has she stopped singing? The pallitor has several wounds that will eventually take his life."

Varis was relieved when Pattie quickly resumed the healing song, but it was soon apparent that it was having no effect on the obviously severe wounds. She kept up the song for a few minutes, plenty of time for her to have cured all of the injuries, but no new healing could be seen. At last, the pallitor's body went limp. Pattie remained kneeling beside the lifeless body and began to cry. Steve (the Summoned One Varis had witnessed growing ever closer to his pupil) rushed to her.

Just as he reached her side, Pattie stood and embraced him, sobbing and crying out, "How could anyone do such a thing?"

By now, Varis had come to stand next to the pair.

Seeing her distress, Varis said with concern, "What is it child? Are you harmed?"

Pattie took a while to regain her composure, all the while repeating her lament between sobs. Once she had control of her emotions, she began to explain.

"When I began to heal his head wound, something called to me, faintly. So I probed his mind. At first, I found it strangely devoid of thought. Then, loud and clear, a plea came to me: 'Please kill me.'"

Pattie paused, fighting back a new wave of emotion. She pressed on.

"I probed into his brain, and I found massive damage. It was old damage. Large sections of neurons were severed, and several others crudely rerouted. I pushed into the area where I though the plea had originated. The man's conscience was locked in that section of his brain. He was fully aware but unable to control any actions of his body."

Pattie sat down in the grass only a few feet from the fallen pallitor. Steve knelt alongside, keeping a protective arm around her shoulders. Slightly less emotional, Pattie continued.

"At first his thoughts were jumbled, fragmented, but after the initial excitement of finally being able to communicate, a logic came to his thoughts. He was a leader among the Carsanicean rebels, who had been captured three years ago. He was beaten and tortured for information. This went on for months. Finally, after giving up no usable information, he was brought before Zybaro. Zybaro immediately used magic to attack his mind but, despite this, he was able to resist. In a final fit of rage, Zybaro turned him into a pallitor. His only solace was that Zybaro was never able to get the information he sought."

Pattie went on to describe how she told the man she thought she could help him. The man was adamant that he didn't want to live. He said he could never live with what he had been forced to do to his people. Still Pattie pressed on, repairing the severed connections in the man's brain. Having limited knowledge of the anatomy of the pallitor brain, began by reconnecting the severed neurons that obviously fit together. That was her undoing, for only a few seconds into the daunting task, she reconnected a bundle of pain receptors. Almost instantly, the man died of shock.

Pattie rose slowly, pulling away from Steve. She turned to the small crowd that had gathered and spoke urgently but quietly. "Zybaro must be stopped. This cannot be allowed to continue."

CHAPTER 19

ZYBARO

Pattie crumpled to the ground after her plea to the small group gathered around her.

She remained on her knees, looking up at Steve imploringly. "He must be stopped," she repeated and covered her face with her hands. Steve knelt behind her, gently holding her shoulders. Tears filled her eyes and rolled slowly down her cheeks. Pattie knew she needed to remain calm, but she was struggling to cope with the flood of emotions she had taken in from the pallitor. This terrifying monster that could feel no pain and wrought such devastating destruction on those who sought to protect her was not a monster after all. He was merely the instrument of the true monster, Zybaro.

The exchange she had just shared with the man who lay dead only feet from her was unlike anything she had ever experienced. She had caught snippets of emotions and fleeting visions from some of the soldiers she healed, but this was quite different. This poor, tortured soul willingly shared complete stories with her. His memories had entered Pattie's subconscious, and she could now recall his experiences as vividly as if she had lived them herself.

She became aware that Brandon and Commander Darnon were staring down at her, deep concern etched on each man's face. For them and more importantly, for herself, she knew she needed to get a grip on her emotions. Pattie did the only thing she could under the circumstances. She pushed the memories aside and forced herself back to the present. These men needed answers. The young woman scrambled to her feet, collected her thoughts, and described the attempted healing from her own perspective.

Commander Darnon listened carefully as she retold the story she had shared with Varis. She confirmed what Darnon had expected for quite some time. The commander had seen men he knew to be good and loyal turned into those monsters. Until now, however, the fact that Zybaro had a direct hand in their creation had not been apparent.

Darnon thought for a few moments after the girl finished her account. Making up his mind, he called for a messenger.

"It's only right that Rayde be informed about this. He should know that one of his officers has died, even if it was in the form of one of these creatures. Bring him to me."

The messenger swiftly departed. In just a few minutes, the somber group saw him returning with the young rebel behind him. Both men were gliding along at a light run. It was obvious that both were comfortable using this loping gallop that chewed up distance quickly. As they pulled up to the group, neither man was winded, apparently able to sustain the pace without obvious effort.

Rayde looked around at the others questioningly. His eyes quickly came to rest on the corpse. As he looked at the body lying in the midst of the small gathering, Pattie saw Rayde grimace ever so slightly. To anyone who had fought these creatures, it was obvious at a glance that this was a pallitor. The light armor had the typical, unkempt look. The body had layers of scars over all exposed skin, and this man in particular bore dozens of open wounds, any one of which would have killed a normal person. There was no doubt in the mind of this seasoned warrior of countless campaigns against the armies of Zybaro that he looked upon a pallitor.

Rayde turned away from the corpse and addressed Commander Darnon. "Your runner told me I was needed straightaway. How may I be of service?"

Darnon pointed towards Pattie. "This young lady was able to communicate with the pallitor, just prior to its death. The creature told her he had been an officer in the Carsanicean army."

The usually self-assured Rayde seemed taken aback by the comment. He stared alternately at Pattie, then the body. Finally, he spoke.

"This man served many years under my father. Weelose was known to everyone as our greatest scout. Each mission, my father called upon him to penetrate deeper and deeper into Malabrim. After one particularly dangerous mission, he did not return to us. We assumed he had been killed. And after seeing him like this, I wish he had been."

Rayde paused, then spoke softly, more to himself than to the others. "Father was never the same after his loss. That's when Jasheal and I started serving more in a field leadership capacity. It's been three years since we lost Weelose. I hope for my father's sake he never finds out about this."

He turned to Pattie. "Please, tell me what you can."

Pattie again went through what she could bear to relate of the scout turned pallitor. She felt certain that the others gathered around did not notice but, she watched the rebel closely as she spoke to him and could see the stoic young man struggling to suppress his emotions. The sadness in his eyes was replaced with pride as he heard how his father's scout, a man close enough to the family to be called uncle, had resisted every effort to glean information.

Rayde was impressed with Weelose's defiance, because the scout would have known that any information he gave up would be of little value. The Carsanicean army had learned long ago that anyone captured would be tortured unmercifully for information. To mitigate the effects, Rayde's father learned to organize his forces into small, autonomous groups of no more than 20. Each group knew their own mission, but no one else's.

Each independent squad had two messengers who traveled back and forth between Carsanic, bringing new orders. Even though they functioned as separate smaller squads, larger groups could be brought together if necessary, as they were now. The squads would simply be ordered to the same location with similar instructions. The squad leader had considerable discretion with most orders, especially ones such as the orders they followed now—disrupt any enemy activity in the Gralicur region.

Rayde was the senior officer of the 23 squads now gathered, a rank earned in combat, not through nepotism. Even though he was only 27, he had fought in all ten years of the struggles with Zybaro.

Rayde had held this large collection of squads together far longer than his rank would normally allow, but he knew intuitively it was the right thing to do. He was determined to continue traveling with the Bericean army. Major victories achieved with minimal losses, along with the possibility of securing allies, were favoring him with more than enough latitude regarding his command decisions. However, there were other reasons he continued to travel with the Bericean solders. He had known instantly that the four young people who traveled with their army were not from any remote province. He knew he was being lied to but, for the moment, he accepted it. He felt deep down that these four were special and in need of protection. Any doubt that may have remained fled as he stared into the passionate eyes of the narrator of Weelose's final story.

Rayde listened intently and asked few questions. Pattie tried to spare him the most graphic details and covered the sad story as quickly as possible. She finished and said softly, "I'm so sorry." Rayde locked eyes with her a moment. He then thanked her somberly and nodded to Darnon. The commander gave the order to begin clearing the battlefield and burying the dead. The clerics proved invaluable in helping the soldiers complete the grim task. Using their earth magic, the clerics excavated three large mass graves, one for each army. Rayde ordered that Weelose's body be brought to the Carsanicean grave, where the scout was buried with honors.

As dusk approached, the clerics and soldiers were finishing up their work erasing signs of the battle. The battlefield still looked as if it had been trampled by many feet, the only indicator that something on a large scale had occurred. Darnon walked among them, inspecting their progress. Finally satisfied with what he saw, the commander gave the order to make camp. He knew that any enemy in the vicinity would have joined the fray. So, he decided to allow the rare use of campfires. True to his cautious nature, however, Darnon ordered them small and smokeless.

Steve kept a close eye on Pattie as they were setting up camp for the night. She was still troubled over the failed healing attempt. Although he tried to engage her in conversation a few times, Steve managed to elicit only a few terse replies. He fell silent. Maybe it was time to give her some space and wait for her to initiate any meaningful conversation.

Steve and Pattie finished their tasks and joined Gloria and Brandon around the modest but welcome campfire. The other two had just washed up the camp dishes after the group's first hot meal in weeks. Gloria was being uncharacteristically pleasant this evening. Earlier, she had jumped in to help Brandon clean up the after the meal, which was totally out of character for the spoiled young woman. Steve sat down next to Pattie and watched Gloria appraisingly across the fire. He had long since given up trying to understand her mercurial moods.

This evening, the topic of their conversation was a recurring one, as they reminisced about home and wondered how their other friends were faring. Steve and Brandon did most of the talking. Gloria didn't join in too often, but at least she made an effort to follow the conversation and held back her typical snide comments. Pattie remained completely preoccupied and withdrawn, which only made Steve worry about her more.

As the talk trailed off and fatigue started to set in among the group, Brandon yawned and got up from the log he had been sitting on. "Well, it's been a long day. I'm turning in."

Gloria stood up as well. "I think I'll take a walk before bed."

This came as no surprise to the others, who murmured their goodnights and watched her go until she disappeared into the darkness. They all knew Gloria wouldn't be back until morning. Brandon climbed into his bedroll and fell asleep almost immediately. Pattie made no attempt to turn in. She just sat silently, staring into the flames. Steve had already made up his mind not to pressure her any further this evening, but he wasn't about to leave her sitting up alone. The two of them sat quietly for over an hour. The only sounds were faint crackles from the low fire, the faint and distant noises of the slumbering camp around them, and Brandon's steady breathing as he slept just 20 feet away.

Seeing the fire burning low and wanting something to take his mind off Pattie, Steve walked over to the small woodpile and grabbed a few small pieces. As he went to move past Pattie to the fire, she reached out suddenly, startling him. She grasped his hand and looked up at him with a sad smile. Steve returned her gaze, not knowing what to make of this. She opened the blanket she had wrapped around her shoulders and gestured for him to join her in her warm enclosure. Trying to hide his surprise, Steve quickly saw to the low fire and sat down beside her. He pulled the corner of the blanket over his shoulder. As Pattie scooted closer to him, he put his arm around her and waited for her to make the next move.

Steve could feel the tension in her body, but it wasn't long before Pattie began to relax against him. Steve could feel her sinking deeper into the crook of his arm. After several minutes of silence, she spoke quietly.

"He didn't talk to me like I told the others."

Caught off-guard by the comment after she had been quiet for so long, Steve's only response was a soft "Hmm?"

"Much like the language tokens, the pallitor's thoughts came to me as images…Well, actually not images so much as memories. It was like I was remembering, vividly, but they were his memories, not mine."

Steve didn't know what to say, so he merely gave her a comforting squeeze. Pattie slid an arm around his waist and responded in kind. She didn't even want to think about the pallitor's memories, let alone talk about them, but deep down she knew she had to.

Feeling secure in Steve's arms and drawing strength from his empathy, Pattie continued.

"The memories were so vivid, not just the sights and sounds, but the smells, tastes, and feelings. By far though, the emotions were the most overwhelming. He loved his daughter so much. That love is what sustained him through all the hardship."

Pattie hesitated, choosing her words carefully. "The torture he endured was something I don't think I can describe. His captors started with intense questioning. He responded with defiance, he wouldn't tell them anything. They quickly escalated to cruelties so severe he had to be healed or he would have died. Regardless of the techniques they used, he was obstinate. Whatever they did, he remained silent."

Pattie continued, Weelose's story pouring out of her now as if she could not stop. The tortures continued at precise times each day, early morning, just prior to noon, and early evening. During each of these sessions, his captors were ruthless but each session always ended with Weelose being healed. After these agonizing ordeals, he was allowed meager rations before he was tossed back into his cramped cell. This routine continued every day for a week. Then, mercifully, two days went by with no physical abuse, though his tormentors would rattle keys outside his door at random times both day and night. At the end of the two days, Weelose began to let himself believe that he may have shown his captors their tactics would not work on a man of his strong constitution, but he was proven wrong when the relentless rhythm of torture began anew on the third day. Only this time, it was replaced with totally random sequences of torture and tormented respites.

Over a month later, on a day when his torturers had already engaged him in five excruciating bouts of brutality, he was thrown into his cramped cell. In his mind, he attempted to reach for the crutch that had sustained him each time before: the memory of his beloved daughter. He grasped desperately to envision her face but, try as he might, he couldn't concentrate enough to recall her image. His morale was at its lowest point, and the only support he had sustained in his titanic struggle now evaded him.

Slumped against the wall, half sitting and half reclining in the cell that was too small to stretch out in, Weelose began to wonder if he was cracking. He felt like crying but couldn't even summon that small release. Suddenly, the door was flung open, and the captors grabbed his limp body, dragging him off to a new round of torture. Fear began to overwhelm Weelose. He knew this was it, he would break for certain.

Stretched out and tied to a table, he was asked the same question he had heard so many times before. "Where are your men stationed?" But unlike all the other times, he was ready to give an answer, to give them anything they wanted as long if they would stop. But just as he started to relent, he was overcome with emotion. He opened his mouth, but not a sound emerged. His tormentors took this as yet another act of defiance.

They didn't notice as tears streamed down his face, intent as they were on pushing a red-hot poker against his flesh, searing through layers of previous scars. The screams formed on his lips but never escaped. Instead, the images of his daughter flooded into his mind: the beautiful, needy baby only minutes after her birth, the little toddler as she giggled and ran into his arms, and the young girl trying desperately to be strong as her father left on yet another long journey. The nearly broken man then remembered his loving young bride. He remembered the sacrifices she made through her difficult and painful pregnancy, knowing all along that the birth would most likely kill her.

These memories changed him, not into a heartless, soulless shell but into someone that knew, no matter what they did to him, he would never break. The resolve he felt was unbreakable. He knew he had won at least a small victory. But at what cost?

Pattie pulled back from Steve and looked searchingly into his eyes. "The bond I felt with him was almost palpable. I could see his wife and his daughter, he loved them so. I'm not sure I can tell you any more of his memories."

"You don't have to. You've been through too much," Steve said, holding firmly to her shoulders.

Pattie eyes welled with tears and in a choked voice, she said, "But I feel I have to, right now, or I may never speak of it again. I don't think I can carry that burden for the rest of my life."

Pattie fell silent, staring into Steve's eyes. Sensing her internal struggle, Steve was desperate to help her in any way he could. Finally, without stopping as he had always done in the past, he leaned forward and kissed her passionately. He pulled back slowly and looked directly into her eyes, determined to finally say it. "I love you."

Pattie's mind was reeling as she struggled with all the emotions of the day. Steve's confession was something she had wanted for years. It didn't come about as she had dreamed, but she knew he was sincere. For weeks now, she had sensed the barriers to their relationship fading. Pattie laid her hand against his face and gazed into his eyes for just a moment before leaning back against him. She felt safe and secure in his arms. She squeezed his arm gently and said softly, "I love you, too."

Believing she now had the courage to continue, Pattie decided to start with Weelose's journey rather than delving straight into the memories that frightened her most.

The captors reached new levels of cruelty and pushed much farther than they had ever gone before, perhaps spurred on by Weelose's indifference to anything they tried. Finally, when the scout was certain he was dying, the agonizing treatment came to an abrupt end. On the edge of consciousness, he could feel himself being healed with magic. When next he gained any sense of awareness, Weelose found himself bouncing in the bed of a wagon. He was on his side, a gag in his mouth, and bound tightly with a rope.

The sides of the wagon were high enough to prevent him from seeing his surroundings. He had no way of knowing how long he had been unconscious, so judging how far he had traveled from the prison was impossible. He had vague memories of drifting in and out of consciousness, seemingly over a period of days. This time he had been lucid for a few hours rather than brief moments, a fact he decided to keep from his captors by remaining deathly still.

Always a scout, even with his eyes shut, Weelose could tell they were approaching a sizable city. The street traffic increased, with wagons noisily bouncing past in the opposite direction. From the sounds, Weelose knew they were empty. Likely, they were supply wagons returning home from their morning delivery. He could hear people talking who were walking close to the road, with an occasional curse at the driver for coming too close. And then the ride became much smoother, suggesting a well-maintained road that, from the sounds of the iron-bound wheels, was paved with stones.

Weelose's worst fears were realized when they reached the gates. When asked their business in the city by the gate guard, his captors answered with words that filled his heart with dread.

"We have a special prisoner in the back. We will present him only to Zybaro himself."

"Move on with the poor soul," came the reply, and the wagon lurched forward.

"Zybaro himself," thought Weelose. "What can this mean?"

The prisoner had over an hour to develop dozens of theories as the wagon wound itself through the crowded streets of Monisteaf, the capital city of Malabrim. From the sounds of the countless people begging for money and the smell of garbage, raw sewage, and an overall unkempt population, Weelose thought the city must be in complete chaos. It was a far cry from the pristine city he had visited as a boy 20 years earlier.

They finally reached their destination and the wagon came to an abrupt halt. Weelose was dragged out and dumped onto the smooth, cool street pavers. Now able to see beyond the sides of the wagon, he realized he was at a side entrance to the royal palace. Unable to walk, Weelose made no attempt to stand. His captors grabbed him under his arms and shuffled with him into the palace. They continued on, alternately half-carrying and dragging him down seemingly endless corridors. After several turns and passing door after door, they deposited him unceremoniously on the floor of a large, ornately tiled washroom.

His guards backed away and servants quickly stripped him of his clothes. They scrubbed him thoroughly from head to toe, cut his hair very short, shaved his scraggly beard, trimmed his nails, and made an attempt to clean his teeth with a mint-flavored paste. Finally, they dressed him in clothing that was fit for a royal court. All the while, Weelose offered no resistance, too weak to fight them.

The servants, unlike his captors, gently helped him to an adjacent room. This finely appointed chamber boasted a roaring fire, a large canopied bed, and, most importantly to Weelose, a small table laden with food. The servants lowered Weelose onto a chair and he began to enjoy his first hot meal since being captured over a month earlier. The spread consisted of a hot hearty stew, a plate of exotic cheeses and nuts, several small loaves of bread, and a bottle of fine wine.

Each bite seemed to give Weelose renewed strength. At one point, he realized that this was likely to be his last meal. He forced himself to slow down and savor every morsel.

The servants stood nearby and waited patiently for him to finish. When he could hold no more, they helped him into bed clothes, advised him to rest, and indicated that someone would be along later for him. Weelose knew that even if he had the strength to escape, he would not get far. Besides, he was bone tired and almost dead on his feet. He did as they instructed and climbed into the canopied bed. He was asleep almost before his head hit the luxurious pillows.

Weelose woke to the welcome smell of breakfast being served, but he was dismayed once he realized that the interior of the windowless room gave no indication of time. He swung his legs slowly over the side of the bed and tried to clear the cobwebs from his head. He had slept deeply and dreamlessly. He dashed some water on his face in the adjoining washroom and made his way to the small table to eat. After savoring a large breakfast, he donned his court clothes with the help of his servants. He thanked them for their kindness and waited expectantly for their next instructions. He did not know what the day would bring, but he felt resigned to whatever came next. A servant took his arm and led him through the door opposite the washroom.

Once through the door, he was reunited with his original captors. They fell on both sides of Weelose, flanking him as the servants led the way. The torturers turned guards were now clean-shaven and in dress uniforms. He surmised they were to appear in the court with him.

Weelose was able to keep up with his entourage without assistance. The two hot, wholesome meals and the sound sleep in a soft bed where he was able to stretch out and relax had gone a long way toward restoring his strength.

The wide hallway they traveled had all the accoutrements one would expect in a royal palace, but something struck the observant scout as being off. Proceeding down the hall, he realized that the palace was poorly lit. He had missed it at first, having spent the last month entombed in a dark dungeon. He noticed for every lit torch, three more holders stood empty. Every window that could have allowed in natural light was covered with heavy curtains, which only rarely offered an open slit through which the morning light could penetrate. Weelose marveled how the beautiful palace of splendor he had visited as a boy had been transformed into something that closely resembled the dungeon he had left.

Weelose was eventually led into an antechamber. Judging from the fine woodwork and massive ornate door opposite the one he entered, it had to lead directly into the royal hall. Four other wretched souls were already in place, their emaciated, bruised, and scarred bodies filling out as best they could their fine court clothes. After seeing the condition of his new colleagues, Weelose guessed he must be in the same deplorable shape.

Each prisoner was granted access to the main hall one at a time, in the order they had come into the antechamber. Servants were on hand to make last-minute adjustments to their ill-fitting clothing. Ten minutes or more elapsed between each admission, during which only the guards that led them accompanied them through the door and into the darkness beyond. More prisoners entered at about the same pace as each left, keeping the antechamber full.

When Weelose's turn came, he reluctantly followed the lead of his apprehensive captors. The royal hall was even more dimly lit than the hallways, the only source of light a series of burning braziers. They were set in pairs spaced far apart, giving the appearance of an eerie hallway down the center of the large open chamber.

These large, cast-iron pots sat atop crude metal frames and were filled to the brim with coal. The coal smoldered more than burned and gave off an unnerving red glow, along with smoke that hung in the air, causing a light haze before rising to the ceiling, which must have incorporated some sort of slits to allow the smoke to escape. The braziers offered such poor light, Weelose couldn't see the other end of the hall.

This scene was particularly distressful to the scout, because he remembered the great hall from his trip as a boy. At that time, the hall boasted row after row of windows, from floor to high vaulted ceiling, with beautiful formal gardens tantalizing just outside. Huge colorful banners representing every providence of the empire had hung from the ceiling's intricately carved beams. Now, the lingering smoke made it seem as if the ceiling was just out of reach, and not one beam of light danced through the windows. He looked down at the brilliant white marble floor of old, now covered by soot that left it dull and gray and countless scuff marks left by an endless parade of victims.

Weelose was marched halfway down the row of braziers and jerked to a halt. The guards tightly bound his hands behind his back and tied his feet together with a short cord, leaving him shackled such that he was only able to walk in a shuffling motion. They had just finished binding him when Weelose heard a scream burst from the darkness ahead. A clicking noise signaled the guards to move forward.

As they neared the end of the crude hallway, Weelose could sense the apprehension of the guards, his woodland skills enabling him to smell their fear. At the end of the braziers, the scout could barely see the outline of the large dais on which the thrones of the emperor and his wife had been located. As they continued, details began to emerge. Weelose could clearly see that the thrones had been removed from the platform. In their place stood over a dozen figures with long cowls, whose hoods and long sleeves covered every detail of their person. A lone figure stood in the center of the dais, his cloak a deep crimson red and secured at the waist with an ornate gold sash.

The only light at this end of the royal hall was provided by two small braziers on tall stands at the base of the dais. Hastening toward that light, the guards gruffly forced Weelose to within a few feet of the first step leading to the dais and shoved him in the center between the two barely burning lights. Using the short rope that bound his feet, they secured him to a spike driven into the marble floor. The guards then unceremoniously hurried away. Looking down, Weelose saw several pools of dried blood surrounding the spike.

The figure in the red cloak turned and with a measured pace made his way down the 20 steps leading from the raised dais. Even when the entity reached the floor and stood only a few feet away, Weelose could not make out any details, its face fully hidden in the shadows created by the deep hood and poor lighting.

"Carsanicean, you find yourself before me because you have proved to be a particularly stubborn guest."

Surprisingly, the voice that came from the cloaked figure was not harsh or threatening. As a matter of fact, it was so pleasant and melodious that Weelose craved the opportunity to hear it again.

"I am not a proponent of the harsh treatment you received at the hands of your captors. I plan to deal with that matter later. I only wish they had made you the offer I now extend to you before you had to endure their brutal treatment," the cloaked figure continued as Weelose stood mesmerized by the soft and almost whimsical voice.

"I am Zybaro. As you can see, I am not the monster I've been made out to be. The empire and I have been misrepresented by the lies of our enemies. I desire only to bring peace to the world. Then everyone can..."

Suddenly, something deep in Weelose's mind triggered and mental barriers against the soothing voice were erected without conscious thought. Month after month of training that at the time he thought a ridiculous waste of time had been activated. His good friend and direct commander, Hintileck, the leader of the Carsanicean resistance, had rightly deduced that magical coercion must have been at play for a tyrant like Zybaro to raise an army as quickly as he did.

Coercion spells could alter memories or cause minor additions or deletions of existing memories. Some spells could completely erase memories of major events or even add significant events whole cloth. A master of coercion could change the most die-hard ally into your worst enemy, and Zybaro obviously was a master. The trick to blocking the attack was to first recognize it for what it was and then deny access to your memories.

The clerics of Carsanic would attack their trainees again and again, pulling out personal and embarrassing memories. It was necessary for the less skilled clerics to physically touch their victims, but masters of the craft needed only to have them within earshot. After several months, a trainee would begin to develop an instinct for recognizing when the attacks were occurring. After the instinct for detection was developed, the trainees were taught the mental barriers, and they too were drilled in this practice repeatedly until they would erect the barriers without thought.

With his barriers in place, Weelose could now understand that Zybaro's spoken words were just projected memories. He could hear for the first time the beautiful, enchanting singing of the cloaked figure. That singing abruptly stopped as the figure's hood flew back.

"Oh Steve, I'm sorry. I need a minute," Pattie said, jolting Steve into the moment.

The fire had died down as Steve still gently cradled Pattie, holding her to his chest. She was sobbing softly, her head turned as she hid her eyes against him. He felt her tears soak into his shirt as he stroked her hair.

Pattie sat upright and looked into Steve's eyes. "He was so hideous. Zybaro has already begun to change. He's not as far along as the others we've seen, but he is becoming a nollax."

Steve gently brushed tear-soaked strands of hair from her eyes. "I can't imagine experiencing these events not just as images, but as actual memories, with sounds, smells, and emotions. It has to be overwhelming. Are you sure you want to do this?"

"I know I have to," said Pattie in a resigned tone.

Weelose stared in fascination at the face just revealed to him. It was dramatically distorted. The mouth was extremely wide, stretching almost from one ear to the other. Those ears were held tight to his head, blending into the skin until they were almost nonexistent. The nose was upturned, not like a pig's but more extreme, almost not a nose at all, only a bump with exposed nostrils. Weelose found he was most disturbed by the eyes. The pupils were slits, much like a cat's, shining in the pale red light, looking like pools of fire.

Zybaro stopped singing abruptly and began to rage at the shackled scout. Then, abandoning his light, whimsical song of coercion, he turned to a sinister tune. Zybaro began to spin an extremely complicated composition similar to one used for healing, but with a much harsher edge.

Pattie shuddered. "The pain Weelose began to suffer was beyond anything I would have thought a person could endure. Even as he lay dying, this gentle man sheltered me from many of the worst memories. But he couldn't hold them all back, nor the emotions he felt." Pattie pressed on.

The pain Weelose felt wasn't isolated to the head where the tissue of the brain was being destroyed. Because massive amounts of nerves were being severed, the pain coursed through every part of his body. He tried to scream, to run, to lash out at his attacker, but found he had lost all control of his body. Suddenly, the pain stopped, but this was no merciful release; instead of feeling pain, Weelose felt nothing.

Weelose was relieved to find his mind and reasoning were intact, but he lacked the ability to control his body. To his horror, he couldn't consciously alter even the most basic function such as breathing. Most cruelly, his vision and hearing were intact, but instinctual reactions to their input were not his to control. Weelose struggled to deal with what was happening to him, shocked at his inability to master his own body, but the worst was yet to come.

Weelose saw a cloaked figure appear beside Zybaro. Flipping back an oversized hood, it revealed itself to be a nollax. Its large head closely resembled that of a goat, but with enough human features to make it grotesque. It reared back its head with its curled horns, emitting a hideous half laugh, half bay.

Zybaro's wide mouth curled into a smile at the sinister sound and addressed the nollax. "This new champion is yours. You have enough now to take into the field. Join the northern forces; I think it fitting this Carsanicean should fight those he foolishly tried to protect."

The nollax sang a brief song and immediately, against his will, Weelose's body walked from the royal hall, led by the nollax.

"Steve, I caught only brief glimpses into what they forced him to do." Pattie stared into her hands before looking up. "He fought to shield those images from me. He was so repulsed by what he had done, he made the choice to die rather than to live with it."

The next morning, Brandon found the two still huddled together by the ashes of the campfire, sound asleep. As he pulled the blanket up

around his friends, he thought, "It's about time."

Curious as to why the camp was so still this late in the morning, he headed off to see what the plans were for the day.

EPILOGUE

Colonel Yonks, the former supreme leader of Malabrim's army, sat patiently in the dark command tent, waiting. He had never trusted those with magic, certainly not the vile nollax that now composed most of the war council. He would not be in their presence now had he not feared for the lives of his wife and three precious children.

In the dim light, the colonel could barely make out the other two humans in the tent seated on his immediate right and left. Like him, they made a feeble attempt to mask their disgust for the remaining members of the war council. Earlier, the five nollax had relented and allowed a single, shielded candle to be lit. The eerie, dancing reflections on the canvas of the tent's back wall at least allowed the humans to discern basic shapes.

The group waited for Ragatheano, Zybaro's trusted liaison, sent to communicate his leader's directives. Yonks believed they had initiated the siege of Karness far too soon. More troops and time to construct additional ladders and siege engines would have gone a long way towards ensuring victory. He knew better than to speak this truth aloud, however, as the order to begin the attack had come directly from Zybaro via Ragatheano. Despite his exemplary leadership skills, Yonks knew he would have lived only a few agonizing minutes or, worse yet, been transformed into a pallitor had he expressed his belief. As terrible as either outcome would have been, that wasn't what held him back; as always, it was the fate of his family.

Despite his reservations about the timing of the attack, Yonks entertained some hope the siege would still be successful. The guardians of Karness had foolishly wasted lives and resources defending the pass itself. They did this without utilizing their single greatest advantage: the roadways above. The high vantage points would have allowed them to cast objects from the switchback passes down onto their attackers. If they didn't use this tremendous strategic advantage to thin the ranks of his army, as Yonks had feared, they should have pulled back and used every available troop to defend the wall.

At this point in the conflict, Yonks was thankful for the light, probing attacks his side had been carrying out over the past 2 weeks. These light attacks allowed them to gather valuable information while minimizing casualties. The nollax typically had no regard for lives other than their own and would have no qualms about sacrificing humans. However, with the losses on the pass, even with the recent addition of 1,000 reserve troops (albeit without much-needed supplies), Yonks was able to convince the nollax of the necessity of the probing attacks.

From all reports, the wall's defenses were not fully manned, yet another strategic blunder by the defenders. Yonks would have had every able-bodied person on that wall regardless of fighting skill. All that his troops had encountered were the uniformed guards of the city. The city surely had merchants, workers, even farmers that could throw rocks over the wall at the very least.

Yonks thoughts were interrupted by a commotion just outside the tent, signaling the arrival of Ragatheano. He remembered the first time the creature had landed near him. It was quite unnerving, even for a seasoned veteran. The tall, thin figure bent to enter through the tent flap. The illumination from the distant campfires was enough to allow Yonks to discern the new occupant's form-fitting cloak. Only he knew it was no cloak, but rather the leathery membranes of Ragatheano's wings tightly folded around his body. Yonks was thankful the tent flap closed before Ragatheano straightened and he was subjected to the full extent of his hideously deformed features.

Ragatheano wasted no time. As soon as he stood to his full height, he issued a single instruction.

"The all-out assault begins at noon tomorrow." With that, he turned and left the tent as quickly as he had entered.

Yonks managed to hide his dismay. He knew the light, probing attacks couldn't go on indefinitely, but he had held out hope that the major assault wouldn't begin until work on their massive battering ram was completed. He had spent the last 2 weeks convincing the war council of its need. Now, if the all-out assault failed and they incurred heavy troop losses, the use of the ram would be fruitless.

Yonks still held out hope that, under the protection of the nollax, his soldiers would have a chance to breach the wall using only scaling ladders. He was heartened by the fact that the daily grind of the probing attacks had been effective in reducing the defenders through attrition. For the life of him, Yonks couldn't understand why the populace wasn't aiding in the defense of their own city. They couldn't fail to understand that once the wall fell, their lives would be forfeit.

Yonks was jolted out of his musings by a not-so-gentle nudge from the human cleric to his right. Looking as best he could into the murky depths of the tent, he realized the nollax were staring at him expectantly.

Guessing they had just asked about his plan, he launched straight into it.

"My men will hit the western section of the wall with six concentrated attacks. To have any hope of success, we will require magical protection. My four remaining units will be held in reserve just out of bow range. If any one of the six attacks can establish a foothold on the wall, these units will surge against that portion of the wall en masse."

In response, Yonks heard the primeval grunts and squeals of the nollax, the only sign of approval they ever granted to humans.

Thank you for reading Book One in *Flight to Bericea* series, *The Summoned Ones*. All the Camp Wyanet friends are out of immediate peril, but they are not safe from the long and powerful reach of Zybaro's forces. Join me in the future release of Book Two, *Perilous Path*. Information about this future release and other background material can be found at

www.darrylawoods.com.

CPSIA information can be obtained
at www.ICGtesting.com
Printed in the USA
LVHW030719300320
651615LV00015B/527

9 780997 905908